THE ANGEL
OF
KNOWLTON
PARK

A Joe Burgess Mystery
Book Two

Kate Flora

Cover and Book design by eBook Prep www.ebookprep.com

May, 2014
ISBN: 978-1-61417-582-7

ePublishing Works!
www.epublishingworks.com

DEDICATION

In loving memory of my mother,
A. CARMAN CLARK.
She modeled courage, tenacity, faith, and character
and inspired a generation of Maine writers.

ACKNOWLEDGMENTS

Thanks go, once again, to the Portland Police Department, and especially to Deputy Chief Joseph K. Loughlin, for all his years of advice and support and to Detective Scott Dunham, Mark Teceno and an unnamed MDEA agent.

I have been the fortunate recipient of so much good advice. Thanks to the Learning Center for the Deaf, in Framingham, Massachusetts, and all the students and staff there for their willingness to share their world and culture with me. I am indebted to Dr. Honore Weiner, for giving me a reading list and answering my questions. To Dr. William F. Hickey for his detailed information and insights.

I will never finish another book again without a nod of gratitude to Joshua Bilmes, who taught me so much about editing and rewriting. Nor can I finish a book without advice from my readers—Joe, Diane, Jack and Nancy, Brad, and my brother John Clark, the world's greatest librarian. I couldn't write without the generous support of my husband, Ken, who really likes Joe Burgess.

I have been well advised. Despite their best advice, I have taken liberties, both procedurally and geographically, and perhaps even botanically. Any mistakes are my own.

CHAPTER 1

The fat, blue-black fly circled lazily in the July heat before landing in the child's open eye. Burgess stifled his instinctive impulse to brush it away. He'd just started working this scene, and he wasn't letting anything muck up his chances of learning everything it had to say about what had happened to this small dead boy.

Forty minutes ago, he'd been on vacation, a packed suitcase by the door and a borrowed canoe waiting on the roof of his car. Asleep until Lt. Vince Melia, head of CID for the Portland, Maine Police Department, called.

"Hate to do this to you, Joe, but we've got a bad one. Half my staff's on vacation or out sick, and I can't find Kyle." An uncharacteristic hesitation, then Melia said, "It's a kid, Joe. Name's Timothy Watts."

The body had been left in a city park, wrapped in a soft blue blanket so new it was still creased from the package, the blue over the torso stained purple by blood. Only the boy's head was visible, a pale, elfin face with a sprinkle of freckles, tangled pale hair, and, where the lips parted, teeth that cried out for orthodontia. It didn't matter now.

Was he seeing too much in the careful tucking of the blanket, covers drawn up to the chin like a mother settling her child for sleep, the edges tucked in to guard against the damp night air? What was it telling him? The body had not been dumped; it had been arranged. But was the arrangement love or hate? Remorse? A kind of "in your face" defiance or a deliberate attempt to confuse the investigation?

The two evidence techs, Rudy Carr and Wink Devlin, shifted in the heat, impatient to start their pictures, but Burgess lingered, taking the time to study the scene. Sure, after they released the body, there'd be the pictures, but pictures were only that. Pictures. They couldn't duplicate the feeling of this time and place, where the body had been placed, the layout of the park and surrounding streets, whether houses overlooked this spot.

This was the moment he usually made his promise of justice to his victim, but this time, it was Terry Kyle's promise to make. As soon as Kyle showed up, this was going to be his case. Burgess turned away, closing his eyes against images already imbedding themselves in his brain, then opened them again, looking downhill toward the crime scene van. The bright orange canoe looked ridiculous parked next to the yellow crime scene tape. Where in hell *was* Kyle? This was not supposed to be Burgess's scene, his body, his problem. Not *his* kid.

Not yet 7:00 a.m. and already his clothes were stuck to his body. They were having an ugly summer. The salty Maine air, normally refreshing even when it was sweltering inland, had been cooked by hot, windless days into a fetid, sour brine. A rank miasma of smells rose up from old brick and asphalt, from dumpsters and alleys, fishing boats and bars, making the port seem seedy and derelict. Two weeks without sea breezes and the city needed a shower.

Burgess preferred winter, however cold and raw. You could always add layers. There was only so much you could take off, especially at a high-visibility crime scene. He'd left his jacket in the car and wore a short-sleeved shirt, but his tie was choking him and sweat had darkened the dull red silk. As he bent over the body again, drops of sweat ski-jumped off his nose onto the blanket.

Finally, with a nod, he stepped back. Devlin and Carr had already taken video and photographs of the body from a distance. Now they moved in for close-ups. Stan Perry, the other CID detective, was sketching the scene. He and Stan had already measured off the distance to the body from a couple fixed objects—a hydrant up above on the street and a square granite post at the edge of the roses that bordered the park—and gotten seriously scratched for their troubles. The roses hadn't been planted solely for horticultural appeal. They kept the public on the paths, meaning there was only one likely way the killer could have approached to drop the body.

Burgess surveyed the growing crowd, edging over as Carr lowered the video camera and mopped his face. "Get me some pictures of the people watching, up there on the street, would you? And those down by Delinsky?"

"Sure thing, Sarge."

Carr was good. He'd drift back to the crime scene van, camera slung casually on his shoulder, and people would never know he was taking their picture when he paused to look back the way he'd come or when he sauntered over to ask a question or study something on the ground.

This was one where the killer might come back. It

wasn't just a cop show cliché. Bad guys did. Sometimes because they were dumb. Sometimes because they thought they were so smart. Often because they couldn't stay away.

"You going to be able to get the dew on the body?" Burgess asked. "On the blanket?"

"Hey," Wink grumbled. "I'm the Annie Leibovitz of crime scenes, remember?" He raised the camera, then lowered it again. "Someday we oughta have a show. Your best pics, my best pics. That would be something."

Burgess's walls were ringed with his own crime scene photos, the ones he took when everyone had left and the scenes were empty. "I hate to think who'd come," he said.

"It might be very instructive." Devlin raised his camera, circling the body slowly like a spider inspecting its prey.

Once their pictures were taken and the sketch was done, everything would stop, like God had hit the pause button, until the medical examiner arrived. It was the law. At a crime scene, the ME owned the body. Burgess hoped Dr. Lee would come soon. Too long in this heat and Timmy Watts wouldn't be the only body on the ground. That was the homicide detective's life. Twenty below or 110 in the shade, the call came, you went and worked the scene. No rolling over for a few more z's. You had to give the dead their due.

He pulled out his notebook, following the path they'd lined out with crime scene tape back downhill to ask Gabriel Delinsky, the first officer on the scene, a question about the damp grass and footprints and what he'd seen when he first arrived.

As he approached, the crowd around Delinsky surged forward. They were pressed back, and then

Delinsky went down. A large figure pushed past and headed up the hill. Burgess shoved the notebook back in his pocket.

"Stan," he called, "we've got trouble. Rudy? Call for more officers. Whatever you do, don't let people up here..."

The figure in the lead was a woman, followed by two or three men, then Delinsky and Lt. Melia and the patrol officers who were protecting the scene. If it was a race, she was the clear winner. She made a kind of roaring noise as she came, her feet thudding on the dry ground like the hooves of a charging animal. She was nearly Burgess's height, an easy 6', and outweighed him by a good hundred pounds. She had to be the boy's mother, though it seemed impossible this bulky creature was related to that small, golden child.

"Timmy," she roared, "my Timmy," her mouth a dark "O" in her broad face. White flesh oozed from the armholes of her torn housedress. As Burgess stepped into her path, he caught the reek of alcohol and stale sweat.

"Move!" she barked, swinging an arm the size of an Easter ham.

Burgess stood his ground. He knew what would happen if she got past. She'd throw herself on the child's body, embrace it, unwrap it, toss it around, claw at the wounds, maybe even try to carry him away. If there was a weapon, she'd handle it. His crime scene would be destroyed.

"Ma'am..." He held up a hand, trying to capture her attention. "I'm sorry, ma'am, but you can't go up there." Keeping his voice steady and firm. "You can't go up there. You have to let us do our job." His words bounced off like balls off a wall.

"Timmy!" She flailed her arms as she tried to push

past. "Timmy. My baby...my poor, poor baby. I've got to go to him..."

Up close, her smell was overwhelming. Graying clumps of unwashed hair dripped from her skull in Medusa coils. Her eyes jumped in her face, wild and unfocused, the pupils gigantic. He'd seen all kinds of bizarre behavior spawned by shock and grief. This didn't look like grief, though. This looked like drugs.

Where in hell was everyone? He stepped back, trying to block her way while avoiding her flailing fists. "I'm sorry, ma'am..." He raised his voice. "Ma'am, I know you're upset, but you have to stay back behind the yellow tape."

Melia was beside him now, other officers around them, but Burgess didn't take his eyes off her. "This is Lt. Melia," he said. "We will keep you informed, I promise, but you need to go with him now and let us finish our work."

"Get the fuck outa my way!" she yelled, spitting words and stinking breath in his face as she drove a vicious kick into his shin. She slammed into his shoulder and shoved past. "Timmyyyy. Timmyyyy!"

But Burgess had been a high school football player, and though it had been thirty years since the local paper called him "lightning and poetry on the field," he hadn't forgotten his moves. He was around and after her, seizing her great, stinking, rubbery mass. He felt her resist, then yield, her weight coming back at him, his feet slipping on the dew-slicked dry grass. There was pressure, then incredible pain in his bad knee as they crashed to the ground.

She began pounding him with fists like softballs full of knuckles, screaming, cursing, spitting, kicking at everyone within range. It took four officers to haul her off and subdue her until paramedics could get in to sedate her.

Burgess sat holding his knee, flashes of pain dancing like Northern Lights in his head, hoping the damage wasn't permanent. He wondered if the media had gotten it on film. If the Maine citizens eating their Wheaties this morning would be entertained by a beefy cop in a sweat-soaked shirt slamming the mother of a homicide victim to the ground only a dozen yards from her dead son's body. How long before some desk-jockey at 109 called him in for a speech on sullying the department's image. What life was like north of the Arctic Circle.

A hand on his shoulder made him look up. "Jesus, Joe. What do you think she's on? PCP? Amphetamines?" Melia looked miserable.

"She's on something."

"You okay?"

"No."

Melia jerked his head toward the ambo. "Need a ride to the hospital?"

"I'd walk before I'd ride with her."

"I could have someone drive you."

"We've got a dead kid, Vince."

"And you're no help if you can't even stand up."

"Oh, I'm a stand-up guy. You find Kyle yet?"

Melia shook his head. "Sent someone by his place and everywhere else I could think of. Even called his ex-wife. You know what she said?"

"Something about child support, I expect. The PMS Queen is kind of one note." Burgess shrugged. "So you're stuck with me, aren't you?"

Melia looked uphill toward the body. "You gonna be okay with this?"

Burgess would never be okay with a dead kid. They both knew that. Not since Kristin Marks. Little girl abducted, raped, strangled with her own underpants and dumped in a landfill. Burgess had just about worked himself to death on that case. When he'd heard the plea deal—guy walked with a slap on the wrist because Captain Cote screwed up a warrant and lost crucial evidence—Burgess had gone over the desk for Cote's throat. The case almost ended his career and left him wondering: was the job worth it if you couldn't get justice for the innocent and most vulnerable? He hadn't stopped trying.

Melia held out a hand and Burgess pulled himself up, pain stabbing in his leg. "You might see if those medics can spare some Demerol and an ace bandage."

"Your face is green," Melia said.

"Goes with the red tie. Christmas in July." Burgess shook his head. "So that was Mother Watts. Can't believe I didn't recognize her."

"She used to be a lot smaller. A real looker. Hard to believe it now," Melia said, looking at the EMTs struggling to load the massive woman. "Family's been over in the Lewiston-Auburn area about ten years. Moved back maybe six, eight months ago."

"Family report him missing?"

"What do you think?" Melia studied Burgess. "Joe, are you sure?"

Burgess made shooing motions with his hands. "Go, go, go," he said. "Ask the medical men for some Demerol, Tylenol with codeine, Motrin. Whatever they've got, but get me something. Like to get through here before we're all toast."

August in Maine wasn't supposed to be like this. They'd all be dehydrated and sick as dogs if they didn't take care. He radioed Delinsky, asked him to arrange a cooler of ice and a lot of sodas and bottled water. Then he limped up to Perry, who knelt beside the body.

Stan Perry was the newest detective in personal crimes. A promising investigator with great instincts and a disconcerting tendency toward impulsive behavior. Despite the heat, Perry wore a zipped-up Portland PD windbreaker. His face was pink as a ham.

"Lose the jacket, Stan," Burgess said. "You're gonna get heat stroke."

"Can't."

"So you've got a tee shirt on. Vince won't care."

"I dressed in a hurry," Perry said, unzipping so Burgess could see his shirt. It was navy blue and in large white letters, read: **Homicide—our day begins when your day ends.** "You think I'm going to parade this in front of the media, you're crazy. I'd rather get heat stroke. Besides, Vince sees this, he'll fire my ass. You know that."

Burgess pulled out his car keys. "In my trunk," he said. "In my suitcase. Lotta tee shirts. Help yourself. Only Stan?"

Perry took the keys. "Yeah?"

"Not the one that says, 'No, but I've hugged yours,' okay?"

"Suitcase in the trunk. Canoe on the roof. I was a detective, I'd think you were going on vacation."

"Soon as Terry shows up, I'm out of here."

"Case of Rolling Rock says you aren't. Not with something like this…"

"I'm burned, Stan, okay. I need to do some fishing, catch some sleep, spend time with Chris when I'm not obsessing about a case or snoring. I've rented a camp. I've borrowed a canoe. She's taking some time off. Come hell or high water, I'm going."

"Oh, sure," Perry said. "Like you'd leave the fate of this little chap in the hands of lesser mortals."

"I'm not the only detective in this city. You and Terry can handle this."

"You're the best."

"I'm going."

"Case of Rolling Rock," Perry repeated. He trudged away, jingling the keys.

Dr. Andrew Lee, the impeccable and efficient assistant medical examiner, arrived a few minutes later. He surveyed the limp, the grass stains, the scraped arm. "So now you're crime scene bouncer, Joe?" He reached in a pocket and handed Burgess some Motrin.

"You got that right. Had to eject the grieving mother."

Stan returned wearing the blue polo shirt Burgess had packed to wear when he took Chris out for dinner, the nicest thing in his suitcase. No matter. Unless this thing broke in a hurry, he wasn't going to need vacation clothes any time soon. Just a shower when he could grab one and a clean shirt. His body felt slick as an eel.

Stan held out a Diet Coke. "Thanks, Dad. Once again you've saved my ass."

"I am *not* your goddamned dad."

He popped the top and went to stand by the boy's feet. He and Devlin had carefully worked a pair of clean white sheets beneath the body, fanning them out on both sides so that when they unwrapped the blanket, anything that fell would be caught. Lying in the center in his blue cocoon, the great white wings spread around him, the boy looked a sleeping angel.

"It's not getting any cooler, gentlemen," Dr. Lee said, "Let's work this body."

On TV, police might find a body, feel it, flip it, assess it and bag it in two or three minutes of plot time. In real life, it was a slow, meticulous process. Every step photographed and videotaped, with frequent pauses for evidence collection, preserving everything for a trial that might come a year or more down the road. That was why they had the white sheets and the vacuum with special filters. Working the body meant just that. Lee pulled on some gloves and started with the boy's head.

As Lee turned the head, Burgess saw blood in the boy's hair. Carefully, Lee felt the skull, describing his observations. In laymen's terms, it boiled down to a big lump and swollen, mushy tissue. "Looks like somebody hit him pretty hard. Hold on. Something strange here." He peered into the boy's hair, parting the curls so they could see. "Here's something for you, Detectives."

Burgess leaned in for a closer look. Caught just behind the ear was a small brown feather. He looked around for Devlin. "Wink, you wanna shoot this before we bag it?"

"What is it, Joe?" Perry asked.

"Feather."

"So we're looking for a chicken?"

"Chickenhawk, more like," Burgess said. But it was something. He waited while Devlin took close-ups of the feather, then carefully removed it and bagged it.

Dr. Lee bounced from foot to foot as Burgess grabbed the edge of the blanket where it was tucked under the boy's left side. "What do you think, Stan," Burgess asked. "Right handed?"

"Or clever."

Perry at the head and Burgess at the feet, they gently pulled the tucked blanket from beneath the body, stepped sideways, and laid it out on the sheet, moving with exaggerated care. The last thing they wanted was to fling some precious bit of paint, fiber, or hair that might tie this child to his killer out into the grass. They waited while Carr vacuumed the sheet and changed the filter, then unfolded the other side.

The skinny little body—bruised white limbs and a

narrow, bony chest Burgess could have spanned with one hand—was naked except for patterned cotton briefs, the pattern mostly obscured by blood, and a Band-Aid on one toe. Burgess stared silently at the wreckage that had been Timothy Watts. Then, in a move that might have been choreographed, he and Perry turned away.

"There appear to be eleven stab wounds," Dr. Lee said. "I'll know better in the morning, but from the evenness of the borders, I'd say it was a double-edge knife, not serrated, perhaps an inch wide? I won't know about blade length until I get inside."

He touched the pale skin with a gloved hand. "You can see here...and here...where the thrusts were sufficiently powerful to leave impressions of the handle." He touched a single cut on the side of the chest, and a small slice on the boy's arm. "Looks like he was trying to twist away, using his arm to shield himself." He examined the boy's arms and legs, pointed to some small cuts on the hands. "A few defense wounds. He was a small boy, possibly stunned by that blow to the head. Couldn't do much to protect himself."

Lee pushed away and stood up. "If you'd like to get your pictures, we can turn him."

"Sweet Mother of God!" Stan Perry said, kicking at the soda can Burgess had set on the grass and sending it flying. "It's fuckin' savage, Joe. How could anyone...?" He turned his face away and stalked to the edge of the roses.

Burgess watched flies circle and buzz above vacant eyes reflecting a sky the color of the blanket. A tiny breath of wind rippled the soft hair. He studied the small form on that sea of blue and knew that Stan was right. He couldn't walk away from this.

They were on the clock here—the critical first

hours, first days—and there was no sign of Kyle. He didn't know where he'd find the energy for a major case, the strength to keep Kristin Marks at bay, or the words to explain this to Chris. He was just so damned burned out. But nobody got away with something like this in *his* town. Someone had to stand between Portland's kids and those who wanted to hurt them.

The sun already felt hot as an iron on his head and neck. The air smelled of dust and death. He closed his eyes. As Devlin and Carr crunched wearily over the crisp grass, taking their pictures, Burgess drew a long breath, pulled deep into himself, and with a pang that was almost physical, kissed his vacation goodbye.

As he exhaled, he knelt and put his hand on the dead boy's shoulder, on bones that felt fragile as a sparrow's, and made the promise he'd made to so many victims over the years. I will find the one who did this to you, Timmy Watts, and I will get you justice.

CHAPTER 2

Perry would have seen his share of ugliness as a street cop, but since coming to CID he'd only handled one child, a crib death. Now, seeing Perry's stark white face, the younger cop's throat working as he fought nausea, Burgess remembered his own first time with a murdered child. Perry needed to get away for a minute, get his balance back, and remember why he was here.

He dropped a hand on Perry's shoulder. "Let's walk back down and get Vince," he said. "He's gonna run this thing, he needs to see this. And let's see if we can get some screens up. I don't want those cameras getting a piece of this. This is not some goddamned entertainment..."

Perry tapped his radio. Sweat gleamed on his shaved head, on his drawn face. "I can call..." His voice choked. "Jesus, Joe. He's so small..."

"Walk with me. Wink and Rudy gotta shoot this thing, anyway, before we can do anything more."

"Don't be long, gentlemen," Lee told their departing backs.

Perry tried for a grin but his heart wasn't in it.

"Thought you'd be running this, Joe."

"Vince'll run it because it's a kid and that'll have the whole city boiling over, which, in this heat, it's primed to do anyway. What you wanna hope is this doesn't bring Captain Cote back." He felt like he was babbling but wanted to keep talking until he got Perry well away and some of that wide-eyed horror faded. Burgess knew his own reputation for meanness, for being impatient with cops who wimped out. He also knew the damage the ugly stuff they saw could do. Knew you had to look after your guys or you'd lose 'em to burnout. Last thing he wanted was for Stan to decide he'd be happier in another unit.

"Jeez, Joe. Cote wouldn't…would he?"

Burgess shrugged. Cote, next up the food chain from Melia, was an asshole. A captain who'd forgotten he'd ever been a cop. When Cote was away, it was like a weight was lifted off the building. Night the guy'd left for vacation, they'd circled up at their favorite bar and gotten seriously drunk to celebrate. "Better light some candles, Stan. Media's gonna be all over this, and that starfucking prick loves the media."

He hobbled down the hill, feeling every year and excess pound, the dry grass under his feet crackling like corn flakes. The city was waking up, news vans circling the park like sharks, distant traffic noises clamorous in the heavy air. Burgess liked night, the peace and quiet and emptiness of it. Not a steamy morning like this, already crowded with goddamned rubbernecked gawkers, gathering like a flock of vultures to gnaw on Timmy Watts.

He stepped down hard on his anger. He could be angry later. Right now, he needed to be cool-headed and clear-eyed. Not miss a goddamned thing. Timmy deserved no less.

Vince Melia was standing in the shade about ten

feet inside the yellow line, talking on the phone. He finished with some abrupt words Burgess couldn't make out and snapped the phone shut. Melia wore an unrumpled summer-weight suit in a subtle blue plaid. Sweat had darkened saddles under his arms and curled his short hair tightly against his skull. His glasses were slipping down his nose. He nodded when he saw them coming, then reached in his pocket and held out an ace bandage.

"We got the kid unwrapped," Burgess said. "You better come look. And get some screens up. It's pretty damned ugly." He opened the cooler and got out a bottle of water. "I'm going to wrap up this knee. Then let's finish this thing."

He swallowed. "Lying up there with those white sheets, Vince, the kid looks like an angel. You tell me. Who would practically gut an angel?"

He swallowed half the water and poured the rest over his head. To hell with glamour. At the best of times, he wasn't much to write home about. Then he climbed in the van, undid his pants, and sat down to wrap his knee. It was like peeing on a three-alarmer— his knee screamed for what the docs called RICE, rest, ice, compression, and elevation—but this might get him through the morning. At least it was cool in the van. Maybe in a while they could take a break, sit in here, cool their brains down before someone passed out.

He was zipping his pants when Rudy Carr came in. "Wrapping my knee," Burgess explained.

Understanding wiped the clouds from Carr's face. "Long as it's not something kinky in my evidence van."

"Thought it was *my* evidence van."

"Yeah, and Vince thinks it's his evidence van." Carr jerked his head toward the door. "That's some ugly thing up there, Sarge." Carr picked up some stuff and headed for the door. "Sometimes, even though you know it can happen, it's still hard to believe."

"We'll get him," Burgess said.

"Him?"

"I'm about 98% certain."

"But how could anyone..."

"Go take your pictures, Rudy," he sighed. "If I knew what made monsters or why they did stuff like this, I'd be retired on the royalties from my books."

Truth was, he knew a lot about what made monsters. Their toxic families, or lack of families. The cruelty of other grownups and kids. And he knew what lay behind different types of killings. Crime scenes spoke volumes, if you took the time to listen. Sometimes they spoke in strange languages, or in sentence fragments, or in the spaces between the words. Sometimes they spoke in contradictions. Sometimes the words were garbled and took time to sort out. Sometimes they even lied. But they spoke.

His job was to figure out what they were saying. His job. Stan Perry's job. Terry Kyle's job. Keep working at the message until they understood it. It helped to have different sets of experience interpreting things. They listened in individual ways and each heard different things, just like in everyday conversation.

Except Kyle wasn't here. Kyle was Burgess's kind of cop—smart, fast, no nonsense, and tenacious as a pit bull. Plus, with his child support killing him, he needed the overtime. So Kyle's absence meant something was very wrong. If Burgess let it, it would worry him until he found Kyle and checked it out. But as with every other distraction, his concerns about Kyle had to wait.

Reluctantly, he went back into the sauna of the day, the water dripping off his hair warm before he was halfway up the hill. Ahead of him, patrol officers were setting up screens. Melia and Perry were standing by the boy's feet, Perry talking and Melia nodding. Lee was listening, then nodded. "Looks like he was lying down when he was stabbed. We'll know tomorrow."

Devlin lowered his camera, signaling that he was through. "Two minutes," Carr said.

Two minutes felt like dozens with the sun scorching their heads. Finally, Carr stepped back and Lee moved in. "Let's roll him toward the left," he said.

Burgess stepped around to the head and knelt down. Perry stood by the boy's feet. Together, they rolled the body so the boy lay on his stomach. Burgess stared at the vulnerable, naked, blood-splotched back, the skinny little spine and shoulder blades, at the blanket, spotted dark where it had touched the wounds. He realized he didn't know how old the boy was, just that he was small, painfully thin, and bruised. Old bruises and new.

He looked at Lee. "He wasn't killed here."

"No," Lee agreed. "And he wasn't lying on that blanket when he was killed. He was wrapped up afterward and brought here. And someone cleaned him up."

"Short knife?"

"We'll know better when we open him up, but it looks like a short knife. None of the thrusts went through."

Burgess squeezed the back of the boy's thigh between a thumb and forefinger. There was no change in color. "How long you think he's been dead?"

Lee grunted, studying the spot where the fingers had squeezed. "More than eight? Not so much to go on, kid bled so much. This heat affects things. See what his family's got to say about when he was last seen, what he last ate." He pushed back on his heels and stood, shutting off his recorder. "See you tomorrow morning, Joe. Seven?"

Burgess looked at his lieutenant. Melia's face was a dull brick red. "You want me at the autopsy?"

Melia nodded. "Sorry, Joe." He didn't need to explain. It only made sense that the detective who worked the scene would attend the autopsy. After that, it only made sense to stay on the case. Burgess shrugged. He didn't know how he'd break this to Chris. Their relationship was so new they were still finding their way. Nor did he know where he'd find the stamina. But he'd made a promise and Mrs. Burgess's boy kept his promises.

Dr. Lee pocketed the recorder and stripped off his gloves. "So I'll see you in the morning," he said. "Gotta run. I'm late for golf. You can send the body along whenever you're ready."

"Golf?" Stan whistled. "God, the people who love it, they sure love it, don't they? Can you imagine golfing in this weather?"

"I can't imagine golfing in any weather," Burgess said. "I'm too young. 'Round seventy or so, maybe I'll take it up. When I'm ready to slow down."

Melia took an unsteady step, then shook his head as though trying to clear it. "Vince, you don't take that jacket off, I'm going to haul it off you in front of God, the media, and everybody," Burgess said. "You're not a lot of good up here passed out on the ground and we don't need the distraction." Melia removed his jacket, folded it lining side out, and set it on the ground. The light gray lining was black with sweat. Carefully, they turned the body onto its back again. Burgess checked the boy's hair for anything else, saw nothing. Then he went around and stood at the feet again, bending to stare at the stab marks across the boy's stomach and abdomen. "We'll see what the esteemed Dr. Lee says after autopsy, but this humble cop thinks we're looking at a wide, double-edged blade, three to four inches long."

He passed a finger through the air above the marks left by the knife handle. "T-handled knife, maybe? Scumbag's weapon of choice? Available in any pawn shop."

He picked up the hands and gently examined the fingers. "All that violence and almost no defense wounds." He looked again at the gaping, raw-steak-colored slashes on the torso, like eleven extra mouths clustered with buzzing flies.

"Stan, you don't want to watch this."

He carefully folded in the white sheet so he wouldn't disturb anything, then knelt down on the grass on left side of the body. He closed his eyes, raised his hand over the boy as if he were holding a knife, took a slow, deep breath. Then he opened his eyes and stabbed up and down eleven times as fast as he could, imitating the pattern on the body, imagining the child writhing and twisting, the killer's unstoppable rage.

Dropping his hand to his side, he heaved himself to his feet, and stepped back, stomach lurching at the ugliness of what he'd done, the greater ugliness of what it confirmed about the crime.

"Overkill." He choked the word out over the sickness closing his throat. "The poor little guy."

Perry and Melia turned away as Burgess and Wink Devlin began carefully folding the blanket and sheets back in around the body, getting Timmy Watts ready to leave his neighborhood for good. Ready for the body bag.

CHAPTER 3

"Sergeant," Delinsky said, "this is a terrible thing."

Patrol officer Gabriel Delinsky's rich black skin was gray with fatigue, his face pinched with responsibility. "I'm sorry about the family, sir," he said. "I tried to stop them." Delinsky's pants were torn, his face bruised, and his lip swollen.

"You're lucky to be standing," Burgess said. "The Watts family's not known for gentleness."

"I should have anticipated..." Delinsky shifted his feet uncomfortably, staring at the ground. "I...uh...didn't think it would be quite the thing to shoot them, sir. Under these circumstances, I mean."

"You made the right call."

Burgess studied the crowd behind the barriers, curious and excited, like this was a street fair. There was even an ice cream truck. "I ought. I should. Don't beat yourself up, Gabe. You've done a good job." He took out his notebook. "You were the first one here? First officer?"

"Yes, sir." Delinsky pulled out his own notebook.

"Let's sit in the van. It's cooler." Burgess summoned the nearest officer and left him in charge, stopping at the cooler for another Coke. The real thing this time. He needed the sugar. He'd come straight here without breakfast and that had been hours ago. There was one soda left and Delinsky hesitated. "Goddammit, take it," Burgess said. "You've worked as hard as anyone." He figured Delinsky, catching this as he was about to go off shift, had missed a meal, too.

He walked back to the officer he'd just put in charge and told him the cooler needed to be refilled. "And get some chips, too, or pretzels. Something salty. Everyone's sweating like crazy out here." Pizza would have been better, never mind that it was only 9:30 and hot as hell. Pizza was plenty salty, but having it delivered to a crime scene? Media wouldn't miss that. The GP could have ice cream trucks and act like they were at a carnival. Cops walked a finer line.

In the van, they opened their sodas and savored the cool. "Summer like this," Delinsky said, "I might as well have stayed in the south."

"You don't sound like south. You sound like Boston."

Delinsky smiled. A perfect smile, warm and comforting. Burgess had seen him use it to good effect on a frightened crime victim. Too bad a smile couldn't do anything for Timmy Watts. "Boston's south of here," he said.

"Who called it in?" Burgess asked.

"Woman out walking her dog." Delinsky carefully read off the woman's name, Grace Johnston, and her address. "Nice lady. Real shaken up. She knew the boy pretty well, said she's had him at her house. She said she wasn't really first. There was this guy in the park before her, but he refused to call it in. Said he didn't want to get involved."

What was the big deal? A phone call and a few minutes of the guy's time? "She know the guy?"

"Not by name. She referred to him as 'that jerk with the big dog.' But she knew his house. We go outside, I'll show you."

Burgess made a note. "Now, this woman—"

"There's more," Delinsky interrupted, "about the guy with the dog. The woman, Mrs. Johnston, says the dog went up to the body, sniffed around, then snatched something and ran away with it."

"She see what it was? What happened to it?"

"Too far away. Something blue, she said. Dog went down by the pond and when it came out, the blue thing was gone. She was across the park. It was only when she'd gotten around the end of the pond that she saw the blanket...went up and looked and realized what she was seeing. She told him he had to call it in. He told her to go fuck herself, he wasn't getting involved. Excuse me, sir, those are his words. She was uncomfortable saying them."

"That's why you set such a big perimeter, to include the pond?"

"Yes, sir. She said the man's dog is always out of control. That he won't keep it on a leash. Sounded like they'd had words before."

Burgess got on the radio to Melia, told him about the dog, and that they'd better get some people searching the area around the pond, looking for something blue. That the pond was a good place for someone to have tossed a knife.

"I was hoping to get out of here sometime before dark," Melia said.

"Oh, poor you," Burgess said. "I was on vacation."

"Nothing like that first day, huh?" Melia shot back. "Putting work out of your mind. Getting into that restful groove."

"Fuck you, Vince."

"I don't think so."

"Any sign of Terry yet?"

"I sent someone by his house again. Car was there but no one answered the door."

When he was finished here, he'd go find Kyle. "Look, it's a hundred and ten out there. The four of you better come cool off before your brains boil. The media'd love a nice front page photo of one of Portland's finest knocked on his ass. Probably print you in color."

Melia didn't respond. Burgess gave up trying to look after a pack of snarling alpha dogs and returned to Delinsky. "The family. Before you got overrun, you get their names? Relationships?"

"Names, yes. Relationships? I'm not sure they know. You met Mother Watts."

"Not so much an acquaintance as a mugging, as you know."

"That's how most people meet her. Family lives a couple blocks over, on Turley. Moved in about a year ago, when her mother died and left the place to her and her brother. She just moved in and fuck...uh...to heck with the brother."

"You know this neighborhood pretty well."

"I live around here. My wife grew up here."

It was good for this part of town to have cops living in it. Portland's downtown was located on a high spine of land in the center of a boot-shaped peninsula. At both ends of the boot, high promontories looked out to sea. The East End, with its parks facing out toward islands in the bay, had some of the city's prettiest views and greatest possibilities but had retained its reputation as tough and gritty long after other parts of the city had gone upscale. Ten, fifteen years ago, they'd be up here three or four times a night, for fights, people setting fires in the middle of the road. Driving down the streets, patrol cops could recite the histories of half the people they passed. Recently, that had been turning around.

"About the house, the inheritance..." Delinsky said. "I guess she and her brother were supposed to split the estate, such as it was. He wanted to sell the house. But Mother Watts...actually, her name is Dawn..."

"Red at morning, sailors take warning," Burgess murmured.

"With that woman, it's not just mornin'. She's a danger 24/7. Anyway, she moved in her extended family, lock, stock and barrel. From what I hear, there's plenty of stocks and barrels lying around, and the brother can't get his money, and he's some pissed..."

"Mad enough to do this?"

Delinsky shifted his broad shoulders wearily. "I can't imagine anyone mad enough to kill Timmy, and I'm a cop. Brother's named Hank. Henry Devereau. Lives out in Raymond, I think. Raymond cops'll know. Compared to his sister, he's a saint. Compared to the rest of us...?" Burgess made a note. They'd have to talk with Henry Devereau.

Delinsky waited until Burgess nodded. "Okay, so there's Mother Watts, and she's got about six kids from various marriages, or relationships, or whatever. There's her husband, wizened up old twist called Pap, only she calls him 'Stinky.' He's got a couple kids, his or his grandkids, I don't know, and there's various boyfriends and girlfriends of their kids in and out of there. Pap and Mother Watts, they had just the one child between them. Timmy."

Burgess thought of that unstoppable juggernaut of a woman, shrieking as she swarmed up the hill toward her child. "The apple of his parents' eyes and the joy of their old age?"

"Not exactly. Mother and Pap were so busy with

their assorted nefarious activities that young Timothy didn't get much raising, except what his brothers and sisters happened to provide when they noticed."

Burgess felt a surprising prick of disappointment. Despite the bruises he'd seen, the undernourished body, he wanted this child to have been loved. "Human Services been involved?"

"I guess a lotta folks phoned social services. Dawn Watts sat down with one social worker who dared to darken their door and scared her so bad she almost wet her pants. Girl wrote it up as an ideal family and never went near the place again."

Burgess made a note to find that social worker. "You might want to take a walk up there before the removal, see what was done to the boy before wasting any sympathy on that social worker."

"Bad?"

"He was butchered."

Delinsky rocked back like he'd been struck. "When I saw him up there, all wrapped in that blanket, I guess I thought...Even with the blood, I guess I hoped..."

Delinsky swallowed hard and squared his shoulders, trying to keep emotion out of his voice. He looked diminished. "Kid kinda wandered the neighborhood like some little lost soul. People were always asking him in, feeding him, taking him along on family expeditions, to the movies and stuff. He was kind of everyone's pet. You go house to house, you're gonna see a lot of tears."

Then Burgess understood. Delinsky hadn't just known Timmy Watts. He'd been one of the ones who looked after him, who'd called social services. "You knew him pretty well, didn't you?"

Delinsky blinked rapidly, then dropped his head to stare at his shoes. Burgess remembered him at another crime scene, a man with a soft spot for kids, and looked the other way. Let the man have his tears.

On the street, you learned to pack it away, not let it get to you. With the public in your face, you couldn't wear your heart on your sleeve. Cops saved that for when they were with their own, people who understood how it could hurt. How that beautiful slaughtered child lying up there could bring on spasms of rage and frustration, discouragement and profound sadness. After a while, every cop had his black holes, places he tried not to go because he knew they'd suck him in.

"Give me the Watts's address." Burgess wrote it down. "Anything else?"

"I can give you some names, people who looked out for him," Delinsky said. "When you see the kid's house, you'll know why he never went home."

Burgess was getting as much here as from five to ten interviews and a neighborhood canvass. They'd still have to do the canvass, though, and he wanted Delinsky involved. "I'd like you with us when we do the neighborhood, Gabe."

The big shoulders hunched as protest came and went on the young cop's face. "I just did a double, Sarge."

"I need you on it." It was part of shaping a cop. Man needed to know how to function when he was eighteen hours out and wrapped in the stink of his sweat. Burgess had little sympathy for a cop who wimped out because he was tired. It wasn't that kind of job. Delinsky sucked it down and nodded.

The door burst open and Perry and Wink Devlin staggered in, holding a limp Vince Melia between them. Melia's face was blotchy scarlet and dead white.

"Won't drink water, won't go stand in the shade, won't even loosen his goddamned tie," Perry complained as they eased their limp lieutenant to the floor. "We've all about hit the wall here. Funeral home's coming to do the removal. Carr's coming down, too. Sheesh. This day is a bitch from hell!"

He looked around with a faint grin. "Nice in here, Sarge." When he grinned, Perry still looked boyish, but otherwise, since Perry shaved his head, Burgess had lost a useful tool. He no longer had a disarmingly attractive, young-looking detective with dynamite interviewing skills to spring on unwary suspects.

"Vince were conscious, he'd tell you to watch your language."

"Vince were conscious, we couldn't get him off that hill. He's got his own boys."

"Get that shirt and tie off him and bring me the cooler," Burgess said. "We've got to get his temperature down. And put that box there under his legs." Delinsky went for the cooler.

"Shouldn't we call medcu?" Perry asked.

"Let's give it a couple." Melia was particularly nervous these days about image, about performance, with Captain Cote breathing down his neck about his stats.

Cote, who sat in an air-conditioned office studying pieces of paper, hadn't noticed they were having the summer from hell, and that the GP was responding the way people who didn't sit in air-conditioned offices did in heat. They drank and quarreled. Dropped the few clothes they wore and screwed the wrong people. Got mad and hit each other with whatever came to hand, robbed each other for money to buy fans and air-conditioners or to buy drugs to forget how miserable they were, and shot each other with little provocation because their tempers were already short. No, Lt. Melia did not want to be dragged off to the hospital instead of managing a crime scene, felled by a mere 110 degree day.

Melia was a good lieutenant. He stood up for his men, cut them slack when he could. He knew when to lean, when to let it ride. Captain Cote came from some antiseptic, stainless steel factory where they made bureaucrats. If he'd ever sweated for hours under blistering sun at a crime scene, he'd forgotten. If he showed up here now, he'd barely see that savaged child up there surrounded by buzzing flies. He'd see how sweaty and unprofessional they looked. Immediately start pressing for preliminary reports. No wonder Melia kept his tie as tight as Cote's ass.

Burgess dipped Melia's shirt in the icy water and spread it over his chest, draped his own soaked handkerchief over Melia's forehead, and slipped an evidence bag full of ice under his neck. It didn't take long. Like Snow White kissed by her prince, Melia's eyelids fluttered and he was struggling to sit up and ask questions.

Burgess pressed him down. "Give it a couple minutes, Vince," he said. "You blacked out. Delinsky's getting some Gatorade."

"Hate that stuff," Melia muttered. "I won't…"

"Shut the fuck up and do as you're told, or we *will* send you to the hospital. Sir."

"What…?" Melia closed his eyes, too weak to finish the question.

"I've ordered a fresh shipment of officers to search the area and drag the pond. Might as well ruin everybody's day. Stan can run it."

"You?"

"I'll talk to the woman who found the body, then go see the family. You and Stan can get the house-to-house together…ask them…" But Melia knew the drill. "Use Delinsky. He knows this neighborhood. Knew the kid."

Melia drank the Gatorade and made a face. "Your

vacation," he said. "I'm sorry."

Burgess acknowledged the inevitable. Today, he would be driving around the neighborhood, talking to people about the murder of a little boy, with an orange canoe on his roof and fishing poles rattling in the back seat, tantalizing him with what he was missing. Then, because a child had been murdered, he would return the canoe, stow the poles, and work this thing until he brought in a killer.

CHAPTER 4

Grace Johnston was a parboiled detective's dream. There was no hemming and hawing and 'keep the cop on the doorstep' with her. She seated him in a comfortable blue armchair in front of an air conditioner, offered lemonade or ice tea, and insisted on fixing him a sandwich before she would talk about what had happened.

"I know how long you've been out there working," she said, "and I haven't seen you visiting that disgusting ice cream truck."

If he hadn't been seriously involved with Chris, he would have offered marriage on the spot, the twenty-year age difference a mere bagatelle in the great scheme of things. This woman clearly had her priorities straight.

She waited, sitting quiet and upright on her chair, until he'd eaten. Then she took away his plate and resumed her quiet sitting. Her hair was thick, silvery and no-nonsense short. She wore white slacks and a short-sleeved blue sweater that matched her eyes. She was middle-sized, wore glasses, and looked both pleasant and smart.

He took her through the preliminaries. This was her house. She lived alone. A widow, unfortunately. She'd been in this neighborhood, this house, for forty years. Had seen it decline and now was watching it rise again, along with her taxes. She walked her dog in the park every morning. Not usually that early, but it had been so hot. She hadn't seen anyone else around, no one on the street, no cars, until she got into the park. Then she'd seen the man with the big dog.

"Is he usually there?" Burgess asked.

She considered. "I've seen him occasionally. I think he normally walks his dog later. Walks?" She sniffed. "He makes no effort to control that dog. Just strides into the park and takes off the leash. I think—" She lowered her voice, though they were alone in the room. "—that the way a dog behaves reflects the owner's personality. That man is undisciplined and uncivilized, and so is his dog."

"Tell me what you saw this morning when you came into the park."

"The park, you know, runs uphill from south to north. I suppose, to be more precise, south-west to north-east. From downhill on the south-west side to uphill on the north-east. I came in from the south side." She spoke with the certainty and precision of a teacher, then did a teacherly thing. She took a pad of paper and drew a quick, accurate sketch of the park, far better than he could have done. An art teacher, he decided, noting the long, deft fingers.

She labeled the streets that formed the boundaries of the park. Munjoy, Wilson, Moody, Beckett. Drew in the park entrances, the fence of black chain and bollards that surrounded it, the paths, the pond, the thicket of cattails on the north-east side of the pond, the wide, undulating swath of roses that lined the upper edge. He hadn't seen clearly before her drawing that the cove where they'd found the boy's body was one of many. The bank of roses edged the park in a scalloped fashion, so that no paths entered from the Beckett Street side. Seven evenly-spaced scallops. Timothy Watts's body had been in the second scallop in from Wilson. He wondered if that was significant.

She pointed to the corner of Munjoy and Moody. "I came in down here. Because of the uphill, and the cattails, I couldn't see that corner at first." She traced a path along the pond, stopping at the end. "Until I got here. The man with the big dog...his name is Osborne. I asked around after I got back this morning. I was so upset with him. Little Timmy was everyone's child. He was part of our neighborhood. When something like this happens, it affects everyone. You can't choose not to be part of it."

She shook her head. "I don't mean to waste your time venting my opinions, Detective. I know you've got a job to do. But I have strong feelings about community and people like Osborne...self-centered people who believe they don't have to be part of society, that they can simply opt out...anger me. I suppose it's classic, but families like the Watts have always been with us. People who are hereditary criminals. But Osborne's bright, educated. He could be so much more if he weren't a selfish clod."

She ran a hand over the sketch, then gripped that hand with the other. "You should say, 'Get to the point, Grace' like my husband did. When I got around the end of the pond, where I could see up the slope, Osborne was standing there, watching his dog. It was running toward...well, at that point, of course, I didn't know what it was running toward."

She stopped, her knuckles knotted. "I thought, I suppose *he* thought, that it was some homeless person who'd spent the night in the park. He probably considered it amusing to let his dog go romping up there. It's a big, frightening dog. It snarls, jumps on people. It bites..."

Tears clouded her bright eyes. "Timmy was so scared of that dog."

"Do homeless people sleep in the park?"

"They used to. Not so often now that we have a police officer in the neighborhood."

"Gabriel Delinsky?"

"He's a nice man. He takes his children to the park."

He wished he could linger in this cool, dark room and let her take her time. He hated rushing older people, always felt his mother's disapproval when he did. But time mattered. "The dog ran up the slope," he said, "and then?"

"Grabbed something from near the man's...I mean, at that point, I thought it was a man...from near his head, then backed off, barking frantically. It was making a fearful racket. Osborne called it, and he was making a fearful racket, too, because the dog wouldn't obey. I wondered why the man didn't wake up. Then the dog plunged down the slope with something in its mouth, right past Osborne, and into the bushes by the pond. Osborne made no effort to follow it, though he saw it had taken something."

"Could you see what the dog was carrying?"

She shook her head. "Something blue." She made a square with her hands, about ten or twelve inches. "About so big. Carried it into the bushes and came out without it. I know I shouldn't have, but I went up to Osborne and I said, 'Your dog took something from that man.' He just shrugged and turned away."

"What did he do then? Did he approach the...uh...Timmy?"

"Yes. He marched up there, bent down and grabbed the blanket like he was going to undo it, then he just kind of straightened up and walked away. So he couldn't help but see..." She stopped, making a conscious effort to suppress her opinions about Osborne.

"At some point you went up yourself and discovered the body?"

"You'll think I'm an old fool," she said. "I went up to apologize for Osborne and his dog. And when I got up there..." She looked toward the window, but what she was seeing was inside her head. "There was blood on the blanket. I wanted to run away then, but I thought maybe someone needed help, and when I got closer, I saw it was Timmy."

Abruptly, she shoved the pad and pencil off her lap and stood. "Excuse me..."

Burgess rested his head against the chair and closed his eyes. Lately he was so tired that some days the haze never lifted. It had been a hard winter and spring. He'd dragged himself through the last month with visions of that peaceful lake, pan-fried trout for breakfast, time with Chris when he wasn't busy or distracted. It was hard to let those visions go. But Timmy Watts was dead and for now, his attention need to be here.

He looked around the room—practical and pleasant, like Grace Johnston herself. He'd been at this long enough to be suspicious of people who were too forthcoming, witnesses too willing to share their stories. But he'd also been a cop long enough to see truth when it came at him. Grace Johnston was the real thing. A neighbor, a citizen, a good person. A bit opinionated, but then, most people who'd made it through seventy years were.

She returned with a box of tissues. "I guess it's all right to cry," she said. "You're probably used to it. My generation, we were raised to put up a good front. To pretend everything was fine, no matter what."

Burgess knew about that. His mother had perfected the art of keeping her troubles to herself, trying never to show her fear of his father or her worries about money to her children. She'd been dead going on three years now, and sometimes his grief was so strong it might have been yesterday. "Yes," he said. "It's all right to cry."

"He was just such an endearing child," she said, her voice shaking. "I don't see how anyone could..."

"How did you know him?"

"Oh, he was always around. Playing with other children. Riding his bike. Looking for bottles he could return for a little pocket money. Back in the spring, when I hurt my wrist, he used to come and walk Popeye. My dog."

"What was he like?"

Grace Johnston considered. Like her drawing, she would want her description of Timmy to be clear and accurate. And she would believe in not speaking ill of the dead. "A diamond in the rough," she said, finally. "The way he spoke, his language, was simply appalling, but he was full of wonder and curiosity. He was so needy it broke your heart, but he had an extraordinary natural generosity. Where he got it, with that family..."

He saw her willfully pull back from this digression. "Timmy was tender toward smaller children and animals. Except he was terrified of big dogs. Well, what would you expect? His family was likely to set their dogs on anyone, including their own relatives."

She wiped her eyes. "Half the time, they didn't even remember to feed him. He's only been around about a year. I don't know how it was where they lived before. But I can't imagine it was any different. He always looked like the rag man's child. Dirty and disheveled.

Always needing a haircut and a bath. I had a special afghan I put on the sofa when he was here because of the dirt, but he thought it was just for him. It was blue..." Her tears flowed freely. "Blue like the blanket he was wrapped in. Blue was his favorite color."

She turned away from Burgess, the closest she could come to privacy, until she'd recovered. "Sometimes he'd come after school and ring my bell. I'd find him on the steps with that adorable little buck-toothed grin, and he'd say, 'Please, Mrs. Johnston, I've came for tea.' I'd fix him cocoa and cookies, make myself some tea, and we'd curl up on the couch and read or watch TV. Not much of a reader himself, but he loved to be read to. He was everybody's child, Detective. Not quite nine years old. How could someone...?"

Burgess didn't have an answer yet. In order to understand what had happened, he had to come to know the victim, be able to picture him, know where he'd go and who he'd see. What his life was like. It was hard with anyone—the young mother working nights in a convenience store, the beloved grandfather bludgeoned with a pipe by a crack-head who wanted his wallet, the shy librarian raped and drowned in her bathtub—but children were the hardest. It was hard to reconstruct their lives, habits, and friendships. He couldn't help thinking of all the living they'd miss.

"Do you know who he played with? Who his friends were?"

"I can't give you names," she said. "A bunch of them used to run around the neighborhood, all different ages, girls and boys. He talked about two boys called Sam and Davey, but he was the only one I knew. When he came here, he came alone."

"Did you see him yesterday?" he asked.

She shook her head. "I went up to Rockport to an art

exhibit. Got back late and went straight to bed. I can't help but wonder if things might have been different if I'd been home."

"You can't blame yourself..."

"Of course I can." She opened the drawer of a small table beside her chair and pulled out a folded sheet of paper. "This was in my door when I got home."

He unfolded the paper. It was a crude crayon drawing of a blond child with a suitcase. On it, the artist had written: "I'm runig away frum hom. Gudby and thanks for all the kukies. Timmy."

"May I keep this?" he asked.

"If you think it might help. Oh," she said. "I never finished about Osborne. When I saw it was Timmy, I ran after him and told him to call the police. He had a cell phone on his belt, while I'd have to go home to call. And I wanted to stay with Timmy. Not that it mattered, but I thought he shouldn't be alone."

"I understand," he said.

"He wouldn't call. He said it was none of his business and walked away like it didn't matter at all that a little boy was dead."

"Thank you," he said, getting up. "Thank you for all your help."

She walked him to the door. He stopped in the doorway, assailed by the wall of moist heat, and looked down at her. She looked diminished and fragile. As soon as she shut the door, she'd be in tears again. "Is there someone you could call to be with you?"

She looked surprised, then nodded. "I should do that, shouldn't I?"

She followed him onto the porch and pointed to a blue house across the street and about six doors down. "That's where Osborne lives." As he stepped into the bright glare of the sun, she called after him, "Find him, Detective. Find the man who did this before he does it again."

Descending the steps reminded him that even the best painkillers have a finite working life. His knee was screaming like an ignored two-year-old. He stopped at his car, snarled at the sporty orange canoe, and grabbed some pills.

He called Stan Perry and arranged to meet him in forty-five minutes to interview Timmy's family. Perry would have had time to touch base with Rocky Jordan, who was searching the records, and would arrive up-to-speed with what the computer could tell them about the various members of the Watts family. Then he limped down the street to Osborne's house and rang the bell.

CHAPTER 5

The flurry of barking exploding inside made Burgess wish he'd brought pepper spray. This particular animal already had two strikes against it. It had messed with his crime scene and it had terrified a small boy. He had a pretty good idea he wasn't going to like the dog's owner much, either. Grace Johnston might not be a neutral observer but she was honest.

The barking continued but no one appeared. The Saab in the driveway had "Ozzie" on the vanity plate, so he had reason to believe the owner was home. He rang the bell again.

Footsteps thudded. The door was jerked open by a man wearing only a pair of chino shorts. His hair was wet and tousled, water beaded his chest and shoulders and ran in trails across a pale, flabby stomach. It didn't take a detective to know he'd just come from the shower.

"What the fuck do you want?" the man snapped. A huge mastiff, echoing his sentiments, stuck its head around his leg and growled.

Burgess flipped out his badge. "Detective Sergeant Burgess, Portland Police. Like to ask you some questions about the boy in the park." He stepped into the house, forcing the man and dog backward.

"Can't help you," the man said. "I don't know anything about that."

Burgess might have been born at night, but not last night. People should know better. Burgess knew what he looked like. He'd seen himself often enough in crime scene pictures. Salt and pepper hair, fierce dark eyes, the unsmiling mouth and scarred cheek, an aging full-back's body. It was neither a pleasant nor welcoming visage and he sure didn't look naive.

Burgess pulled out his notebook. "You are Mr. Osborne?" The man nodded. "Could we sit somewhere, sir? It's been a long day..."

Burgess could almost hear the words bubbling up in the man's brain. "I don't give a shit about your day." Some feeble vestige of manners or self-protection stopped them. The only difference between Osborne and the scumbags who normally uttered such sentiments was this guy had a nice house with shiny floors and leather furniture, a Saab in the driveway, evidence of a regular paycheck. Osborne waved a hand toward the living room. "I don't know why you want to talk to me, but have a seat," he said. "I'm going to put a shirt on."

Burgess started toward the living room.

The dog, growling, positioned itself between him and the doorway. "Rogue!" Osborne said. "Come." Rogue gave his master the canine version of eye-fucking attitude and stood his ground.

Burgess, watching the struggle between man and dog, heard Grace Johnston. "The man is undisciplined, uncivilized, and so is his dog." Finally, Osborne grabbed the dog's collar, dragged it down the hall, and shut it in another room. Then he stomped up the stairs. Between man and dog, Burgess didn't think the shiny floors would last long.

Osborne's living room had the unlived-in quality of a furniture showroom. Smart, uncomfortable sofa, a coffee table with carefully arranged books, two blond wood coasters and an ashtray, a black iron floor lamp with a mica shade and the price still hanging from the switch. The only personal touches were two blue and yellow needlepoint pillows. Maybe Osborne had a doting aunt. The generic 'Coast of Maine' painting over the sterile fireplace was too neat and pastel to be real. It needed a rusting piece of farm machinery, a derelict barn, or an overturned boat in a state of disrepair. Mainers weren't neat and pastel. They had projects. They had *stuff.*

Overhead, a hairdryer whirred, a door slammed, a toilet flushed. Eventually, Osborne reappeared wearing an ugly olive and tan plaid polo shirt and boat shoes without socks, his thinning blond hair moussed into place. "Sorry about that," he said, settling into an expensive leather chair. "Thought you were one of those damned college students from Greenpeace or the Sierra Club. Every time I get in the shower, the doorbell rings. Unless it's kids, selling candy or cookies or collecting bottles. The kids in this neighborhood." He rolled his eyes.

Burgess clicked his pen. "What's your full name and date of birth, Mr. Osborne?"

"Jeffrey. Jeffrey Davis Osborne. 7-10-69."

"You've lived here how long?"

"What difference does it make?" Burgess waited, pen poised. "Eight months."

"And before that?"

Osborne clearly didn't want to answer, which struck Burgess as odd. Finally, the man said, "New York," without elaboration. Burgess let it go. There were other ways to find out.

"You work here in the city?" Osborne started to protest again, then gave the name of a small brokerage firm.

"I understand you were in Knowlton Park this morning, walking your dog?"

"Yeah."

"About what time was that, Mr. Osborne?"

"Six-thirty, seven."

By six-thirty, the park had been sealed off. Was this guy lying only because he didn't want to be involved or was there something else? "While you were in the park, did you observe the body of Timothy Watts?"

"Who's that?"

This went beyond stupid. Even if Osborne hadn't known him from the neighborhood, by now, everyone in the state knew the identity of the dead child. "You weren't acquainted with Timmy Watts?" Osborne shook his head, an innocence on his face that wouldn't have fooled a first grade teacher. "Let me put this a little differently. While you were in the park, did you observe the body of a child, wrapped in a blanket?"

"No."

"You never observed anyone wrapped in a blanket, lying on the ground."

"Oh, yeah. There was someone on the hillside, up by the roses. I thought it was a homeless person."

"You never approached this person?"

"They give me the creeps."

"You never approached this person?" Burgess repeated. Osborne shook his head. "What about your dog? Your dog approach this person?"

"Rogue? He went up and sniffed around."

"I'm confused," Burgess said. "You tell me you never went near the person. Then you tell me your dog approached the person and sniffed around. How can that be?"

"Dog was all over the place," Osborne said. "I was down on the path."

"There's a leash law in Portland."

"Oh, shit. No one pays any attention to that," Osborne said. Then he flushed. "I mean, I...Look, what are you trying to pull here?" he demanded. "You said you were investigating a homicide. What difference does it make whether my dog was on a leash?"

"I don't know yet," Burgess said. "I'm just trying to find out what happened to that little boy. Starting with what happened in the park this morning. It would help if I could get some honest answers."

"Hold on." Osborne reddened, rising from his chair. "Are you calling me a liar?"

"Witnesses have stated that your dog took something from the area around the body and carried it off. That you were close enough to the body to touch the blanket. I want to know what really happened. What you saw. What you did. What your dog took."

"That old bitch is lying. I never touched him. And Rogue never took anything..."

Eventually, he'd find out why this man was lying. "When you came into the park this morning, did you see anyone?"

"Not until that old bag and her prissy little mutt showed up."

"What about on the streets? Anyone getting into a car? Any unfamiliar cars?"

"No. It was dead...uh...quiet...this morning." Somewhere in the house, a phone rang. Osborne bounced up. "Excuse me. I'm expecting a call." He hurried away.

Burgess used his absence to collect some dog hairs

from the pillow beside him and the rug at his feet, then collected a few damp blond hairs from the back of Osborne's chair. He put everything in evidence envelopes, slipped them in his pocket, and checked his watch. Almost time to meet Perry for their visit to the boy's family, and he wasn't finished. No matter. He wasn't getting any cooperation, and it wasn't worth the pushing it would take to move the guy off first base. These first hours mattered too much.

He'd visit the gentleman again, give his speech about interfering with a crime scene, obstructing government administration, abusing a corpse, make Osborne regret getting snotty with a tired cop. Maybe he'd bring Kyle with him. People claimed Burgess was scary, but it was Kyle who really spooked them. Maybe they'd ask why Osborne's coffee table books all featured pictures of naked men or naked children.

He limped to the door. Damned pills sure were taking their time kicking in. Or maybe they *were* kicked in, and this was as good as it was going to get. He pulled out his card, wrote 'to be continued' on the back, and set it on the hall table. Before leaving, he allowed himself a peek through the closed dining room door. A cheerful room, soft yellow with dark, modern furniture. Eight or ten large photos on the walls, all of prepubescent boys.

He swam through the thick air to his car, found Stan Perry leaning against it. "Nice canoe," Perry said.

Burgess ignored him. "Be with you in a second." He called back to 109, gave Osborne's full name, address and DOB, and asked for a records check. Then, though maybe it was locking the barn door after the horse had been stolen, he asked for surveillance on the place in case Osborne got spooked and started moving things.

"Looks like maybe we've got ourselves a

pedophile." Perry nodded. "So what do we know about these people we're about to visit?"

"Got a couple hours?" Perry said. "This is a one-family crime wave..."

"Just the highlights."

"Let's sit in my car," Perry said. "It's already cool."

"Can't argue with that. How's Vince?"

"He'll live if he stays out of the heat. He never should have gotten so involved, you know? The twins are what? Seven? Eight?"

"Eight, I think. They find anything interesting when they searched the park?"

"Lotta junk out of the pond. Your usual assortment of soda cans and bottles, candy wrappers, stuff like that. No knife. Didn't find the blue thing that lady talked about. But those cattails are a real snarl. We'll send people back early tomorrow, when it's cooler. Keep the place off-limits until then."

"Gonna be a lot of angry dog owners."

"Screw 'em," Perry said. "Not our problem, is it? Personally, I never thought we maintained public parks so people's pets would have somewhere to take a dump."

Inside the cool car, Burgess closed his eyes and grunted with satisfaction. "Nice," he said. "So. The Watts family..."

"Beginning with the matriarch," Perry said, "we've got prostitution." He smiled at Burgess's reaction. "That's an old one. Lots of larceny by check, robbery, blackmail, extortion, child endangerment, assault and battery, possession of a controlled substance, possession with intent to sell, criminal threatening. Nothing since they came back to Portland, but that's unlikely to be reform. She's probably got her kids doing the dirty work now."

"And the kids are?"

"Hers? Daughter, Shauna, age 30. She's got a short sheet. Mostly prostitution, drug sales, couple OUIs. Parole officer says she's living at the house. Shauna has a baby. Son, Michael, age 28. He's a thug, pure and simple. Started knocking old ladies down and stealing their groceries, their purses, what ever he could get, at age 12. He's progressed from there. PO says at one point, he was pimping for his sister. Currently doing time for murder. He wanted a beer. Girlfriend told him to get it himself, so he shot her."

Stan shuffled the papers. "Let's see. Next you've got Dwayne, age 26. Minor drug stuff. He's mostly into home improvement scams. Roofing, driveways, things like that. Collects deposits, never does the work. He's living at home. Probably working on the place."

Burgess rubbed the back of his neck. "They know we're coming?"

"Thought I'd give 'em a chance to get the hardware and drug paraphernalia out of sight, they being the grieving family and all. Didn't want to have to arrest any of 'em today."

"Kind of you."

"Oh, I studied in the Joe Burgess school of public relations. And anyway, didn't our training talk about the importance of the detective's relationship with the grieving family?"

"Sounds like the Terry Kyle school to me. Aren't I supposed to be a heartless oaf?"

Perry's humor fell away. "What's up with that, anyway? Where is Terry?"

"Wish I knew," Burgess said. "He's compulsive about checking messages. He's always looking for overtime, looking to keep Wanda the PMS Queen off his back. He'd never miss a chance like this."

Even if Kyle hadn't been a dynamite cop and badly needed here, he was their friend. Friends looked after one another. Cops looked after one another. "When we're done here, let's swing by his place," Burgess said.

"Sounds like a plan," Perry agreed. "Let's see. Then there's Jason." Perry consulted some papers. "He's 24. Real light-weight compared to the others. Just a few minor drug things. But dollars to doughnuts, he's just better at not getting caught. How many's that? Four? Okay. Then there's sweet 19-year old Ricky. His specialty seems to be sexual assaults. Just got out for good behavior." He shook his head. "Ricky's one of those charmers thinks if the victim smiles in relief as he's leaving, it means she wants to see him again. His PO gives him three or four weeks before he falls off the wagon or whatever it is rapists fall off of."

"I think they fall into," Burgess said. "It's never their fault, poor things. The girls are asking for it."

"Yeah," Perry grinned. "It's those breasts. If they'd just leave 'em at home instead of wearing 'em out in public and driving us poor guys wild." He paused to consult his list again. "Last, and by far the least, is Iris. She's 17. And as far as I can tell, clean as a whistle…"

"How did that happen?"

"She's deaf. Away at a special school."

"In the summer? I'm surprised they let her go," Burgess said. "Sounds like a deaf girl would be handy to that lot. You'd think, in the Dickensian tradition, they'd at least teach her to be a pickpocket or something. That all?"

"Dickensian?" Perry, used to Burgess's idiosyncrasies, shrugged off the lit ref. "Then there's Pap's kids. Frankie's 40. He's up in Thomaston, but his daughter, Adele, used to live with Pap. She's 21. A working hooker. PO didn't know if she was around or not. Pap has a daughter, Alice, but she's on the West

Coast somewhere. And then there's Lloyd. He's a mechanic. About 30. Lives there with his girlfriend and their baby. He specializes in stolen cars and the drug trade."

"Place must be like a rabbit warren," Burgess said.

"More like a den of iniquity."

"Iniquity, Stan? You *are* sounding like Kyle."

Perry made a face. "Gosh, Dad. I was trying to sound like you."

Burgess cuffed the side of his head. "Okay, son. Let's go ask these people some questions."

Perry put the car into gear. "We could walk," he said, "but I don't mind having my ride there. Makes me feel safer, walking into a den of iniquity and all. Think they'd mind if we asked them to wear name tags?"

Someone banged on the window and Burgess looked up to see a teenager standing there, awkward, red-faced, scared-looking. He rolled down the window. "Yes?"

"Sir. Excuse me. Are you one of the police officers working on Timmy's murder?" The boy's hands crept into his pockets, made fists, and shifted up and down, taking the shorts with them.

"I am."

"Then please, sir." Another nervous shifting of the shorts. "I'm scared as heck of Timmy's family, but I've got something I'd like to tell you."

"Get in."

Perry shoved the car back into park as the boy, sweaty and panting like he'd been running, climbed into the back seat. Burgess pulled out his notebook. "Go ahead," he said.

CHAPTER 6

This had better be good. Hours into this thing, they'd learned little about Timothy Watts's last day. Maybe this kid knew something. "I'm Detective Sergeant Burgess. This is Detective Perry," Burgess said. "What did you want to tell us?"

The boy's eyes darted from one to the other and then to the door handle like he regretted his impulse to hail them. "I don't know if I can tell you," he said. "I mean, like if that jerk Dwayne ever found out I'd talked to you, he'd kill me."

He was thin, his body just beginning to show the muscling of the adolescent male. Could have been any age from 15 to 19, but hairy calves and the tailored wisp of soft beard suggested the older end. He wore baggy cargo shorts, an open Hawaiian shirt, and a tight sleeveless undershirt. His gold-rimmed glasses gave him a slightly nerdy look.

"Dwayne doesn't need to know it came from you."

The boy pushed a shock of hair back from his face and looked at Burgess hopefully. "I guess that's right, isn't it? I'm Matty. Matthew McBride. I live over on Morning."

"What number?"

"226. No. Sorry. 236."

"Date of birth?" The information, when divulged, made him eighteen.

"Your phone number?"

"Hey," the boy said, surprise, and something— concern, maybe—in his voice, "you aren't going to like....come there, or call me up, are you? Because my mom wouldn't like that. She wouldn't want me involved in this. She's uncomfortable with the Watts family, you know. They may be ignorant thugs, but it isn't smart to underestimate people with a propensity for violence. She tried talking to Mother Watts once." His eyes flitted from one of them to the other. "Timmy's mother, I mean, trying to tell her that she ought to keep better track of Timmy. I guess you can imagine how that went."

He tugged at his hair and flopped over onto the other side of the car. "I mean, do you, like, *know* about that family? I figured, being cops and all, you must."

He trailed off, obviously overwhelmed by the possibility of having to explain the Watts family. Then he blurted out his phone number and began to button his shirt.

"I think we've got them figured out," Burgess said. "What was it you wanted to tell us?" They were late getting to the victim's family and this little twerp was taking his sweet time getting to the point.

"It was maybe a week ago. A week, ten days...I forget." The boy settled into story-telling mode, the busy fingers now unbuttoning. "I was coming back from the park. I'd been over there tossing a Frisbee with Timmy. He was..." He hesitated. "Timmy was a pretty good athlete for such a little shrimp. Coming up toward their house, there were loud voices. Timmy was timid, you know. He tried to avoid fights and stuff."

Burgess could feel the clock ticking, forced himself to be patient.

McBride tapped his lips. "That's why he spent so much time wandering around the neighborhood, even at night, or like when it was raining and stuff. Trying to stay out of their way. So when he hears loud voices, he says 'Let's wait here, Matty. Dwayne sounds angry' and pulls me into the bushes. So, we're crouching there, listening to Dwayne and this other dude arguing, and the mosquitoes are eating us alive."

He shrugged. "I don't suppose I'm really much use to you, you know. I can't describe the other guy."

The boy almost seemed to be enjoying this, but maybe it was only that nerves were making him scatterbrained. Or he was one of those pitiful characters who hoped to be a hero, and the hesitations were coyness. Burgess knew anything could be their big break, but this didn't feel promising. "That's okay," he said. "Just tell me what you saw."

"Like I said. Dwayne was arguing with someone. A big bulky man. Dark. He had his back to me, but their voices were loud. I heard him say, 'You'd better get me what you owe me, Dwayne. What I paid you for. Or something very bad's gonna happen.' Dwayne yells at him that he'll get his fuckin' stuff soon as it's ready. Then the man says, 'That's what you said last week, asshole,' and Dwayne says, 'Get the fuck outa my face,' and the guy says, 'I mean it. I ain't waitin' much longer. You'll be sorry you fucked with me.' Then he jumps in his truck and peels off. Dwayne goes inside and slams the door. Me and Timmy come out of the bushes. He goes inside, and I go home."

Something to ask Dwayne Martin about. "You notice anything about the man? Age? Height?"

"No." The kid was twisting his buttons like they were control knobs.

"What about the truck?"

"I don't pay much attention to trucks. They're kind of a working class thing."

What did the kid expect? It was a working class neighborhood, except for some gentrification around the park and up along the Eastern Promenade.

"Did you see Timmy yesterday?"

One of the buttons popped off. McBride stared at it, surprised, then tucked it in his pocket. "Not for a couple of days. Yesterday, my mom wanted me to spend some time with her. It's her vacation, see, and I'm her only child."

"Who might have seen him? Who should we talk to?"

McBride shook his head.

"We appreciate your coming forward like this, Matty," Burgess said.

He looked back at the boy, trembling like a terrier in the back seat, buttoning the shirt. Didn't add 'We'll be in touch' although they would. About this incident and about Timmy Watts and his habits. Talk to the boy, and, whether she liked it or not, talk to his mother.

Matty McBride exhaled like he'd been holding his breath the whole time, opened the door, and jumped out. He watched them drive off, his fingers hooked through the belt loops of the improbable shorts the boys all wore—the ones that perched precariously on their hip bones, showing a generous swatch of their Joe Boxers—twitching them up and down.

"Something creepy about that kid," Stan said. "He doesn't seem upset enough. And he's an arrogant little snot."

"We don't have to like 'em for them to be useful."

"Not very useful."

Burgess hadn't formed an opinion yet. He'd wait until they'd talked face to face, not looking over his shoulder into a dark back seat. "We'll take another look at him, Detective. And have a chat with his mother."

"He won't like that."

"Nothing new there," Burgess said. "Nobody likes a cop 'til they need one. Let's visit that den of iniquity. And let's tell dispatch where we're going."

"Aye, aye, sir," Stan barked, saluting and picking up the radio, all while pulling away from the curb. A remarkably dexterous lad.

The Watts's place stood out like a red dress at a funeral. It was a quiet street of plain houses fronted by small yards, many with low hedges or some kind of decorative bushes, many with some attempt at grass and flowers. Not the Watts's place. It was impossible to see whether the front lawn had grass. It was covered by parked vehicles. The driveway was blocked by several rusting metal barrels, large blue plastic barrels, beer kegs, a rusting bedspring, an eviscerated sofa, and a small mountain of plastic trash bags. Some of the bags had burst and the place stank of garbage.

"We'd better check and see if there have been complaints by the neighbors," Burgess said, making a note.

They pulled in along the curb behind the vehicles. Before Perry had the engine off, the porch door flew open and a shirtless red-faced man with long, greasy hair and a torso so heavily tattooed it looked like the funny papers stormed down the walk. He had a knife in a sheath on his belt. He was at least 6' 6" and an easy 350. "Get that shit-heap the fuck outta here! You're blocking my truck." He pounded on the hood with a basketball-sized fist.

Burgess stared calmly at the hammering fist. "That's public property," he said.

"I don't give a good goddamn! You're blocking my truck."

"You live here?"

"Wadda you think? I park my truck on somebody else's lawn?"

"Your mother home?"

"Last I heard, she was moanin' and carryin' on like she gave a damn about that little twerp." Abruptly, the man turned and went back inside.

Burgess followed, unsurprised. Nothing he'd ever heard about the family had led him to expect civilized behavior. They went up steps jumbled with litter— empty fast-food wrappers topped a thick layer of cigarette butts, discarded matchbooks, candy wrappers, and canine feces. The entrance was through a glassed-in sun porch shared by bulging trash bags and two German Shepherds.

What they'd find inside wouldn't be much different. People who live like pigs don't stop at the door to the sty. He'd seen too much in twenty-eight years to be very shocked by the squalor in which some people lived. So he wouldn't be shocked. But on behalf of Timmy Watts, he would be angry. He raised a fist and knocked. Waited no more than a breath, and knocked again. Suddenly, the door flew open. An old man stood there, poking absently at his mouth with a toothpick. Delinsky's description had been right on the mark. A dried up little twist of a man.

Burgess showed his badge. "Detective Sergeant Burgess, Portland Police. Detective Perry. About your son, Timothy. May we come in?"

The man stepped back, his head bobbing in a nod. No reaction on his face. Cops on the doorstep were common in this house. "Mother's the one you want to see. She's through here." He jerked his skinny neck, pointing with his chin. "She's takin' this real hard. They hadda give her drugs." He stepped over a dog and disappeared down a dark hallway.

Burgess followed, his hand on the butt of his gun. He'd seen bad, but this was beyond squalid. Obviously, no one took the dogs out. They simply did their business wherever they happened to be. The stench, simmered by the damp summer heat, was worse than a six-day corpse. He pulled out a tube of Vick's, touched up his nostrils, and passed it to Perry.

In a back bedroom, the woman who had wiped out his knee lay on the bed, her housedress rucked up to her waist, a fan at her feet. Her vast lard-white thighs were roped with bulging veins and explosions of purple spider webs. "The police, Mother," Pap Watts announced.

She snatched a tissue from the box beside her. "Catch him, officers. Catch the monster who did this to my baby!" The television on the dresser was showing cartoons.

There was no place to sit. The only chair was occupied by a sullen woman with a rat's nest of black hair, nursing a filthy baby. She glanced at them, then shifted her eyes back to the television.

Burgess leaned against the wall, wondering which would terminate the interview first—his knee or the overwhelming sense that he was going to be sick. He was an experienced professional here to collect facts from a victim's family, but envisioning that brutalized child in the park living in this hell hole sickened him almost beyond endurance.

"Mrs. Watts," he pulled out his notebook, "when did you last see your son Timmy?"

"Last night," she said mournfully.

"What time last night?"

She struggled to sit up and, perhaps remembering that being a grieving mother demanded a certain dignity, tugged her dress over her thighs. "Hanged if I know," she said. "He was always in and out. Playing with the neighborhood kids. Summertime, you know."

"What time does he usually go to bed?"

She pondered the question. "Ain't got a bedtime. Just goes up when he's tired."

"Did he sleep here last night?"

Mother Watts looked at the other woman. "Shauna, you see Timmy come in last night?"

The woman glared at her mother. "Fuck, no," she said. "I was busy with the baby, then I hadda work."

"What about earlier, Mrs. Watts?" Burgess said. "When did you last see him?"

"Dinner time, maybe."

"Timmy was home for dinner? What time was that?"

"I dunno if he was home. Lotta times, he ate at a friend's. You know how kids are."

"You don't recall?"

She shook her head. "'fraid I don't."

"What did you have for dinner last night?"

"I don't recall," she said. "Pizza, maybe?"

"Did you fix Timmy's dinner?" She shook her head. "Who normally gives him dinner?"

"Ain't no normal," she said.

They could have burned that sentiment into a board and hung it over the front door. "What about other family members? Who would have been home who might remember?"

"Maybe Pap can help you. Boy was always in and out. I just don't recall..."

This family was well versed in not recalling. "Pap was home last night? He might have seen Timmy?"

She reconsidered. "No. Now that I remember, Pap was playing cards with friends."

"What about your other children?"

Her face went vacant as she sorted through the residents. "Lloyd's girlfriend, Darlene, maybe? She kind of took a fancy to Timmy. Used to read to him and stuff." She turned to her daughter. "Shauna? Was Darlene around last night?"

"I told you already," the girl said in a bored voice. "I was busy with the baby, then I hadda work. Ask Pap. Or Lloyd. I think he's upstairs asleep. Darlene's workin'."

This was getting them a lot of nowhere. "Let's back up," Burgess said, still addressing the mother. "When do you last remember seeing him...that you're sure of?"

"I can't rightly say."

"What about the kids he played with? Can you give me some names?"

"Sam and Davey. They're two doors down." She pointed toward the left. "Mother's a real bitch, but Timmy liked to go there. Otherwise?" She shook her head. "There was a whole pack of 'em, boys and girls. Ran around like wild Indians."

"What about adults? Were there grown-ups he was friendly with? Liked to spend time with?"

"Everybody loved Timmy," she said. She sounded a little surprised and for the first time, there was a touch of real sadness in her voice.

"Can you give me some names?"

"'fraid not."

Burgess looked at Perry. They were getting nothing here but a big goddamned zero. It made the door-to-door that much more important, the hope of finding someone who'd seen the child yesterday. Tell some bleeding heart member of the GP about the Watts's reaction and you'd get tutt-tutting disbelief and the assertion that it surely *must* be grief. Tell 'em about the house, and they'd say 'no way.' Sometimes he wished he'd kept pictures, but unless it was a crime scene, that would invade people's privacy.

"How old was Timmy?"

She had to think about that, too. "He was eight," she said, finally. "Gonna be nine in October. Third grade in the fall." She sighed and closed her eyes, exhausted by the strain of using her brain for something legitimate.

Burgess turned to the woman on the chair. "Where does Darlene work?"

"She's a toll taker. Out there at Exit Eight."

The answer surprised him. "And her last name is?"

"Packer."

"Thank you. Do you suppose you could show us Timmy's room?"

"Ain't got a room."

"Where he slept," Burgess amended.

"Pap'll show you. He ain't busy." She shifted her eyes back to the screen.

Burgess closed his notebook and forced out the words, usually so hard to speak in the face of people's grief, that here were hard to say in the face of such indifference. "Thank you for your time, Mrs. Watts. We're very sorry about your loss. You know we'll do our best to find out who did it."

"Who did it?" She roused herself and stared at him. "You don't know who did it? It was that faggot lives over by the park. One that drives a Saab? He's had his eye on Timmy ever since he moved in. Timmy said so. Said the man invited him in, give him pizza, and made him look at dirty pictures. Timmy loved pizza. Cheese pizza. But Timmy didn't like to go there. He was afraid of that dog. It bit him once. Timmy's brother, Dwayne, he hadda go over there, give that faggot a piece of his mind. We didn't have no trouble with him bothering Timmy after that. But I bet it was him."

Burgess opened his notebook again. "What makes you think the man by the park might be involved?"

"That's what faggots do, ain't it? Screw little boys."

"You think you know who killed your boy, but you weren't going to mention it?"

"Didn't ask, did ya? I figured you knew."

"You have any reason to think Timmy was at this man's house last night?"

Another mountainous shrug. "Said he was gonna have pizza with a friend."

So now she recalled. "This man by the park. Mr. Osborne. Was he the only person around who ever gave Timmy pizza?"

"Shit no. Everybody give Timmy pizza. People knew he loved it."

"So you don't know that Timmy was at this man's house?"

She shook her head. "Do you have any idea where Timmy was last night?"

"I'll bet it was with that faggot."

What kind of mother lets her child wander unsupervised in a neighborhood where she believes there's a pedophile? He wondered whom the boy might have gone to for comfort in a house like this? Was overcome, for a moment, with a childish desire to turn back the clock. To make it yesterday, when someone could still have rescued Timmy Watts. He didn't stay there long. "Do you know of anyone else around here who might have harmed Timmy?"

"Everyone loved him."

God! It was like a knife in his *own* guts. This great sow could actually lie there and say, without irony, that her child had been loved by everyone. Someone had even loved him enough to kill him. Then again, thinking about the tender folds of the blue blanket, maybe she was right. Maybe someone had loved him to death.

"Do you have any idea why Timmy might have wanted to run away from home?"

"No call for that," she grunted, hardly considering the question. "He wasn't hardly here as it was."

"He ever run away before?"

"He went to see Iris once."

He tried the friends question again. "Who did he hang out with?"

The big hands moved indifferently through the air. "I can't rightly say."

"Do you mind if we take a look at Timmy's room?"

"Ain't got a room. I told you." Shauna, from her chair.

"He's got a corner, up to the attic," Mrs. Watts said. "Iris fixed it up for him real nice. You can go on up. Don't need no one to show you." She made a sound that was somewhere between a sob and moan, and closed her eyes. Before they'd left the room, she was snoring.

CHAPTER 7

Up one flight of stairs and then another, jarring his knee and making him want to go down and twist *her* goddamned knee, see how *she* liked it. The attic was hot enough to cook eggs on the floor and mostly as cluttered as the rest of the house, but it wasn't as dirty. Maybe the dogs didn't like the steep staircase. One small corner was neat. A mattress on the floor was covered by a faded quilt with cars and trucks. A fuzzy yellow backpack made from a character he didn't recognize served as the pillow. There was a scrap of green rug. Stacked wooden produce crates, painted white, served as a dresser and separated the space from the chaos beyond.

On another painted crate beside the mattress was a lamp shaped like a giant crayon, a photograph, and a small, neat stack of books. Burgess looked at the meager space life had allotted Timmy Watts—the pathetically small stack of clothes, shabby sneakers, a plastic crate holding a few toys, including a red wooden car with three wheels and a small box of crayons, and his throat got tight. Crumpled shorts lay on the rug beside threadbare socks and a stained dinosaur tee shirt. Otherwise, everything was neat, suggesting Timmy had changed in a hurry.

"Oh, Jesus," Stan Perry muttered behind him. "Oh, sweet Jesus. He gets a miserable little corner of the friggin' attic! This case, Joe...this case...I've seen plenty, but this one could break your heart."

"It's not doing mine much good," Burgess agreed. "But look. This isn't like downstairs. It's clean. Painted. Someone took some time here." He stayed outside Timmy's corner, taking it all in, not ready to touch anything. A person's private space, even a child's, could tell him a lot. This told him that Timmy Watts had been neat for a small child. Particular about his space.

He sucked in a breath, knowing the pain in his chest wasn't just from breathing scorching, dusty air. "Someone loved the poor little thing after all."

"Iris," Perry said. "The deaf sister. His mother said Iris fixed it up."

"I wonder if anyone's thought to tell her, or if they'd even bother," Burgess said. "It would be awful for her to read it in the papers."

"Being deaf in this household was probably an advantage."

"Even Helen Keller had a nose."

Burgess was ready to enter Timmy's corner now. He wished Perry would be quiet, or that he were alone. He believed if he listened carefully enough, this place would tell him about Timmy Watts. But he couldn't listen if Perry kept talking. "Can you give me a few minutes, Stan? Maybe talk with Mr. Watts, see if he has any recollection of Timmy's day yesterday? And any information about the boy's friends. Find out how to contact Iris."

Perry went, as glad to be released as Burgess was to have him go, despite the stench below. They both knew it didn't take two detectives to go over that small area. That Burgess worked best alone. Perry was good at the people stuff, at getting them talking. He was more use downstairs. It was hard to strike the necessary balance between investigative caution and cop's intuition. Alone in the room, Burgess could sense things, learn about Timmy Watts by the stuff he kept and how he arranged it, but in an era when so many cases were made or broken based on evidence, vital evidence was collected under the watchful eyes of another cop. It might be months, even years down the road before they knew what mattered.

As Perry's footsteps retreated, Burgess sat down on the mattress and massaged his knee. Legwork, he thought ironically, was what solved cases like this. Watchful, persistent legwork. Going through the neighborhood like a human filter, talking to people, snagging the important bits, then fitting them together like the pieces of a puzzle. Was the fact that he was starting with only one good leg a sign? Sighing, he pulled on gloves and picked up the stack of books.

He realized, thumbing through them, that he had very little idea what Timmy Watts had been like. In an ordinary case, if there was such a thing as an ordinary child murder, there would be family members who could talk about the child—his personality, his friends, his schedule. They might talk through tears, around the lumps in their throats, and their talk might be punctuated with long, terrible silences broken by sobs and shudders as the child was remembered, but they would talk. Here, his brother, only hours after the death was discovered, scoffed at the notion that someone had cared about the little twerp. His sister couldn't tear her eyes from the TV. His mother couldn't recall when she'd last seen him.

The books were worn and tired, with price stickers

from the Salvation Army and yard sales, except for one pristine, hardcover copy of *The Polar Express,* inscribed "Merry Christmas to Timmy from The McBrides," two coloring books labeled "frum Iris" in a child's labored printing, and a copy of *Miss Rhumphius* from Grace Johnston. He held them by their spines and riffled through the pages. Nothing fell out except a note from Timmy's teacher saying he often dozed off in school and urging that he be put on a more regular schedule.

Burgess checked the pockets of the few pairs of pants and shorts. Found some candy wrappers, elastics, a movie ticket and a stubby pencil with the name of a miniature golf course. Under the clothes, he found a heart-shaped candy box which contained Timmy's treasures—a small, hand-held game with a dead battery, some beach glass, a Star Wars figure, two dollar bills, some letters and postcards which appeared to be from Iris, alphabet letters from an old keyboard, and a lethal-looking pocket knife.

Burgess sat back down on the bed and prepared duplicate receipts for items taken, one for himself and one for the family, listing the things from the pockets, the teacher's note, and the contents of the treasure box. It was tedious, but many a criminal has walked because some cop was too lazy, rushed, or careless to document evidence or maintain the chain of custody.

Then he picked up the photograph. There was a resemblance to the two women downstairs, but it was faint. The girl in the photo—he assumed it was Iris— was plain and slight, but there was something courageous in the lift of her chin, a vital warmth in her smile. Finally, a family member he looked forward to meeting.

There were footsteps on the stairs and Perry came in. "Anything?" Burgess asked.

Perry shook his head. "Pap thinks maybe Timmy was home for lunch yesterday, but he can't swear to it."

"You talk to the brother? Dwayne?"

"He's gone out."

"Without his truck?" Perry shrugged. "What about...what's his name? Lloyd?"

"Sleeping. I tried, but I don't think Gabriel's horn would rouse him."

"Detective Perry, I'm going to search the room."

Methodically, he went through it, collecting the things he'd already identified—the stuff from the boy's pockets, the treasure box, the note. Then, though these were not usual hiding places for a child this young, he checked underneath the backpack-pillow and under the mattress. The child had lived in a household where being secretive was the norm, as natural as failing to recall the events of a given day or the whereabouts of any family member.

Under the pillow, he found a smooth rock with the word "love" carved into it. Handling it carefully by the edges, he slipped it into an envelope and added it to his inventory. Under the mattress, he found nothing. Finally, he unzipped the pack. He took out a ratty beach towel and bathing suit. Below was a Ziploc bag of what looked like dirty rock candy.

He sighed, knowing, even before he unzipped the bag and inhaled the foul stink, what he'd found. What was it doing in a child's room, even in this house? Had Timmy taken it by accident, thinking it was candy, then been afraid to put it back? Had his taking it, or even knowing about it, had something to do with his death? He looked at Perry. "What smells like cat piss, looks like dirty crystals, and doesn't belong in a child's room?"

With a gloved hand, Perry took the bag by the

corner, and sniffed. "Crystal meth?"

"How do we list this on an inventory of items taken from a child's room?"

"Think we oughta call Vince? Get a warrant?"

"We'll talk to him when we get to the station," Burgess said. "We've got permission to search."

"I'd like to take this house apart."

"You think he was killed here?"

"Those stab wounds...that level of violence. That's someone out of control...could be a shithead on speed," Perry said.

"It's Vinnie's call," Burgess said. "And it's a tough one. Let's give these people a copy of the inventory and head back downtown."

"How you gonna list it?"

"Ziploc bag of crystals. Rock candy? With a question mark." He put it into an evidence bag, then carefully logged it onto both inventories. He pulled out his handkerchief and mopped his face. "I could use a shower." He limped toward the door, carrying the stuff they'd found.

"After this place, I'd like to burn my clothes, shower, and down a six-pack."

"Gonna be a while before you get to do any of those things. Besides, that's my shirt, and I'm fond of it." Burgess thought of the canoe on his car. The fishing poles. He could shower at the station, but all he had to change into were casual clothes. He needed to grab a minute to call Chris. Tell her what was going on. That their vacation would at least be delayed and might not be taking place.

He hoped she'd understand, but even though she was wise about relationships and flexible about his crazy schedule—a refreshing change from other women he'd known—it was hard for anyone to understand the all-consuming nature of the detective's job. Hard to live with. That's why detectives had such a high divorce rate. People expected them to be normal. They acted normal. Looked normal. Even lived normal until something like this came along. Then it swallowed them up. Even if they loved their wives, girlfriends, kids, their passion was for the job—the adrenaline, the problem-solving nature of it, the competitive good guy versus bad guy thing. Detectives had too many reasons they needed to win.

They found Pap Watts at the kitchen table, staring at a bottle of beer. They gave him the inventory, and Burgess made his speech about calling if he remembered anything that might help, especially information about Timmy's last day. Burgess left his card on the table by Watts's elbow, not sure the man had heard anything he'd said. He didn't ask that they have Darlene call when she finished work. Iris might be the only one who was clinically deaf, but the rest of the family might as well be.

Pap never acknowledged them or took his eyes off his beer. Burgess had seen enough people struck dumb by shock, paralyzed by grief to discount people's behavior right after a tragedy. Sometimes they did strange things, said strange things. Pap seemed neither shocked nor grieving. He'd given no sign that he'd cared for his son, asked none of the usual questions about suffering, would they get the guy, or about planning the funeral.

"I'll call you tomorrow, when the Medical Examiner is finished," Burgess said, "so you can make funeral arrangements."

Pap raised his head. "Don't the state take care of that?" he said. "All the taxes people pay, I should think they oughta."

Burgess doubted anyone in the Watts family had ever paid a cent in taxes. "Families usually..."

Decided to save his breath. "The Victims Witness Advocate will be in touch."

Back in the car, Burgess called Vince Melia and told him they were coming in.

"Find anything?"

"Another big headache."

"Meaning?"

"Tell you when we get there."

"I already have a headache," Melia groaned, which he probably did. The heat had given them all headaches. "You're gonna keep me in suspense?"

"A few minutes longer."

"You had permission to search? Stan was there? Witnessed everything?"

"I'm not a virgin, Vince. I get something, I'm not letting some lawyer screw me out of it. Isn't that why you pulled me back from vacation?"

"A bit testy, are we?"

"We'd like to take that place apart."

"This is the dead kid's family."

"They're not exactly Ozzie and Harriet. Oh, and Vince?"

"Yeah...?" There was hesitation in Melia's voice. An 'Oh, Vince' from Burgess usually meant trouble. "Rouse whoever you have to at the Department of Human Services. I want the file on Timmy Watts. I want to know who signed off on leaving that child in such filth and neglect...what lily-livered asshole signed that boy's death warrant."

"Take it easy, Joe."

"Easy! If you'd seen."

"When you get here," Melia repeated. It didn't belong on the radio.

"And can you send out for food."

"Sandwiches. Good call," Perry said, pulling in

behind Burgess's car.

Burgess got out, watched Perry drive away, then, despite the heat, stood in the street. His head was pounding. He should start the engine, get his air conditioning working. He should cool down, drink water, take Advil. But he didn't want to carry the stink of the Watts house into his car where it would linger for days, greeting him with rotting garbage, dirty diapers, stale beer and dog crap. As he knew too goddamned well, describe that shithole to some citizen and they'd say, 'Oh no, you're exaggerating. That's impossible.' But cops knew. Cops saw the impossible, the intolerable, the inhuman all the time.

He'd kept a lid on things while he was there, but now it boiled over. He pounded on the car in frustration, kicked his tire, knowing he hurt only himself. He couldn't help it. Even in the scumbag world he traveled, some things were almost unendurable. Leaving a helpless child in that violent and filthy den of thieves was one of them.

Wearily, he unlocked the door and climbed into the car. His knee didn't want to bend. He had to drag it in after him, gritting his teeth against the pain. That cloud, though, had a small silver lining. He was so tired he could have dozed off standing up. The pain kept him on edge. This many years into the bad-guy business, his vacation wrecked and his disposition not far behind, he needed a little silver lining.

Cops, like shade-growing plants, learned to thrive on small things. Just a little light was all they asked. Maybe, while he and Stan had been wading through the garbage, someone had turned up something. He cranked the air up to max, swigged some disgustingly warm water, and pulled away from the curb. Fishing poles clattering, canoe ropes straining, he headed back to 109.

CHAPTER 8

He backed his car in next to Perry's, got the box of stuff he'd gathered from Timmy Watts's room, and took the elevator upstairs. Devlin, Perry, and he were a rumpled, sunburned, sorry-looking lot. Melia had a fresh shirt and a worn look. Joining them were "Rocky" Jordan, their computer jockey, who'd done the records search on the Watts household and was checking the neighborhood for sex offenders, and Lt. James Shaheen, the day shift commander. Shaheen had secured the scene and was coordinating the neighborhood canvass.

Shaheen was a heavy man whose sandy crew cut was making a graceful segue into gray. Burgess's hair was graying in clumps, his colorist a kindergartner with a clumsy paintbrush. They'd come on the force about the same time. From day one, Shaheen had wanted his current job. He loved the day-to-day stuff of managing personnel, liked being a gruff father figure to scores of young cops. Burgess had taken longer to know he wanted to be a detective, not so much finding it as it found him. Now being watchful and suspicious had become as natural as breathing. An empty car beside the road could send his mind racing. He faced the door in restaurants, like a gunslinger in the old west.

"You might wanna keep an eye on Delinsky," Burgess said. "He's going to run himself into the ground on this one. His neighborhood and all. And he knew the boy."

"I'll take care of it." Shaheen patted his shoulder with a beefy hand. "Had two guys pass out on me today," he said. "Rather not lose a third."

His eyes drifted to the window, where even this late in the day, the sun still had bite. "Heat's gotta break soon. I can't remember a summer like this. Even nice people are in piss-poor moods. My wife's a bitch. My kids are sitting on their lazy asses while I'm working mine off to keep a roof over their heads. Can't even get the little ingrates to mow the goddamned lawn!"

"Too hot to mow," Burgess said. Complaining about the weather was something they did. Cops had to go out, no matter what the weather was. It gave them complaining rights. "When I was a boy, the summers were cool and perfect, with wide blue skies and fresh sea breezes. Must be this damned global warming, you think?"

Melia cleared his throat. "You two old farts wanna stop reminiscing about the good old days, when men were men and sheep were nervous? Can we get started? I've sent for sandwiches and coffee. Anybody need anything else?"

Burgess dropped his bulk into a chair, feeling ugly. Soon as he got some energy back, he was going out there to shake something loose. You didn't kill a kid in Portland, Maine and get away with it. Not on his watch. "I could use a bag of ice for my knee."

"Okay." Melia *wanted* him out there being ugly. "How's it doing, anyway?"

"Hurts like a bastard. She musta weighed three hundred. Beyond that? Who knows? Long about Wednesday, I might get around to checking it out."

"Don't be a hero," Melia said, but it was perfunctory. With Kyle missing and people on vacation, he couldn't spare another detective. Not with a rape, a domestic shooting, and a barroom brawl with a vic hanging on by his fingertips. The heat was making everyone crazy. Otherwise he would have taken Burgess to the hospital himself.

A box of sandwiches and coffee, like manna from heaven, came through the door, and Melia asked the officer who delivered it to get a bag of ice.

"Okay," Melia said, "I've got the media crawling all over me. As this gets out, every mother in the city will be in a panic. So what do we know? Joe?"

They were on the clock, tension warring with weariness as the ascendant emotion in the room. All their eyes were on him, waiting for him to tell them what they'd seen and begin to make some sense out of it. This was the process. Sum up what you know about the victim, the crime scene, and what you speculate from that. What you've learned since and where you're going next. It was frustrating to know so little.

"We've got an eight-year-old boy, wearing only underwear, with multiple stab wounds to the stomach, abdomen and chest, as well as evidence of a significant blow to the skull. Body was wrapped in a blanket and left in the park. Lee says at least some of the wounds were antemortem and there would have been significant bleeding. From the state of the blanket and the ground beneath it, we know he wasn't killed where he was found. Lividity and rigor suggest the boy was dead at least eight hours when we found him, and that for part of that time, he may have been lying on his stomach.

"It's a confusing crime scene," he said. "We don't have enough information yet to know if that was deliberate. We've got a murder that's consistent with rage. We've got overkill, frenzy, a killer who got going and couldn't stop. When we find the murder scene, there will be blood, no matter how hard they've tried to clean it up. The weapon looks like a double-edged knife, three to four inches long and three-quarters to one inch wide. Not serrated. We'll know more about that, and the manner of death, after the autopsy."

He looked at the circle of strained faces. "If he was lying on his stomach, he was lying in a pool of blood, yet his face, his torso and arms and legs were remarkably clean. Someone cleaned the blood off that child's body, then wrapped him carefully—you might almost say tenderly—in a brand new blanket. A torn piece of plastic we found under the body suggests it was then put in a black plastic trash bag, driven or carried to the park, and arranged there among the roses. Look..."

He used Grace Johnston's sketch to show the layout of the park and the careful arrangement of the body. "Seven of these coves, or bays, and he's in the second one. Not closest to the road, where it would have been easiest to dump him. And centered. Almost perfectly centered, the blankets smoothed and tucked. Someone went to some trouble." He looked at Shaheen. "Any luck finding that trash bag in any of the barrels?"

Shaheen shook his head.

"So we've got a kid from a filthy house, a kid who was always dirty, scrubbed clean and shampooed when we found him. We've got a family so indifferent they not only can't tell us the hour he was last seen, they're not even sure what day. Can't tell us when he last ate a meal at home or what that meal might have been. Can't tell us what his schedule is or who his friends are. Delinsky says the boy spent little time at home. He wandered the neighborhood. People looked after him, took him in, fed him."

He nodded to Shaheen. "I'm hoping your people are going to bring us some better information to help us build a timeline. Best we've got so far is the note he left for Grace Johnston, she's the one who called it in, saying he was running away from home."

He stopped. "Delinsky should be here. He knew the kid. Knows the neighborhood."

Shaheen rose. "I'll have him here in ten." He left the room, stopping to hold the door for a patrol officer who deposited a big bag of ice in the middle of the table.

Burgess stared at the wet bag and down at his aching knee. It might be cooler, but even in this heat, he wasn't going back out there with wet pants. He might not be the fashion plate Melia was, but he had a few standards. "Stan," he said. "You suppose you could fetch me the liner from that wastebasket?"

They ate their sandwiches while they waited for Delinsky, who came through the door exactly ten minutes later. Melia told him to eat something, then nodded at Burgess.

Burgess reported on his interview with Grace Johnston and held up her sketch again, pointing to the cattails. "So far, we haven't found what the dog took. We'll keep the park sealed off and search again tomorrow. I interviewed Osborne after I spoke with Grace Johnston. He insisted he hadn't approached the body. That his dog hadn't taken anything. And that he had never heard of Timothy Watts."

"He's lying," Delinsky said. "His dog bit Timmy once. I spoke with him about it. Told him I was reporting the incident and the next time his dog bit somebody, the dog officer would be taking it away."

"He's lying about a lot of things," Burgess said. "Boy's mother, Dawn Watts, says she's sure Osborne's the one who killed her son. She says she knows he's a pedophile. He's had Timmy at his house for pizza and made the boy look at dirty pictures. She says her son, Dwayne, spoke with Osborne and told him to leave Timmy alone."

"That's Dwayne Martin," Rocky Jordan said. "He's the second son. Dawn Watts's second son. Age 26. Minor drug stuff. Home repair scams. I haven't had a chance to run a check on Osborne yet." He hunched defensively and looked at Burgess.

Jordan was their budding cybercop, methodical, careful, and good with computers. But Jordan was slow, and Burgess was impatient. He wanted information quickly, before new things intervened, memories faded, evidence got lost, or crime scenes got messed up. "Osborne's dirty," Burgess said. "Even if he's not involved in this, he's dirty. We toss his place, we'll find something."

"Can't toss it without a warrant," Melia said. "In the good old days, or bad old days, depending on which side you're on, a cop's instinct and a few manufactured facts were enough for any judge. These days, an affidavit from God isn't always enough. Delinsky, you got anything concrete we can use?"

Melia was getting cynical. They all were. Staying on top of the Fourth Amendment was enough to make any cop crazy. "He's got coffee table books with pictures of naked children," Burgess said. "His dining room's wall-to-wall with oversized photos of prepubescent boys." He pulled out the envelopes. "I've got hair from the man and hair from his dog. All right out there in plain sight. Let's see what hair and fibers turn up from the body and the blanket. So far, we have no idea where the boy was yesterday."

"I'm with Burgess, sir," Delinsky said. "Osborne's dirty. He's also smart. When he first moved in, I noticed young boys going in and out of there, so I started watching. Since I've been watching, I've seen nothing I could use. Not even as an excuse to ring the bell and peek inside. Other than the time with the dog, and then he never let me in the door. Maybe he moved his operation elsewhere."

He looked hungrily at the remaining sandwich. "Anyone mind if I eat this?"

"Go ahead," Melia said. "Joe, fill this out a little. You and Stan went to the Watts's house. Did you talk with Dwayne Watts?"

Burgess shook his head. "I interviewed the mother, father, and sister. Mother couldn't recall when she'd last seen her son. She could barely recall how old he was. The sister, Shauna, had nothing to say. She wanted to watch cartoons. Dwayne was there briefly but left before we could talk to him. Our exchange was limited to an instruction to do the anatomically impossible. Pap Watts's son Lloyd was there, asleep, but Stan couldn't wake him. Stan, you talked with Pap Watts. You get anything more?"

Perry shook his head. "Pap Watts had trouble remembering the boy's name, let alone the last time he'd seen his son. Sometime in the last week, he thought. He had no idea who the boy's friends were. That boy lived in a pigsty with a pack of indifferent morons. I did get this." He pulled out a small school picture of Timmy Watts, which Melia seized and sent off to be copied. Burgess was pleased. Perry was getting good at pulling rabbits out of hats.

Melia shuffled his papers. "All the people in that house, no one could help?"

"It's not a normal family," Burgess said. "Darlene

Packer, Lloyd Watts's girlfriend, was at work. Dawn Watts says she took an interest in the boy. I'll go by later, see if she's back. There's a deaf sister, Iris. You find out how to reach her, Stan?"

"Best Pap could do was school for the deaf. He didn't have a number."

"The others?"

"Pap says the other two brothers, Ricky and Jason, are living in a trailer somewhere. He wasn't too clear where."

Not being clear was a skill the Watts had perfected. Burgess looked at Delinsky, feeling mean and bitter on Timmy Watts's behalf. "That social worker you told me about? I'm going to take her there, make her crawl through the dog crap on her hands and knees. There are two babies in that house, and it's the filthiest place I've seen in all my years as a cop."

Delinsky looked like he wanted to disappear through the floor. Burgess knew Delinsky couldn't be everywhere and do everything, but the guy definitely needed a heads-up on this one. If DHS had done their job, Timmy Watts might still be alive. Even a bad foster family had to be better than what Timmy had had. And if Delinsky couldn't make them take notice, he should have kicked it up the food chain. The Chief was no fan of Human Services.

"We also looked through the boy's room," Burgess said. "With permission."

"Room!" Perry interrupted. "Kid had a fuckin' mattress on the floor in a corner of the attic. Hot as Hades. Windows nailed shut. Not even a fan."

Melia gave Perry a cool look. He'd told Perry repeatedly to rein in his language. "Permission from whom?" Melia asked.

"Mother Watts." Melia nodded, satisfied. "We found a couple rather interesting things," Burgess continued. "A rock with the word 'love' carved into it, under his pillow. A pocket knife. And this..."

The last thing they'd found at the Watts house had the potential to put the case in a whole new light. It looked like a sex crime. Stabbing, particularly the kind of overkill stabbing present here, was usually sexual. And they'd learn tomorrow whether the child had been molested. But bringing drugs into the picture muddied everything. There were drug dealers clever enough to make a warning crime look like something else. Vengeful drug dealers and users, and druggies so depraved, strung out, or high they might do anything. "Inside the backpack the kid used for a pillow, we found a plastic bag with a substance that resembles dirty rock candy." Everyone around the table sat up straighter. "And smells like rotten eggs and cat piss."

"Holy shit!" Rocky Jordan rolled his eyes. "Methamphetamine in a child's pillow. Knowing the Watts, they're probably cooking it themselves. Just what we need to cap off this rotten summer. Turn the city into a bunch of jazzed up, hyper-sexed, go-go-go tweakers until a lab blows up and sends a bunch of our citizens, innocent and guilty, to kingdom come."

"Jazzed up, hyper-sexed, go-go-go tweakers," Perry intoned, nodding thoughtfully. "Rocky, you are a veritable poet of the mean streets, you know that?"

"Which reminds me," Burgess turned to Delinsky as he flipped through his notebook. "Matty McBride. You know him?"

"Scrawny kid, looks a little geeky?" Burgess nodded. "Yeah, I know him. He's a computer jock, lives up near the Eastern Prom, spends a lot of time playing computer games. During the school year, he runs an after-school program at the elementary school for kids who are interested in computers. Teaches them some basic programming stuff. Mother's kinda strange. Cold. Controlling. Treats Matty like he's about twelve. Before Ricky Watts went away for his brief stint with corrections, he and Matty used to hang around together. Matty was one of the big kids who looked after Timmy, taking him to the park and stuff."

Burgess told McBride's story about the argument between Dwayne Watts and a customer about a late delivery. About the customer's threat.

"You want me to follow up with Matty?" Delinsky asked.

"With him and with any of the other kids who used to hang around with Timmy. Ask if anybody remembers seeing him on Friday. And everyone you talk to? I want names. Addresses. Phone numbers. I want it in writing, on my desk, soon as you can."

"Yes, sir," Delinsky said wearily.

"Got anything else for us?" Burgess said.

Delinsky's uniform was limp and sweat-soaked and his shoulders drooped. An athletic man who normally moved with a brisk and powerful stride, today he was moving in slow motion. Burgess knew how that felt. He'd done a canvass in heat like this, in an area where cops were as welcome as five-day-old fish. Just a baby cop back then, fresh from Vietnam, trying to police an America angry at cops and vets, trying to hold his head up and do his job in a world that was often confusing. He knew what if felt like to trudge down hostile streets, soaked with sweat, meeting an endless succession of blank or hostile stares.

He also knew Delinsky had been looking forward to finishing this day, going home, and getting some sleep. Having breakfast with the wife and kids. He might as well learn. Homicides didn't work like that.

"Besides sore feet?" Delinsky consulted his notebook. "Grace Johnston's neighbor, that's a Miss Tina Beaton, age 85, says she saw Timmy on

Johnston's porch yesterday around five, five-thirty. Said he was wearing shorts and a blue tee shirt and carrying a backpack. She said when he left the porch, he was heading down toward the park. She saw a blue car stop and Timmy heading over to it. She doesn't know whether it was a friend, or someone asking directions, or what. Her phone rang and she left the window."

"That's it? Small car? Large? Old, new? Light blue? Dark blue? One she recognized? One she'd seen before?"

"We were lucky to get that. She doesn't see very well."

"Talk to her again," Burgess said. "So, things we want to know are: What was Timmy's schedule yesterday? When was his last known meal? Where are his clothes? His backpack? Who was driving that blue car? Got anything else for us, Gabe?"

Delinsky shook his head. "It was hot yesterday. People went to the beach or the mall, or stayed in with their shades drawn and the fan on, watching TV. Nobody saw a goddamned thing. Spaceship could have landed and taken the boy, for all they noticed."

"Who's doing Timmy's street?"

"Gabriel Delinsky, I think. We're still doing the houses near the park. Next, I'll do the Watts's neighbors. There's one place up there should've been a gold mine. Old lady who lives there, Anna Pederson, sits on her porch all day, or in her window. But she went to the hospital this morning."

"So visit the hospital."

"You bet I will," Delinsky said. "Soon as I—" He broke off. Burgess's reputation for being the meanest cop in Portland was passed like the myth of Santa Claus from one class of recruits to the next. "Just shuffling along in your footsteps, Sarge."

"As long as you don't burn yourself out. We need you on this."

Delinsky managed a tired smile. "Thank you, sir."

"Those boys he played with—Sam and Davey? What's their parents' name?"

"Gordon. Alan and Julie," Delinsky said.

"I want to talk with them."

"So where do we go from here?" Melia asked.

Burgess had forgotten how the heat took it out of you, how much harder it was to push on when your brain had been cooked and your head was pounding. He remembered Nam as one big headache. He looked at Melia, who'd had a worse day than the rest of them. The lieutenant looked drained, and he would be standing before TV cameras in twenty minutes.

"Stan and I'll go back to the Watts place, see if we can locate Darlene Packer. Then we'll do the immediate neighbors." Delinsky's face fell. He'd planned that for himself. "Okay. After the Watts, we'll split up. Delinsky can go with Stan and follow up with any kids who hung out with Timmy Watts. Rocky's going to work on that list of sex offenders, topped by our friend Osborne. I'll see the Gordons. And Wink?"

Devlin looked up warily from his contemplation of the oils on his coffee. "Don't look at me with assignments in mind. I'm going to be logging in evidence for the next six hours," he said. "Every bottle, bag, can, and candy wrapper in that whole damned park."

"Wouldn't dream of it," Burgess said. "I'll be seeing you soon enough. At what ungodly hour did Lee say he was cutting?"

"Seven. Wants to get out early for golf. Before it gets hot."

"It's always hot these days. Seven. That means six for us, leaving here around five? I'll meet you there, okay?"

The Medical Examiner's office was in Augusta, the state capital, 45 minutes north. Despite the valuable information it gave them, autopsies were always grim. Tomorrow's would be grimmer. Even with all those horrific wounds, Timmy Watts had been beautiful and touchingly small and helpless. Like Kristin Marks, the child who haunted him.

Melia conferred with Shaheen. Then Shaheen left the room. The rest of them sat in silence, gathering themselves to go back to trudging down hot streets and ringing doorbells, back to logging in cans and bottles. Back to being alone with their visions of Timmy Watts. Pushing themselves to go hard because time mattered.

The door burst open, admitting a blitz of speech before the new arrival was even in the room. "Burgess, is that your car with the canoe on top? Do you have any idea how that looks to the public? An official police vehicle, parked in the police garage, with a canoe on top? I want that thing out of here. We've got the media in fifteen minutes."

Paul Cote, unable to let anyone else have the limelight, had returned from vacation to snatch the press conference from Melia. At least he hadn't arrived in time to interrupt their meeting or muck up the crime scene. More than once, Burgess had carefully collected Captain Cote's hair and fibers from his clothes from victim's bodies. Despite their efforts to educate him, Cote steadfastly refused to learn about crime scene investigation. He still had to get in there and contaminate everything he could.

Burgess observed with satisfaction that Captain Cote was getting fat. Fat and bald, and, judging from his red face, choleric. Perhaps a heart attack was in the cards. Or a stroke. It was the only satisfaction he could take from Cote's presence. Working a homicide around Cote was like hiking up a path strewn with boulders, except in Cote's case, every time you stepped around it, the same boulder just moved back into your path.

"You can't feel worse about it than I do, Captain. I *was* on vacation." Emphasizing 'was.' "I've got my suitcase. My fishing poles. Soon as we wrap this up, I'm out of here."

He lifted the ice pack from his knee and hefted himself to his feet. "I'll move the car."

Melia looked like his sandwich didn't agree with him. Cote had an uncanny ability to make healthy people feel unwell. Burgess didn't feel too badly letting Melia handle things. That was what Melia got the big bucks for. He felt worse that Cote would be taking the press conference. Cote thought he was a media darling. His self-perception in this, as in many things, fell far from the mark. He also thought people liked and admired him. Cote wouldn't notice that Burgess was limping, or, if he did, he'd just be annoyed that Burgess looked less professional. A canoe on his car and a gimpy walk. Burgess was offending on several fronts.

"Wrap this thing up?" Cote leaned toward Burgess eagerly. "You're that close?"

"Captain," Burgess said, "we haven't got a fuckin' clue."

CHAPTER 9

The crime lab staff was busy and Wink said he'd log it in later, so Burgess put the stuff from Timmy Watts's room and the envelope with the hairs from Osborne's place in an evidence locker. Heading for the elevator, he met Andrea Dwyer, the "kiddie cop," coming the other way. In brief nylon shorts and a tank top, she didn't look much like a cop. With her long, tanned limbs, shiny short hair, and an entire 6' 2" of wonderful muscle definition glossed with a sheen of sweat, she looked like her other avatar, the triathlete.

"Joe, I heard about the little boy. I'm so sorry it had to be you." Her voice was husky, her face solemn as she hugged him, surrounding him briefly with a potpourri of shampoo, soap, and deodorant.

The hug and expression of sorrow were more overt, but otherwise she only echoed what he'd been seeing on faces all day, beginning with Melia's apology at pulling him back from vacation. Melia hadn't been apologizing for spoiling the vacation; he'd been apologizing for assigning Burgess another dead child.

"I'd like to help, Joe," she said. "What can I do?"

As a youth officer, she was constantly in contact

with Portland's kids. She saw things, heard things, received confidences the rest of them didn't necessarily get. "You coming or going?" he asked.

"Sometimes I wonder. Going. I was just checking on a hunch. It didn't pan out."

"There is something you can do." He pressed the button. "Ride down with me."

"I don't think I've ever been in the elevator," she said as the door rolled open.

"Don't rub it in," he grumbled, stepping in and holding the door for her. "I was once young and beautiful myself." He looked around warily. "No offense or harassment intended. That gonna bring the PC police down on my head?"

"I took it as a compliment," she said, watching him rub his knee. "You okay?"

"My retirement injury," he said. "Three hundred pound grieving mother mowed me down on her way to muck up my crime scene. Soon as I put this one to bed, I'm taking my pension and limping off into the sunset."

"And if I believe that, you've got a bridge to sell me. So, what can I do?"

"There's a guy named Jeffrey Osborne, lives over by Knowlton Park. Got a big mastiff named Rogue." He gave the street address. "Dead boy's family says Osborne tried to put moves on Timmy. Invited him in for pizza and showed him dirty pictures, prequel to posing for same." She nodded, attentive. "Maybe you could ask around, see if anyone's heard about this guy. If any kids have complained, or teachers, or parents. See if there's talk about guys in that neighborhood who like little boys."

"You think this was a sex thing?"

"It's a possibility. Other than their families, why do people usually kill young boys? To keep them from talking about the nasty things the grown-ups did. I'll know more in the morning, after the autopsy. Oh, and the boy's family. Extended family—"

He broke off as the door opened on a lobby crowded with reporters on their way upstairs to hear Cote's golden phrases. Several, recognizing Burgess, shouted questions at him. "Sorry," he said, pushing his way through, "all information about the case will be handled by Captain Cote." One enterprising photographer took a picture of them, which he hoped wouldn't end up in tomorrow's paper. No reason it should—Dwyer wasn't working the case—but in his experience, "newspaper" and "reason" didn't necessarily belong in the same sentence. Burgess in the paper, in any form, and Dwyer, in her abbreviated costume, would both be magnets for Cote's wrath.

They paused outside the door. "About the family?" she said.

"Most of 'em have been involved with us for one thing or another. Rocky can give you the names and the breakdown. I just wonder if there are any rumors out there. Anyone with a Jones for the family who might have taken it out this way."

"I'll check it out." She swung onto her bicycle. "See what I can come up with." She paused, a smile playing around her mouth. "I've always wondered, Joe. Is there a female equivalent of 'a Jones'?" She put on her helmet and rode off.

He didn't know. He lumbered into the garage and climbed into his offending automobile. He was tempted to swing by his house and drop off the canoe, but there was no place to put it. He might get lucky and someone would steal it off the car. The East End could be that kind of neighborhood, but then he'd have to put up with complaints from his sister Carla, who'd perfected the art of complaining, until he'd replaced it.

He had no more time for that than to return this one.

He left the lot, crossed Franklin, and drove up Munjoy Hill, pulling into the empty space in front of the Watts's house. Funny how, in a crowded neighborhood, these spaces always stayed empty. Just like on a TV cop show—always a place to park right where the officer needed it. Dwayne's truck was in its place, along with another car on the lawn. He observed with satisfaction that the vehicle his car didn't block, Stan Perry's did. He gave it a minute, to see if Dwayne would come out and curse at them again, then got out of the car, and he and Perry climbed the steps and knocked.

This time, Shauna answered. Transformed from the sullen girl in the bedroom, she now had glossy curls, bright make-up, and a tight white dress that showed off her tan and most of the rest of her. Not so much a dress, he decided, watching her step back to let them enter, as the kind of sleeveless tee shirt some guys called a 'wife beater.' Same skinny straps, same rib knit. Just long enough for minimum decency, and short enough to keep someone looking. Fruit-of-the-Loom had never looked better. Terry Kyle would have said, "She cleans up good." She did. And he knew exactly what kind of work she was going to.

Kyle's absence had been lingering in the back of his mind all day, irritating as a splinter. Soon as he got a break, he had a bunch of things to do. Check on Kyle. Call Chris. Return the canoe. Folly to imagine he'd get a break any time soon.

"Darlene come home?" he asked.

"Yeah." She snapped her gum and assessed him the way she'd assess a customer. "She's upstairs feedin' the baby." She shifted her gaze to Perry, lifting her chin and sticking out her chest, making Burgess feel old and invisible. "Want me to get her?"

"We'd appreciate that," he said.

"You wanna sit?" She looked dubiously around the room. The one chair that wasn't heaped with junk was missing the seat. She shrugged. "Guess not, huh?"

Burgess watched Perry's eyes follow her, knowing how much his colleague wanted to go stand at the bottom of the stairs. "Ran into Andrea Dwyer at the station," he said, "in running shorts and a tank top."

"Some people have all the luck," Perry said. "Bet she looked like a million dollars."

"Two million. You should ask her out."

"I did. She said 'In your dreams, Stanley. I'm not interested in being another notch on your belt.'"

Five minutes of waiting in the fetid heat brought another surprise. Darlene Packer, who entered the kitchen carrying a very small baby, was black. Burgess chastised himself for his surprise, for making the assumption that no one in this family could have a black girlfriend because they were the Downeast equivalent of rednecks. He knew better, knew this work was a crazy combination of experience, your gut, and keeping an open mind, yet it was a lesson he forgot and relearned all the time.

In this case, especially, he'd have to watch himself. He didn't want to miss something important because of what he thought he already knew. Cote'd come back from vacation to look over his shoulder, longing, as Cote always did, for Burgess to make the mistake that would finally get him canned. It was that much harder to move forward in a careful, observant way while simultaneously watching his back.

She stopped in the doorway, cocking her hip and giving them a cool nod, "I'm Darlene and this is Kanesha." She was small and wiry, dressed in cut-offs and a tee shirt, her hair in braids. Despite the polished display of attitude, she didn't look a day over twelve.

"You're investigating..." She stopped then, not so cool, looking for words to avoid saying "murder" and "death," settled on "...what happened to Timmy?"

"Detective Sergeant Burgess. Detective Perry. Yes, we wanted to ask you some questions about Timmy."

Perry cleared a chair for her, but she shook her head. "Either of you gentlemen like to buy me a cup of coffee?" She managed to make "gentlemen" sound unsavory. "Or maybe you have air-conditioning in your car?"

"Whichever you prefer," Burgess said, stepping to the door and opening it for her, happy for a reason to leave that wretched kitchen.

As they followed her down the steps, she said, "Car'll do fine. Place down the street has good coffee, but I wouldn't want my friends and neighbors to see me talkin' to the police." She put the emphasis on 'po.' A fleeting smile lit her solemn face. "It would ruin my reputation."

Perry unlocked his car and opened the door for her. She climbed into the front seat, Perry started the car to crank up the air, and Burgess got in the back. "That air feels good," she said, looking curiously at all the gadgets. "I can't rightly recall another time when I was in the front of a police car and a cop was in the back. But everything's topsy-turvy today."

Her edgy bravado fell away and Darlene Packer began to cry. "I just can't believe it...not Timmy. He was so sweet." Perry handed her a tissue.

"We have very little information about the boy," Burgess said gently. "We were hoping you could help us."

"You already talked to Mother and Pap," she said. "Didn't they...?" She trailed off, staring out through the windshield. Then she drew her daughter more tightly against her chest. "Nope. I don't suppose they did. Guess I don't have to pretend with you all, do I? I...he...look," Her voice softened, lowered. "I don't know how to do this. Tell you about him. I even say his name and I get this pain," Her thin fingers stroked her throat. "Right in here. Makes it hard to talk, you know."

"We know," Burgess said. "He was a lovely little boy, and we know you cared about him. We wouldn't ask you to do this if it weren't important, but to find Timmy's killer, we need to know him. We need to understand what he was like, what he liked to do. Who he spent his time with. You can help with that."

She nodded, reaching down with one finger and stroking her baby's hand. The tiny fingers opened and the entire fist wrapped around her finger. "He was so neglected it used to break my heart," she whispered. "I did my best. When I could, I'd play board games with him, or read stories. Sometimes I'd fill the tub with bubbles and get him to take a bath. He was always so dirty, and none of them cared. Lloyd thought I was wasting my time." Her smile wavered as she looked for understanding. "He thought I should be paying attention to *him*. It wasn't a big deal. Timmy didn't spend much time at home."

"Why was that?" Burgess asked.

"You've seen the place," she said. "It wasn't just the dirt. He was afraid of the dogs. Afraid of all dogs. There's a man in the neighborhood, lives down near the park. He set his dog on Timmy one time. That time," She shook her head, as though it still surprised her. "Dwayne went and talked to the guy." A sharp laugh. "The way Dwayne would talk to somebody. Creep didn't bother Timmy after that."

"Do you know where Timmy went when he wasn't at home?"

She shrugged. "Around. Hanging with the

neighborhood kids..."

"Can you give me some names?" Burgess asked, "or point out some houses?"

"Sure." The finger the baby wasn't holding stabbed the air, pointing out a couple different houses. "And there's a couple kids named Gordon, in that house there, boys about Timmy's age. Before Ricky went away, Timmy used to trail around after him and his friends, when they'd let him. They thought it was kinda cute, like Timmy was a pet or something. But they thought it was funny to give him beer and make him sick, too, so I asked Lloyd to stop them. Mostly they did. Then it didn't matter, 'cuz Ricky was gone."

"How often did Timmy eat meals at home?"

"Almost never. Not that there were meals. Like in a regular family, I mean. But he wasn't around much. Even if he wasn't with somebody, he'd just stay out until it got real late, then come creeping in and go upstairs to his...to his room, and sleep."

"The door wasn't locked?"

"Nope. I mean, seriously, who'd rip off the Watts?"

"Where did he get food, then, if he didn't eat at home?"

"People fed him."

"Like a stray cat?"

"It wasn't like that," she said. "People loved Timmy. You would have loved Timmy, if you'd known him. That's why this thing...what happened...it doesn't make any sense. Who would kill such a sweet little boy?"

"Tell me what he was like," Burgess said. "Why would I have liked him?"

"He was so small," she said. "He was eight, and I could still pick him up and carry him. Like if he fell asleep on my bed when I was reading or something, I could carry him upstairs and tuck him in. And his hair! Most kids by the time they're his age, it's gotten dark, but he had these silver-gold curls, like something from a picture book. Usually it was all dirty and tangled and you couldn't see how pretty it was, but sometimes he'd let me wash it. He was real quiet. Shy like, I guess, from being yelled at so much. I mean, if every time you opened your mouth, someone shouted 'Shut the fuck up!' you wouldn't talk much, either."

She looked down at her baby. "I know what you're thinking. Why should it be any different for her, growing up in a place so dirty and violent? Well, she's not growing up here. This is temporary. I've got me a real job now, a regular salary and benefits. Soon as I've saved enough for the security deposit and stuff, I'm out of here. Lloyd can come with me or not. Kanesha isn't growing up in this house, with people like this."

Her bright, round eyes darted between them. "I'm not just talking big, either," she said. "I got a sister who watches her while I'm working."

"So Timmy was quiet and shy. Was he ever talkative?"

"Sometimes. When we were alone, he'd talk. Then I could hardly get him to stop. He'd chatter like a magpie, giggle hysterically. He could get pretty wound up. Sometimes I got annoyed, when he'd get really goofy and wouldn't stop. Then I'd send him upstairs. Yeah, sometimes he could be real gooney."

"Were there particular grownups in the neighborhood who looked after him?"

"There was Mrs. Johnston, the art teacher. Timmy used to go over there for tea." She crooked a finger and mimicked la-di-da. "He liked that. And sometimes he'd go two houses down, to Sammy's, and have pizza. That big cop, Delinsky? If he was taking his kids to the park, he'd take Timmy along. Timmy loved him. Said he was going to be a cop when he grew up. That used to make Mother and Pap howl. Then Timmy would get all weepy and someone would smack him and send him to his room."

Her baby whimpered, and she raised it to her shoulder. "He used to go to the McBride's sometimes, but lately he hasn't been doing that. Matty's been busy with a summer job. And Matty's mother, she don't like nobody. Thinks she and her precious son are too good for the rest of us."

"That's all the adults you can think of?"

"There are probably others. I just don't remember." Her hand crept toward Perry's, then sprang back like she'd remembered you didn't touch cops. "I don't know if you can tell me this, but...you were there, in the park? You saw him?" Perry nodded. "Was it awful?"

Burgess watched Perry struggle with his answer. At this stage, with everyone a suspect, they kept details under wraps. But this girl had cared about Timmy. And she was family, sort of. They were supposed to be supportive of the family.

Perry put his hand over hers and squeezed. "Darlene, the way you described him? That's just how he looked. Like a little angel, sleeping there on the grass."

She'd been holding her breath. Now she slowly exhaled. "That's Timmy," she said, pressing the tissue against her eyes, her voice thick. "Just like one of God's little angels, tumbled down off a cloud." She grabbed the handle and jumped out of the car, clutching her own child tight against her chest. "I've gotta go," she said. "I've gotta go." She ran up the steps and into the house, slamming the door behind her.

CHAPTER 10

"So what now?" Perry asked as they watched the door close behind her. "A little chat with Dwayne?"

"Might as well," Burgess said. "I'll just check my messages, see if there's anything from Terry."

He called his house, punched in his code, listened to some crackling and static and then heard Chris. "Joe? I know you're not there. You're supposed to be on vacation, and I know you're not there, either, because I heard about the little boy. Look. I'm coming back. From Boston, I mean. I'll be at home. At your place. I wonder, does this sound as disjointed as it feels? I hate talking to a machine. Anyway. I know you'll be looking for whoever killed that boy. But I know you, remember? So I'll be here in case you need me. A meal or a hug or... I don't know. Whatever." She laughed. "Band-Aids?"

Her voice. From the first, it had drawn a response, something visceral within him. Now that he knew her, there was also her smile, the flow of her hair, the simple generosity of her body, her amazing equanimity. But from their first conversation, he'd reacted to her voice, and that remained true, even in a disjointed message on an answering machine.

There was more static. "Joe? My cousin's got tickets to this art thing at the Museum. Yeah. Like you care, huh? Anyway, the tickets weren't cheap, so I've got to go to that or she'll feel mistreated. Then I'll drive back. I'll be home by seven. So call me. Or whatever. I'll be here. And Joe?" She spoke in an embarrassed rush, "You be careful. Please?"

Nothing from Kyle. Burgess checked his watch. Almost seven. A whole day gone and Kyle hadn't checked in. Even if Kyle had taken his kids to the beach for the day without his phone or been out of cell phone range, he should have surfaced by now. But he'd been missing this morning, too.

"Nothing from Terry," he said. "But Chris is coming back. I'm not sure why."

"She thinks you can't take care of yourself."

"I've managed for forty-nine years."

"Right. And look at you." Like all his friends, Perry liked Chris, thought she was good for him. "Be nice to have a nurse around. She can take care of your knee."

"A choir of angels couldn't do much with this knee."

Being seriously involved, at least with a living person, was a rare experience for Burgess. He'd managed to get through most of his life as a solitary man, his energy and his passion going to his work. The demands of being responsible to, and for, another person, made him profoundly nervous.

"A little ice. Anti-inflammatories. Some good sex, you'll be a new man in no time."

"It's because you're so young," Burgess grunted, reaching for the door handle, "that you still believe in miracles." He'd often puzzled over the phrase, "a new man," and the pleasure people took in the idea of becoming one. Why would anyone want to be a new man when the "old man's" calluses and wisdom had been so hard won?

"Oh, lookie there." Perry whistled softly. "Her nice brother's driving her to work."

"My brother, my pimp," Burgess said. "What a family." He shut Perry's door and walked back to his car.

Shauna Martin was heading for the truck, followed by her brother Dwayne. She hadn't noticed that their way was blocked, but Dwayne had, and he was charging toward them, waving an angry fist and spewing a flood of foul language. Burgess, noting the loose flesh on the arms and around the stomach exposed by the man's upraised arms, realized that big as Dwayne Martin was, until recently, he'd been significantly bigger.

Before Burgess could react, Dwayne Martin had decided against charm and persuasion and the truck began backing rapidly toward Perry's car.

He looked to see if Perry was aware of what was happening. Perry was on the phone. He shouted, "Stan!" as Martin's truck hit the car with an explosion of crushed metal and glass and Perry's head slammed against the window.

He called for backup and medcu, then drew his weapon, and forced Dwayne Martin out of the truck and onto the ground. He wrestled Martin's arms around and cuffed him, his cuffs barely fitting around Martin's thick wrists, resisting the urge to kick him in the head. He left the man bitching about police brutality, rushed around Perry's car, and opened the door. Stan Perry, dazed and bloody, was slumped over the steering wheel. In the background, Shauna wailed loudly that she'd be late for work. Like hookers punched a time clock.

He pulled out his handkerchief, pressing it against the wound, and eased Perry back against the seat.

Head wounds were nearly always gushers. Perry's chest, neck, and Burgess's favorite shirt were drenched with blood.

"Important phone call?" he asked, grabbing some tissues and wiping the blood from Perry's eyes.

"Michelle," Perry grunted through clenched teeth. "She's at Terry's. Says she can't wake him up."

"What is it?" Burgess asked. "Drink? Pills?"

Perry closed his eyes, gathering the words with an effort. "She doesn't know."

"I'd better get over there."

When he backed out of the car, Melia was there and the place was swarming with cops. He filled Melia in quickly and concisely about what had happened, then nodded at Dwayne Watts, who was stumbling around the yard, cursing. "Take that piece of crap downtown and hold him until I get there." Shauna, her elbows pulled in to enhance the scenery, was trying to charm one of the officers into giving her a ride. "Better take her, too."

He stepped aside so the EMTs could get to Perry. "Good thing young Stanley has a hard head. I've got to go check on something...I shouldn't be long."

Melia gave him a sharp look and didn't ask. Sometimes it was better not to know. "See you downtown." Almost as an afterthought, he added, "Watch your ass on this one, Joe. Cote's got such a hard-on for you it's drained what little blood used to get to his brain. I'll do my best." He shrugged. They both knew Cote didn't want Burgess working high profile cases. It was nuts, what they were all supposed to be about was solving crime, but Cote was who he was, and neither of them had been born yesterday.

"I'll do my best."

"You can start by losing the canoe."

Burgess sketched a salute. "Yessir, boss. I'se tryin."

He steered carefully through the massed patrol cars and the ambulance, and past the curious crowd, heading for Kyle's place.

Michelle had the door open before he could knock. She grabbed his arm, the pressure of her fingers telegraphing desperation. "Joe. Thank God. You've got to help him." She looked past him. "Where's Stan?"

"You didn't hear?" he said. "We've got a dead kid."

She recoiled like he'd hit her, shaking her head. "Terry didn't say. I haven't seen him for a couple days. He's been in a rotten mood. Yesterday, we were supposed to have the girls, so when I picked them up, I took them to my place for a girls' sleepover, and today we went to the beach. I dropped them off at Wanda's and when I got here, I found him like this."

The living room was dark, shades drawn against the heat, the air still and thick and smelling sour. "Where is he?"

"In the bedroom. I didn't call 911...I was afraid if it was drugs...an overdose...or drinking...that he'd get in trouble with the job." Her voice veered between uncertainty and defiance. "Terry's got enough trouble right now."

He followed her into the dim bedroom, catching a bottle with his toe and sending it clattering into the baseboard. "He was on the floor," she said. "I got him onto the bed, but he won't wake up."

Detective Terry Kyle, wearing only gray gym shorts, sprawled face down across his bed. His skin was a waxy yellowish-white, and Burgess could have counted every vertebrae and rib. Kyle always ran at high revs and was whippet thin, but now, seen unconscious and vulnerable, Burgess realized Kyle was thin to the point of emaciation. He grabbed Kyle's shoulder and turned him over. The body rolled loosely, without reaction or resistance.

"I'm scared, Joe," she said. "I hope I did the right thing, calling you."

Burgess checked Kyle's face, his eyes, his pulse. "Turn on more lights," he said. She moved to the wall switch and flipped it on, then turned on the second bedside light. The floor was strewn with clothes and covers that had been flung off the bed. There was an empty Jack Daniels bottle on the floor. He checked the bedside tables, dresser top, and wastebasket for empty drug containers.

"He taking any prescription drugs you know of?"

She shook her head. "He's been real depressed. And angry. But you know Terry. He'd rather hurt than do something about it.

"Call my number," he said. "See if Chris is there. If she is, tell her what's happening and ask her to come over. Then make some coffee."

He went into the bathroom, turning the shower on, full-bore cold. He levered Kyle to his feet, half-dragged him to the tub, and dumped him in. It was awkward with his bad knee, and he got soaked in the process, but it was so hot in the apartment the soaking felt good. Then he lowered the lid and sat on the toilet, watching Kyle's face. This wasn't medicine. Burgess didn't know much medicine. This was shock treatment, what one cop did for another who didn't want it on record that EMTs had dragged him out of his house comatose with drink. If this didn't work, and Kyle didn't wake up, he still might have to call for help.

This wasn't the day for him to play Clara Barton. His mind was crowded with images of a slaughtered child, with lists of things to do, people to see, all the mental triage of a murder investigation. He needed to be four other places, asking questions and gauging reactions, writing reports, reading reports, considering what they knew and where to go next. But Kyle had been there for him when he needed help. If Terry needed him, even in the middle of an investigation, he had to help. Even with Cote and the media looking over his shoulder, snapping at his heels for answers. Because the living mattered.

He focused on Kyle's lean face, watched the water pour down, waiting for the sharp, cold gray of Kyle's eyes. People always said Burgess's face was fierce, but he looked like a pussycat next to Kyle. Kyle had a way of going dead behind the eyes, showing only anger and disbelief, that Burgess didn't have. Mate that with the bristly dark hair, narrow mouth, and sharp cheekbones, and Kyle was one scary piece of work. A cop whose whole being said that lies hurt him, and that hurting him made him angry. *At you. Scumbag. So think twice about what you just said.*

Burgess watched the eyelids, willing them to move. Open. "Goddammit, Terry," he said. "What's going on here? What do you think you're doing to yourself?"

Water poured over the bruised-looking cheekbones and down over Kyle's bony chest, soaking the gray shorts a darker gray. Burgess thought about how vulnerable Kyle looked and how he'd hate it if he knew. The room was stifling and smelled of sickness. He imagined Terry sitting in this miserable, sweltering place, shades drawn, drinking himself sick, sleeping it off, and starting all over again. Cops were good at being professional alcoholics—sober for work, drunk the rest of the time. Had Terry been doing that? And where had they all been?

In the bedroom, he heard Michelle moving around, cleaning up. Changing the bed.

"I've been here, Terry," he said. "I've been right here. Why didn't you call?"

"He didn't think anyone could help him," Michelle said, from the door. "He's such a goddamned stoic."

She took a few steps into the room and stopped, staring with tragic eyes at the man in the tub. "He's always liked to drink. But lately, this thing with Wanda, it's just gotten worse and worse. Is he going to be okay, Joe?"

"Let's give it a little longer," he said. "You find Chris?"

"She's coming over."

"You make that coffee?" She nodded. "Good. Bring me some. Cream and sugar and pour it over ice. Thanks."

He didn't want coffee. Not on top of the last bad coffee and hastily gulped sandwich. He wanted her out of the way, leaving him alone with Kyle. Kyle wouldn't want her seeing him like this. It was the downside of serve and protect—they tried to protect the ones they loved from the ravages of the job, the toll it took on them.

"Sure, Joe. Sure." She backed out of the room. Afraid of him, he thought, though he'd never given her any reason to be.

"I'm here for you, Terry," he said. "Whatever it is. But you've gotta wake up and talk to me. I can't help you otherwise." Stretched out like this, with those purplish-blue lids in a gaunt, exhausted face, long pale limbs ending in long, bony feet, only a drape of gray cloth around his loins, Kyle reminded him of pictures of Christ taken down from the cross. Policing was so intimate sometimes. They got to see each other at their worst, most strung out, most vulnerable. Had to trust each other with that.

"Jesus, Terry...Talk to me. Please!"

Kyle's lids fluttered, fluttered again, then lifted from red, glazed ugly eyes. Thin hands flailed at the falling water, trying to keep it away. Burgess reached out and turned off the shower. After a while, Kyle's eyes opened again. "Hey, Joe." He grabbed the side of the tub. "Sick," he muttered.

Burgess flipped up the toilet seat and gave Kyle his arm, supporting him, holding him, wiping his face. Then he stripped off Kyle's wet shorts and put him to bed. For better or for worse. In sickness and in health. It was a lot like a marriage.

He led Michelle into the kitchen, sat her down at the table, and took a chair across from her. "He's gonna be sick as a dog, but I think he'll be okay," he said. "And you'll have Chris. She's steady."

Now that the crisis was over, she put both hands over her face and sobbed. He went around the table, knelt beside her, and pulled her close. Like a kitten, she worked her face into his neck and stayed there, sucking up whatever comfort he could offer. He was glad to help. Kyle had a hard life. His ex-wife made it her life's work to try and turn their girls against their father, constantly jerking him around about support and visitation. He'd seen plenty of domestic situations in his years as a cop, and Wanda Kyle was up there with the worst of them. Michelle was about the only good thing to happen to Kyle in years.

When she'd calmed down, he said, "What's going on?"

"It's Wanda, of course. She can't stand it that Terry and I are happy. He's tried to enforce the visitation in the separation agreement, so he's got regular times with the girls and some time to be with me." She grabbed a paper napkin off the table, dried her eyes, and blew her nose. "She's so mad that she can't jerk him around day and night, that he isn't always at her beck and call...now she says she's moving to Texas."

Her big eyes swam with tears. "It's killing him, Joe,

just thinking about losing the girls. I was trying to help, so I...I moved out."

She gripped his arm, her eyes intense, determined that he not misunderstand. "Not because I don't care about him. Terry means everything to me. Enough to leave him, if it meant he could keep his girls."

Burgess felt his own throat get tight. Life was just one damned thing after another. Not just the investigation that wasn't catching any breaks. Few of the people he knew were, either. The harshness of their lives just kept scouring them until they were all sore and bleeding. "Has he seen a lawyer?"

"Finally. The only way to stop her is to get custody of the girls himself. That means fighting dirty. It means he's got to show she's unfit."

"Which she is!"

"Which she is," Michelle agreed. "But he's always believed he shouldn't try to poison the girls against their mother, to let himself be dragged down to her level. And he's never thought he could raise them himself. Not with his hours, his schedule."

She played with the salt and pepper shakers, a pair of English Bobbies someone had given Kyle as a joke. "I suppose he could get a different job, maybe even a different job in the department, but you know how much he loves what he does. So..." She knocked over the salt shaker, automatically picking up a pinch of salt and tossing it over her shoulder, as if, at this late stage, she could ward off their bad luck. "Terry being Terry..."

"He's been letting it eat him up inside instead of talking to people about it."

"It's not so hard to understand, Joe. A cop being stoic, protecting his private life? I told him we should get married. The court would like to see him as a stable, married man. But Terry's scared to get married again. And after Wanda, who can blame him? I moved out, so he wouldn't be—"

She tipped her head sideways, and smiled, shyly. A lovely, honey-haired, All-American Homecoming Queen. All she had to do was enter a room and Terry lit up. "Living in sin. Only...only I miss him so, when I'm not with him. And then he goes and does this. Whether he likes it or not, I'm moving back in. I don't see how he does anyone any good if he drinks himself to death. Do you?"

"I'd miss him."

"Miss him! Joe Burgess, you're such a jerk. You love him like a brother, and you know it."

There was a sharp rap on the door. Michelle hurried to get it, threw it wide, and then, continuing her forward movement, threw herself into Chris Perlin's arms. Chris looked at Joe over the quivering blonde head. "Thought I came back from Boston to take care of *you?*"

"This *is* taking care of me."

"Right." She nodded, and he could see her mentally rolling up her sleeves. "You want to fill me in a little before you jump on your steed and go charging off in search of bad guys?"

"Out here in the hall?"

She led Michelle into the apartment and disengaged long enough to wrap her own arms around him. He stood a moment, savoring the perfume of her hair. She'd been gone three days, and he desired her with an almost adolescent desperation, a degree of need and desire that scared him. He filled her in quickly, then said, "Do you mind if we put the canoe on your car? Cote's having fits about it. He says it's not professional."

She narrowed her eyes and gave him a mean look. The canoe represented their time together away from all this. She'd been talking about this vacation for months. "On my car? I wouldn't mind shoving that canoe up Cote's ass."

The three of them moved the canoe to her car. He checked on Terry one more time before handing him over to an experienced nurse, then kissed her, knowing it would make him want to stay. All the way downtown, he distracted himself from missing her by thinking about the canoe and Cote's ass.

CHAPTER 11

The long summer evening was drawing to a close, darkness moving softly in, bringing no relief from the heat. As Joe drove past people sitting hopefully outside, waiting for the breeze that wasn't coming, he saw a city settling in for a long, restless night. Last night, under cover of the steamy darkness, an immense evil had moved through the city. He hated to see another night fall without some hope of a solution.

Maybe he'd get back to headquarters and there would be news. Maybe someone else would have shaken something loose while he was tending Kyle. But he didn't think so. If it was important, they would have called him. And anyway, this case felt like dogged persistence and endless questions, infinite tiredness and sore, swollen feet.

The weariness he felt wasn't just from a long day, though it certainly had been that. It came from such intimate knowledge of the details of this terrible crime and awareness of how much the resolution depended on him. In a case like this, he walked a peculiar emotional tightrope. To understand the crime, he had to understand the victim. Learn about him, imagine him, recreate him so that his personality, his habits, his relationships became clear. At the same time, he had to keep his distance in order to see clearly and objectively. He was supposed to avoid becoming emotionally involved.

A cop's job really was to keep people safe. With that went a particular duty to protect society's most helpless and vulnerable that made it hard to be objective and distant with children. Having stood there on the crisp grass, in the simmering heat of the park, and looked down at Timmy Watts, clasped in the certainty and stillness of death, how could he not feel it? Now, sealed in the icy quiet of his car, rolling mechanically toward the station and the next phase of interviewing and evaluation, he had a surreal moment, like the pause at the top of the roller coaster. It seemed like the spirit of the dead boy screamed once, somewhere deep in his brain, a cry for justice or resolution that reverberated like an echo.

He didn't want this case getting its claws into him. This morning, he'd given in and engaged. He'd begun to work the case, to pile up the facts and details in his brain so he could play the adult version of that card game where you flipped cards, trying to remember where the other cards were so you could make a match. But even this deeply in, and despite the promise he'd made to Timmy this morning in the park, he wished he could declare that it wasn't his problem, that he could simply write his reports and hand it off.

He pulled into the garage, backed into his space, and sat a moment before turning off the engine. Why didn't he walk away? Because it was bullshit to think the case didn't already have its claws into him. Because Timmy Watts, given so little, had tried so hard to be a survivor. Struggled to make a normal child's life of pleasure and adventure and play in the midst of overwhelming squalor and disinterest. He had been a rather heroic little boy. Didn't he deserve a heroic response, one that didn't include driving off into the sunset with a canoe atop the car?

Burgess snapped off the motor and got out of the car. He couldn't help seeing the irony of it—if half this effort had gone into Timmy while the boy was alive, this might not have happened. He'd been joking when he spoke to Andrea Dwyer about retirement, but sometimes lately he really felt his age, when his spirit and intention moved forward and his body came behind like an afterthought. That was how he felt now, moving through the sluggish air. His mind was rushing upstairs, ready to check on Stan, interview Dwayne Martin, make some phone calls, and skim the early reports, while his body was still plodding across the parking lot.

Eventually, all his constituent parts arrived upstairs. He walked out of the elevator into a less-than-friendly conversation between Melia and Paul Cote. Cops read faces. He didn't need to hear the words.

"Where the hell have you been?" Cote demanded. "Right in the middle of investigating a child's murder, suddenly no one knows where you are."

Burgess shrugged. "You told me to get rid of the canoe." To Melia, he said, "How's Stan doing?"

"Eight stitches and a bad headache. They're probably still taking pictures of his head, just to be sure nothing's broken. When the doc suggested he go home and rest, I thought I'd have to arrest him. He wanted to skip the stitches, leave right then. Guess you trained him well."

Melia, whose skin was the color of putty, was the one who needed to go home and rest. Stan Perry could still take a licking and keep on kicking. He was a kid. "He going home?" Burgess asked.

Melia shrugged. "I told him he should."

That left Perry the option of coming in, since he hadn't been *ordered* to go home. "Dwayne Martin," he said. "You take him or save him for me?"

Melia made an expansive gesture. "I've been at the hospital with Stan. He's all yours. I did have a run at the sister, though."

"And?"

"Nice tits," Melia said. Cote made a gagging sound and got redder. "Turns out she was in a hurry to get to work 'cuz that sexy look's spoiled once she starts leaking milk."

"Yeah," Burgess agreed. "Hard for a guy who said he was going for cigarettes and actually got a quick blow job to explain to his wife how he got those two big milky spots on the front of his pants. She say anything useful?"

Before Melia could answer, Cote hauled up his sleeve and made a show of checking his watch. "I want all your preliminary reports on my desk first thing tomorrow," he said. "Anything breaks between now and then, I expect a phone call. At home. Not to my voice mail. And Burgess..." He cleared his throat, as though saying the name choked him. "The minute you get back from the autopsy, I want a full briefing." He turned on his impeccably polished heel and left.

"Anything useful?" Melia said. "She said everyone, including the parents, considered the boy a real nuisance. That his habit of being absent was one of his only good qualities. She said he was incredibly irritating, that he used to sing, and dash around, getting underfoot, and that he chattered like a magpie when other people were trying to watch TV. That he used to take things. When I asked if she knew of anyone who might have hurt him to get back at the family, she snapped her gum and said the list was too long to bother with. I tried to get her to be more specific but she couldn't. Or wouldn't."

"You ask her about the blue car?"

"Yeah. She said maybe it belonged to the witch."

"You get a name or address for this witch?"

"Nope. She just said, 'You know. The witch. The witch.' Like we all knew about the witch."

"Any description?"

Melia rolled his eyes. "Witchy. You can watch it yourself. Whole thing's on tape. How's Terry?"

"Sick. Heart sick, soul sick, gut sick. Chris is looking after him."

"That's good news."

"She's supposed to be on vacation, too."

"Every cloud..." Melia muttered.

"Don't," Burgess said. "There's nothing good about this wrecking *her* vacation. Look, go home, Vince. Get a little rest before you fall on your face or blow lunch all over Cote's shiny shoes. You can only push things so far, you know."

"This from the guy who should have taken his knee to x-ray twelve hours ago."

"Not my fault," he said. "Mrs. Burgess raised her boy to be tough." In truth, Mrs. Burgess had raised her boy to be compassionate and observant. Dealing with his violent, drunken father had made him tough.

"You should go over there now."

"And have 'em tell me what? Stay off it? Keep it elevated and use lots of ice? How the hell I'm gonna do those things in the middle of a murder? Huh? Go home, Vince. I've got enough worries without losing you as a buffer between me and that asshole. One of these days, he'll push, I'll push back, and I'll be a retired policeman."

"I hope not." Melia put a hand on his shoulder,

jerked his chin toward the conference room. "Let's sit. Talk a minute, go double team Dwayne Martin. Then I'll go home. Deal?"

"You're the boss."

"Right, Joe. I'm the boss. That's why *you're* telling *me* to go home."

"Bad habit," he said, dropping into a chair. He tipped his head back and closed his eyes. "So, sir. What was it you wanted to talk about?"

"Hold on." Melia gave instructions to move Dwayne Martin to an interview room. "Timmy Watts. Your impressions. What are we looking at here, Joe? Should the mothers of Portland be locking up their kids?"

"The parents of Portland," he emphasized "parents," "should be paying more attention to their kids, that's for damn sure." He rubbed his forehead with one hand, his knee with the other. It reminded him of the old thing where you tried to pat your head and rub your belly. He felt about that coordinated. The rubbing that satisfying. "Do I think we've got a child killer on our hands who might repeat the act? Too early to tell, Vince."

But Melia wasn't letting him off that easily. "What's your gut tell you?"

"My gut tells me whoever stabbed that kid would do it again. That whatever Lee finds in the morning, we're dealing with something perverted here. Then again, my gut tells me the person who wrapped that child in a clean, soft blanket and carried him to a park where he loved to play was trying to make things right and restore order. So my brain tells me this won't be simple, and to wait a while before drawing conclusions. Talk to the families who knew him best. Talk to his sister, Iris. See what the autopsy tells me. I'd lay odds the kid was sodomized."

Melia winced and looked away, probably thinking about his twins. Cops are tough. They can take it. But most of the cops Burgess knew—the good cops—had a mission. They really did want to make the world a safe place. They might put their own spin on it, sometimes make their own rules, but they were serious about being there to serve and protect. And occasionally bust a few heads that needed busting.

He pulled out his notebook, flipped through some pages, and studied something he'd written. "Ask me again tomorrow. I don't think this was done by some witch, and I don't think we've got a Satanic cult, and I don't think this kid was killed by a woman. But I could be wrong. It's happened."

Melia changed the subject. "Kyle gonna be able to work tomorrow?"

"He'll come in," Burgess said, "even if he shouldn't. Maybe he can drive a desk. Work with Rocky. Review the canvass paperwork, see where we need to follow up, but he's in bad shape. He's got to stay out of the heat or he'll go down for the count. While we had our heads up our asses, enjoying the view, Kyle's lost ten or fifteen pounds he really couldn't spare, and pushed himself right over the edge. What's up with that? We're supposed to be observant."

"I'm supposed to be observant. Life's too goddamned busy." Melia got to his feet.

Burgess heaved himself up and followed Melia out of the room. Slinging Kyle around hadn't done his knee any good. He felt like tearing into something, and Dwayne Martin was a good place to start. He found Rocky, sitting in the dark, his face illuminated by the bluish light of a monitor. "Do something for me?" he asked.

Rocky turned, startled, coming slowly back into the world of people, away from the world on-line. "Sure thing. What do you need?"

Burgess scribbled a name and address. "Call these people and ask whether, even though it's late, I can come by in a while and talk to them?"

Time in the cooler hadn't improved Martin's disposition. He was restless and agitated, sweating despite the air-conditioning. Also a professional. His first words when they entered the room were, "I got nothing to say to you assholes. I want my lawyer."

Burgess knew the drill. Suspect lawyers up on you, you can't ask him anything. But everyone pushed the envelope a little, made sure the suspect understood he was passing on a chance to tell his side of the story, make a deal, the whole malarkey. And he wasn't here to ask Martin about a crime, at least, not the crime Martin expected them to ask about—assault on a police officer. He didn't need to. He was an eyewitness.

He identified himself and Melia for the tape, gave the necessary information, then said, "Before the unfortunate incident with your truck, I was coming to ask you some questions about your youngest brother, Timmy Watts, whose body was discovered this morning in Knowlton Park. That's what I'm here for. So let's just be clear, okay. Are you refusing to talk about Timmy?"

Dwayne Martin stared, pursed his lips, said, "Huh?"

"Timmy Watts," Burgess repeated. "Your little brother. Murdered this morning. I wanted to ask you some questions about him. Are you saying you won't talk about Timmy without a lawyer?"

Martin blinked, shook himself, blinked again, the hand that was cuffed to the table shifting restlessly. When Burgess was a boy, there had been a wrestler on TV called Haystack Calhoon, weighed about 600 pounds. What had impressed him was not how well the man wrestled, but that he could move at all. Dwayne Martin wasn't that big, but he was damned big, and clearly had been bigger. He filled his side of the table, stinking up the room with the fug of sweat, unwashed skin, and the stench of the house he lived in. He wore cut-offs and a sleeveless tee shirt, his tattooed arms like jiggling pink hams, his hairy white thighs spreading over the chair like melting Crisco. He looked a lot older than 26.

He stared at them, puzzled, then said, in a voice surprisingly light and high for such a massive man, "I'm here because you wanted to talk about that little fairy?"

"Fairy?" Burgess repeated.

"Fairy. Artsy-fartsy little thing, skippin' and prancin' around like a faggot. Faggots had their eyes on him, too."

"Mr. Martin," Melia interrupted. "Earlier you asked for a lawyer. Are you willing to talk to us about your brother Timmy without a lawyer present?"

"Why the fuck not?"

Given Martin's experience with the criminal justice system, Burgess decided that constituted a knowing waiver. He looked at Melia to see if he agreed. Melia nodded. "If, at any time, you do decide you want that lawyer, you let us know, okay?" Martin grunted what Burgess took to be an affirmation. "Tell us about your brother and the faggots."

"Guy down by the park. Osborne. He's a faggot." Martin's eyes darted around the room, checking the walls. Then he looked around behind him. "Started hanging around Timmy when he was at the park, invited him back to his house for pizza. Starts showing him dirty pictures and trying to get Timmy to take off his clothes, take a bubble bath. Timmy won't, so the guy sets his dog on him. Dog's as big as

Timmy. Kid came home hysterical." The massive shoulders shifted as the body moved restlessly on the chair. "I hadda go to talk to him."

Martin, figuring they'd hear it anyway, added, "It was that colored cop, lives in the neighborhood, always got his nose up everybody's ass. He brought Timmy home, told us what had happened. I told him it was a family thing and we'd deal with."

"When's the last time you saw Timmy?"

Martin stared blankly at the table, tapping the side of his head, trying to jar a thought loose. "Last night, I think. Or maybe it was the night before, I dunno. Little bastard come in looking for something to eat. There wasn't nothing, so he started in crying. I was eight years old, I didn't cry about nothin', but Timmy, he was always whimperin' and whinin'. He's Pap's kid, is what it is. See, all them Watts is whiners. He grabs my arm, and he's saying how he's hungry..."

He looked nervously back over his shoulder at the empty wall, but Burgess didn't think Martin's demeanor had anything to do with the questions. "What did you do?"

"I told him to shut up. He wouldn't, so I hit him."

Burgess waited, keeping his disgust off his face, but that was all Martin had to say. Timmy Watts, a pitifully undersized child, had come to somewhere just above this man's knee. "You hit Timmy very often?"

"He weren't home very often. Knew enough to stay out of folk's way."

"What did Timmy do after you hit him?"

"He just lay there in the dog shit, starin' up at me with those eyes. He was the most pathetic lookin' thing you ever saw. He didn't cry or nothin', just looked at me, like it was my fault he was hungry. I took out my wallet, got out a ten, and dropped it. Told him to buy himself a pizza."

Behind him, Burgess felt Melia's anger, though he knew that if he looked back, Melia's expression would be neutral. "Yeah," he said, "sounds like he was a real irritating kid to have around. What did he do? He pick up the money?"

"Oh, yeah. Grabbed it before it hit the floor." Martin looked around again, drummed his fingers on the table, swiped at his nose, and went back to drumming.

"When you gave him the money, about what time was that?"

Another shrug. "Six, maybe."

"Six," Burgess repeated. "You remember what he was wearing?"

"Yellow shirt. Shorts. Them shoes that light up when you walk." Martin smiled proudly. "I bought him those."

"And that's the last time you saw him?"

"I already said that."

"Timmy wasn't at home much, right?" Martin nodded. "Where did he go?"

"Around the neighborhood." His hand scrabbled restlessly on the tabletop. Plucked at his shirt. "You got a cigarette?" he asked.

"Marlboro okay?" Burgess asked, pulling out a pack. He passed one to Martin, lit it, waited while the man inhaled. It was like watching a religious experience. "Any people in particular he liked to visit?"

"That school teacher. The kids down the street. That asshole cop." Martin shrugged. "Lotta people. Kid was so pathetic, people took pity on him. Not that he needed it. He was treated okay at home. Timmy liked the attention."

"Anybody else?"

"I dunno. Lots of people."

"Mr. Martin, even if he was annoying, he was only a little kid. Can you think of anyone who might have wanted to hurt him?" Martin looked at him blankly. "Someone who had a grudge against another member of the family, anything like that?"

Martin's eyes shifted suspiciously from one of them to the other. Then he shook his head. "Ain't nobody got a reason to do something like that."

"Nobody with a grudge against you or your brothers, or against Mother or Pap, who might have taken it out on Timmy?"

"It would take a pretty low son-of-a-bitch to..." Martin trailed off, staring at the blank wall, rocking back and forth on his chair.

Burgess could only guess at the thoughts in his head, wondered what the standards for low-down behavior were for a man who casually cuffed a hungry little boy down into dog crap. "Can we get you a soda or something? Some coffee?"

Martin scratched his chest, then his head, pulled at his ear-lobes, then scratched some more. Finally he said, "You got Dr. Pepper?"

Melia stood up. "I'll get it," he said. He looked grayer. Probably needed the air.

Burgess moved his chair closer to Dwayne Martin. "It seemed like such a good lead," he said, loading his voice with disappointment. "See, we heard that a few days ago you were arguing with some guy, out in front of your house, and the guy you were arguing with threatened that if he didn't get what he wanted, something terrible was going to happen. And this, what happened to Timmy, I'd say that's pretty terrible, wouldn't you?"

Martin stared. He had a stunned-ox look, like some beefy creature that's been hit in the head. It was pleasantly cool in the room, but his face was red and the part that wasn't covered by beard was shiny under the lights. Shiny and plagued with acne. "Who the fuck told you that?" he grunted.

"A witness."

"The fuck's name?"

Burgess smiled. "I think we both know people supplying information about you prefer to remain anonymous. This gentleman with whom you were arguing...is there any reason to think he might have hurt Timmy?"

Martin considered, rocked some more, then shook his head, dismissing the possibility. "Nah. That ain't his kinda thing." He paused. "You got another cigarette?" When Burgess had lit it, he said, "He ain't that creative."

Creative. Hell of a word choice. "And there's no one else? Nobody else who's mad at your family?"

Martin laughed. "Shitload of people mad at my family. None of 'em I know of would dare do anything about it."

Melia came in then with the soda, popped the top, and set it on the table. Burgess was glad for the interruption. For a moment, he'd been losing it, afraid his opinion of the despicable piece of scum he thought Martin was might be showing through. He knew the drill. You could feel any way you wanted. How you acted depended on the result you were looking for. He'd been looking for information; knew he wouldn't get it if Martin clammed up or asked for a lawyer again. He'd hoped for a vestige of family feeling, at least an us versus them, but Timmy might have been an annoying neighborhood dog that got hit by a car for all his brother Dwayne cared.

Martin grabbed the soda and emptied the can. He was getting more agitated, starting to rock faster. His eyes were bloodshot with deep circles below them, like a man who hasn't slept for a while. He looked unhealthy. And he kept looking over his shoulder even though there was nothing there.

"What were you and this other guy arguing about?"

"Nothing important."

"Must have been a little important. You were shouting in the street." Martin shook his head. "What time did the argument take place?"

"Who the fuck cares?"

Burgess moved his chair a little closer. "Who were you arguing with?"

"None of your damned business."

"I'd just like to find him...ask for his side. Make sure he wasn't involved."

"He's got no side. He's an asshole. A loser."

Burgess moved closer. "A customer?"

"A loser."

"He gave you money for something, and you couldn't deliver? You stiffed him?"

"I don't stiff people," Martin said angrily. "I said I'd take care of him, didn't I?" He pushed his chair back. Burgess pushed forward.

"What did he give you money for?"

"None of your fuckin' business."

"He give you money for drugs?"

"None of your fuckin' business."

Don't let him lawyer up on me, Burgess thought, keeping his questions fast and short. "He gave you money for drugs, didn't he? And then you couldn't deliver."

"None of your..."

"You couldn't deliver because your drugs disappeared, didn't they?"

"How the fuck...?"

They continued their chair dance. Martin back and

Burgess forward. "Your drugs disappeared, didn't they? Know where they went?"

"How the fuck...?" Martin was on his feet now, leaning toward Burgess, his uncuffed hand raised in a fist.

"Oh, we found them. You want to know where?" he taunted, ignoring the fist.

"You shithead cops had no right to search my fuckin' house." Martin moved forward, dragging the table with him.

"It's not your house," Burgess said, standing his ground.

"Where did you find my shit!" Martin roared.

"What shit?"

"My fuckin' crank," Martin raised his arm, lifting the table right off the floor.

"In Timmy's room." Martin and the table continued to move forward as Burgess and Melia backed toward the door. "Did you kill him?" Burgess asked.

"If I'd known the little shit had taken it, I woulda fuckin' killed him," Martin said, turning to pick up a chair. By the time he'd swung around, they were safely out the door.

"Joe," Melia said, stopping to catch his breath, "I sometimes wonder whether sending you to that interview and interrogation course was a good idea."

"Hey, that's as much cooperation as anyone's ever gotten from Dwayne Martin. And he just confessed on tape that the stuff in Timmy's room was his."

Melia winced as something crashed against the door. "Joe, he's destroying my interview room."

There was a roar of laughter from Melia's office. Stan Perry stuck his bandaged head around the doorframe. "You guys gotta see this."

On the TV monitor, they watched Dwayne Martin, perched precariously on two chairs, the up-ended table dangling from his wrist, peering into the ceiling vent, trying to find the camera. He was yawning and his eyes were at half-mast, a disjointed stream of curses flowing from his mouth.

"Five minutes," Perry said. "And he'll be out like a light." Burgess covered a yawn of his own. "We should all be so lucky." He'd love to be out like a light. But he still had places to go.

CHAPTER 12

It was a very modest house, the furniture tired and the carpet worn, but there were books on the coffee table, dozens more in the bookcase, and children's drawings had been taped over the screen of the silent television. Burgess knew, even before they'd exchanged names, that this family cared about children. This was a place where a little boy like Timmy Watts had mattered. He shook hands first with the man who had opened the door. "Detective Sergeant Joe Burgess," he said.

"Alan Gordon." The man's handshake was steady, though he held himself with the tenuous caution of someone recovering from a body blow. "This is my wife, Julie."

Julie Gordon was small and strong, with no-nonsense short hair, a warm smile and tired brown eyes. Her eyes were red, so was her nose, and her shoulders slumped as though today the weight of the world, which she normally carried with grace and firm resistance, had won. Burgess took her hand between both of his and said the words that had meant so little a few houses away. "I know how much you cared for him. I'm terribly sorry about what happened."

Her eyes filled with tears. She lowered her lashes, and then her whole face, as grief crumbled it. She turned away with a sob and stepped into her husband's embrace.

"I'm sorry," she said. "I've been trying all day...I just can't seem to stop crying. He was...such..." She struggled to get the words out, "...such a special little boy...and I feel..."

Her husband rested his head on hers, rubbing her back in a gentle rhythm. "I feel..." The words were exhaled on a sob. She turned her stricken face toward Burgess. "I feel like what happened is my fault. If I'd only..."

"Jules," her husband said, "You've got to stop. This is not your fault! You did your best. His family failed him. The State failed him. Not you."

Alan Gordon lifted his head and looked at Burgess. "I'm sorry, Sergeant. I'm afraid she's...we're both...taking this very hard. Timmy was..." He pulled out his own handkerchief and wiped his eyes. "He was like a third son." Gordon's voice was rough and strained. He had a big, tawny Mark Twain mustache, a matching thatch of tawny hair and tragic spaniel eyes. He wasn't an especially big man, but he was a sturdy, scrappy one, and scars on his face and arms made Burgess think he'd been a pretty good brawler until domesticity had settled him down.

Gordon led his wife to the couch and sat beside her, taking her hand. "Jules, listen to me. Whatever Timmy Watts had that resembled a normal life...a childhood...he had because of you." That only made her cry harder. She pulled her hand back, covered her face, and sobbed. The agonized sobs of someone who's lost a beloved child.

"I'm sorry," Alan Gordon said again, both helpless

and accepting in the face of his wife's grief. "She wants to help. I just don't think she can do this right now."

Burgess understood. He'd been the bearer of bad news too many times. Like all cops, he hated it. He'd take a dozen ugly crime scenes, or a dozen autopsies, over one conversation like this. Over having to watch someone's terrible grief, witnessing about the worst pain that can be inflicted on the living.

His mother, who had worried about what being a police officer was doing to his soul, had asked once how he handled notifying families that someone was dead. "I understand why you have to do it. You have to do it for them. I just worry about you, Joseph," she'd said. "About what it does to you. Doesn't it bother you?"

"Of course it bothers me," he'd said. "But it's part of the job. And it's important they know the police care. Important that they have us there to help them through it. We can help, you know."

She'd nodded in her quiet, thoughtful way, her knitting needles clicking over a sweater for one of her grandchildren, and said, "Yes, but Joseph, who helps you through it?"

There were two answers to that question. "No one," and "We help each other." Oddly, though he could remember where he'd been sitting, where she was, the color of her yarn, he couldn't remember how he'd answered.

The Gordons hadn't asked him to sit, but it wasn't a lack of manners. Everything about Julie Gordon said she was a caring person. That was why he was here. He sighed, knowing that if they could have talked to him, they would have had a lot to share about Timmy Watts. "I can come back, Mr. Gordon," he said. "Tomorrow, the next day. But these initial hours are so crucial. It's the end of the first day and I've learned so little about him. Maybe we could talk in the kitchen, the two of us, if you think you could leave her."

Gordon put an arm around his wife and spoke quietly near her ear. Julie Gordon nodded. "Go on," she said. "Go ahead. Anything we can do to help...I'll be okay." When he hesitated, she looked over at Burgess. "I'll be okay. Really. I'm much tougher than I seem right now. I'm sorry to be so much trouble. I never thought, when they called..." She massaged her chest with a shaky hand. "I never thought this would be so hard."

"There's nothing harder, Mrs. Gordon," he said.

She blinked at him, a little surprised, then nodded. "You do understand. I wish I could...if only I could talk without it hurting." Her brown eyes were moving, but she wasn't looking for anything in the room. She was looking for a reprieve, for mercy, for the magical stroke that would take back what had happened and make the world right again. When you're little, people tell you to find a cop when there's trouble, and the cop will fix it.

He'd seen that look many times, always wishing he could turn back time and give them what they wanted. Cops were realists. They had the seamiest side of life stuck in their faces daily. But that didn't mean they didn't feel. He wanted to hug her and tell her it would get better. Over time, it would. But it would never go away. He'd been mourning Kristin Marks for years. She still came to him in his sleep and stood watching with her sad, innocent eyes. When you worked a murder, the victim was yours for life.

"You never knew Timmy?" she asked. Burgess shook his head. "He was actually older than my younger son, Davey, but much smaller. Everyone called him Little Timmy. We've got the two boys, Sammy, who's nine, and Davey. He's seven. Timmy was right in the middle." She looked at her rough hands twisted up in the fabric of her skirt. She was that kind of proper woman who would wear a skirt for a visit from the police. "I wish I could talk about him, bring him to life for you...Oh, God! What am I saying?" Emotion choked her.

When she recovered, she said, "Alan, there's lemonade in the kitchen. Maybe the policeman would like that, or some coffee? Excuse me, I'm going upstairs to wash my face."

She was going upstairs to throw herself across her bed and release the choking sobs she'd been holding back. To wail and beat her fists and feel, in privacy, the overwhelming hurt. They all knew it. Burgess and Alan Gordon stood watching as she fumbled her way blindly across the room, hands over her face, then clung to the railing to haul herself up.

"This isn't like her, you know," Gordon said. "You're not seeing her as she is. Jules is a real brick. Solid as they come. She don't...doesn't give way to emotions like this. But Timmy...well, we can ill afford it, but she would have taken him in a minute. She did her best by the boy. There's no call for her to be accusing herself now because the social services wouldn't do their job..."

"She's the one who called?"

Gordon gave him a level look. "I'd think she was one of many, wouldn't you, not that it did any good. You've been in that house. Met those people. It's no fit place for a child."

"No," Burgess agreed. "It's not." In the sixteenth hour of this investigation, he was so tired his clothes felt heavy. "Do you mind if we sit?"

"There's a fan in the kitchen. I could make

coffee..."

He hadn't even noticed the heat. He'd been focused on the emotion. "Coffee would be nice." He followed Gordon through a doorway. The contrast with the Watts's place couldn't have been greater. Even with two young boys around, everything was spotless and orderly and, as in his mother's house, you could have eaten off her floor. "You wife's a marvelous housekeeper," he said.

"She is that," Gordon agreed. "Best thing that ever happened to me."

Probably it was. Burgess liked to see relationships that worked. It gave him hope. He lowered himself carefully into a kitchen chair, favoring his knee. "Did you see Timmy yesterday?"

"Oh, sure," Gordon said, busying himself with the coffee. "We see him most days. Found him once sleeping on the step when I went out in the morning." His hands went still for a moment. "Can you imagine? That about broke my heart." He clutched the edge of the counter, knuckles white. In the living room, he'd had to be strong for his wife. Without her, he was stumbling. "Boy that young sleeping on a doorstep when he's got a home...uh...a house and a family almost next door. I brought him in and put him on the sofa. He didn't even wake up. I was awful glad Jules didn't see that."

Gordon went back to work, measuring, pouring. At least it wasn't going to be instant. Burgess drank it to be polite, but he hated instant. "Most times," Gordon said, "he shows up for breakfast or lunch, and then stays on. Showed, I mean. Stayed." He turned his face away, but Burgess could see him reflected in the glass, fist pressed against his mouth. "Officer? Uh...what am I supposed to call you, anyway? Sergeant? Detective?"

"Either one's fine." Better keep the man talking or he'd break down, too. "Can you tell me what time you last saw Timmy?"

"Yesterday afternoon. Sometime between three and four, I think, maybe a bit later. We had to go to a cook-out. People Julie works with. We don't really know them, and she wasn't comfortable taking an extra child along, so she sent him home. I mean, what else could she do, really? But now, with what's happened, she'll never forgive herself for leaving him behind." Gordon leaned on the counter, bracing himself with his arms. Burgess didn't need to see his face to know he was crying. It was there in the shaking back and shoulders. In Gordon's voice. "Jesus, Detective, Jesus, we should have just taken him. What difference would one child have made?"

A coffee mug shot across the counter and plummeted to the floor, exploding into shards. Gordon turned, slightly crouched, fists cocked like a boxer. "Goddammit!" he said. "Goddammit! Who did this to him? I need to know, Detective. I've got boys of my own."

"That's what I'm trying to find out," Burgess said quietly. "You got any ideas?"

"Yeah. Yeah. Maybe I do." Gordon got another mug from the cupboard, poured them each coffee, and set Burgess's down in front of him. "You take cream or sugar?"

"Both."

"Look, I don't know. I mean, me, I can't imagine how anyone could hurt a kid, let alone kill one. I heard..." His voice dropped as he leaned forward. "I heard it was really awful." When Burgess didn't respond, he said, "Oh, yeah. You can't talk about it, can you? Who I think might of done it? If it wasn't one of his own relatives? Which I wouldn't put it past them, you know what I mean? Kid was always black and blue. Mostly from Dwayne, but the parents weren't much better. Only time Timmy was treated half-decent was when Iris was home."

Gordon sat back in his chair, worry puckering his forehead like corrugated cardboard. "Has anyone told Iris yet? The deaf sister? She's not like the rest of them over there. She really loved him, Detective. When Iris was home, he was clean and fed and kept regular hours, like a normal kid. I hate to think of her all alone in her room, hearing it on the news. Except, she don't...doesn't hear. But she can read. They got newspapers. They get captions on their screens, don't they? My God! Bad as it is for us, think how it must be for her. She can't even run to a phone and call home and ask what's really happening."

He tugged at his mustache. "I dunno. Maybe she can use a phone." He shrugged. "But who would she call? Them? I don't guess any of that lot would think to call her."

Burgess hadn't contacted her and wasn't sure anyone else had. "I don't know if she's been told," he said. "I'll have to check with the Lieutenant in charge. So, you were going to tell me who you suspect?"

"Right. Well, like I said, there's Dwayne. He's a mean son-of-a-bitch and he didn't like Timmy. Lately it's been worse. Timmy's had more bruises, and Dwayne was even out in the street, screaming at him. Dwayne thought Timmy was stealing his stuff."

"What stuff?"

Gordon shrugged. "When I asked, Timmy just said he didn't fuckin' take nothin'. Those were his words. He didn't talk nice. Jules was always after him about it, like she'd be with Sammy or Davey. Once or twice, he got to swearing so bad she sent him home. But she's got a soft heart, and Timmy was real needy."

He lifted the cup to his lips, then set it down without drinking. "So, Dwayne. And there's that creep down by the park. We wouldn't let the boys go down there alone. Weekends, he'd sit there on a bench, letting his dog run loose, watching children. Once Sammy went into the bushes to pee...I know, we shouldn't of let him, it being a public park and all, but little kids, they gotta pee, you let 'em pee, right? Can't be worse than all those dogs running around, and we let them pee. Anyways, Sammy says that this guy, the creep, followed him and watched. That's not normal."

Gordon allowed himself a smile. "I'd watch their mothers."

"The creep down by the park, you know his name?" Gordon shook his head, then gave a description that was clearly Osborne. "Anybody else?"

"Yeah, I'm getting to that. But there's something you should know." Gordon folded his hands together and looked down at the table. For a second, Burgess wondered if he was confessing. "You bring up a list of sex offenders, you're going to find me." He watched Burgess's face. "See...when I was younger...before Jules, I spent a lotta time in bars. Used to get pretty drunk. One time, I'm taking a piss against a lamp post...cop comes along, tells me to knock it off. I give him some lip, get arrested for indecent exposure." Gordon shrugged. "So it looks bad. But all it was was pissing."

"Thanks for telling me," Burgess said. "Dwayne Martin. The guy down by the park. Anybody else?"

"Couple days ago," Gordon said, "Dwayne was having a screaming match out there in the street with some guy."

"You hear what they were fighting about?"

"The word they used was 'stuff' but you ask me, they were arguing about drugs."

"What makes you think so?"

"Because the other guy said...oh, yeah, he didn't say stuff. Guess Julie's been getting to me, too. He said 'shit.' He said if he didn't get his shit that he'd paid for before Friday, something real bad was going to happen." Gordon shrugged. "And something real bad happened."

"You know this guy?" Gordon shook his head. "Seen him around before?"

"Yeah."

"Can you describe him for me?"

"Sure. I got his license number, too. I'm pretty damned sick of that family and the way they're bringing down the neighborhood. Me and Jules, we're trying to raise kids here. You don't wanna raise kids next door to a bunch of drug dealers spouting filth day and night. And all that garbage gonna bring rats. Lemme find the number." He rummaged through a drawer, saying, apologetically, "Jules don't let me leave anything lying around."

God bless you, Alan Gordon, you'd better not be lying to me. And you'd better not be mixed up in this. He liked Gordon for a lot of reasons—for his caring, for his observations, for his decency. Even for his scrappy past. He'd committed a few acts of public indecency in his day. So had every man who'd ever drunk too much and relieved himself in a public place. He'd also had people lie to him well and convincingly. The cop who tells you he can always spot a liar is lying himself, whatever flavor-of-the-month detection method he says he's using. Good cops can do it most of the time. No one bats 1000.

Gordon came back with a scrap of paper. Burgess copied the number into his notebook. "Mind if I keep this?" Gordon shook his head. "What did this guy look like?"

"It was dark," Gordon said, "I didn't get a good look at him. Mostly, I was seeing him from behind. He was big. Bigger than you. Dark hair. Heavy-set. Wearing jeans and a tee shirt. And his pants rode real low."

"You didn't see his face?"

"Just his butt crack."

"Could you tell anything about his age? Old? Young?"

Gordon considered. "Older than me, I think."

Burgess put Gordon at about 33. "What was he driving?"

"Truck. Big Dodge Ram, double cab, fancy sumbitch. Black. New."

"Who did Timmy hang around with, besides your boys?"

"There was a whole gang of 'em, used to run around the neighborhood. Couple kids lived down near the park. Family named Lane. Big yellow house. The boys are Sydney and Leo; the girl is Gretchen. Sydney can be a bit rough sometimes, Sammy's come home crying once or twice, but kids are...well, you know."

"Anyone else?"

"The art teacher. Timmy really liked her. She gave him books. And Gabe...uh...Officer Delinsky. He was great with all the kids. Him and me, we were going to get a baseball team together, try and do something for these kids...lotta kids who don't have fathers around, and the mothers aren't much for getting out and tossing a ball around."

"You know a kid named Matty McBride?"

Gordon made a face. "He used to pal around with Timmy, when Timmy first moved in. But Matty, he's..." He picked up his coffee cup and crooked his little finger. "A snob, I guess. Thinks he's too good for the rest of us. Poor kid's gotta live here with us working folk 'cuz his rich daddy took off. That's their story, anyway. He used to pal around with Ricky Watts. I don't know what that was about. Ricky's scum. Then Ricky went away. After that Matty mostly treated Timmy like an unwanted pet. But that might have been his mother. She's an even bigger snob."

"You know of anyone in the neighborhood people call 'the witch'? Woman who drives a blue car?"

"I don't," Gordon said. "Maybe Jules does. You want me to ask her?"

"If she's up to it."

"I'll see." Gordon pushed back his chair and went upstairs. Burgess hadn't found out what he did for a living, but whatever it was, it was physical. His workboots were worn and his muscles hadn't come from a gym.

As soon as he heard the heavy feet on the stairs, Burgess dumped out his coffee. He liked it strong, but this stuff would take the enamel off his teeth. Gordon had drunk his without noticing. He filled the cup with water, drank it, and set the cup in the sink, thinking longingly of a cool shower, a soft bed, and Chris. He still had reports to write. By the time he got to bed, if he got to bed, it would be time to get up again.

He sat again and tipped his head back, his lids sliding like fine grade sandpaper over his tired eyes. But it wouldn't do to have Gordon return and find him snoring in the kitchen. There were photos on the refrigerator. He walked over for a closer look. On top, secured by a Ronald McDonald magnet, was one of three boys, a sturdy boy with Gordon's tawny hair, a dark-haired boy with Julie Gordon's smiling eyes, and a third with a mass of white-blond curls. He carried into the light for a closer look. The other two boys were smiling broadly for the camera. Timmy looked uneasy.

Gordon returned as he was studying the picture. "He

had that deer in the headlights look a lot, Detective. Too many years getting hit for anything he did." He took the picture and put it back on the refrigerator, then rummaged in the drawer again, turning to hand Burgess another picture. Timmy Watts was standing on top of a climbing structure, grinning hugely, his arms raised in triumph. He looked vibrantly alive and completely happy. "Take it," Gordon said. "Put it on your desk. It'll help you remember what that bastard did."

He tugged at his mustache. "Oh, and Julie says that she hasn't heard of the witch either, but she'll ask around and call if she learns anything. You got a number we can use?"

Burgess gave him a card. "If I'm not there, please leave a message." He had two more questions. "Did Timmy eat here yesterday?"

"You know kids," Gordon said. "Julie didn't want 'em cranky at the cook-out, so she fed them peanut butter and jelly. Timmy, too. She knew he wasn't likely to get fed at home."

"Timmy say anything about running away from home?"

Gordon shook his head. "Not to me. I'll ask Jules."

It was time to go. "Thanks for all your help, Mr. Gordon."

Gordon nodded. "Julie says to tell you Timmy was a pack-rat."

"Do you know what she means?"

"Yeah. Timmy liked to take things. He didn't mean anything by it. I always thought it was just that he'd never had nothin', and he longed for things."

"He take stuff from you?"

"At first. Julie got him to stop. But a packrat, you know, they don't just take stuff, they leave stuff. So sometimes he'd leave us things, too."

"Like what?"

"I dunno. Julie, she kept it all in a box for him like they were his treasures."

"I'd like to see that box."

Gordon looked dubious. "Can it wait 'til tomorrow? She's almost asleep. I'd just as soon not disturb her."

"Tomorrow's fine," he said.

Gordon didn't see him out. He stood by the refrigerator, staring at the picture of the three boys. Burgess pitied his sorrow but took some comfort in knowing that somewhere in Timmy Watts's miserable world there had been smiling faces, loving hearts and a decent, welcoming home.

He gimped his way through the body-temperature air to his car and paused, looking back at the house he'd just left. A man crying in the kitchen. A woman crying upstairs. And two small boys safely asleep, boys whose parents wouldn't sleep easily until Burgess and his team had done their job. If their rough guesstimate was right, by this time last night, someone had repeatedly plunged a knife into a boy's body and Timmy Watts was dead.

CHAPTER 13

He got home at 12:30, four and a half hours to sleep before he had to start all over again. He showered and went into the bedroom, his skin puckering as he crossed the room. The window air-conditioner was working flat-out and the room was as cold as a meat-locker. Chris had bought the air-conditioner, saying, "You want to have sex in a summer like this, you need air-conditioning." He wasn't complaining.

He slid in, put an arm around her, and pulled her close. Ever the detective, he deduced she was wearing something silky and that there wasn't very much to it, that the secret parts of her body were easily accessible. She turned, feeling for his face in the dark, and kissed him, pressing the length of her body against him. She'd been sharing his bed at least a few days a week since February. Five months and he still got an electric thrill when they lay like this which was almost adolescent.

"I've missed you so much," she said.

He put his hands just below the small of her back, where her hips began to flare, and pulled her tighter. "You feel so good," he said.

"I'm going to feel even better." She touched him, uttering a low murmur of appreciation. "What are you waiting for?"

He fell asleep wondering if he was an irredeemable oaf. Too often, despite the pleasure he took in both her body and her company, they had sex and he fell asleep. Sometimes he fell asleep on top of her. She said she didn't mind, claimed she found it endearing. But didn't she deserve more?

They were already like an old married couple in one unfortunate way—they didn't find time to talk. She was busy, he was busy, they were both tired or had too much on their minds. And there were all the things he didn't want to tell her because they were so ugly. As a nurse, she dealt with some pretty ugly things herself, but he still had that urge to protect her. Like cops everywhere, he tried not to bring the job home. This was a new experience for him. Until now, his life had been his job.

This was his first homicide since the one that brought them together, and it could be a true test of their relationship. He wasn't only worried about their vacation. When he worked a homicide, it was pretty much 24/7. How would she handle his absence, his obsession with the case? Recovering from Kristin Marks, he'd destroyed half his furniture. He had a better handle on himself now, but these cases generated a lot of emotion. Home was where he could be alone and decompress. What would it be like to have company, an audience? What if he lost control and screwed everything up?

He knew Kristin Marks would come tonight. Sometimes he'd stay awake, a bleary-eyed next day preferable to the God-awful visions his brain served up, but tonight he needed sleep. Tomorrow's autopsy would be bad. Then he was stopping at the school for the deaf to see Iris Martin, which would be no picnic either. When he got back, Captain Cote would be waiting. Not a ray of sunshine on his whole horizon. He gritted his teeth as he burrowed down into the pillow.

The dream began on that early morning when he'd responded to an anonymous call about a body and found Kristin lying there in the dump. Even in a dream, Burgess still felt the outrage he'd felt at that moment, staring down at a dead child who'd been snatched off the street, raped, sodomized, and suffocated with her own underpants, then thrown on a trash heap. The dream began the way their video of the crime scene did, at a distance and moving closer.

Unlike the video, his dream had all the sensory aspects of memory. There was the striking quality of slanted early morning light, with its incredible contrasts of blinding brightness and dense, purple shadow. There was the strangely deep quality of silence, of being alone in the world, a silence disturbed only by his footsteps crunching over garbage and the shrilling of gulls overhead, the distant susurration of the sea. There was the distorted sense of time intermingled with feeling, of wanting to slow things down, to stop there, in the cool emptiness of the morning, and not take that next step toward what certainty told him lay ahead. There was the fresh tang of sea air corrupted by the smell of refuse, and, as he got closer, the unmistakable smell of death.

Whenever that picture began, Burgess would try to wake, to stop the dream. Sometimes he couldn't. As the dream camera panned in, he saw Kristin, standing on a mound of trash, naked except for the veil she'd worn for her confirmation, her fair hair and the veil billowing back behind her. She came toward him, what looked like white foam coming from her mouth.

As she got closer, the foam resolved into maggots, and maggots crawled down her thighs.

This time, she held a small boy by the hand, fair-haired like her, his curls blowing in the breeze, Kristin with her slender child's body, the boy painfully thin. The boy wore bloody patterned underpants, the red slits of his gaping wounds opening and closing like mouths as he walked. They were making high, keening noises, like the shrieks of hawks, and their eyes were soulless and opaque. They came at him at dream speed, as inexorable as zombies.

As he'd done so often, Burgess pushed off the covers, stumbled into the bathroom, and threw up. He brushed his teeth and stood, leaning on the sink, waiting for his stomach to settle.

"The dream?" she said from the doorway.

"This time, there were two children."

She stared at him with troubled eyes, little frown lines in her forehead he wanted to smooth away. "Why did it have to be you?" she asked. "You're not the only detective..." She was wearing something silky blue that dipped low over her breasts. Her long hair was tangled. She looked younger than her thirty-eight years and deeply unhappy.

"It would have been Terry's."

"I see," she said. "Do I blame Terry for ruining our vacation, then?"

"You could blame Vince. He called me. But the real one to blame is the killer. How is Terry, anyway?"

"Miserable. He kept some soup down. A start. But how could things get so bad without you noticing?"

"Just what we asked ourselves." He looked at his watch. "I've got to leave for Augusta at five. The autopsy."

"Why such an ungodly hour?"

"You're a nurse. I thought you understood doctors."

"What's to understand?" she said. "There are some nice ones and some saints and a lot of arrogant assholes. Why five?"

"ME wants to cut at seven so he can go play golf, and we've got to finish working the body first."

"Cut?" she said. "Work the body? That's an ugly way to talk about the death of a little boy. And who plays golf in heat like this?"

"Golfers. And it was an ugly death," he said. "Come back to bed. I won't survive in there without you. I'll freeze to death."

"Yeah," she said. "Nice, isn't it."

"Another way you've changed my life."

"I do what I can. Speaking of which, you want me to get up with you, fix breakfast?"

He shook his head, still feeling shaky, beginning to feel trapped. "Look," he said, "the next few days, the next week, nothing's going to be normal. The way I work these things, it's day and night. I just follow everything as far as I can, push as hard as I can, see what I can make happen. I don't do stuff like breakfast."

"I know," she said. "Terry told me how this was going to be."

Good old Terry. Dragging himself back from his own depths to help someone else. No wonder the guy wore himself out. "Even I don't know how this is going to be," Burgess said. "Just that it will be intense, and I'll be unavailable. I don't know how it's going to be for us, either. I only know that you can't get in my way. You can't lay expectations on me, like being home for dinner, or breakfast, or even to sleep."

He studied her, trying to see how she was taking this. He was not articulate about relationships. All he knew was truth. That it wouldn't help them through this for him to play Mr. Nice Guy and try to let her down easy. There was no easy. He had to call it like it was.

"You know I've always been a loner." He waved a hand toward the bedroom. "I'm trying, with you, with this...but this case, this little boy...it's gonna snap me right back where I was when we met."

She pushed her hair back over her shoulders. "I'm not a sweet young thing with her head full of dreams about the perfect romance and the ideal man, Joe. I've been around. I can take care of myself. I can still eat dinner if you're not across the table. I can read a book if you're not here to talk to. And I can sleep alone without sobbing into my pillow. You go do whatever you have to do, and don't worry about me, okay?"

He still wasn't sure she understood. "My reputation for being mean?" he said. "I earned it during cases like this. I will get mean. I won't let anything get in my way. Not even you."

"You trying to scare me away?"

"I don't know."

She folded her arms, her chin lifting. "Then we'll just have to see, won't we?"

"Ms. Tough guy, huh?"

"Mr. Bloodhound, I presume?"

He tried to sweep her a bow, but pain from his knee caught him mid-motion and stopped him dead. "Pleasure to make your acquaintance," he said.

She stepped past him, opened the medicine cabinet, and handed him some Advil. "You go back to bed," she said. "I'm getting some ice for your knee. And tomorrow, I'm buying you a knee brace. You know..." She stepped up until her breasts were touching his chest—a sweet, decent, generously-made woman— and looked straight into his eyes. "You're good at taking care of other people, Joe Burgess, but you don't know a damned thing about taking care of yourself."

CHAPTER 14

It hadn't cooled off overnight. At five a.m. the air had the congealing quality of semi-set Jell-O. The air smelled of rotting vegetation and everything was faintly slimy to the touch. A few streets away, there was a sudden, explosive crash. For a moment, he was in the jungle again, dropping into a defensive crouch and scrutinizing the world around him. Nam had only been a year of his life, over a quarter century ago, but it still happened, leaving him awash with adrenaline and memory. He straightened up and went to the car, the driveway and walk slick and oily under his shoes.

Running on four hours sleep, he felt dopey and slow, lacking edges. He'd heard when people got older, they needed less sleep. He seemed to need more. At least he spent more time in bed. Maybe it was just the novelty of having Chris there, a reason to linger, something to offset the dreams. It was a gray morning, the overcast sky a dingy blanket overhead, the world wrapped in a faint haze. He drove north under a gray sky down a gray road through a gray world. No surprise. He'd long ago recognized that little he encountered would be black and white.

Wink Devlin was already there, taking close-up photographs of deep bruises on the boy's upper arms. "Hell of a lot to do in an hour," he muttered. "I should have brought Rudy. You see these?" He set the camera down and motioned for Burgess to look at the bruises. "What do they tell you?"

Burgess studied the bruises, then lifted the stick-thin arm and looked at the other side. He lowered the boy's arm carefully and measured the bruise pattern with his own hands, picturing the child being held down. "I'm not surprised."

Devlin shook his head. "Nor am I. Sorry, though."

Sorry. A meager word for such an immensely brutal thing. Together they went through the process. Scraping under the fingernails. Combing the hair for trace evidence, then securing standard hair samples. Soft, silky clean hair, still a young child's hair. Burgess sniffed and smelled herbal shampoo. Carefully, they removed the underpants and put them in a paper bag. Took oral and anal swabs and examined the skin for semen. Photographing every step. The many bruises. The wounds. The body, front and back. It was a grim process. The boy was so small, the wounds so ugly.

The room helped. It was cold and clinical, all hard-edged, shiny and utilitarian. Stainless steel and tiles, saws and tools, knives and scales. Nothing soft or worldly. No hooks for sentiment.

A small scrap of white paper fluttered to the floor. Burgess picked it up. Read: Inspected by 117. He took the underpants from the bag and smelled new cloth. He looked at Devlin, who was preparing to fingerprint the boy's hands. "Let's think about this for a minute," he said. "After the boy's dead, someone cleans up the body, dresses it in new underpants and wraps it in a clean new blanket. There's a chance, if we haven't already screwed it up, that we might get fingerprints from the skin."

"Wish you'd thought of this yesterday," Devlin grumbled. "We'd have a lot better chance if the body wasn't cold, the interval wasn't so long."

Burgess didn't lob the ball back. Devlin should have thought of it; he was the evidence tech. But Burgess was the scene detective. It was on his shoulders. It was a long shot anyway. It was hard to get prints off skin. But if the child had been cleaned and dried, the killer nervous, sweaty, on a hot night.

"It's worth a try," he said. He helped Wink with the process, pointing out the likeliest places. Mostly they got a lot of nothing. Then they raised one on the boy's shoulder another on his arm where the bruises were.

"Where's the blanket?"

"Over there." Wink indicated a large paper bag. "Got the blanket and the sheets. I've got five filters from yesterday, unwrapping him. Even vacuumed out the body bag. If there's anything there, I'll find it."

"Get Dani to help. She loves playing Nancy Drew."

Wink smiled proudly. He'd recruited Dani Letorneau, trained her, and took an avuncular pleasure in her success. It didn't hurt that she was Sally Field cute and brave enough to face down a mob of Hell's Angels. "Will do."

Burgess watched him print the boy's fingers and got another idea, imagining small damp feet on a bathroom or bedroom floor. Footprints the perp might not have thought to clean up. "Do his feet, too, would you?" As Wink moved to the boy's feet, he saw the Band-Aid around the boy's big toe, something he'd noticed at the scene. "And get that Band-Aid."

Wink removed the Band-Aid, grinning a bandit's grin. "Maybe this time, the good guys will get lucky," he said as he took plantar prints from the child's feet.

A Band-Aid. A thin rectangle of flesh-colored plastic. It seemed so unimportant. But it was very difficult to apply a Band-Aid without leaving friction ridge impressions, which meant it might offer them a good partial print. The Band-Aid had been carefully applied, making it unlikely Timmy had done it himself. There was no one in the Watts household except Darlene Painter who would have bothered, and that was something he could check. Finally, there was the fact that the Band-Aid was clean, as was the skin underneath. By all reports, Timmy Watts had rarely been clean.

A picture of the events on the night Timmy Watts died was beginning to form. At least some of the events. A lot more would be filled in by Dr. Lee's autopsy. Someone had taken Timmy Watts to his home and persuaded him to take a bath or shower and wash his hair. That person had then held him down forcefully and raped him. Either before or after the rape, his assailant had hit him in the head. When the blow to the head didn't kill him, the man had taken a knife and stabbed him repeatedly. The washing afterward had been to clean the blood off the body, probably so it could be transported without too great a mess.

The door swung open and Dr. Lee flew in, moving, as always, at twice the pace of normal folk. He was followed by his assistant, a silent, stolid fellow who'd always struck Burgess as someone who should be following Dr. Frankenstein. The contrast between the slender, dark-haired, athletic Lee and his hulking, pale assistant couldn't have been greater. Lee greeted Devlin with a nod. "Morning, Wink. I see you've been messing with the little fellow. He looks like a chimney sweep."

Wink assumed a self-mocking hangdog look and

pointed at Burgess. "I just do what he tells me."

"Yeah," Lee agreed. "People do, don't they." His quick gaze rolled up and down Burgess's body, doing a visual autopsy. He turned to his assistant. "Al, can you get the sergeant a stool, then clean this boy up a bit?"

"I don't need a stool."

"I know you, detective, you've got a long day ahead. Save yourself for the bad guys." Al hadn't moved. Lee gave him a fierce look. "Al. The stool?" The man hunched his shoulders and slouched out of the room. Lee stared after him a moment, animosity plain on his face, before he looked down at the body and then at them. "My turn?"

Burgess nodded. "You know what we're looking for. Cause of death. Evaluation of the head injury. Any information you can give us about the weapon. Weapons. Whether the child was standing or lying down when he was stabbed. How long since his last meal. Whether he was molested." The block under Timmy's neck thrust his bony chest forward, reminding Burgess of a painting he'd seen once of Icarus. Yesterday, for a while, the boy had even had wings.

"Whether the assailant was right-handed or left-handed, a member of Mensa, and a vegetarian." Lee looked down at the boy on the table. "This child is unnaturally clean. Look at his fingernails. At his toes." He cleared his throat and began to dictate. Al came back with the stool, dropped it a few feet from Burgess, then stumped sullenly forward and gave the body a cursory wash.

Wink photographed and videotaped. Burgess, from the comfort of his stool, observed, and Lee went through the protocol. There was a moment after he'd finished the external exam, when Lee picked up his scalpel but before he began to cut, when they all stood silently and stared down at the body, thinking their individual thoughts. The purplish wounds glistened on the pale skin like lipstick kisses. It was the moment when Dr. Geller, the pathologist who'd done the first autopsies Burgess had witnessed, had given his silent prayer for the departed. In his memory, Burgess still did. Then Lee began the Y-incision, slicing cleanly through the thin white skin.

By that time, Burgess knew that the boy weighed 45 pounds, small and underweight for a child almost nine, and had definitely been sexually assaulted—there was trauma and tearing and traces of KY. A dark piece of him was pondering what kind of adult could force himself on a 45-pound child. He'd expected it. Over the years, he'd seen so many unimaginable things that little *was* unimaginable. People raped two year olds. Raped babies. But it was always hard in the moment when he first confronted the blunt reality.

Lee conducted the autopsy with frightening speed and precision, keeping up a running staccato commentary on what he was doing and his findings. Unwillingly, Burgess found himself remembering the Kristin Marks autopsy, the sickness he'd felt, not at the procedure—he'd grown used to seeing the human body dissected this way—but at the information about how she'd suffered. To do his job, he had to imagine the scene, but no one comfortably imagines of the violent rape of a child. Burgess tried to keep his rational and emotional sides far apart. Today, he failed, anger and impatience arcing between them as Lee's brisk voice reported his findings.

Timmy Watts had been stabbed eleven times with a smooth, doubled-edged blade, approximately three to four inches long. "How wide?" Burgess asked.

"Inch at the hilt, maybe," Lee said.

"Standing or lying?"

"Lying down." Lee's hands described the angle of the knife. Then he pointed to one of the wounds. "Looks like he tried to roll away from the knife, curl up to protect himself. That's why this one's way over here to the side. Probably a right-handed assailant." He didn't miss Burgess's grimace. "You're not letting this one get to you, are you, detective?"

"What killed him?"

Lee pointed to a wound higher up the chest and toward the side. "This one. But the others did enough damage that together, they would have."

"The head wound?"

"Single blow with a blunt object. You've got some nice impressions here if you knew what to match them to. Coke bottle would be my guess. One of those small ones. But that only stunned him. It wouldn't have killed him."

"I've got a Coke bottle in the car," Wink said.

Lee glanced impatiently at his watch. "Small one?" Devlin nodded. "Go get it." Lee paced impatiently while they waited, eager to get on with it and get to his golf.

"Golf means that much to you?" Burgess said.

"You think I'm moving too fast?" Lee said. "You think maybe I'll get careless and miss something?"

Burgess had never seen Lee anything but cool and detached. Entertaining, at times, but always distant. Today he seemed angry. "I'd hate to see another child-killer walk, that's all," Burgess said.

"No one's ever walked because of my mistake."

Devlin returned with the bottle and gave it to Lee. Sensing something in the air, he looked curiously at Burgess and the assistant ME. When no one said anything, he picked up his camera and filmed Dr. Lee comparing the bottom of the bottle with the marks on

Timmy Watts's skull. Filmed Lee's triumphant smile, decisive nod, then changed cameras and did a series of still shots.

"Here's one of your weapons," Lee said, shooting a challenging look at Burgess.

Burgess wasn't playing the game, wasn't sure Lee wanted to play it either. He was too old for verbal versions of my dick's bigger than your dick. "The sexual assault?"

"Don't let the KY fool you," Lee said. "Perp did that for himself, not for the kid. It was violent. Brutal. There are tears and bruising. The boy would have been in pain. And I'll be surprised if you find sperm." Lee went on with the autopsy but now, clearly in response to Burgess's implied criticism, he did it at half speed—half-speed for a normal person. He did everything slowly and carefully, dictating lengthy, detailed and precise descriptions of every step, shooting Burgess the occasional look to be sure he understood what was going on.

Burgess knew all about malicious obedience. He practiced it himself occasionally, especially with Cote. Didn't much like finding himself in the same class as that asshole. He didn't think there was any more care or reverence in this slow technique than there had been in Lee's Vegematic style. What was missing from the room was a sense of shared purpose, of mission, something he thought had been there earlier. But maybe Dr. Lee's only mission was reading the entrails, getting the slice and dice right; his only goal that his ego be satisfied, that if the case came to court, he wouldn't be found lacking. Maybe what had brought them all here—a child's death—didn't matter so long as the essential information was obtained. He thought of Kristin Mark's autopsy, with a different ME, of the profound sadness in the room.

His neck and shoulders were stiff. Stools weren't much good for sitting after the first twenty minutes or so. He stood, shifting his shoulders, trying to work the kinks out. Standing wasn't better, only different. The pain shifted to his leg. Devlin was tired, too. The camera wasn't light and they'd been at this a long time. He was sure Wink had put in a day as long as his yesterday. Wink didn't like to go to bed until all his toys were put away.

His mind drifted to Iris Martin and the news he was bringing; the questions he'd have to ask. It seemed a cruel thing to do to a sheltered young girl, but it was a necessary cruelty, just as this was. It had been a while since he'd done an interview with a deaf witness and never with one so young. He couldn't imagine how the interpreter would handle the information he was bringing, or elicit the information he was seeking. He wondered whether Iris Martin was profoundly deaf or only partially. How she'd communicated with Timmy.

He yawned. Dr. Lee smiled sardonically. "We keeping you up, detective?" Lee had never been like this before. Usually, the doc called him Joe. Maybe this wasn't personal. Maybe someone was chewing on Lee's ass and he just needed an ass of his own to chew.

Maybe they could call a truce. "Four hours sleep," he said apologetically. "I'm getting too old for this."

"Almost done." Lee took the blood and urine samples he needed and turned to the stomach, which he'd set aside in a pan. "Let's have a look at his last meal, shall we?" He sliced and a sour smell filled the air. After all these years, Burgess thought he could probably track the course of an autopsy with a blindfold on, purely by the smells and sounds. Lee peered in. "This isn't a clinical opinion, detectives," he said, "but it looks a lot like a couple of hot dogs to me."

Burgess crossed the room, looked, and added another item to the list of things he'd never eat again. "Care to comment on the interval between last meal and death?"

"An hour, maybe?"

"And the time of death?" Lee hesitated. "If you can," Burgess urged. "Anything to narrow the time."

"Between 10:00 p.m. and midnight. That's very rough. I wouldn't take that one to the bank, Detective. Too many variables."

Burgess understood that. He was still hoping for witnesses. Real live humans who'd seen Timmy Watts on the night he died after he left Mrs. Johnston's house and headed toward that blue car. For now, he'd take anything he could get, even a reluctant guess from a cranky medical examiner.

"That's all, folks," Lee announced, deftly putting the sampled organs back in the body. "We'll get you toxicology as soon as we can." He stepped back from the table and nodded at Al. "You can finish up." Al hung back, waiting for Lee to leave.

"Wink, you need any help?" Burgess asked.

Devlin nodded. "Can you bring the blankets and the sheets?"

As Burgess bent to pick them up, he spotted something on the floor by the wall and knelt down cautiously to examine it. "Wink, you got some tweezers and a plastic bag?"

Devlin handed them down. "Whatcha got?"

"I don't know." He captured it, bagged it, and handed it over. "Do you?"

"Looks like something mechanical, maybe?" Wink lowered the bag. "Goddamn! Found on the floor of the autopsy room. We don't even know if it came from the boy. Could have come in on a shoe."

"Then let's hope it's not the crucial link." He'd be nearly an hour late for his appointment with Iris Martin and Cote would be pitching fits. He'd better do a preliminary report by phone. Better than looking at that revolting face anyway. He picked up the bags holding the blue blanket and the sheets, and walked slowly out of the room, pausing at the door for one last look at the remains of Timmy Watts.

He put the bags in Wink's car, then headed toward his own, swimming through the turgid air like a shipwrecked sailor still a long way from shore. He felt as drained and hollowed out as that child on the table, his mood dense and ugly. He closed his eyes and reached inside himself for something that would carry him through the next few hours—compassion and patience for Iris Martin, clarity and resistance for Cote. Heard the jingle of keys and looked up.

Dr. Lee was standing a few feet away, watching him. They stood in a moment of silent appraisal. "I hate doing kids," Lee said. He got in his car and drove away.

CHAPTER 15

Until that moment, watching her expressive hands swooping with grace and punching emphatically, and the elaborate facial expressions accompanying them, Burgess had had no conception of signing as something beautiful and unique. He hadn't understood it as a language, only as a tool. Iris Martin sat in an ugly orange institutional chair, tears running down her face, and the movements were so eloquent he hardly needed the interpreter to know what she was saying. How much she had loved her brother, how concerned she'd been that he was allowed to run wild, her fears that something like this might happen, how helpless she'd been to prevent it. And then, in contrast to that last, that it had all been her fault.

Something he hadn't seen from the photograph was her resemblance to her brother. She had the same slight build, the same fine-boned face. In her face, he saw what Timmy Watts's blue eyes would have looked like with life in them instead of staring empty at a hot summer sky. Her last name might be Martin, but she was clearly a full sister. The picture in Timmy's room had been unflattering. In person, Iris

Martin had a fragile loveliness, with a grace and dignity far beyond her seventeen years. Even as her hands and face moved and her tears flowed, he got a sense of steadiness and calm. He felt that Iris, who had already survived much, would weather this as well. Growing up in the Watts household had made her a survivor. He also felt the incredible depth of her sorrow. Here, as at the Gordons', was a proper place for his expression of regret.

Before the interview began, he'd met with the interpreter, Missy Steinberg, a warm middle-aged woman with an explosive mop of curly gray hair, and she'd explained the protocol. "I'll be interpreting," she said, "but although it is my voice, it is Iris who is speaking, and you should be looking at her, not me, when you ask your questions and when you hear her answers. My job is to ask your questions exactly as you put them, not interpreting them or editing them, and to do the same with her answers. I will not try to explain you to her, nor her to you. I won't answer questions about her for you, nor about you for her."

She considered. "The timing may seem strange. Between when she answers, and when I tell you her answer, I may have to ask some questions, to be sure I've got it right. Speak slowly and be sure she can see your face. In her presence, I'm only an interpreter." She'd paused, slightly uncomfortable, as people often were in the presence of the police. "Iris is not profoundly deaf. She has some hearing, and her oral skills are quite good. She's more comfortable with signing, more fluent, and given the stressful nature of the interview, we felt it would be easiest for her."

Her hands flew out in a self-deprecating gesture. "What am I saying? How could this possibly be easy for her, no matter what we do? She loved her brother so much, tried so hard to care for him. She blames herself for what happened. She wanted to live at home this summer so she could take care of Timmy. You've seen that place?" Burgess nodded.

Missy Steinberg touched his arm. If touches had voices, this one would have been insistent, loud. "If anyone's at fault, I am. I persuaded her to stay for the summer, for another year. I convinced her she could take better care of Timmy if she finished high school and got the skills to get a job." She pulled her hand back into her lap and knotted her hands together. "If she'd gone home, this might not have happened, but her life might have been ruined. Abandoning her education? Living with those people in that hell hole?" Her shoulders rose and fell. "Hindsight is always 20-20, isn't it? If I'd known it would save a life…"

"Ms. Steinberg, few of us make our daily choices assuming we, or someone we know, might be killed tomorrow."

"I know," she said, "but still."

"Something like this happens, we all wonder what we might have done to prevent it. Tell me about Iris Martin. What's she like?"

"There's something ethereal, other worldly, about her." She caught his look. "Oh, I know that sounds odd, but you'll see what I mean when you meet her." She sighed. "Oh. All right. Like Audrey Hepburn, then. That slight, light quickness. The delicacy…and she's very artistic." She stopped. "Am I being a complete ass?"

"I've met a fair number of people who are complete asses. You're not even in the running." He changed the subject. "Does she know why I'm here?"

Missy Steinberg nodded. "I'm afraid so. She has a lot of questions she wants to ask you. No one from the family has been in touch. I'm afraid she learned it from the papers...that horrible picture."

He hadn't seen a paper yet. "Do you have the paper?" he asked. "I left this morning too early to read it."

"But you already know..."

"But I don't know anything about this picture. I don't know what she's seen, what she's read."

She got the paper for him. "I can't believe you allow photographers to do that." She bit her lip and turned away as Burgess looked at the front page photo—a large, color close-up of Timmy Watts's body, cocooned in the bloody blue blanket, the two white sheets spread out on either side of him. Clear enough to show the vacant eyes, the gapped teeth, the flies. The caption was: "The Angel of Knowlton Park."

Blind rage at the photographer, at the paper's editor, at this second violation of the child, surged through him. Timmy Watts's death was a tragedy, not a spectacle. The GP shouldn't be seeing this. He and Vince hadn't allowed photographers near the scene. That's why they'd cordoned off the park, put up screens. They'd never allow this. But after seeing this, would Cote and the Chief believe that? He'd expected to return to a wall of impatience, questions, the inevitable 'How do we quell public fears?' Now he'd be returning to hell.

"You didn't know?" Missy Steinberg asked.

"Do you think I'd ever allow...?" He checked himself. Wrong place. Wrong person. He folded the paper and stood. "What I'm asking, what she's answering, you understand it's confidential?" She nodded. "Let's do it."

So they were doing it. Burgess in his own ugly, uncomfortable chair, speaking slowly and carefully to Iris, and Missy, to the side, translating his questions into sign and her answers into voice. He asked the same questions he'd asked Grace Johnson, the Gordons, Delinsky, her family. Did she know of anyone who might have wanted to hurt Timmy?

"My brother, Dwayne, was very angry at him," she said. "He thought Timmy had taken something from him." She lowered her eyes. "Timmy did take things. He didn't mean any harm. He just liked to collect things. Or he'd take something from one person and give it to another. Like a packrat. Dwayne wouldn't tell me what was missing, so I couldn't really help, but I searched Timmy's room and couldn't find anything that would matter to Dwayne."

Iris Martin hesitated. "Have you seen his room?" Burgess nodded. "It was all torn apart. I put it back together. Timmy liked things neat." There was a desperate sadness on her face and her tears flowed freely, but her hands continued to move, and Missy to interpret.

One advantage of sign language. People in these circumstances had trouble speaking because their throats closed. Even though that was happening to Iris, she could still communicate. It was Missy who was having trouble, Iris who suddenly stopped signing and put her hand over Missy's, made a sign like a little animal running up into the air.

Missy looked apologetic. "I'm sorry, Detective. I didn't expect...I'm not supposed to..." She covered her mouth. She'd broken the rules.

"To have feelings?" he asked. "Because you're only the interpreter?" She looked at Iris. Interpreted what they'd just said.

"What was the sign you just made? It looked like a mouse."

Iris Martin gave a shaky smile. "It was," she said. This time, she used her own voice. "Mouse was his name-sign." She signed something to Missy.

"Little bright-eyed fellow, creeping around the edges..."

Burgess nodded. "You think your brother Dwayne could have done this?"

She considered. "I don't know. When Dwayne does drugs, he might do anything."

"Other than Dwayne, can you think of anyone who would hurt Timmy?"

"Why would anyone want to hurt him? He was just a sweet little boy."

"How did you and Timmy communicate?" he asked.

"I have some speech, some hearing," she said. "He'd learned a little sign." She swiped at her tears with the back of her hand. "He was my brother. It just worked."

"Did he ever mention a man named Osborne? Lived down near the park?"

"The dirty-pictures man? He took pictures of Timmy. Naked pictures. He used the big dog to scare Timmy so he took off his clothes."

"Timmy told you this?"

She nodded. "But Dwayne took care of him."

"What about your other brothers?"

She just shrugged, then signed something. "She doesn't know," Missy said.

"Some people in the neighborhood tried to do what you did, to look after Timmy, didn't they?" She nodded. "Can you tell me who?"

"The Gordons. Mrs. Johnson. Officer Delinsky."

"Anyone else?" She shook her head. "Who did Timmy play with?"

She named the same children the Gordons had named. Burgess was disappointed. He'd hoped Iris Martin would know more, would have something to add, because she'd been close to her brother, the only person in the family likely to have been observant. She read his disappointment, and did to him what she'd done to Missy—reached over and took his hand. Then she pulled hers back, her forehead furrowed.

"He used to spend time with the McBrides. Matty and his mother. But not lately. I don't know why. I think Mrs. McBride decided she didn't want to be involved with our family after she had trouble with my mother. Timmy was sad about that. He used to have fun with Matty. But I wasn't sorry. Matty's nice but he was bad for Timmy. At least, he was when Ricky was around. They got him drunk once." Iris pulled herself up straight, her hands swooping and stabbing. "It was a very bad thing to do to a little boy. Timmy was so sick. But that was Ricky, I think, not Matty. Ricky doesn't care about anyone."

The hands faltered and fell still as she considered the very much worse thing that had been done.

"Any enemies of the family..." Burgess began.

Her hands rose again, then fell back into her lap. Momentarily sign-less. Her clear blue eyes focused on Burgess, the tears welling up. "I need a moment," she said.

"Take your time," he said. "I know how hard this is."

She gave him a trembling smile. Then her hands rose. "You aren't at all what I imagined. I expected to be afraid of you. I thought you'd treat me like a dummy. But you're kind." A pause, then her hands swooped. "And sad."

Burgess nodded. She swallowed, and he could see her gathering her courage. "Why did you let them take that picture? The one in the paper?"

She deserved an honest answer. "We would never have allowed a picture like that. Someone must have got up high somewhere, at a distance, and used a special lens. It was a low-down, despicable thing to do. I'm so sorry you had to see it." He repeated his question about enemies.

Her hands swooped wide, words flying faster than Missy could talk. "Enemies of the family? Everybody's got enemies. All of Dwayne's customers. People he's cheated. Jason's customers. My uncle, Henry Devereau, once said he'd kill us all off, one by one, until he got the house. But I didn't believe him. Uncle Henry's not as bad as he seems. I don't know. The family of the girl that Ricky..." Her hands were still. She raised her eyes to his face and the hands spoke again. "I know you're disappointed. I wish I could be more help. May I ask some questions now?"

"Of course." Burgess knew what was coming. It was never easy. A detective had a special duty to the family, serving as their conduit for essential information and their link to the criminal justice system. At the same time, many of the details of the death had to be kept confidential, often others were too painful for the family to hear.

"How did he die? Was it awful?" She wanted to know what Julie Gordon had wanted to know— whether Timmy had suffered. He knew more now than he had then and the answer was 'Yes, it was awful.' He wasn't about to tell her that.

"Are you sure you want to hear this?" he asked, immediately feeling ridiculous for using the word "hear." She nodded. "He was stunned by a blow to the head, then stabbed. He probably didn't feel the stabbing." It was a lie. There were marks on the child's back, and on his arms, showing he'd thrashed, turned, tried to evade the plunging knife, defense wounds on the small hands. But how would it help her to know that? To sit alone in her room and replay that in her mind?

"Why was he left in the park?"

"We don't know."

"Was he killed in the park?"

Burgess shook his head. "Ms. Martin, your brother left a note in Grace Johnston's door, telling her he was running away from home. Has he ever run away before?"

She looked away, then, reluctantly, back at Burgess. "Only once that I know of. He came here. Such a long way. He said he wanted to live with me."

"When was that?"

"A month ago."

"How did he get here?"

"Got someone to drive him."

"Who?"

"I don't know. He just showed up." Her eyes returned to the window.

She knew. Burgess was sure of it, and puzzled. Why would she lie? Who was she protecting? He was aware, suddenly, of the awkwardness of doing this with a third party in the room. He shot a look at Missy Steinberg. She didn't seem to find anything strange about Iris's answer. "Timmy didn't tell you?"

Iris shifted on her chair, looking everywhere but at him. "No."

"You weren't expecting him? You didn't know he was coming?" She shook her head. "Did you ask him how he got here?"

Now her eyes were darting. He waited until they came back to his face. "Ms. Martin, I don't want to make any mistakes or fail to ask any question which might let your brother's killer go uncaught. Someone Timmy knew well enough to ask for a ride out here, someone who was willing to bring him—that's a person I need to talk with. Do you understand?"

Was he treating her like an idiot? Was he insulting her? He didn't know the rules of her world. He didn't know how to pressure someone through a third person in a situation like this. How to figure out what Iris was holding back, or why, and say the things which would persuade her to tell him. He looked at Missy, but her focus was on Iris, who looked terribly shaken and fragile. It was evident she'd had enough.

He had two more questions. "Was that the only time Timmy ever came here?"

"Yes."

"And you're quite sure you don't know who brought him?" When she didn't respond, he tried a different question. "Do you know anyone with a small blue car?"

Suddenly, Iris Martin made a flurry of signs, jumped up, and rushed out the door. Missy Steinberg said, "I'm sorry. I'm feeling sick. Excuse me," and hurried after her.

Burgess waited a while, but neither of them returned. The clock was running. Cote was waiting. He had a million things to do. If necessary, he'd come back. He closed his notebook, crossed the empty room, his footsteps echoing heavily, and let himself out. The hot, moist air wrapped him like wet Kleenex.

He felt like a blind man trying to put together a jigsaw puzzle.

His mother had always said life would be dull if you didn't face new challenges and learn new things, but sometimes Burgess longed for dull, for peaceful and routine, for easy. Today, the first full day of his vacation, he'd planned to do some sleeping, some reading, and some fishing. Actually, he *was* doing some fishing. And so far, not catching anything he could use.

CHAPTER 16

He stopped at Mickey D's for a chicken sandwich and coffee, fretting at the time it took to produce what was supposed to be fast food. By the time food and drink were finally handed over, he figured he could have gone home and made himself a sandwich. All his impatient jittering hadn't done his knee or his disposition any favors, either. He took a moment in the garage to wolf the sandwich. Once he got upstairs, there wouldn't be time.

Prioritizing his next steps from worst to least worst—there was no best—he decided to go first to Cote, stopping in Melia's office for a barometer reading of Cote's reaction to the photo. He didn't need words. Melia's sagging shoulders and set face were enough. "He gave you a hard time?" Burgess said, skipping preliminaries.

"Damned near gave me my walking papers. How'd that happen, Joe?"

"Second, third floor window. Telescopic lens. I'll find out. We can't block out the sky, Vince. Or keep numbskull citizens from letting reporters into their homes. I'm on my way up. Pray for me." He said it flippantly, but as soon as the words were out, he wondered. Maybe he did need someone praying for him. Maybe they all did. This was that kind of case.

"I will," Melia said. Burgess thought he meant it. That the lieutenant, father of twin boys, would stop at church on his way home, have a private talk with God. "See me when you're through. We've got to get moving on this thing, give him something for the press."

Like Burgess had spent the morning playing footsie with Chris and then gone rain-skipping instead of watching a small boy being carved up. "I'll be as quick as I can."

"I'll bet you will," followed him down the hall.

Cote's office was neat as a pin and deliciously cool, but the man wasn't enjoying it. He sat glaring at a stack of papers, his face a dangerous red. Burgess knocked, entered, and dropped into a chair, waiting for the opening salvo. Cote wasn't going to cut him any slack because he'd just come from the autopsy of a child and a brutal interview with the child's heartbroken sister. He didn't give a damn how many black things swam in Burgess's head or how many walking wounded his detectives had dealt with. When he wasn't crunching stats or formulating rules and regulations designed to keep them from catching bad guys, Cote lived to chew ass. He slapped the folded newspaper down and stabbed the picture. "How in the hell did this happen?" Same thing Melia asked, yet an entirely different question.

"I don't know," he said, "but I can guess. You want to hear about the autopsy?"

Cote shook the paper spastically. "I want to know about this."

"You call the paper and ask them? You tell them exactly how devastating and painful that photo is to those who knew and loved the victim?" He saw Iris Martin's face—her tears, the small teeth biting her lip to stop its trembling, her diminished, stricken look. "Did you tell them how unnecessary such a graphic illustration is to the reporting of the story? Or how the information revealed could compromise the investigation? You threaten to cut them off?"

He knew the answer. Cote thought his job was to harass the men in his own department, not to manage the media or help with the investigation. When Cote didn't respond, he moved on to his next agenda item. "Lee will fax in his report as soon as it's ready, but basically, the child was stunned by a blow to the head and killed by a series of penetrating knife wounds including one which pierced the pericardium and punctured the left ventricle of the heart. Causes of death: exsanguination and cardiac tamponade. And yes, the boy was sexually assaulted."

There was more he could have shared but didn't. He'd learned from experience that Cote couldn't be trusted. It would all be in his reports, but he'd found that if he buried details in the middle, chances were Cote wouldn't read them. Unlike his predecessor, and unlike Vince Melia, who would know names, facts, and details, Cote didn't read reports, he acquired them. A fat, miserable, mean little paperwork miser.

"Sexually assaulted?" Cote said it as though the idea delighted him because it made the crime more lurid. As though they needed it to be worse. "I'm briefing the press at four. I wonder—" He broke off. "You and Melia need to put something together for me."

Burgess felt the itch in his palms that made him want to grab that wattled throat again. He forced his fists open, squeezing his knees hard enough to hurt. "Was there anything else, sir? You've got my preliminary reports there?"

Cote, frustrated by his inability to pick a fight, only sighed, already looking for a new way to make Burgess snap. "It's been more than twenty-four hours," he said. "And you haven't got anything for me?"

Burgess looked at the thick folder of reports, representing so many hours of hard work by so many people. "Everything you see there."

"I'm talking about a suspect."

"We're looking at some people."

Cote shook his head like a disappointed parent. "Keep me informed, Burgess. Keep me informed."

Burgess supposed, given the theatrical way it was delivered, that the words were meant to be a threat. Goddamned fool wasting his time in here with puffery when he ought to be downstairs with Melia and the other detectives, working out their strategy for where to go next. He got up to leave.

"The family," Cote said. "How are they taking it? Are they doing all right?"

Confirmation that Cote hadn't read their reports and wasn't likely to be on board when they wanted a warrant to toss the house. Cops often walked a fine line in situations where family members fell into the pool of suspects; here that line seemed somewhat less fine, given the amphetamine and Dwayne Martin's assault on Perry. It was in his report. It was on the master evidence list. Sighing inwardly, Burgess put on his best solemn face. "Frankly, sir? Except for the deaf sister, Iris, I'm not sure they've even noticed."

He left before he said something he'd regret. Could the captain really not know that one family member had sent a cop to the hospital and been locked up for assault? Maybe Cote, uninformed and unwilling to be, thought Dwayne Martin's attack resulted from grief.

In the face of death, it was important to check on the

living. He found Perry, bandage prominent on his shaved head, glowering over a chaotic desk. "How you doing, Stan?"

"Got a bitchin' headache."

Terry Kyle, dead white and skeletal, hunched over another. Burgess asked the same question. Got a brusque, unamplified "fine."

"Gonna give us a team name," he said as he limped past, signaling them to meet him in the conference room, "build up some morale in you sorry lot. Gonna call us the Crips. I'll round up Vince and Wink."

"Hey!" Perry complained. "They can't be on our team. They ain't crips!"

Burgess picked up a baseball bat someone had taken from a drugged out teenager, and socked it into the palm of his hand. It made a pleasant sound, reminiscent of simpler days and times. "We can take care of that." Swinging the bat, he stuck his head into Melia's office. "Got a few minutes, Lou?"

Melia's eyes fixed on the bat. "You got the wrong guy. Honest."

Burgess thwacked the bat into his hand a few times, wishing he could really hit something. "I know that. I'm going to get Wink."

"Don't hurt him, either. We need him."

He went down to the lab, couldn't find anyone around, finally found Dani Letorneau in a back room, bending over the blue blanket, carefully putting things into envelopes. She made shooing motions. "Get out, Joe. You're gonna contaminate things."

He knew she meant with hair and fibers, but the real contaminating thing about him was a virulent case of bad temper. "Seen Wink?"

She gave him a smile, the first bright spot in his day. Sometimes it was striking how valuable a smile could be. "He suddenly jumped up, muttering something about a cheeseburger, and went flying out the door. Is there a message?" She eyed the baseball bat. "If you want to know can he come out and play, he can't. He has to stay in today and clean his room. You've seen the mess out there." Sure he had. Bags and bags. Envelopes. Jars. Cartons. Dani held out a pale white arm. "Just when I was planning to work on my tan."

Burgess checked his watch. "If he's back in the next twenty minutes or so, send him up to the conference room, would you?"

"Sure thing." She bent over the blanket again. Willing to spend a minute to share a smile, but not much more. Carefully plucking something up with tweezers, she said. "We gonna get him, Joe?"

"Absolutely."

Melia wasn't there yet. It was just the Three Musketeers, Perry ragging on Terry Kyle, light-hearted, profane, and heartfelt.

"I know a good hit-man, down Saco. Take out Wanda the PMS Queen faster than you can shake the drops off your dick. You want me to call him?"

Kyle stared out at the pearl gray day. "I blew it," he said. "I'm sorry."

Burgess slid into his seat, looking at his team. Neither of them looked first string today, The Crips, but collectively, they were good. He opened the case folder. Masses of paper since he'd left last night. Reports from the neighborhood canvass. Reports from Delinsky, Devlin, from Stan Perry. Logs of evidence from the crime scene and the name and rank of everyone who had entered it. The list of sex offenders. Copies of the criminal records of the victim's family. He didn't see anything about Osborne or Timmy's file from the Department of Human Services.

Melia entered, opened his own file, and nodded at

Burgess, content to have his sergeant run things. Rocky Jordan followed, slipping quietly into a seat, carefully aligning a stack of papers on the table in front of him. Compared to the rest of them, Jordan was the picture of health. He looked liked he'd slept, washed, and shaved, like he hadn't dressed in the dark with fumbling, exhausted hands. Maybe he'd eaten something healthier than fast food in the last twenty-four hours. Burgess pulled out the license number from Alan Gordon. "Rocky, can you run this for me, see who the owner is and if he has a record?" Rocky nodded.

"Lee says we've got a right-handed stabber," Burgess said, holding up his hand to show how the knife had been held. "Eleven wounds. Couple good impressions of the hilt, in case we ever find the weapon. Boy was molested. Lee says probably no semen. Guesstimate of time of death, between ten and twelve. Last meal, hot dogs. Last known meal, he picked at a peanut butter and jelly sandwich between 3 and 4, so someone fed him later. I've got last sightings variously at five-thirty, six and seven. That last is from his brother, Dwayne, so it's not very reliable."

He looked around at the others. "Updates?"

"Did another search around the pond this morning," Perry said, absently fingering the bandage. "I think we found the thing Osborne's dog took."

"What?" His chair was uncomfortable. He couldn't find a position for his knee that didn't hurt. The chicken sandwich sat like a rock in his stomach.

"It's pretty disgusting, between dog saliva, pond scum, and mud." Perry set a plastic container on the table. It held a dirty pillow, eight or ten inches square. The color was obscured by dirt, but it had once been cheerful yellow and blue needlepoint. Burgess knew immediately where he'd seen a similar one.

"What is it, Joe?" Melia asked.

"Osborne's got two just like this in his living room."

"He'll claim his dog brought this one to the park," Perry said.

"When I interviewed him yesterday, he said his dog had taken nothing from the body, carried nothing down into the cattails. Where'd you find it?"

"In the cattails." Devlin slipped in and took a chair.

Kyle shuffled his papers. "Osborne? Nothing on him but some calls from worried parents, but I talked to the PD in his old town, outside Boston. Same story. He hung around playgrounds, showed an inordinate interest in kids. They thought he was dirty. Never could get anything to nail him. Before that, Jersey cops got him there for soliciting sex from a male minor. That got misdemeanored. Delinsky's going through the field observation cards." Kyle's voice had the whispery weakness of someone recovering from a long illness. He sagged in his chair like a resting stork. Only his eyes alive.

Burgess checked his notes. "You figured out who we should re-interview, Ter?"

"Still working on it. Canvass just got done. Lotta people in that neighborhood playing hard to get."

"Sex offenders, Stan?"

Perry plucked at his bandage again. "Averages about one per house. Oughta rename that part of town Sodom and Gomorrah."

"Vince, what's the story on that Human Services file? They don't want to give it up, let's get a warrant. We can't wait for interdepartmental politics on this one. I need to know who made reports about the family. When. And what their response was." Melia nodded and made a note. Melia was his boss, but on a case like this, Melia usually gave him his head and only asked to be kept up-to-date. "Delinsky around?"

"Night shift commander wasn't happy, but we've got him as long as we want."

"Okay, campers. This is a bad one." Their eyes were on him, their pens poised. Kyle was breathing like someone trying not to heave, Perry picking at the bandage again, everyone waiting for what they didn't have—a good lead. Burgess said, "For starters, let's check out those sex offenders, anyone with a history of kids or kiddie porn. Terry will make a list of people to re-interview, or people who weren't home who still need to be seen. We've still got nothing on those last few hours. We're looking for someone called the witch. That blue car. Anyone who saw Timmy after he left Mrs. Johnston's porch."

Perry's fingers worked the bandage loose. "Stan, stop picking at that thing!"

The hand dropped like a stone. "Sorry, Dad."

"I'm not your goddamned dad."

He summed up his interview with Iris Martin, her confirmation that Dwayne was mad at Timmy for taking something, her information that Timmy had run away before. His sense that she was hiding something. "She says Osborne used the dog to frighten Timmy into taking his clothes off, then photographed him naked. We got the pillow, we got this, we got the family's story. Vince, can you ask the AG's office if that's enough for a warrant? Who's on it, anyway? There was no one at the ME's." In Maine, even in a big city like Portland, the Attorney General's office prosecuted all the homicides.

"I'll ask Paul," Melia said.

Their crime scene photos were pinned up on the board, spread out on the table. Burgess flipped the picture of Timmy on the climbing structure onto the table. "Just so we all remember. This is our victim."

It landed next to a close-up of the stab wounds. Kyle looked from one to the other, lurched from his chair, and left the room. Melia watched, his eyes dark and worried in a sea of tiny wrinkles. He stroked the dark stubble on his chin, fingers rasping in the silence. "You need more help on this, Joe? I could..."

"No." Louder than he'd meant to be. "We're okay. It's just going to take time. Worst thing we can do is let Cote's impatience infect us. We rush this, we'll get sloppy."

Maybe he was wrong, not wanting more people on it, when Perry should be home nursing a concussion and Kyle was half-dead, but they were the team he wanted. Cut Kyle out of this, after he'd already screwed up once, he'd brood himself into a hospital bed, and Young Stanley liked to play through the pain. Cut him loose, he was apt to do something impulsive, like a half-trained puppy.

Burgess looked at Wink Devlin, calmly eating the last of his fries. "Get anything on those prints off the body?"

"Two different ones. Haven't had time to run them yet."

Two different prints? Did that mean they were looking for two people? "Everyone at the ME's got their prints on file?"

"Yeah," Devlin said.

"The feather?"

"I'm betting on parakeet. Could be pigeon. We'll send it to Quantico, soon as we get everything together. In just six short months, the world's greatest crime solving organization might have an answer for us."

"Can't you dig up an ornithologist at one of the colleges?"

Before he could answer, Kyle returned, face and

hair beaded with water, eyelashes wet, white knuckles wrapped around a can of Coke.

"We got two sets of prints off the body," Burgess said. "You want to get the prints from Osborne's arrest in New Jersey?" Kyle nodded. "How soon you think you'll be ready to talk about that canvass?"

"Half hour, forty minutes?"

"Good. Find me then. Stan? Perverts?"

"We're almost there."

"When you're there, grab Rocky, get out there and start asking questions." Rocky nodded, pleased. He loved his computer but sometimes felt a need to get out of the office. "Anyone seen Delinsky?"

"He's been helping me," Kyle said. "I'll send him in."

"Impressions?"

"I still like Dwayne Martin for it," Perry said. "But would he rape his own brother?"

"High on drugs, he might do anything," Melia said.

"That's what his sister says," Burgess agreed. "For now, my money's on Osborne."

Kyle was holding pictures of Timmy wrapped and unwrapped. "This just doesn't make sense," he said.

"No," Burgess agreed, "Unless it's remorse. Let's go," he said. No one wasted a minute getting out of there. The pictures, the time-line on the whiteboard represented a puzzle for which they had too few pieces. Everyone went to find more.

CHAPTER 17

On top of the flurry of slips on his desk was a message to call Chris. He picked it up, annoyed. He didn't want the world intruding on his focus. Working something like this, the rest of life went on hold. He'd meant it when he'd said he'd be unavailable. Had times like this accelerated Wanda Kyle's spiral into a wallow of bitterness and revenge? How would Chris handle it? She wasn't Wanda, but what she was hadn't been tested yet. Neither had he.

He stood in the busy, noisy room, staring at the mass of paper awaiting his attention, the sea of pink message slips. He wanted some peace and quiet to listen to the inside of his head, to tune in to the faint keening sound lingering there since yesterday. Timmy Watts's call for justice. This case felt like an insistent scream, the slow pace of their progress like an unscratchable itch. Sighing, he reached for the phone.

She answered on the first ring. "I just wanted to tell you Michelle and I are cooking dinner here, in case you guys can get away." When he didn't respond, she said, "You've got to eat, Joe, and this will be a heck of a lot better than McDonald's."

She had that right. "I appreciate it," he said. "I just don't know. I can't promise." He hesitated, wanting to say her name. "Chris. We're swamped."

"If you can," she said, "I wasn't asking for promises." Her voice did that thing where it dropped a register. "I just wanted to hear your voice." She hung up.

He muttered a confused "goddamn" and picked up his messages. One from Andrea Dwyer, asking him to call when he came in. She might have something for him. He scanned the reports. Not a lot of crazies calling up and confessing to this one. Not many people who might have seen anything, either. It was damned depressing that someone could take a child, brutalize him, stab him, and dump him, and no one saw anything. He had a thought, went into Vince's office.

"DPW do the storm drains around there, looking for that knife?"

Melia shook his head and reached for the phone.

He found Stan Perry standing by his desk, looking at the chair as though wondering if he'd been abducted by aliens. Everything about the posture suggested immediacy, news. "What?" he asked, feeling a tiny flutter of hope.

"Kids collecting bottles," Perry said. "Found some clothes in a trash can on the Promenade."

"Think they could be ours?"

Perry shrugged. "Patrol didn't touch them. They're waiting for us."

He got a radio, checked for his gun, and was out of there, glad to be doing something besides shifting papers. Knowing his impatience was a mistake, that if he were giving himself advice, he'd say settle down and focus. He couldn't stay calm with Timmy Watts perched on his shoulder like Tiny Tim. God help us, every one. They stopped at the lab, grabbed Devlin, and were gone.

"Bad news, Joe," Devlin said. "I logged in everything you took from the kid's room. The amphetamine is gone."

"Gone? How could it be gone? Who else touched it?"

"No one else touched it," Devlin said gloomily. "That is, there's no record of anyone touching it."

"Who was on last night?"

"Bascomb."

Burgess gripped the wheel. The amphetamine was their ticket to searching the Watts's house. Maybe a key to this whole thing. Finding it was important, and Bascomb would be less than useless. Fat Wayne Bascomb had carried a Jones for him ever since Burgess had found him sleeping on the job and reported it. Bascomb still gave him dirty looks when Burgess brought things in. Maybe Bascomb was trying a new form of revenge.

Perry might have been reading his thoughts. "You think maybe Bascomb...?"

"Be pretty damned stupid if he did."

"Bascomb *is* fuckin' stupid, Joe. That's why he sits on his fat ass and eats candy bars and catches zs while we get our brains beat in. It wouldn't be safe to let him out on the street. He'd stumble into the nearest Dunkin' Donuts and arrest a cruller."

"You kidding?" Devlin said. "Crullers would get together and cuff him to the bakery rack."

The screaming in Burgess's head was getting louder. He did not want to think about Fat Wayne right now. He pulled into the curb behind a patrol car, its light bar flashing, and shut off the engine. "This better be something," he said.

Here by the water, the air was redolent with the

stink of lobster bait, fish, and decaying seaweed. Restless waves smacked the shore in a crabby way that echoed his mood. Devlin's news hadn't improved things. He wanted to smack something himself.

The patrol officer had cordoned off a small area around the trash can and stood now, shifting nervously from foot to foot, facing down a small, noisy crowd. "What is this?" Burgess grumbled. "Stan, call and get the guy some help. What was he thinking?" As he watched, two kids tried to sneak under the yellow tape. The officer turned, voice snapping like a whip, and they backed away and faded into the crowd.

"Probably got too excited about maybe finding some evidence." Stan ducked back into the car and called for more officers.

Burgess approached the officer, whose wild eyes and flared nostrils reminded him of a frightened animal. Up close, he realized it was a woman. Short haired, pleasant-faced, the equipment-draped uniform blouse only slightly suggesting breasts. It was the vests that did it. Flatted the breasts and made everyone look like a pigeon. What hair he could see was wet with sweat and curled tightly around her face. "Detective Sergeant Burgess," he said. "Where are the kids who found it?"

The officer, whose nametag said "Beck", looked around, first easily, then nervously, swiveling her head from side to side as she eyeballed the milling crowd. "I don't know, sir. They were here a minute ago." She pointed toward an empty bench. "I told them to sit there and stay there." She swung on another kid who was pulling on the tape. "Hold it right there! You want a free ride in a police car?" The kid hunched his shoulders and slunk away.

Burgess's anger flared. Turning his back on the

crowd, so his words were only for her, he snapped, "Jesus Christ, Beck. You didn't call for back-up. You didn't detain the witnesses. You roped off an area the size of a postage stamp. What were you thinking?"

"I'm sorry, sir," she said, her shoulders rigid, eyes straight ahead, only the slightest trembling of her jaw betraying her. "I was about to go on break when I got the call." Two spots of red brightened her cheeks. "I've got my period real bad today, sir. What I was thinking was I wonder if I'm going to be able to get out of here before I bleed right through my clothes. And that was about thirty minutes ago."

He didn't know what to say. He'd dealt with female emergencies before. Cops did, but this, coming as he was about to bite her head off, took the wind out of his sails. "Next time, call your supervisor, explain the situation, get yourself some help. It's nothing he or she's never seen before. Understand?" She nodded, tight-lipped, her eyes fixed on his shoes. "The witnesses," he said, "you get their names and addresses?"

"Yes, sir." Her eyes were teary and there was a defensive hunch to her shoulders.

He had such a salutary effect on people. "Goddammit, Officer Beck, don't you dare cry on me," he said. "Now, I want you to look around carefully, see if you see those kids." Behind him, Perry yelled at the crowd to move. He looked back, saw Perry's fierce, sweeping gestures, watched the people move away, thought how Perry relished being big and mean.

Officer Beck studied the crowd, hopeful but not expectant, then looked the other way, toward the sea. "Down there," she said, pointing to where the land began to drop off. "The taller one's a girl, smaller one's a boy. Brother and sister. Nina and Ned. She calls him Neddy. They were looking for returnable bottles, trying to get enough money to rent a movie. She called it in." She forced herself to look at his face. "When you talk to her, well, you'll see. She's really spooked." She wanted to tell him to go easy on the girl but didn't dare. Fine with him. He didn't need advice from some rookie.

"Thanks," he said, turning abruptly back toward the crowd. She jumped when he moved, telling him he still had her spooked. Every time he thought he'd finally begun to live down his reputation, something like this happened. At crime scenes, he liked it that way. He wanted people to be extra slow and careful to avoid his wrath. But times like this, it pained him. He wasn't mean or irrational, and found it no sin to be demanding. He didn't ask anything of others he wouldn't ask of himself. He'd occasionally bled though his clothes. Didn't think the knowledge would be much comfort to Officer Beck.

He motioned Stan over, pointed toward the water. "I'm going to talk to the kids who found the clothes. Soon as back-up gets here, Officer Beck needs to be relieved." He looked at the trash can, sitting like a dented icon in the middle of the small yellow-taped area. She'd used a bench, a tree, and a lamp post for her corner posts. He could see why she'd chosen such a small area. Otherwise, she would have had to cordon off an enormous square. He would have preferred that.

He tugged on some gloves, slipped under the tape, and lifted the cover on the can, releasing a heat wave of rotten food smells and a noisy swarm of flies. Bending over, he took a pencil from his pocket and teased open the cheesy plastic K-Mart bag. On top, he saw a blue and white tee shirt with a bright, busy pattern, spotted with a blackish substance which could be blood. He replaced the lid, leaving it for Devlin.

He watched two more patrol cars arrive. Nodding to Stan to handle it, he turned and walked toward the water. If not for his cynicism about human nature, he would have been surprised by the crowd. The overcast skies were a reprieve from yesterday's scorching sun, but the hot, stale air made breathing difficult and moving worse. The walk to the two children was perhaps half the length of a football field, but by the time he got there, he'd sweated through another shirt. He checked his watch. Mid-afternoon. The day felt like it was passing in slow motion.

He crunched up to them across the dry grass. They stood together, the boy's shoulder tight against the girl's side, watching his approach with tense faces and scared eyes. Same faces. Same frank, greenish eyes with profuse lashes. Pale skin. Freckles. The boy had rusty red hair; the girl's a softer color.

When he got close, she said, "Are you the detective? That lady police officer said we had to wait here until a detective came to talk to us. Now we're going to get in trouble. We were supposed to be home already." Her tone was matter-of-fact, as though grown-ups doing things to get her in trouble was normal.

"Who are you going to be in trouble with?" he asked. "Your mom?"

"Our foster mom. She doesn't like us wandering around the neighborhood. Not after what happened. I got us half an hour to come down here looking for bottles, so we could rent a movie for Ned." She shrugged, an elaboration of bony shoulders in a thin white cotton tank top. The nipples of her small breasts were visible through the cloth. It was something he couldn't understand. Why adults who were otherwise protective let girls go around dressed like hookers. Showing his age, he guessed. Even his own nieces dressed like this. One had even gone and gotten a tattoo.

"I'll call her," he said, "explain what happened. Or I can drive you home, tell her then. You live far from here?"

"Not too far," she said.

Her brother, still stuck to her side, hadn't said a word, just stood there with his eyes wide. Burgess bent down and held out his hand. "Joe Burgess," he said, "and you are?"

The small hand came out and fitted itself into his. "Ned."

"You got a last name, Ned?"

"Mallett. Two l's and two t's," the girl said.

Burgess kept Ned's hand in his. "You like ice cream?" he asked.

The solemn face crinkled in an impish grin. "Hate it," the boy said, his eyes dancing. "I could hate a great big ice cream cone right now. Orange sherbet, maybe?"

"Sounds good to me," Burgess said. "I could hate a great big mocha fudge. How about you, Nina?"

She considered. "I could hate a chocolate shake."

"Then let's go. We can talk as well over ice cream as we can here. And it'll be cooler." He released Ned's hand.

"We're not supposed to talk to strangers," Nina said. There was a note in her voice that made him suspect a wicked, thirteen-year-old sense of humor, but he gave her a serious answer.

"It's all right. I'm a police officer. We're the one type of stranger you can talk to."

Another bony little shrug. "Okay," she said. She turned on her heel and headed back toward the street, holding out a hand to her brother, a clanking plastic bag dangling from the other. The cans and bottles they'd collected. He'd done the same thing as a kid, first by himself, then supervising his little sisters. On a good day, they'd felt like millionaires. Gone nuts at the penny candy store.

The ice cream place was heaven. At least fifteen degrees cooler and the moisture had been wrung out of the air. They sat in a booth, waited on by a heavy-featured teenaged lout who eyed Nina's breasts—nipples erect from the cold—with undisguised interest. He had to struggle to take down their order. When he left, she rolled her eyes and muttered, "Jerk."

With great restraint, Burgess refrained from suggesting more clothes. He knew the rules—a woman was entitled to dress however she pleased and still be free from sexually harassing behavior. He also knew reality. That men had only recently come down from the trees and were regularly flooded with the desire to throw women over their shoulders and do a bit of recreational procreating. Politics always ran ahead of evolution.

"Tell me about finding the clothes in that trash can," he said.

Nina gave an affirmative nod, pleased to be getting down to business. "We have a routine," she said. "We start at one end and work our way down, doing all the cans. We like to do it around this time of day, in the summer, when we don't have school, because the street people come later. They creep me out." She twisted a strand of hair around her finger, held it a second, and released it. "There's not much to tell. When we got to that can, we opened it and started digging. Just under some newspapers, we found that bag. I thought maybe someone had thrown away something good. We do find good stuff sometimes, so I opened it." She stopped, eyeing her brother and then looking up at Burgess.

"Ned," he said, "would you mind going up to the counter and telling the man to make that a double cone?"

"Sure." Ned jumped to his feet, started away, and turned back. "Can I tell him I want a double cone, too?"

"Of course."

Ned scampered away and Nina said, "As soon as I looked in the bag, I saw they were little boy's clothes. Neddy loves the Power Rangers, too. And they had what looked like blood on them. First thing, I thought we should just get out of there, you know?" She twisted up the hair again. "But then I thought, if it had been Neddy, instead of that other little boy, I wouldn't want someone to just walk away, would I?"

Newspapers and TV were always full of apocalyptic crap about how teenagers had all gone to hell and the future of the nation looked bleak, but Burgess had found many a hero and heroine among them. He was a lot more cynical about adults. "You did the right thing," he said, "and we appreciate it."

She narrowed her eyes. "You're awfully nice. You sure you're a cop?"

"You want to see my badge?"

"I dunno." A little wriggle on the seat. "Maybe I should. I mean, anyone can say he's a cop, right?"

"Right." He showed her his ID.

She took it with a big grin, studied it, and nodded. Very much a thirteen-year-old, but also a cautious, methodical child. "That's so cool." She handed it back as the waiter stumped up, delivered a chocolate shake to Nina's chest, and stumped away again.

Burgess watched the waiter walk toward them again carrying two cones piled high with melting ice cream. As drops of chocolate and orange dribbled onto the floor, he thought of the debacle that would occur when Ned and the cone got together. He grabbed a handful of napkins, wrapped some around the cone, and handed it to Ned, who'd followed the waiter back to the table. He piled the rest in front of the boy.

He gave a series of quick licks to contain his own cone, and asked the pro forma question, "Did you see anyone around the trash can before you checked it? See anyone put anything in?"

It was the question she'd been waiting for. She peered at him between her dark lashes and said, "Yes. Someone parked at the curb, got out of a car, and put something in the can. A white plastic bag."

"Could you tell anything about the person?"

Nina shook her head emphatically. "We were too far away."

"No, we weren't," Ned insisted. "You were talking to that boy, so you didn't pay any attention." He ran a quick pink tongue around the edge of his cone and smiled shyly up at Burgess. "I saw who got out of the car."

"Who?"

Ned looked suddenly very serious, sitting there with an orange face, holding his cone carefully in two hands, melted ice cream running over his fingers and down the backs of his hands. "I didn't know her," he said. "Some lady."

CHAPTER 18

It didn't make sense. This wasn't a woman's crime. His mind zipped through possibilities as ice cream dripped down his hand. He leaned forward, reining in his eagerness. "How do you know it was a woman?"

Ned gave him the "you are a stupid grown-up" look. "She just was."

"How far away were you?"

He spread his hands wide apart. "This far," he said.

"Nina?"

She looked out the window, spotted a fire hydrant about 100 yards away. "Here to the hydrant, maybe?"

She looked away, suddenly interested in what was happening outside. "I was talking to this boy."

"Someone you know?"

She shook her head. "Not really. I've seen him around."

Another witness, Burgess thought. "Know his name?"

"No." She wouldn't talk to him about boys. To her girlfriends, she could giggle for hours, but not to some strange male cop. This might be a job for Andrea Dwyer.

"The boy was talking to me," Ned declared.

Nina rolled her eyes. Then she looked at her brother and sighed. "Oh, Neddy, look at you! Auntie Mary's gonna kill you. She's gonna kill both of us. That's a brand new shirt!" She shot Burgess a look. "Brand new Salvation Army shirt."

Burgess got up and dumped his cone in the trash. He liked ice cream, and those first few bites had been great, but he didn't have much appetite, and he had no patience with the mess. When he was on a case, he ate to live, mostly too busy to eat. He returned to the table, grabbed a handful of napkins, and tried to make Ned presentable.

Nina, watching him, said, "You must have kids."

"So you didn't see this person?"

"Well, yeah. I mean, someone got out of the car and put something in the trash. It was like a blip on the screen, you know. I guess all I thought was maybe it was some bottles. That would have been okay."

"Did you notice whether it was a man or a woman?" She shook her head. "What about the car? You notice the car?"

"Look," she said, her face had acquired a nervous, pinched quality, "I was happy to tell you about the clothes. I mean willing. Because it was a kid. But me and Neddy, we don't want to get involved. Neddy's been through enough bad stuff. You understand?"

Thirteen going on forty. Nina dipped a napkin in her water glass and scrubbed at her brother's face and hands. She didn't want to get involved because she was afraid for her little brother. "I understand," he said. Understood enough, would learn the rest from Auntie Mary. "Here's my problem. I need to catch that little boy's killer. I can't do it without help. Help like you making that phone call when you found the clothes. Maybe the person you saw dumping trash didn't put the clothes in that bin. But I have to check it out. And to do that, I need all the information you can give me."

"It was a blue car," Ned said, crunching on his cone. "Not very big."

"Neddy..." his sister cautioned.

"Nina, it's okay."

"You don't know that," she said, her eyes clouded with worries a child her age shouldn't have been carrying. "Look. Neddy's all I've got."

Now it was Burgess's turn to stare out the window. "Can you tell me anything about the woman?"

"She was regular."

"Medium height. Medium width," Nina explained.

"Hair color?"

"She was wearing a hat."

"What else was she wearing?"

"A tan coat."

A hat and coat on a hot summer day. A peculiar way to avoid being noticed, if Nina's information was accurate. "She stopped the car, got out, put something in the trash bin and drove away. Is that all?"

"She looked around," Nina said. Her voice dropped. "She might have seen us."

"I want you to stay away from those trash bins for a while," Burgess said.

"You bet."

Ned's face crumpled. He set the gnawed tip of his cone on the table and said, "Then how will we rent a movie?"

"Come on," Burgess said, getting up. "I'll drive you home. We can rent a movie on the way."

"You don't have to do that," Nina said. "He'll survive. He's kind of whiny since..." She didn't finish the sentence.

"I don't have to," he agreed. "But it would be nice, don't you think?"

"I don't believe you're a cop," she said.

He sighed. When he came on the force, America's disenchantment with the police was just beginning. The messes the LA and New York police got themselves into hadn't helped. He'd spent his entire adult life trying to help people, solve their problems, keep them safe. It hurt to face a child who believed a police officer couldn't be nice. "What can I say?" he asked her. "I am. I've been a cop a long, long time."

"You are pretty old, aren't you," she agreed.

A KO punch straight to the gut. In his heart, he was always eighteen. Could still remember goofing around with his buddies, trying to attract the attention of girls like Nina. How much a girl's look or smile or encouragement mattered. Those nostalgic memories of how impossibly hopeful and insanely stupid they'd all been never entirely went away.

He had a crime to solve. This was no time to be walking, trip trap, trip trap down Memory Lane. "Come on," he said, heading toward the door.

"Jeez," she said, coming after him, dragging her brother by the hand. "You don't have to get sore, you know. Being old's not so bad. It's better than..." She stopped. Like him, she had places she wouldn't go, and she was only thirteen.

They rented *Finding Nemo* and *The Princess Bride.* Then she directed him to a shabby white three decker. She hesitated before getting out of the car. "Will you come up with us and explain?"

He walked them up onto the porch and rang the bell. A plump, red-faced blonde with black roots answered, a baby on her hip. Her mouth tightened when she saw them, and she snapped, "You said half an hour, Nina. You're old enough to tell time." Her eyes shifted to

Burgess. "Who are you?"

"Detective Sergeant Burgess. Portland Police."

"Nina!" The woman's tone was somewhere between anger and a whine. "What have you done now?" Implying that Nina was habitually in trouble? He wouldn't have thought so.

"And you are?"

Her eyes shifted back to him. "Mary Turner. I'm their foster mother."

"May I come in?"

She blinked and stepped back. "Of course. Of course. Come on in. I'm sorry. After what happened with that little boy, I was just worried."

"I understand." He followed her into a dim, stuffy room with shades drawn against the heat. A large oscillating fan sent out brief, tantalizing bursts of cool. A toddler in a playpen was earnestly arranging soft cloth blocks. A small boy lay on the sofa, asleep.

"We got a movie," Nina said. "Could we watch it?"

The woman shrugged wearily. "Just don't wake Patrick. He's been a beast today."

Nina nodded her understanding. "He just misses his mother."

"Why don't you come in the kitchen," Mary Turner suggested. "I've got a fan out there. It's not too bad." He followed her through a doorway and was waved into a chair. "You want some coffee?" When he hesitated, she smiled. "Look, I'm sorry I was crabby...this heat...all these kids...you'd be crabby, too." She put the baby down in a crib, wound a mobile, then grabbed the coffee and a filter, and raised her eyebrow.

"Sure," he said. "I'd love some coffee." As she turned to fix it, he said, "They didn't do anything wrong."

"I would have been surprised if they did," she said.

"Nina's such a little old lady when she's with Neddy...but she's still a kid. They're all terrible about time. I let her take an inch, one day she'll take a mile. She's thirteen, after all. So what happened?"

"Picking through the trash cans, they found some clothes that might have belonged to Timmy Watts. Nina figured it out and called us."

She set the coffee pot on the counter with a crash and sank into a chair, fumbling for a cigarette. She shoved it in her mouth, lit it, and inhaled deeply. "Oh no," she said. "Oh hell. They really didn't need that."

He waited. She inhaled again and blew it slowly out. "Last thing they need's more death and violence in their lives. Their father's up in Warren now, sent there for killing their mother. Nina and Ned were home when it happened. Father had no family. No one in the mother's family would take 'em. Court gave 'em to the state. State sent 'em here."

"All I need is a statement of what they saw," he said. "I can send a juvenile officer. But Nina knows more than she's saying. Something that happened out there spooked her."

She stubbed out her cigarette abruptly. "You'd be spooked, too, if..." Remembered she was talking to a cop. "Sorry. She's a funny kid. Sometimes she's happy go lucky and acts her age, other times, she goes all silent and broody. I keep telling her social worker to get her some therapy. Social worker says everything's fine. Shit...excuse me...but how could things be fine when you've seen your father beat your mother to death? When you tried to stop it and got beat on yourself for your trouble?"

She pushed back her chair and went back to the coffee. "I know you gotta do your job, but keep her name out of this. Both their names. Last thing those poor kids need is to be chased by reporters. It's taken me months to get Neddy out of his shell. He used to curl up on the couch and huddle there, just like Patrick, that little boy you saw out there." She poured the water in, flicked the button, and got out cream and sugar and two mugs. "You ask me, they ought to pay me for therapy. State don't hardly pay enough to keep 'em in food and clothes, let alone the things kids need, like toys and books."

He didn't need any more reasons to dislike the Department of Human Services. "I don't see why their names should become public," he said, meaning it, knowing how badly things could go wrong. Knowing Cote might do anything, even put kids in danger, if it meant he could tell the press he had a lead. Already thinking how he'd bury this.

"Damned straight," she said, and grinned at his surprise. "Can't swear around the kids. Gotta do something to stay in practice."

"It's good of you to take them."

"Someone has to." A shrug. "I figure it might as well be me." She scooped up the pot, poured his coffee, and set the mug in front of him along with a spoon. "Fix it the way you like it." She took a step toward the refrigerator. "You hungry?"

He shook his head. "We had ice cream."

"And you rented them movies." She leaned back from the waist, stretching, her hands on her hips, and studied him curiously. "You sure you're a cop?"

"That's what Nina asked. Since when are cops not allowed to be nice?"

"Since as long as I can remember."

"I'm sorry to hear that," he said. "Is Nina interested in boys?"

"As far as I know, she's at the looking stage. She doesn't date. Why?"

"It looks like they might have seen the person who

dumped those clothes. Ned told me it was a woman. Nina claims not to have noticed anything. Ned says it's because she was talking with some boy. When I asked about the boy, she clammed up."

"Her private life's all she's got that's hers, you know. That might be all it is. You want, I'll see if she'll tell me anything. Sometimes she does, sometimes not."

"I'd appreciate that."

"Ninety-nine kids out of a hundred, they wouldn't have bothered to call you at all," she said. "Nina's special." Then she said, "I don't know. What I read in the paper, that wasn't any woman's crime. Maybe Neddy was wrong. I worry about his eyes sometimes. He squints a lot. Can get 'em checked if I just make ten thousand phone calls and fill out a thousand forms."

He nodded.

They finished their coffee in a companionable silence. He thanked her and left, pausing in the living room to say good-bye to Nina and Ned. They were deeply immersed in *The Princess Bride,* Ned curled up against Nina's side, the sleeping Patrick on the other. Hardly more than a child herself, Nina had become a little mother.

CHAPTER 19

Back on the waterfront, things were finishing up. Stan Perry was snarling at the dispersing crowd. Devlin, hot in his blue Portland PD jumpsuit, stood off to one side, his evidence kit around him, directing two gloved officers loading the trash can into a public works truck. Burgess parked at the curb, opened the trunk so Devlin could load his gear, and walked over.

His throat was scratchy from the constant temperature changes, his knee gnawed like a toothache, and his head ached from heat and lack of sleep. He hadn't looked in a mirror, but it felt like he wore it all on his face, that the world, looking at him, got back nothing but bad news.

"Detective Perry," he said, "could I offer you a lift somewhere?"

"Mars is looking good. Can't be hotter than this shit hole. Or is that Mercury?"

"Mercury. And it is hotter." Burgess waved an admonishing finger. "You know what Vince says about language."

"No. I've forgotten. I've forgotten everything except being hot and miserable. I can't even remember why it was I didn't go into my father's office and sell real estate like my brother. I must have been out of my expletive-deleted mind." He pulled down the last of the crime scene tape, looked around for the trash can, remembered that they'd taken it away. He started for the car, yellow streamers trailing behind him. "We gonna get this fucker, Joe? Before he does another kid?"

Burgess stopped abruptly. "Do you doubt it?"

Perry's big shoulders rose and fell under his sweaty shirt. "Just seems like we got nothin'."

"We've got plenty. We just have to work with it. Remember, Stan, put a lever in the right place, you can move the earth."

"You know where to put it?"

"Not yet. But I will."

"I get as old as you, will I have your certainty?"

"Probably." He didn't bother to explain that it wasn't certainty. Nothing was more uncertain than a case like this. It was faith. Faith that with hard work and persistence, it could all work out. That experience and determination counted for something. That if they did it right, the good guys would win.

Perry stalked up to the car, untangled the tape, and threw it in the trunk. "I don't know what it is," he said. "I just feel like beating on something."

Burgess slammed the door and fired up the engine. "You're not alone," he said.

"No," Devlin agreed. "You're not alone. Some cases do that to you. You get anything from those kids?"

"Little boy says he saw a woman drop a bag in that can."

Perry snorted. "No woman did that. Kid musta made a mistake. What'd the girl say?"

"She was talking to some boy and didn't notice."

"Get the boy's name?"

"Said she didn't know it."

"You believe her?"

"No."

"You push her?"

"Girl's already watched her father kill her mother. I thought I'd take it easy. Maybe send Andrea."

"Let's hope Andrea can get something," Perry said. "We got a family of know nothings, a neighborhood of see nothings. Anyone who might know something, like the sister, Iris, or this girl, they all got lost memory syndrome. This case is like swimming in a cesspool. Every time it looks like there's something solid to grab onto it turns out to be shit."

"Nicely put," Devlin agreed.

The rest of the ride back they were silent, Perry and Devlin drinking in the cool air, lolling against the seats, eyes closed, more than halfway exhausted. Devlin never complained. He was a workhorse of a man, who, like Burgess, didn't distinguish between work and life. Behind the closed eyes and the slack face, Burgess knew an eager mind was already looking forward to the challenge of lifting prints off that plastic bag, fibers off the bloody clothes.

Perry was something else, still burning with the youthful passion to "do something." The problem was that the something to be done was steady and ponderous spade work, not shoot outs and fireworks. The challenge was keeping Perry's nose to the grindstone, not letting him go larking about, chasing his theories, getting himself in trouble.

"You know, Stan," he said, "we haven't finished with the family yet. No one has talked with Jason or Ricky Martin or Lloyd Watts. Maybe you should see if you can track them down."

Perry's "Sure thing, Sarge," was pleased and eager.

"Captain Cote wants to see you," the desk sergeant

told him.

Burgess nodded. He had a couple things he wanted to do first. He went straight to Melia's office. Melia was on the phone, so he waited, leaning his head back and closing his eyes. The instant he relaxed, he felt the ugliness of the case settle around him like Perry's metaphorical cesspool. The stink of it, the density, the utter filthy darkness. Competing with that scream in his head, which he knew was Timmy Watts, was another voice, the deep, rasping voice of doubt. Was he too tired, too angry, maybe too haunted by the Kristin Marks case to do this one justice? Was Perry right that he should be pushing Iris Martin and Nina Mallett? Was he going to miss something, screw this up, not because of indifference, but because he cared too much? The thought unnerved him.

Melia cradled the phone and gave him a hard look. "What's wrong?" he asked.

"Afraid I'm going to miss something."

"Don't go there, Joe." Melia ran a hand through his crisp, graying hair. Younger. And grayer. It was all that responsibility. "Get anything from our witnesses?"

"A little. The boy said he saw a woman drop something in that can, girl said she saw someone drop some trash but can't say if it was male or female. She was talking to some boy and didn't really notice. Can't—or won't—give us the boy's name. They're two scared kids, already had the crap kicked out of 'em by life. Girl didn't want to talk, I didn't want to push it. Thought I'd see if Dwyer could get somewhere."

"Good thought. She was looking for you a while ago."

"I'll see if she's still here." He got to the point. "Wink says the meth's disappeared. I don't know if this is Bascomb trying to screw me, someone else trying to screw me, or general incompetence that has nothing to do with me. But it's critical evidence. That meth's our ticket to search the family house; it's our lever into a whole branch of inquiry—was the boy killed because of a dispute over drugs?"

Melia sighed, a cop too long to be surprised by things. "I've got your report on your visit to the boy's house? Your search of his room?"

"And my signed copy of the inventory, including the meth. Plus you all saw it yesterday afternoon, before I put it in the locker."

"Who was on duty when you put the stuff into evidence?"

"Bascomb."

"And who was on duty when Wink went to retrieve it and log it in?"

"You'll have to ask him." He wanted to drop this in Melia's lap and get back to the important things.

Melia gave him a probing look. "You sound sullen. That's not like you."

"I'm just so fucking mad. We don't need this right now."

"Like we needed the murder?"

He hadn't come in here to play tennis; he'd come to offload the one piece of administrative bullshit that could get kicked up the food chain. If Melia was just gonna give him a hard time, he could go upstairs and get that from Cote. He headed for the door.

"Sit down," Melia said. "What is this? Suddenly you're a Prima Donna?"

"I've got a dead kid waiting on me," Burgess said.

"We've got a dead kid waiting on *us,"* Melia corrected. "This isn't a western and you aren't the Lone Ranger, okay? I need you to settle down and work this thing without drama. Kyle's hanging on by his fingertips, and Wild Man Perry's ready to beat a

confession out of somebody. You control this thing and keep your guys on task or I'll bring in another team."

"Do that," Burgess said, "Then I can put that canoe back on my car and go fishing."

"Then you can sit at your desk and write nice little memos for me and Captain Cote."

Burgess understood. Case like this put everyone's balls in a vise. Sent reverberations all the way down the food chain. Melia *wanted* to solve this case because it was a kid; he *needed* to solve it to protect his ass. "My guys are tired."

Melia gave him a stony look. "Everyone's tired. When did that ever stop you?"

"Stopping? Who said I was stopping? All I'm saying is maybe you could help out here. You find the meth. We'll find the killer."

"Go see Cote."

"Soon as I find Andrea."

"Before."

Burgess shambled out. For years, his doctor had been after him to lose weight, take some of the burden off his knee, screwed up since high school football. Now he'd finally lost weight and he felt worse than ever, screwed up by Timmy's mother, the great sow. And it wasn't even like she cared. He dialed the number on Andrea Dwyer's note. "It's Burgess," he grunted. "You got something for me?"

"Coming from you," she laughed, "I know that's not a pass. You in the building? I'll be right up."

Today she was in uniform. Unlike Officer Beck's, Andrea's uniform didn't have a unisex effect. She looked distinctly female and distinctly professional and neat enough to have stepped out of a recruiting poster. She just looked too goddamn good. For a moment he resented it.

"It's Sunday," he said. "What are you doing here?"

"Same as you, I imagine," she said, puzzled by his tone. "Trying to keep kids safe."

"What have you got?"

"Kid over at the community center," she said, "comes edging up to me last night, says can he tell me something. What he wants to tell me...this kid is fourteen, got a little brother who's ten...is about a month ago his brother's in the park hanging out and this man comes up to him, wants to know if he likes pizza, invited the kid to his house..."

"You talk to the younger brother?"

"Yeah. Kid's name is Lonnie Mitchell. He doesn't know the man's name, but he could identify him if he saw him again. From Lonnie's description, it sounds like the guy who took Timmy Watts home. Osborne."

"He go to the man's house?"

She looked sorry, sorrow for the kid, he figured, then said, "Yeah."

"Anything happen?" She nodded. "Anybody call the cops?"

"What do you think? Kids I deal with don't have parents in any meaningful sense of the word." She sounded unusually bitter. "A million times, I find myself thinking, 'How could anyone let their kid' and then I recall who's doing the parenting. Or not doing it. There's no 'let' involved. Half the kids in this city are raising themselves. Anyway, Osborne told Lonnie if he said anything, his family would get hurt. So he wasn't going to say anything. Only I guess he sort of knew your victim."

"Lonnie say whether the guy took pictures?"

"He took pictures."

"Great job, Andrea. It's just what we needed." It was ugly but now he could do an affidavit, get a warrant, toss Osborne's house. He looked at the stack of papers on the desk. "I got a report on this?"

She opened the folder she was carrying, pulled out some sheets, and laid them on top of the others. "You do now."

"Something else I could use your help with." He told her about Nina Mallett, the boy she'd been talking to, her reluctance to identify him. Shared the home situation and Nina's background. "I was hoping you'd talk to her. Maybe she'll tell you stuff she wouldn't tell me." He gave her the address.

"It's worth a shot." She didn't tease him or chide him or remind him that he was supposed to be the best. She just nodded, solemn. "God...kids these days. They go through so much. I hope I can help."

She turned away, giving him a nice look at her backside—he'd forgiven her her youth and beauty by now, since she was also such a good cop—then she turned back. "I know I don't have to tell you. Bring his computer back here for Rocky to play with. Rocky can coax porn from a stone."

He thought she had that right. The intricacies of computer forensics completely escaped him, but Rocky would salivate at the chance, if not the way she'd put it. "I'm not sure he'd be pleased to hear you say that."

She dropped one eye in a lewd wink. "He loves to hear me say that."

He went back to Melia's office, set her report on the desk. "Now can you get me a warrant to search Osborne's place?"

Melia scanned the report. "Your gut tell you this is the guy?"

Burgess spread one hand across his stomach, used the other to cup his ear. "My gut's not telling me anything, Vince. Scares the hell outa me. But whether he's our guy or not, this is one place to start. We've got a lot of ties between Osborne and the kid. Whether he killed Timmy Watts or not, he's dirty. Make it broad. We're going in to follow up on this, looking for pornography, evidence of sexual abuse of a minor. If there's anything else, we'll find it."

"How do you want to play it?"

"Assuming he's home, I'll take Kyle with me and reinterview Osborne. You get the warrant, let me know as soon as it's ready, and we move right into tossing the place. Give me the house, the garage, the car. Give me his goddamned trash cans. Computer equipment. Photographic equipment. Dwyer can give you an affidavit."

"You see Cote yet?" Burgess shook his head. "This is my ass, too, Joe."

"I'm on my way."

He stopped to give Kyle a head's up about Osborne. Kyle gave literal meaning to the expression, 'death warmed over.' He ought to send Kyle home, but Kyle was as stubborn as he was, and Burgess knew how he'd react if someone tried to send him home. Besides, Kyle here he could keep an eye on. Kyle at home was one more thing to worry about.

He took some of those deep, calming breaths the shrink had taught him and went to see Cote.

CHAPTER 20

His tete-a-tete with Cote went too smoothly. Cote had something up his sleeve that kept him from the usual nagging and gnawing. If Burgess had to guess, he'd bet on the missing meth. Looking at the man's plump, self-satisfied face, Burgess vowed he wasn't going to let Cote get to him. If Cote wanted him off his stride so he'd screw up, Burgess wasn't giving him that. The small-minded asshole might have lost sight of the big picture, but Burgess hadn't. This wasn't about them; it was about a murdered boy.

Before he left 109, he paid a visit to another small-minded asshole, Bascomb, just to remind him that Burgess wasn't someone to screw around with. No sense having a reputation as the meanest cop in Portland and not using it when circumstances demanded.

Melia wanted a couple hours for the warrant, given the challenge of finding a judge on a summer Sunday, but he had some news. "Human Services finally called back. Twenty-four hour turn around. Not bad for an emergency, huh?"

"They got the file for us?"

"Not exactly. They can't copy it until someone higher up has approved it. But we can see it if we go to their offices." Melia checked his watch. "Guy who was Timmy's case worker will be there in fifteen minutes, ready to be a good little doobie and show you anything you want. But nothing can leave the office."

"That's bullshit."

"That's bureaucracy. That's interdepartmental cooperation. That's life."

"I thought his caseworker was a woman. That's what Delinsky said."

Melia only held out a fluttering pink message slip. His normally meticulous office looked like a bale of paper had exploded. "You going or shall I send someone else?" Burgess snatched the paper. "You saw Cote," Melia said, "And?"

"He seemed way too pleased about something. I don't see that we have much to be pleased about. Do you?" Melia shook his head.

Burgess grabbed Kyle from a desk as littered as Melia's. "Take a ride with me?"

"I thought you'd never ask."

"Seen Stan?"

"When he went out the door, he said something about K-Mart."

Wayne Bascomb, that repulsive toad, squatted in a chair reading a comic book. The only time he left the chair was to search for donuts. Anyone in the city lost a donut, they could have used the man like a bloodhound. Bascomb could have found a donut in a sewer. Even as a new recruit, when he wasn't so heavy and hadn't yet proved himself intractably stupid, Bascomb had been pudgy and phlegmatic. Whoever hired him might have mistaken inertia for calm and silence for sagacity, but his employment application hadn't been harmed by being the city manager's nephew. The wonder was how he'd gotten through the academy.

Political connections had kept him on the force despite a series of misadventures over the years that had become legend. Twice, as a patrol officer, he'd lost his gun to the bad guys. Once they'd taken his pants and used his handcuffs to fasten him to a light pole on Cumberland Avenue, one of the city's main drags. The second time, they'd used his gun to rob a convenience store. Any other cop would have slunk off in disgrace and shot himself in the nearest stand of trees. Bascomb, in perhaps the one smart move of his career, figured they wanted him off the street and asked for this job.

Burgess stood in the doorway of the evidence area, his hand resting lightly on the butt of his gun, smiling at Bascomb. "I hear there was an evidence mix-up last night."

Bascomb scratched his nose. "Don't know what you mean." He lowered his eyes to the comic.

"Last night," Burgess reminded him. "I brought in a box of stuff from that homicide. The Watts boy? Stuff Devlin was too busy to log in. You remember that?" Bascomb looked blank. "You've got a record of it, haven't you, Wayne?"

Bascomb scratched his nose again, then shuffled through some papers, trying for attitude. "Yeah. I've got a record."

"Devlin came down for it, and when he got it, something was missing. How do you account for that?"

Kyle slid past, quick and sinuous as a snake, and went to stand beside Bascomb. Very close to Bascomb. "Yeah, Wayne. How do you account for that?" Kyle asked. Burgess was the bigger man but there was something in Kyle that unnerved people. Something about his manner and his cold eyes. In the way he seemed to vibrate even when he was still. Bascomb felt it. Kept trying to shift his chair away when there was no place to go.

Bascomb looked at Kyle and Burgess and shrugged. "Maybe the stuff wasn't there?"

Kyle slowly and deliberately settled his belt on his narrow hips, his gun, and his hand, about parallel with Bascomb's nose. "Lotta people saw it, Wayne."

"I was only on until twelve," Bascomb said. "Maybe someone took it after that."

"Devlin says he picked up the box at 11:45. Isn't that what your records show?"

Guy behind Burgess, wanting to get in the room, cleared his throat, "Excuse me, sir?"

"Come back in five," Burgess said.

Bascomb checked the records and grunted a reluctant, "Yeah." He looked at Burgess, his chin hard and stubborn. "Maybe Burgess took it out on the way down."

"But I didn't, Wayne," Burgess said. "Why would I? I'm a cop working on a murdered kid. You think I'd want to screw that up?"

"Beats me." Bascomb turned a page.

"You know," Kyle said, shifting his hip so his gun was right in front of Bascomb's nose. "You haven't been on the street in a while, Wayne. Maybe you forgot we look out for each other. Someone trying to set Joe Burgess up? I don't think the guys'll let something like that go down without taking a real hard look at what happened, do you? Way they'll see it, this time it's Burgess, next time one of them."

Bascomb glared at the gun and tried for tough. "You wanna get that fuckin' thing outa my face, Kyle?"

Kyle flashed a mean grin, eager as a hungry wolf

scenting blood, and stepped back. "Yeah. You know...lotta guys around last night. I wouldn't be surprised if someone noticed who was in and out of here, saw what happened to that missing evidence." He took another step back and adjusted his belt again, giving Bascomb a twisted smile. "You remember that time you got cuffed to the lamp post? I've still got pictures of that." Some joker, finding Bascomb cuffed to the pole in his shorts, had snapped a couple shots before setting him free.

Bascomb glared at Burgess. "You guys threatening me?"

"You're kidding," Burgess said. "Threatening you how? With what? I just came to see what happened to my evidence. Thought maybe it fell into the back of a locker or something." He left Bascomb to ponder on that.

"We're going after some bad guys," Kyle said. "Catch you later."

"He damned near wet his pants," Burgess said.

"We just have to be sure he's more scared of us than of Cote," Kyle said. "Let him sweat a while and then we'll crank it up. I'll see who was on early out last night."

"Aucoin's been on early out. He'll know."

They drove out Forest Avenue, watching the poor confused Portlanders trying to cope with the way the lanes on the road appeared and disappeared like mirages in the desert. Trying to go straight was like broken field running. Zig left. Zag right. Probably part of some new traffic calming strategy. It was enough to drive anyone into a rage.

They parked in front of the Human Services building, a decaying white edifice as down-at-the-heels as the citizens who came through its doors. At least, it being Sunday, they didn't have to look for a place to park. They got out and stood on the steamy sidewalk amidst a litter of cigarette butts and discarded coffee cups. One reliable thing about the welfare population—they might not be able to afford food or clothes or shoes for the kids, but there was always money for cigarettes and coffee.

Burgess shook his head. He was becoming too damned cynical. Too sure he'd seen it all before. He was supposed to be keeping an open mind and a kind heart. He was the champion of the downtrodden, wasn't he? The man people told their children to seek out and rely on? "I'll do the talking," he said. "You be ready to shoot him if he tries to justify leaving the kid in that shithole. Okay?"

"If you say so." Kyle patted his gun. "But I've grown fond of old Nelly here. She's been traveling with me a long time. Hate to turn her over to those cold-eyed fellas from the AG's office, all because of a little deadly force. I think they overreact anyway. Oughta get a quota, like hunters. More than one shooting per year and they investigate."

"That's inspired, Ter. You should put that one in the suggestion box."

"I did. Weekly. Vince asked me to stop. Rank has had a deleterious effect on him. He used to be fun."

Together they pushed through the door and followed the signs until they found the child protection offices. The place was dark and hot and smelled of poor hygiene, cheap scent, desperation, and smoke that had traveled in on people's clothes. He called, "Hello," a few times, got no response. "Probably went to powder his nose. Cops make some people nervous, and this asshole *should* be nervous."

Finally a door slammed somewhere in the building, and a man hurried toward them, carrying a can of Coke and a thick folder. He was sweaty and balding, with thick glasses perched on a fleshy pink nose. His remaining hair and eyebrows were curly, dark and wild. He wore navy athletic shorts and a white tank top, but the body thus revealed hadn't had contact with a gym in a long time. He looked from one to the other. "Detective Burgess?"

"Present," Burgess said.

The man thrust out a soft hand as pink as a baby mouse. "Jim Taylor. I was Timothy's social worker. It's a terrible thing." He went behind a desk and put the file down.

Kyle was eyeing him, probably waiting for the cue to shoot, so Burgess didn't say what he wanted to. That Taylor was almost as responsible as the killer for what had happened. Taylor's conduct and competence didn't matter right now. They were here to see the records. Burgess reached for the folder. "This is Timmy's file?"

Taylor laid a protective hand on it. "Won't you sit down?"

Were they about to be handed a ration of administrative bullshit? They perched on a pair of rickety welfare chairs designed to make anyone using them feel unwelcome. Legs of four different lengths, so you got distracted trying to find a balance point. Upholstery spun from a mixture of old hair and straw, fabric that pricked your thighs and made your butt itch so you couldn't sit still for the hours the system required. Not that Burgess was ever in a waiting mood. He reached for the file again. Taylor pulled it back.

"We came to see the file," Burgess said.

"I just need to establish some ground rules first." Jim Taylor's coke bottle glasses had thick black rims hooked over large ears. He smelled like he hadn't showered recently. It was hot. Everyone sweated.

Considerate folks showered. Used their Right Guard. Flossed and brushed. Tried not to get pissed off and shoot at each other.

"Ground rules?"

Taylor sighed. "I explained all this to your boss. You're welcome to look through the file; however, you may not take anything, and we can't make you copies until we have written permission from the Commissioner." Those who can, do, those who can't work for Human Services. Taylor probably had a degree in accounting or art history. Clearly not phys. ed, not with that body. But Burgess had met some whose degrees *were* in phys ed.

"Which will be when?" Kyle asked.

Jim Taylor tented his thick fingers together. "And you are?" Perhaps his mother had taught him not to speak to anyone unless he was properly introduced, making a job like his rather difficult.

"Detective Terry Kyle, Portland CID. Investigating the murder of Timothy Watts." Kyle's voice was slow and portentous, like he was reading off a celestial teleprompter. When Kyle got mad, he could get very formal.

Burgess reached for the file again. Taylor didn't move his protective hand. "Maybe Lt. Melia didn't make our situation clear, Mr. Taylor. Time is of the essence right now."

"I'm sure it is." Taylor gave a small laugh. "Otherwise, would I be here on Sunday?"

His laugh stirred a flash of anger in Kyle that seemed to Burgess to crackle in the stale air. Taylor didn't notice. Burgess opened his notebook. "So what's the problem? Does something need to happen before we see the file? You want us to sign a form or something?"

"Oh. I thought you'd want to talk with me first,"

Taylor said. "Get some background on the situation."

"Background?" Burgess said. "On what situation?"

"The family situation, all that."

"It's not documented in the file?"

"Well, my reports are in the file, of course, but I thought you'd want my impressions."

Burgess had had enough pussyfooting around. He pulled the file out from under Taylor's protective hand, flipped it open, peeled off half the papers and handed the rest to Kyle. "You don't mind if we spread out? Use your desk? We've got a lot of stuff to go through, and some pressing business awaiting us."

Taylor looked disappointed. Evidently, he'd planned to be their guide through the intricacies of the Human Services world. Burgess just wanted to know what the department's contacts with the family had been, who'd reported Timmy might be in jeopardy, and what the department's response had been. "I want the names of anyone who made a report concerning any of the children," he told Kyle. "Those are people we want to talk to."

He pulled out the top report and started reading through it. It documented a recent visit by Taylor to the Watts home. It appeared that he'd been responding to a complaint from Julie Gordon. He read the report, set it on the desk, and looked at Taylor. "You were there two weeks ago?" Taylor nodded. "It says here you found no problems in the house?"

"That's right."

He scanned the report. It did note the presence of two infants in the house. "What about the filth? The animal feces? The garbage?"

"No worse than many of the places I visit."

Burgess, who'd waded through three decades of filth, wondered what Taylor used as a measure. "What about the absence of food in the refrigerator?"

Taylor only shrugged. "The child didn't seem malnourished."

"You take him to a physician? Get a professional opinion?"

"No."

"You consider that soon those infants would be crawling?" The thought turned his stomach. The infants were still in the house.

Jim Taylor picked absently at a scab on his hand. "I suggested they clean the place up," he said.

"That's not in your report. There's nothing about the physical state of that house."

Taylor picked at the scab some more, then shrugged. "It's in the earlier reports. That's how these people live, Detective. You must know that. You're in and out of these places all the time. I don't claim to be a miracle worker. I'm just trying to do my job."

"What is that, exactly?" Burgess asked. He looked over at Kyle, whose hands were shaking. Saw a muscle working in Kyle's jaw. Fifteen or twenty years ago, they might have taken Taylor behind the building, pounded the crap out of him, and gone home knowing they'd done a good day's work. These days, a harsh word could constitute police brutality, especially to a sensitive man like Taylor.

Instead of answering, Taylor plucked up a picture of Timmy Watts from the papers Burgess had discarded. "He was a beautiful little boy, wasn't he? I used to take him out to eat sometimes. He loved pizza."

Another flag fell on the field. "What about the lack of supervision? The fact that no regular meals were served? The fact that the boy was bruised and filthy? The obvious overcrowding? Blatant drug and alcohol use?"

"Detective..." Taylor's condescending tone implied that Burgess simply didn't understand. "If we took every child who lived in a dirty house with alcoholic parents into custody, we'd have no place to put them."

Burgess thumbed through the file. Complaints from Grace Johnston, from the Gordons, from other neighbors, from Timmy's teacher, Sally Mitchell, about him being dirty, hungry, falling asleep in class. She had written the note Burgess found in Timmy's book. There was a lengthy, articulate complaint from a Regina McBride about the lack of parental supervision. Even a letter from Iris, explaining that no one took Timmy for physicals, got him his shots, cared for him when he was sick. There was a letter from a physician some social worker had taken Timmy to, stating that in his professional opinion, Timothy Watts was the victim of repeated physical abuse.

What on earth did it take? He wrote down names and addresses, phone numbers where he could find them, and looked up. "You've read this file?"

"Of course. I was the boy's case worker."

"And despite the volume of complains, the physical state of the house, and a physician's statement that Timmy was being abused, you did nothing?"

"Our goal is to keep the family intact wherever possible."

What family? "Well, you did a hell of a job here, didn't you?"

He made some final notes. Couldn't bring himself to look at Taylor again. The impulse toward violence was just too great. "Terry? You finished?"

Kyle made a note and looked up. He looked sick. This time, though, Burgess thought it was from what he'd been reading. "Three broken bones in two years," he said. "One severe burn. Two wounds requiring stitches. That didn't raise any red flags?"

"Most of that was from the Lewiston office," Taylor

said, as if that meant it wasn't a signal to keep a close eye on Timmy. "You have to understand. We have a huge caseload. Far more than our regulations call for. The union has complained repeatedly. And then, of course, Timmy was an active boy."

Kyle's chair landed on one of its uneven legs with a bang. Burgess shot him a cautioning look. "We know about those ridiculous caseloads," he said sympathetically. "Being a social worker's a hard job. People burn out pretty quickly, we know you really need your weekends to recharge. Just a couple questions and we'll be out of your hair. You've been here how long?"

"About a year."

"What did you do before?"

"I taught in a private school."

"One hard job to another. Around here?"

"Out in Oregon." Burgess got his phone number, then asked, "And who is your supervisor?" Got that name and phone number. He finished making notes, put his papers back in the file, and reached for Terry's. "Thanks for coming in so we could see this, Mr. Taylor. We appreciate the help. You live in the city?"

Taylor nodded. "Condo in the Old Port. I like to be where the action is."

"Like Jeff Osborne. I think he's got a place somewhere around there."

"Oh, no," Taylor said. "Jeff's in the East End. Up by the park, near where..." Too late, the light dawned. He fumbled the papers together and stood up, clutching the file to his chest. "I'll just see you out," he said, "so I can lock up."

"Give us a call," Burgess offered Taylor a card, "when that file's available. I'll send someone to pick it up."

They stood out on the sidewalk, waiting while

Taylor locked the door behind them, watching him disappear into the dark building.

"What do you want to bet the majority of his cases involve young boys," Burgess said. Looking from the dirty gray sky to the dirty gray street, he thought about something his sergeant used to say, back when he was on patrol. Only thing about this job that was black and white was the car. This case might still be gray, but what Jim Taylor was seemed pretty black and white. "Let's see how Vince's doing on that warrant."

"Jesus fucking Christ," Kyle muttered, kicking at a coffee cup and sending a shower of mud-colored liquid onto the sidewalk. "Fox in the fucking chicken house. We ought to get a warrant for *his* apartment, too."

CHAPTER 21

This time, Osborne answered at the first knock, but he was no more eager to let them in. Burgess showed his badge and introduced Kyle. "We have a few follow-up questions about yesterday. May we come in?"

Osborne hesitated, tipping forward on the balls on his feet like a runner about to make a dash for it. Kyle, sensing the fleeing impulse, stepped behind Burgess and to his right, so that between them they made a wall. Eventually, Osborne stopped trying to read their faces—they wore cop faces, there was nothing to read—and stepped reluctantly backward.

"Come in," he said. "Should I call my lawyer?"

"Afraid I can't advise you about that." Burgess followed him into the living room. "Do you think you need a lawyer?"

"Of course not." Burgess and Kyle took the chairs, forcing Osborne onto the sofa, a place from which he could only watch one of them at a time.

It was late afternoon and Burgess was grouchy as a bear just out of hibernation. The day's sauna-like plunging from extreme heat to icy cold, had not, as a sauna might, refreshed him; it had only yo-yoed his overtaxed system in a state of deeper weariness. He looked at Kyle, sitting still as a statue. In the death mask face, Kyle's eyes were the only animated thing about him. He reminded Burgess of Kevin McHale, with his gaunt saint's face, playing brilliant basketball for the Celtics, even with broken bones. Must have come from being raised Catholic. Burgess found the face of suffering aesthetically pleasing.

Osborne sat tentatively on the edge of his own sofa, his eyes shifting from one of them to the other, then down at his watch. "I hope we can make this short," he said. "I have a prior commitment." The two colorful needlework pillows were gone.

Burgess made a show of pulling out his notebook and slowly flipping through it. "When we spoke yesterday, Mr. Osborne, you stated you didn't know the little boy whose body was found in the park, is that correct?"

"No."

Burgess raised his eyebrows. "No, that's not correct, or no, you didn't know him?"

"Neither, really," Osborne folded his hands together and clamped them between his knees. He wore tennis shoes with short little socks that left his ankles bare, and another ugly polo shirt. His body had the look of a workman who drank too much beer—strong shoulders, soft gut. "I knew who he was from the neighborhood. That's all."

"You never spoke with the boy?" Osborne shook his head. "Never approached him down at the park?" Another shake. Osborne's high forehead gleamed with sweat, a heel tapped the floor. "Never invited him into your house?" Another, more vigorous shake.

"You never invited him here for pizza?"

"Of course not. I told you. I didn't know the boy."

"Did you ever take photographs of Timmy Watts?"

"No." Osborne's hand crept toward the cell phone on the coffee table. Kyle shifted on his chair and Osborne pulled his hand back.

Burgess flipped slowly and loudly through the pages. "Have you ever met a man named Dwayne Martin?"

"Not that I recall."

"Did a man ever come here, identifying himself as Timmy Watts's brother, and threaten you?"

Osborne studied his knotted hands, as though the answer was written there. A streak of afternoon sun illuminated a scalp glowing pinkly through the thinning hair. "Yeah. Martin threatened me. I believe he said something about punching my lights out. But that was just a misunderstanding. I'd yelled at some kids down at the park for teasing my dog. They must have gone home and told some bullshit story. That's what kids do these days. They watch stuff on TV and suddenly they're accusing innocent people of all sorts of awful things. I saw a TV show last week where that happened. Ruined a man's life."

"Where is your dog, Mr. Osborne?"

"With a friend. It turns out he's really not a city dog." Osborne ran a hand through his hair, checked between his fingers for deserters and looked from Burgess to the door.

Burgess thumbed through the pages again, wasting time, making Osborne nervous, waiting for his radio to tell him that they were ready with the warrant. "What about Officer Delinsky? He ever speak with you about Timmy Watts?"

"Why don't you ask him?" Osborne snapped. "Man's got his nose up every ass in the neighborhood."

"I'm asking you."

"Yeah. He came here. I told him what I just told

you. That it was bullshit. That the kids were the problem, not me and my dog."

"When I was here yesterday, you had two needlepoint pillows on your couch. Today they're gone. Why?"

"I hardly think my decorating decisions are a matter for the police."

Burgess smiled. "You're probably right about that." He flipped back to his interview with Grace Johnston. "Yesterday morning, when the body was discovered, you were walking your dog in the park?"

"If you say so."

"You're saying you weren't there?" Osborne didn't answer. "I asked yesterday whether your dog had taken anything from the vicinity of the body. Do you recall that?"

"I'm not sure. I'm not accustomed to being questioned by the police. I was flustered. I might have said anything."

"You don't deny that your dog was near the body?"

"No."

"At some point, your dog picked something up and carried it down to the pond?"

"No." Osborne was getting combative.

"No? We have a witness who..."

"I already told you. That old bitch doesn't know what she's talking about. The thing Rogue carried down to the pond had nothing to do with that boy. It was a little pillow, like the ones that..." Osborne looked around, but the other pillows were gone. "Like the ones you saw yesterday," he finished lamely. "Rogue likes to play with them."

Burgess nodded. "Yesterday you said the dog didn't have anything in its mouth."

Kyle made a sudden move and Osborne's eyes jumped to him, shoulders tensing. Kyle was staring at something on a low bookshelf. A blue Power Ranger. "Timmy Watts loved the Power Rangers," he said quietly.

"All the boys that age love Power Rangers." The words were out before Osborne could stop them.

"You like young boys?" Kyle asked.

"I like children. Most people do. So naturally I notice things about them."

"You ever invite young boys to your house for pizza?"

"That's not a crime," Osborne said. "I told you. I like children. There are lots of them in the neighborhood. Once or twice, I've invited passing kids in to share a pizza."

"You know a boy named Lonnie Mitchell?" Burgess said. Osborne shook his head. Burgess dropped his voice down, low and mean. "You think we're stupid, Mr. Osborne?"

"Excuse me?"

"You think we don't know what you are?"

"That's it," Osborne said, getting to his feet. "You're leaving. I've tried to be cooperative, but I won't tolerate being insulted in my own house. How I live my life is my business. I had nothing to do with what happened to that boy."

"Which boy?" Burgess began. His radio crackled. "Joe? We're ready to go." Burgess nodded to Kyle, who opened the door, admitting Melia and some uniformed officers.

"Hey!" Osborne said. "Hey! What the hell's this? What's going on?"

Melia stepped up to Osborne. With the suit, the hair, the glasses, everything but the hard cop eyes, he looked like an expensive lawyer. He handed Osborne a paper. "Detective Lieutenant Vincent Melia," he said, "Portland CID. This is a warrant to search the premises."

"A warrant? Search?" Osborne was strangling on the words. "You've got no right. No right! I'm calling my lawyer." Melia took a step toward him. "Keep away from me, asshole," Osborne yelled. He stepped swiftly into the living room, snatched up the phone, then rushed across the room and through a door, slamming it behind him.

Melia turned to Burgess. "What's that room?"

"I don't know. Another way to the kitchen, I'd guess."

"Keep an eye on him," Melia told one of the patrol officers. "We don't want him destroying anything." The officer seized the door handle. It was locked.

"We blocked the garage, so he can't use his car," Melia said, "and I've got an officer in the back."

But Burgess was already moving down the hall to another door. It, too, was locked. "Terry, come on!" He raced past them, out the front door and down the steps, running along the side of the long, narrow house to the back. The back door stood open, a very surprised uniformed officer lying on his back at the bottom of the steps. "Which way did he go?" Burgess yelled. The officer pointed toward the rear of a neighboring house.

Burgess jumped the low fence separating the two yards and ran toward the street through an obstacle course of plastic vehicles and toys. It was like a football drill, and his knee didn't like it one bit. He made it to the street and stopped, looking both ways. Nothing. Kyle, panting, appeared beside him. "You go left," Burgess said. "I'll go right."

He headed down the street, walking now, checking each parked car in case Osborne was hiding inside or underneath. Periodically, he stopped and listened. In the distance, Kyle was doing the same. It was a quiet afternoon, everyone inside out of the heat, the damp air muffling sounds. He heard the faint scrape of shoes on rough cement. Holding his breath, he tried to pinpoint the sound. It came from somewhere behind him. Driveways. Dammit. He'd been paying too much attention to the street.

Stepping onto grass to muffle the sound of his own feet, he backtracked, holding his breath and listening. There it was again. That rasping scrape. He was coming to the end of a high hedge. Too good an ambush spot. He stepped across the sidewalk, between two parked cars, and into the street, moving carefully along the outside of the car until he could see down the driveway. It was empty, but at the back a garage stood open.

Years ago, he might have charged right in. Age and experience had taught him caution. He hovered behind the car, acutely aware of the incongruity of it all. A beefy, over-the-hill cop with a bum knee, chasing a wily pervert through a breathless gray afternoon, backed only by Kyle, the Knight of the Living Dead.

He wondered where the uniforms were. And Melia. Whether his intuition was right and Osborne was in that garage, not already disappearing into the distance, laughing his ass off at their incompetence.

Osborne was probably unarmed, but it was something one never assumed. Too many cops sent to their eternal rest that way. Spend years on the job with your antennae up and nothing ever happens, then one day you let down your guard, and wham, it comes at you.

Crouching so that he was sheltered from the garage by the car, he eyeballed the street again. It was as quiet as if the whole world had fallen under a spell. No people, no cars, not even a bird. There was a good-sized rock by his foot. He picked it up, hefted it, then flung it into the garage. Just his luck, he'd probably break some innocent homeowner's priceless collection of antique glass. People stored the strangest stuff in their garages.

There was an exclamation, silence, some rustling. Suddenly, Osborne burst out of the garage on a bicycle, coming straight at him, swinging something curved and lethal. A hand sickle. Burgess fumbled for his gun, getting the holster unsnapped, the gun sticking in a holster swollen from the heat and humidity. Those fumbling seconds made all the difference, he was still bringing the gun up as Osborne was on top of him. Too late to shoot. He stepped aside as the sickle rose and fell, shoving his gun away as he grabbed at Osborne's other arm and pulled him off the bike, trying to hold him at an arm's length as he screamed for Kyle.

The bike clattered to the street as Osborne came at him. Burgess sensed the empty afternoon filling with people, bodies and voices surrounding them as they circled each other. Now there was no way he could use his gun; neither could Kyle, all these goddamned people waking up just in time to be in the way. Suddenly, Osborne lunged at him, the sickle blade glancing off the edge of his vest, tearing down through flesh. As Osborne's arm fell, Burgess moved in, swinging his fist, connecting with Osborne's face. Blood gushed but Osborne didn't fall. Burgess hit him again, hard and fast, and backed away from the swinging sickle.

He heard Kyle's feet racing, voice calling. Felt the hot flow of blood, the fierce bite of pain. Watching the blade, he didn't see the foot coming until it landed and his knee gave way beneath him. Fumbling again for the gun, he heard his own voice yelling, "Stop.

Police," as Osborne snatched up the bike again and began peddling away.

He searched through the crowd for a clear shot. They stood, dumb as sheep, none of them with the sense to move out of the way. That and maybe a slight desire to favor the criminal in a neighborhood that had had its share of entanglements with the police.

Suddenly, Osborne's body jerked, one arm flying up. A cry, loud in the still air. The bike dipped, wavered, one foot slamming the pavement. Someone had thrown a rock. Burgess ran gasping in the thick air, still gripping his gun, waiting for Osborne to fall, his own blood rushing hotly down his arm,. No third arm to grab his radio and call for assistance, no shoulder mike on a detective's suit. Kyle's pounding footsteps not far behind.

Then, astonishingly, Osborne's foot came up off the ground, the bike righted and surged forward. Osborne pulled away. Burgess reached down for more speed and came up empty. He steadied his gun but suddenly, everywhere he looked, the street was full of people.

Kyle shot past him, feet flying, and disappeared around the corner after the bike. Why were they the only police officers out here? Where in hell was everyone? He grabbed his radio, gave the call for an officer down, and the particulars of the fleeing suspect, possibly injured, on a stolen bike. Then, recognizing the futility of chasing after a bike already out of sight, he sat down on the curb, rivulets of blood running between the spread fingers braced against the granite. His other hand still held the gun. Doing it all, as he had so often, before a staring crowd. Like he could have told Officer Beck. *Sometimes you bleed through your clothes in this business. You might as well get used to it.*

"You happy now?" he yelled at the crowd. "You

happy? I hope none of you are parents, 'cuz that guy you just helped get away, he rapes little boys."

Kyle returned, winded and retching. After the expletives were deleted, there wasn't anything to say except the criticisms they were heaping on themselves in the privacy of their heads. After a minute, bored with watching his blood pool, Burgess got up and put his gun away. "Might as well go tell Vince." They headed back the way they'd come.

CHAPTER 22

He'd never understood why they didn't market adrenaline as a drug. Maybe they couldn't synthesize it. Maybe everyone already thought they had enough of their own. Police officers, in the course of their roller coaster days, grew familiar with the adrenaline rush, that blast in the pit of the stomach that spread through the body, endowing it, temporarily, with super powers. Like many drugs, though, it had a negative side. When the rush subsided, you could find yourself in surprisingly bad shape, like he was now. Limping down an urban street on a summer Sunday afternoon, dripping scarlet blood onto the dirty gray sidewalk.

Dammit, he wanted to have shot Osborne. To have dragged that child-raping sucker off that bike and ground his smug face into the pavement. He resented the rules on using deadly force—the rules and that crowd of useless gawkers preventing him and Kyle from firing their guns.

Kyle marched tight-lipped beside him, holding the sickle by the narrow part where the handle met the blade. "Figured if I left it there, one of those worthless jerks'd take it as a souvenir." Kyle was self-contained, taciturn, but normally he was lit by a cold intensity, like a lightning bug. Now he drooped like an old man, his gaunt face beaded with sweat. Kyle wouldn't complain. He wasn't the complaining type, but he'd be beating himself up because he hadn't outrun a perp on a bike on this sodden hot bitch of a day.

Burgess cradled his arm like a sick child and cursed himself for letting this happen. Maybe if he hadn't insisted on the Crips? But it wasn't just him. The whole thing was screwed up. Why was only one goddamned officer covering the back? Why hadn't he gotten up and come after Osborne? What was Melia thinking? This was a teamwork thing. You couldn't fail to plan, or have back-up. You couldn't sit on your ass and not use your head and expect to catch bad guys.

He smoldered like a banked fire, needing only the slightest thing to fan him into a blaze again. "I can't believe we let that fucker get away," he said.

"You called it from the first," Kyle reminded him. "You said it was going to be a bitch." He looked at the bloody wound. "That must hurt."

"Puts me in touch with my mortality."

"And keeps you awake," Kyle said, yawning.

How many times over the years had they been at this point? So damned tired they could have gone to sleep on their feet? And if they did, that's just what the GP would see. Not the 18-20 hour days, the heartbreaking, ball busting interviews. Not the gut-wrenching chore of attending a small boy's autopsy. Nah. They'd see two seedy-looking cops in rumpled clothes, leaning against a building or a car, eyes closed, sleeping on the job.

On feet heavy as cement blocks, they retraced their steps down the driveway strewn with plastic vehicles, over the fence, and into Osborne's yard. Melia met them at the door. Burgess had planned to ask, straight away, why no one had come to back them up, but Melia's appearance answered his question. The dapper suit was smudged with soot and water, Melia's hands and face a grimy black. "You didn't get him?" he said.

"I hit him," Burgess said. "Bastard wouldn't fall. Slashed me with a sickle and rode off on a bicycle."

"Hit him with what? Fist or gun?"

"Too many people around for a gun."

"Good. We've got enough paperwork already." A brief show of white teeth in the blackened face. "I think the bad guys are winning today. And Paul was salivating for an arrest." Then, taking in Burgess's bloody arm, he said kindly, "Don't bring that blood in here, okay? I've got enough contamination already."

"I blew it," Burgess said, "letting him get away." His arm felt like he'd been gnawed on by rats and hurt like a bastard. He felt blacker and meaner and uglier than ever. Furious with himself at having to take time to go get stitched up. Furious with Osborne. Disturbed at how badly he'd wanted to shoot the man.

"Osborne destroy much?"

"Don't know yet," Melia said. "I hope not. He had a little study off the kitchen, stuff sitting in boxes like he was ready to move it out. Mostly photographs. That's where he started the fire. The real fire. He set some others as distractions. Fast on his feet, that one."

"You should have brought Dwyer. She would've caught him."

"She was invited. Something came up."

Too bad. She would have knocked that sucker off his bike, hog-tied him, slung him over her shoulder and brought him back like a cartoon caveman returning with dinner. Cavewoman. Still, the idea of someone slashing her with a sickle aroused vestiges of male chauvinism. He preferred women's rippling muscles under unscarred flesh. "His computer?"

"Rocky says it should be okay. He's coming over."

"We're looking for two small needlepoint pillows. Yellow and blue. Be sure you check his trash."

Burgess wanted to help with the search, but traipsing through the house in his present condition was dumb. There was nothing for him to do here. Might as well go get sewn up. "Terry, I'm going over to the ER, get a little mending done. You may as well stay here, help Vince. You hear the girls are fixing us supper?"

"They're what?"

"Over at my place, fixing a nice, nourishing meal. They're worried about us."

Kyle looked away, then back, his face tighter, more worried. He shrugged. "You tell 'em we were working a murder?"

"What do you think? Chris said we still gotta eat, and it'll be better than Mickey D's."

"She's got that right."

"So when you're done here, and I'm done there, we could meet up and go over." He wasn't even sure why he was suggesting this. Kyle's reaction mirrored his own when Chris called. Worse for Kyle because he was already on the shit list for missing yesterday. Kyle was using all his energy to push himself through the day. He had nothing left for chit chat and a dinner party, for humans who weren't on the same wavelength. "Just to eat, Ter. I told her we had no time."

Kyle gave a weary shrug. "Okay." He went up the steps and into the house.

Burgess walked to the car, the pain in his knee matching the one in his arm—a fearful symmetry. He wanted to search the city, block by block, until he found Osborne and beat the crap out of him, needed to stay focused, get his arm fixed, get back to work. Thirty-six hours in, there had been a fair amount of drama and bloodshed; otherwise things were moving like that famous molasses in January. He thought of Delinsky's watchful old lady, who'd been taken to the hospital. Might as well kill two birds with one hospital visit. He got on the radio.

He'd been in the ER at Maine Med more often than he'd been in a church the last few years. Hell, he'd probably logged more time here than he'd spent in church in the last decade.

He'd come to get repaired, come plenty of times to interview victims and their families, even to interview the docs. He'd done the death watch for his mother here—endless sterile hours in the ICU, watching her life's ebb measured in colored lines, in plastic bags and bottles filled and emptied, in the ceaseless whoosh of the respirator. He hated the feel of the place, the smell, the numbing glare of the lights.

He parked close to the door and marched up to the receptionist. He knew most of the people—CID was in and out of there almost as much as street police— but she was a stranger. Without giving her a chance to speak, he said, "Detective Burgess, Portland Police. I'm in the middle of a murder investigation. You got someone who can sew me up real quick?"

They found him a young doc who seemed more pained by the process than he was, someone who wanted to give him care when all he wanted was mending. Many stitches later, he went to the information desk to get directions to Anna Pederson's room. Charlie, the security guard, surveyed his torn, bloody shirt and bandaged arm. "Don't tell me someone's killed another doc?"

"Don't you read the papers?"

"The kid?" Burgess nodded. "That's a sick one," Charlie said. "I've never seen anything like that picture."

"Me neither. I hope I never do again."

"Pissed you off, huh. I don't blame you. No way that was necessary. I hear—"

Burgess was impatient to interview Anna Pederson and get back to the station, but he'd known Charlie a long time. Security guards were invisible to a lot of people, so Charlie often heard useful things. He cradled his torn arm and waited. The stitching had been brutal, but he hadn't wanted pain killers. He needed to keep his remaining wits about him. "What?"

"Paper's got itself a new reporter. Cute little thing. Looks like a sixteen-year-old kid—fresh-faced, adorable little turned-up nose, lots of Shirley Temple curls, got moves like Magic Johnson. She'll do anything to get a story. She's everywhere. Into everything. She'll be behind that picture. You'll find her in your car, in your house, in your face, on your desk. So watch yourself. She'd crawl up your ass if it would get her a story."

"Jesus. That's all we need."

"I'm surprised you haven't met her yet."

"Guess she was too busy sweet-talking someone into letting her into their attic so she could get that picture. Plus, the department keeps my ugly face out of the paper. Thanks for the warning. You hear anything else I should know, you'll call, right?"

"You bet."

He took the elevator to Mrs. Pederson's floor, checked in at the nurses' desk, and ran into a brick wall. Her nurse, a sensible middle-aged woman named Lynne, said, "I'm sorry, but I can't let you see her." Sober, determined, planting her blocky body directly in his path. Had his bull-headed reputation preceded him?

"I've got a murder," he said.

"And Mrs. Pederson's got a bad heart. She's still unstable and I'm not letting you in."

"It won't take long."

"It won't take any time at all, Detective, because it's not happening. Quite aside from her condition, you go in looking like that, you'll scare the hell out of her. She's a frail old lady. Give me your card, and I promise I'll call as soon as she's able to talk. If you promise to clean up first."

"You think I want...?" She didn't move. Didn't even blink. You gotta know when to fold 'em. He pulled out a card. "It's important," he said.

"I know." She wasn't sure of him yet. She was watching his body, his feet, the way an opposing player might watch for a sudden move on the field. When he shifted his foot toward the elevator, and she relaxed a little. "I will call you."

"Day or night," he said. "They know where to find me. Wait." He took the card and scribbled his home number with a little "H" next to it.

He was going through the Emergency Department door when a woman came up to him. She had the squeaky-clean good looks of a high school cheerleader. A pink, scrubbed look. Soft, bouncy blonde curls. Sweet blue eyes and turned-up nose. Thanks to Charlie, he knew exactly who she was—a bloodsucking vampire in a girl suit. She planted herself in his path. "Detective, I'm Charlene Farrell, from the paper. May I ask you a few questions?"

He didn't even slow. "You're the one who arranged that picture?" he asked.

"Yes."

"I have nothing to say. You know the protocol. All department comment goes through Captain Cote."

"I understand you and Captain Cote don't get along," she said. "I don't think he gives a damn about this case. I was hoping you might give me something real."

Ignoring her, he walked to his car and opened the door. Charlene Farrell blocked his way, still smiling. "How did you get injured, Detective?"

"Excuse me." He stepped around her, got in, and started the engine. She must have mistaken him for someone who had scruples about running over reporters, who worried about bad press. She didn't move. "Is it true that you were attacked by a fleeing suspect? That even when he slashed you with a knife, you drew your weapon but never fired it, and let him escape on a stolen bicycle?"

It sounded bad and stupid—what police department lets a suspect escape on a bicycle?—and was intended to provoke a rash response. "Ms. Farrell," he said, "I'm in the middle of a murder investigation and you're in my way. Would you please move?"

"You have no comment on your failed attempt to apprehend Mr. Osborne?"

"Interfering with a police investigation is a crime, Ms. Farrell," he said. "I'm asking you one more time. Please move out of my way."

The pretty face was sullen now. Reluctantly, she stepped onto the sidewalk, but she had the parting shot. "Is it true, Detective, that some drugs you say you seized in a search of the victim's home have mysteriously disappeared?"

Was this what Cote had been so cheerful about, a nifty little leak to the press designed to make him look both corrupt and stupid? He was wearing his trained cop's face, no emotion there for Charlene Farrell to record, but his mind spun. Fucking Cote pressuring him to solve this thing, then doing every damned thing he could to get in the way. He put the car in gear, pulled away from the curb, and headed back across town.

CHAPTER 23

He walked back into 109 and into an administrative road block. One of those witless, get-in-the-way civilians had alleged that he had fired his gun. He had to write a lengthy report on the incident, which grated on already sore nerves and wasted time he didn't have. Sometimes the job felt like a game of Simon Says. Your boss says go do something. Then you can't get out the door because you forgot to say "May I?" When he was done with the issue of deadly force—luckily, a punch in the nose didn't qualify—he went to Melia's office and tried to hand off the meth problem again.

"We've got a serious news leak, Vince."

Melia, who'd washed but still wore his dirty suit, raised an eyebrow and leaned back in his chair. "What now?" Whatever it was, he didn't want to hear it.

"More shit flowing in my general direction." He told Melia about the reporter's parting shot. "How the heck would something like that get out? No one in the lab would talk. I didn't talk. You didn't talk. Terry and Stan wouldn't."

"Told you to watch your back on this one."

"Meaning I shouldn't have brought the stuff in at all?"

"Meaning yes, someone's trying to screw with you. Meaning play it by the book. Keep someone with you. Have a witness to everything you do."

"Fuck it. We don't need this."

Melia gave him a smile filled with pity for the naive and simple. "We needed a murder? We needed this heat?"

"Vince, I can't work like this."

"You can work any way you need to, if it will help a case. Besides, I thought you were asking for my advice."

"I was."

"Look, I'll cover you as best I can, but the food chain's the food chain. It were me, I wouldn't just stand there and let some asshole stab me in the back. You're older, smarter, and more experienced. Use that." Melia stared at his window, which gave him a view of nothing. "I could sure use some results."

That hurt. "Hell, Vince. We busted a pornographer, a child molester."

"Maybe a pornographer. *Maybe* a child molester. *Maybe* our killer. There's no sign the boy was killed in that house. Not even in the basement or the garage. We're still going over the car. As for busted, I don't see any one arrested."

Burgess was striking out on every at bat. Didn't need his nose rubbed in it. If the results so far were any test, he couldn't find his own ass without help. He felt as tattered and mean as a mangy old dog and just as ready to snap at whatever crossed his path. Vince was right. He was letting peripheral stuff distract him. He had to get out of here, somewhere he could think about the case without a desk load of administrative bull. He heaved himself to his feet.

"If outward appearances are a mirror of inner thought, you might as well hand Cote your resignation right now," Melia said. "Turn in your badge and gun, go home and play with Chris and forget about slaughtered kids."

"You trying to make me lose my temper?"

"Near as I can tell, your temper's neither lost nor found. It swarms around you like a big, dark cloud. I'm trying to make you lose your self-pity, get your attention focused on something besides your own sorry ass."

"Someone's trying to set me up here. You saying I shouldn't care?"

"I'm saying move carefully, but keep moving. I'm saying a dead kid's a big deal. I've got a city holding its breath. I've got the brass breathing down my neck. I've got reporters camping on my doorstep. And I haven't a goddamned thing to tell 'em."

"So *you* can focus on *your* ass, but I'm supposed to ignore mine?"

"That about sums it up." Vince pushed his chair back. "You know I've never given a damn about anyone but myself. Now get out of my office. Go find me something."

Downstairs, he found Rocky Jordan sitting at a conference table in a room off the crime lab, playing with a blackened computer. "Getting anything?"

"Remember when that question used to mean something pleasant?" Rocky said. "Give me time, I will."

"You get me a name and address on that license number?"

"It's on your desk."

He stuck his head into the lab, saw Dani patting a dirty, disheveled Devlin on the shoulder. "Don't worry," she said. "We'll handle it." She looked up and saw him. "Go away, Joe. We're busy. We've declared a moratorium on crime until next week."

"Got anything for me?" He folded his hands in front of him like a penitent and lowered his head. "Something. Anything. For the love of God. My fearless leader, Lt. Vincent Melia, is decompensating." Trying not to beg.

Devlin had turned away, so Dani took the question. "Rudy's finishing your pictures. Been in the darkroom so long he's turned fish-belly white, purely out of devotion to you. If you can't wait, there's video. Doesn't the bad guy always return to the scene of the crime?"

She shook her head, masking a smile with a latex-gloved hand. "You want something? How about an amphetamine-cooking or using, Dorito and Oreo-addicted, knifeaholic who lives in a house with purplish-gray carpet, uses coconut-scented shampoo, keeps a pet eagle and drinks Coke in bottles?"

"Just what I was looking for," he said. "Can't be too many of those in the city. I'll just organize a house-to-house. We should be done by Christmas." Then he realized what he'd heard. "Eagle?"

"Yeah." Wink said. "I took your advice. Gave a guy at the university that feather."

Burgess wished it could have been a more common bird. One people kept as pets. It must have showed on his face. "Look, Joe," Dani said. "We're sorry. We want this as much as you do. We haven't had much time. We can't be here, playing with our beakers and our spatulas and tweezers and our super glue, and out there crawling through yet another house. This isn't CSI, you know."

"And I'm not finished yet."

"We didn't think you were," Devlin said. "Now go away and leave us alone."

"What about the K-Mart bag?"

"When we can. Now get out."

"Your eagle feather," Dani said. "What about those dream catchers people have? Don't they use eagle feathers?"

He found the name and address Rocky had left on his desk, unsurprised to find it was Mother Watts estranged brother, Henry Devereaux.. He picked up Kyle and Delinsky's analysis of the house-to-house, Perry's reports on his list of perverts, and some individual reports. Perry and Delinsky were still out. He told Melia he and Kyle were going ten seven. "Anybody needs us, we're at my place."

"Do us all a favor," Melia said. "Get some sleep. Tell Stan to do the same. Everyone back here at 0700?"

He called Chris. "We're on our way but don't expect much. We're pretty ragged."

"I'll take what I can get," she said. "We'll take what we can get."

He couldn't believe her even temper could last. His own rotten mood would rub off. And she'd be furious and protective when she saw the stitches. Like his mother trying to keep him inside when he had a cold. It wasn't fair to make assumptions. She wasn't his mother. His sisters said what he knew about women wouldn't fill a thimble. But he was a cop. His life was making assumptions. He gave it up. So far, Kyle hadn't said a word.

"We're going to be great company," he said.

"What did they expect?"

"Chris says they just want to see our handsome faces."

"You believe that?"

"Trying to."

"They're checking up," Kyle said.

They rode in silence through streets wrapped in a sullen layer of briny fog that looked like cotton candy and reduced visibility to zero. A good night for Osborne to lose himself in the city. Uniforms had found a trail of blood drops and the abandoned bike, but no sign of the man. Where would he go? Who would take him in? One of his own.

Burgess passed the radio to Kyle. "See if Rocky can give us a list of anyone in the area involved in child pornography. Anyone even suspected of such activities. See if he's found anything in Osborne's computer. Anything that looks like names or addresses or phone numbers of his porno pals. That's who he'll go to. He was carrying his cell phone. He must have called someone to pick him up."

That set off another light. "His cell phone. It's Verizon. Get the records. Find out who he called." His mind was racing now.

"Call Stan, tell him where we're going with this, that we'll be calling him to follow up if Rocky has anything. Get an address for that social worker. Jim Taylor. See why he left that private school in Oregon."

Kyle made the calls, ignoring Rocky's whining complaint and Stan's objection he was in the middle of something. Left it that if Rocky didn't come up with something, Stan should go home, be back for the meeting at seven.

He pulled into his driveway, shoved the car into park, and sat there, lacking the energy to open his door. Kyle didn't move, either. "We getting too old for this, Terry?"

"It's not age for me. I'm curdling," Kyle said. "Getting all sour and rotten inside. Can't find my decency, never mind any optimism. Case like this doesn't help. I don't know, we go up there, if I can even be civil. It's like Wanda's poisoned me and the only antidote is in a bottle. Sheesh, Joe. Some days, seven a.m., I'm already dreaming of that first drink."

Wanda was poison, but Kyle had done this to himself. "You have to fight back."

"I know. But Joe, being brought down to her level. Thinking about doing to her what she's been doing to me..."

"You've got Michelle."

"And how long do you think she's going to put up with a mean as a snake drunk with two kids and the bitch from hell calling at all hours of the day and night?"

"I think she'll stick."

"Why would any woman want to stay around, taking care of someone else's kids? Living with a guy who hasn't had a decent mood in months? I'm just like my goddamned father. Life gets tough, I crawl into a bottle."

"You want her to leave?"

"Shit, no. I want normal. Normal and decent. I want Cheerios with my kids. I want Michelle to keep smiling like seeing me matters. But what about her? Doesn't she deserve better?" Kyle got out and slammed the door behind him. He'd had as much conversation as he was good for.

Burgess used his right hand to open the door. His left arm wanted to be babied and he figured it was allowed a little down time. He was starving and craved protein, something raw and bloody. Just thinking "raw and bloody" took him right back to the crime scene. He'd forgotten to ask about the knife. He really wanted that knife. He called Melia. "They find anything in those storm drains?"

"Haven't done 'em yet, Joe. It's Sunday."

"We're working."

"We're cops. Joe?"

"Yeah?"

Vince sounded harassed and explosive. Maybe he'd had a visit from Cote, looking for something to feed the media. "Catch me a bad guy."

"Go home, Vince," he said. "After we eat, we'll see what we can stir up. We get anything, we'll call you."

He trudged up the stairs. Chris, in gym shorts and a tank top, was bending down, getting something from the refrigerator, treating a row of frosty green Rolling Rocks to a view of her cleavage and him to a lot of bare leg. He came up behind her, wrapped his good arm around her, and pulled her against him, wishing he wore shorts so he could feel her smooth skin.

She reached past him, slid a plate onto the counter, and wrapped her arms around his neck, pressing her body against him. He felt a flicker of excitement and wondered how she did it. He only had to be in the same room and he got aroused. She pushed away, laughing, shoving her hair back from her face. "I guess you are glad to see me."

Her laughter stopped abruptly when she saw his torn and bloody shirt. "Oh, Joe. What now?" The caretaker in her studying his face, insisting that he sit.

He wanted to stay pressed up against her. "I'm okay," he said. "Don't baby me."

She folded her arms and stepped back. "Is that what I was doing?"

Excitement to acrimony in a few short sentences. "Please," he said. "Let's not fight. We haven't got a lot of time."

"No. I don't suppose you have. Not even enough for a phone call to let me know what happened."

"No," he agreed. "Not even enough for that. Case like this, we've got so much on the line. People get hysterical. Jobs are at risk. It's real heavy going." He wasn't used to discussing his work with anyone who wasn't on the job. He wasn't doing this well, didn't know how to do it better. "We went to execute a search warrant. The guy ran. I went after him. He came at me with a sickle."

She let her breath out with a sigh. "You get him?"

"No. Then I go to get stitched up and find a reporter in my face, accusing me of stealing meth from an evidence locker."

"That's ridiculous. Everyone knows you're a straight arrow. How many stitches?"

"I'm not sure. Twenty, maybe?"

"I don't get it." She reached back absently and undid her barrette, letting her hair fall free. "They spoil your vacation. You get attacked and need twenty stitches, and they're still making you work? How can they do that?"

"Not they, Chris, me. I'm making me work."

She looked down at the counter, intent on unwrapping a platter. "I knew that. I just don't understand. Why can't you take a break, let someone else do it?"

"Someone else is Terry, and you know what shape he's in. Terry, Stan, and Vince. I'm not the only one going at this hard. That's how these things are. You just keep working it 'til something breaks or it's so clear nothing's going to break that you lower the intensity."

"There are other detectives." She abandoned the platter and came over to him, pulling his head into her chest. "But none of them are you, I know. I just hate to see you hurt. Not," Her voice dropped to a whisper, "...that it seems to slow you down."

"Let's forget about dinner." He stood up, taking her hand, remembered Kyle had come home with him. "Where are Terry and Michelle?"

"In the bedroom."

"Our bedroom?" She nodded. Pleased he'd said 'our.' "That means they've got our air conditioner."

She held onto his hand, pressing her hip against him. "We've got a guestroom."

He pressed back, suddenly wanting her so much he could have pulled her right down onto the kitchen floor. "Just thinking we might want to bring a fan."

"I'm your biggest fan," she said. "I just wish you'd remember it."

Afterwards, showered and dressed, he found Chris and Michelle on the back porch, Michelle pink and pretty in a short blue sundress. Chris was pulling a steak off the grill. A feast was spread out on the table. "Where's Terry?"

"In the shower," Michelle said. She looked down at her feet, curling her bare toes under in embarrassment. "I'm sorry about…uh…taking your room. That was rude." Her toes curled tighter. Her cheeks got pinker. "I just thought he needed something alive and good." She looked up at him, then, her lower lip caught between her teeth. "To know I still wanted him. That even if he's gone through a black patch, we've got more than a fair weather thing."

"What are friends for?"

"In your case, everything."

Terry came out, barefoot and smiling, followed by Chris with the phone. "It's Stan." She handed it over, adding, "Whatever it is, you're not leaving until you eat."

Like Michelle, she wore blue. It was nice with her honey brown hair. Everything about her seemed nice just now. The restorative powers of sex. He'd pushed his black mood away, gotten a little of his balance back. And drained off the last of his energy. He took the phone. "Yeah?"

"Dispatch got a call from a car rental place out at the airport. Guy came in a while ago, tried to rent a car with cash. Got real upset when they told him he needed a card. Said he'd forgotten his, he'd be back in an hour. Description matches Osborne. I'm sitting on the place." Perry gave the details. "Get here when you can."

"You call Vince?"

"Not yet."

"I'll call him. Get whoever's around to call the other places. He might be too spooked to come back there."

"I'm on it."

Burgess terminated the call. He and Kyle tore into their steaks like lions at a kill, hugged the kind ladies in blue, and headed back into the fog. He didn't think Osborne would be back, but they had to check it out.

CHAPTER 24

"You want me to drive?" Kyle asked. It was six of one, half a dozen of the other, Burgess figured, handing over the keys. They were both walking wounded. He got in the passenger seat, reclined it, and shut his eyes. "Wake me when we're close," he muttered.

Drive was hardly the word for what they were about to do. As darkness fell in, the fog had deepened until they couldn't see twenty feet in front of them. It wasn't so much driving as an act of faith. Time was tight and they couldn't hurry. The only comfort was that Osborne would be slowed, too.

These were hard times to be a child. Not just Timmy Watts, but Andrea Dwyer's abused little boy, lured in and violated by Jeffrey Osborne, and Neddy and Nina Mallett, who'd watched their father kill their mother. His own childhood had been hard, but there had been neighbors and community. Kids could wander the neighborhood safely and go to the store for bread and milk without worrying about gangs, guns, or predators. He thought of Yeats's "Second Coming." It seemed, indeed, that a blood-dimmed tide was loosed, that innocence was being drowned.

"Did you know you're making a weird humming sound?" Kyle said.

"It's anger."

"I'll drink to that," Kyle said, "Of course these days, I'll drink to anything."

"Our father's legacy. It's about all mine gave me. That and my temper."

"I didn't get a temper."

"Bullshit. You're just using it on yourself instead of where it belongs. On Wanda. Osborne. Taylor. The entire Watts family. You wanna pull out of that slump, get mad about this case. Get mad for Timmy Watts. You're a dad, for God's sake. Use that."

The fog thinned as they got away from the coast. As soon as staying on the road didn't require all his concentration, Kyle hit the radio and found a country station, a man singing that he should have been a cowboy. "This stuff's our lives in a nutshell, Joe," he said. "You think I made the wrong career choice? Maybe I should have been a cowboy."

"I'm sleeping."

"You want it off?"

"Nah. I can sleep through anything." He closed his eyes again, his body surging toward sleep like a vacuum was sucking him in. He slipped over the edge into numbness.

Numb for maybe ten minutes. He woke abruptly when Kyle jammed on the brake, nearly putting both of them through the windshield.

"Fuckin' skunk in the road," Kyle said. "I'm not driving with that in the car the rest of the night."

"Night, hell. The rest of your life. Except it's my car, my life. I don't think they wash cars in tomato juice when they tangle with skunks."

"V-8," Kyle said. "Cop cars like V-8."

"I was young, I used to like a big V-8 myself. Boy could you leave rubber with one of those babies."

"You're dating yourself," Kyle said.

"I feel dated. Antique. Ready for an overhaul, a new trannie, retirement."

"Weren't you just in for a Jiffy-lube?" Kyle swung suddenly to the curb and shut off the engine. They were at the airport. Kyle parked so they could see the front of the terminal, the row of rental car agencies, and they got out. It might be an international airport, but this time of night, with the fog socked in, flights would be canceled or delayed, and you could probably have safely grazed cattle on the runway. Grazing seagulls were a bigger problem. That and drivers so disconcerted by landing planes as they dipped low over the highway that they ran into things and each other.

They found Perry tucked unobtrusively into a corner, still as a cigar store Indian. "Anything?" Burgess asked.

"Nah. I doubt if there will be. Guy's not stupid."

"How long's it been?" Burgess asked.

"Since he said he'd be back? Hour, hour and a quarter, maybe? Rocky says when we're done here, if we feel like it, we might wanna drop back and look at some of Osborne's pictures. Says he's got some doozies."

Kyle grunted. "I wonder what his standards are?"

"Probably not aesthetic."

"This doesn't pan out, what do we do next, Joe?" Perry asked.

"Sleep would be good," Kyle said.

"Sleep," Burgess agreed. "Get all bright-eyed and bushy-tailed for 0700. We can run it all down then."

They stood in silence, watching the occasional car come and go. Waiting wearily under the cold, bright lights, things took on a time-altered, surreal quality that the distortions of the gauzy night only deepened. The gray night was prettier than the gray day had been. Hell of a lot more dangerous, too. Things came at you suddenly, disappeared just as quickly. It was hard to get your bearings.

"Well, well," Stan said quietly, satisfaction in his voice. "Looks like our guy may be stupider than we thought. I'm going to slip inside and get in front of them." In a flash, he was inside walking through the airport, wearing a baseball cap and carrying a duffle bag.

Ahead, a teal Jetta had stopped at the curb. The driver came around to the passenger side and bent down to confer. "It's that social worker, Taylor," Kyle said. The scumbag world was like a small town. Everyone in a particular area of wrongdoing knew everyone else. Drug dealers knew dealers and users. Thieves knew thieves and fences. Pimps knew hookers and pimps. Pedophiles knew other pedophiles. Cops eventually came to know them all, giving the "yeah, I see you" salute to the regulars on their beats.

The passenger door opened and Osborne got out. Moving stiffly, Burgess was pleased to see. He hated to think Osborne would have walked away unscathed while *he'd* bled from one end of the neighborhood to the other. Kyle spoke quietly into the radio, alerting Perry and the uniforms who were waiting. Then the two of them began walking down the sidewalk toward the car. Perry coming at them the other way. A patrol car, closing in too soon, spooked Osborne. In an instant, he was in the Jetta's driver's seat and moving, the patrol car in pursuit. Taylor stood on the sidewalk, staring in dismay at his departing car.

Perry waved at them, pointing to his car. "Let's go!"

he said. Burgess stepped into the street, stopped a second patrol car, and indicated Jim Taylor. "Hold him," he said. Then he sprinted to the waiting car, Perry moving before he was in the door.

The airport, which straddled the Portland/South Portland line, was built on a patch of land isolated by three rivers, Long Creek, the Fore River, and the Stroudwater River, as well as by the Interstate. There weren't many roads and no neighborhoods for Osborne to lose himself in. But Osborne had obviously been watching Volkswagen commercials. They wanted drivers, he would give them a driver. He led them on a merry chase through the fog and darkness, from tarmac to dirt road to barely visible track, the cruiser and Perry close behind, rocking and rolling over the rough ground, the world around them black as sin. Suddenly, the cruiser's brake lights slammed on. Perry slewed sideways to avoid hitting it.

"You drive like a cop," Kyle said, as he jumped out.

Perry flashed a grin. "Thanks."

The uniform's flashlight illuminated Taylor's car nose-down in a watery ditch, driver's door standing open. Splashing and crackling sounds told them Osborne had struck out on foot through the sucking mud and razor-sharp grasses of the salt marsh. Burgess recognized the uniform—Remy Aucoin, a rookie just finishing his first year on the force. "Call dispatch and get us more cops, Remy. Tell 'em to bring plenty of flashlights. Then call Lt. Melia and tell him we're out here chasing Osborne. And next time, let us get in place first."

Aucoin ducked his head, embarrassed. "Sorry, Sarge, I..."

"No excuses," Burgess said.

Aucoin raised his radio, looking longingly after

Kyle and Perry, who had taken Burgess's flashlight and were disappearing into the darkness. Aucoin was young, fit, and eager. A better candidate for the job than Burgess. "Oh, go ahead. Go get him. I'll make the calls," Burgess said. "Just, for God's sake, don't shoot him if you can help it."

"Thank you, sir." Aucoin plunged into the high grass, taking his flashlight with him, leaving Burgess in a world lit only by the occasional lightning bug and the piercing beams and blue strobes of Aucoin's cruiser, in a night alive with the impassioned screams of insects and amphibians searching for mates and the deadly whine of mosquitoes. No one was going to have fun out here; when they caught Osborne, he was in for some rough handling for putting them through this. Like the cops say, "Make me run, I'll hurt you."

As he got on the radio and called Melia, Burgess felt a wave of regret. Dangerous as it was—and he knew Osborne was plenty dangerous—a chase through the darkness after a fleeing suspect always held vestiges of that most sublime childhood experience, being outside in the dark, late at night, playing games. Even aside from the atavistic stuff, one of a cop's driving forces was that adrenaline rush. You spent the formative years of your career as a street cop, getting hooked by those surges. Dispatch mutters something over the radio. You hit the siren and lights, and go.

Even with the heat, a bum knee, and a bad shoulder, he wanted to be in the game, wanted to be the one to grab the back of Osborne's neck and push his sweaty face down into the oozing mud. He wanted to vent his rage screaming curses, using language he normally excised from his daily speech. He wanted to pull those flailing arms back, plant a knee in the middle of that flabby back, and snap on his own cuffs. He wanted the collar.

Leaning against the car, its metal slippery from fog, he wished he smoked. At least it would keep the damned bugs away. In a summer so dry, they should have died out. But swampy spots, marshes and wetlands, were their last resort. Funny expression, last resort. People always talked about going to a "fancy resort" or a "world-class resort." If they went there and died, had they gone to a last resort?

He heard the distant rise and fall of a siren, the sound distorted by the fog. Looking in the direction Osborne had gone, he couldn't see anything, not even the glow of flashlights. The marsh had swallowed them up. There was a place farther along where the water almost met the road. Once this end was covered, he'd head down there with some people, pinching Osborne between them.

He turned the car around and got himself facing out, waiting as the cars came up to him, Melia in the lead. Burgess rolled down his window, gave a succinct report, and told Melia what he wanted to do. With Melia's approval, he drove back to the road past the line of cruisers, telling the last ones to follow him.

They parked just past the elbow in the road, gathering around as Burgess filled them in. "We don't know if he's armed, so assume he is," he said. "Everyone wearing vests?" There was a murmur of assents. "If you've got gloves, wear 'em. That grass can slice like a knife." In a thin line, they headed into the grass. This time, he slogged through the muck with the rest of them.

It was rough going with his knee and more than once he cursed his macho stupidity. All the same, he needed to be here. Bringing Osborne in was important. Something to hand Melia and stick in Cote's face. To show the media the Portland police weren't a sorry lot. They all took insults to the department personally. All the venom in the world spewing from a suspect's mouth might roll right off, but a nasty word in the press hurt everyone.

They were all doing the same thing—walking a few paces, then pausing to listen and survey the area around them with their lights. Step. Stop. Step. Stop. He'd borrowed a spare flashlight from one of the cruisers. Ahead, there were rustling sounds that might have been the approach of Osborne, or other cops, or the agitated perambulations of disturbed nocturnal creatures. At times, he felt like a nocturnal creature.

Step. Stop. Listen. The backs of his hands oozed from grass cuts. Sweat plastered his shirt to his chest. Clinging muck made his steps heavy. Step. Stop. Listen. Every step transporting him farther from Portland, Maine, in a new century, back to Nam and the seventies. Shaving decades off his life and giving him back the metallic taste of fear, the perpetual burden of dread. It was the place, the air, the heat, the smells. The rasp of grass against his clothes and the stinking, sucking mud. Awareness of his surroundings and their potential danger stirring his nerves like a subtle current. He sniffed the air and felt the night like he hadn't in a long time.

Off to his left, he heard splashing, faint as waves on a beach. Butt down, thighs dropping into an automatic crouch, he moved that way, swinging his flashlight in a steady arc in front of him. Left to right. Right to left. Holding it far from his body, in case someone decided to shoot. He was coated with slime to mid-thigh, the mud sucking at his feet like Mother Nature giving a blow job.

A big splash to his left. Switching his light off, he moved toward it. Everything went silent. He stood on the slippery bank, hearing the water lap, the crashing in the grass behind him. Holding his breath and listening the way he'd listened as a nineteen-year-old in the jungle, aurally probing the darkness for the sounds of living bodies. Over the lap of the water and the noises around him, he heard the sound of muffled breath and then, acute as anything, the scent of another man's fear. He turned toward it as Osborne threw himself up the bank and pulled him down into the river, forcing his head into the brackish water.

Osborne was younger, uninjured, and desperate, but Burgess was bigger and madder and he'd spent a lifetime subduing people who didn't want to be restrained. As soon as he got his head above water, he called for help. They were like eels wrestling, and the mud gave them no decent footing, but in the end, it went exactly as he'd envisioned it.

When he finally got his feet under him, he dragged Osborne upright and sank fist after first into the man's soft stomach. The others held back and let it happen. It wasn't a one-sided contest. Somewhere, despite the stockbroker image and the yuppie Saab, Osborne had acquired some street fighting experience, but Burgess had a point to make. He pounded Osborne until there was no more resistance. Then he grabbed him by the elbow and hauled him up the bank.

"Lie down on your stomach and put your hands behind your back," he ordered. Osborne tried to run. There were cops all around, ready to help if they were needed. He grabbed an arm, swept Osborne's feet out, and slammed him down on his stomach. Osborne tried to crawl away.

"Give it up, you dumb fuck," Burgess ordered, planting a knee in the middle of Osborne's back and pushing his face down into the mud. Through his knee and his hand, he felt furious resistance turn to surprise and then to flailing panic as Osborne realized he couldn't breathe. What did the asshole expect, after the trouble he'd given them—warm tea and a snack?

"Hold still," he ordered. "Put your hands behind your back. As soon as I get these cuffs on, I'll let you up." Osborne continued to struggle, trying to turn his body, to kick his captor away. Burgess put a hand on the back of his head and pushed him deeper into the mud, grinding his face down into it. "Listen, asshole. Make it easy on yourself and do what you're told. I said hold still. Understand?"

Then Remy Aucoin was there, grabbing Osborne's arm and forcing it back, while Perry took the other. When Osborne resisted, he got an extra twist on each arm, his groans muffled by the mud. Burgess snapped the cuffs on, tight enough to hurt.

"It's okay. We've got him, Joe," Perry said. He held out a hand.

Burgess grabbed it and hauled himself up, feeling primitive and evil and elated. He'd lost the flashlight during the struggle. Didn't need light to know what a mess he was.

Osborne bared his teeth in a face glistening with mud and tried to spit mud from his mouth. "I didn't hurt him," he said. "The kid. I didn't hurt that kid."

"Hold on." Kyle, in the voice of revival preacher, recited the Miranda warning, his cadences slow, perfect, and elegant, as they stood in a congregation of the righteous, staring at the trash they were removing from Portland's streets. "Do you understand these rights?" he concluded. Custody and interrogation. If Osborne said something useful, they didn't want to lose it. Osborne nodded.

"Didn't hurt him or didn't kill him?" Burgess said.

"I didn't kill that kid."

"What kid?"

"Timmy Watts. I didn't kill him. I never killed

anybody."

"What did you do to him?" Burgess asked. "Use your dog to scare him into getting naked? Take pictures of him? Fuck him in the ass and then kill him because he cried?"

"I didn't kill him." Osborne had finally recognized the mess he was in. "I didn't kill him. I like kids. You've got to believe me. I like kids."

"We already know that, Mr. Osborne." Burgess turned away, disgusted. "Anyone have a clean handkerchief?"

"Why?" Kyle asked, handing him one. "You want to surrender?"

"Surrender? I thought I won." He didn't feel like a winner, only like a grunt during a lull in the battle. He took the cloth, waded into the water, and washed off the worst of the mud. As an act of hygiene, it was fruitless, but at least he could open his eyes and mouth. He staggered up the bank and held out his hand. "Kyle. Radio?" His own was too muddy to bother with. He called Vince. Told him they had Osborne.

As the fact that he was caught sank in, Osborne went crazy, whirling around, trying to kick and head-butt everyone within reach. Kyle slapped a hand on his shoulder. "Give it up, Osborne," he barked. "Calm down." Osborne tried to bite him. "Aucoin, if you've got pepper spray, for God's sake use it before this asshole hurts someone besides himself."

That prompted Osborne to attempt another escape. Unfortunately, his chosen route was right through Kyle, bringing him face to face with Kyle's wrath, Aucoin's pepper spray, Perry's eager fists and a bunch of cops who weren't too happy about a muddy trek through a salt marsh on a sweltering summer night.

Burgess stood aside, wishing he felt a greater sense

of triumph. He wanted this scumbag to be the killer so they could tie this up, Cote could have his press conference, and they could all get some sleep. But he had a cold, empty feeling in his gut, a sense that the Timmy Watts case was still wide open. It was something to give Cote—busting a couple child pornographers, one of them a social worker, would give him days of material for the press—but Burgess feared their troubles were far from over.

It was a bruised and blubbering Jeffrey Osborne who was half-led, half-carried back through the marsh to the waiting police cars. Eight filthy, bloody police officers were photographed in all their muddy, bug-bitten, grass-cut glory—Melia was taking no chances on a police brutality charge. Then Osborne was put in the back of a transport van—no one wanted him and his muddy mess in a patrol car—and they all headed back to 109.

CHAPTER 25

Burgess showered in his clothes, including his shoes, then stripped down and washed the mud off himself. God, the stuff was tenacious. It ought to have cosmetic promise, but when he checked his skin for improvement, he saw only bruises and the ugly stitching on a shoulder that needed mending again. He was too damned tired to bother.

He dressed, put his filthy clothes in a bag, and squished upstairs in wet shoes. He found Vince looking grim and furious. "They lawyered up on us. Won't say a word. You might as well go home. Get some sleep. Maybe a night in jail will wear them down."

Burgess looked at his watch. "It is tomorrow."

"No shit."

"You going home?"

Melia's tight mouth lifted for a second. "I have a home?"

"You do. And a wife. Nice wife. And kids."

"And kids," Melia echoed. "That's why I'm here."

"I'll just write it up, while it's fresh," Burgess said. "Then ride off into the sunrise."

"That's a new one. You know you're bleeding?"

"Just a slow leak. We're running a pool on which happens first—I bleed out or I retire. Betting's fierce."

"Go home, Joe."

He called Chris, filled her in, said he'd be home soon. Then he wrote it up, clumsy fingers slipping on the keys. He collected some stuff from his desk to read over and went home consumed by a nagging sense of unfinished business.

She was waiting in the doorway in that little blue thing she wore, looking sleepy and totally desirable. "Hi, Superman," she said. "You know you're bleeding?"

"Been told."

"I can help."

"You bet," he said. He dropped his papers on the table and himself into a chair, letting her gentle fingers patch him up. She fixed him, soothed him, lit him up. He was too tired to do anything about it but appreciated the sensation of knowing he was still alive.

Just as his head hit the pillow, she said, "I was just wondering. You know how it's your job to be curious about people? Are you ever curious about me?"

"Yeah."

"I know you're beat," she said. "I'll keep it short." Her exhalation was a little like a sigh. "I was married to a doctor once. He came. He went. Did his thing and never let me in on it. He never talked about what he did or how he felt. I was just supposed to be there, smiling and supportive, with dinner ready whenever he came home. He thought he was giving me the good life. I thought he was giving me no life. So I left." That whisper of a sigh again. "Just so you'll know." Her wonderful voice in the darkness, a woman who kept stabbing him in the heart.

"Told you I was going to be bad at this," he said, "but I'm trying."

"You called tonight." She wiggled closer, fitting her body to his. "Try is all I ask."

He slept hard, woke up hurting and alone. Chris had left a note. "Might as well save my vacation for when we can be together. I'm at work. Call me."

"Call me" was underlined. In the tissue-wrapped package beside the note, he found a knee brace. Going through the painful process of dressing, he decided he'd give a lot for a day when some part of him didn't hurt. Maybe this was what growing old was like. Not hoping for pain free days, but simply for less painful ones.

Another gray day with not a breath of air stirring the tired leaves on the tree outside. The thermometer read 89. He poured coffee and scanned the papers he'd brought while he jawed his way through a bowl of granola. Chris was trying to improve his diet, but he didn't have the energy for all this chewing. Food was a means, not an end.

Breakfast. Something he got to eat. Something Timmy Watts never would again. He could picture the skinny limbs, the animated elfin face bent hungrily over a bowl of cereal, bony shoulders hunched against the possibility of a blow or a harsh word. "Goddammit," he shook the papers, his voice loud in the empty kitchen. "Give me something."

Perry and Delinsky's follow-up of sex offenders had netted them a big, fat nothing. The canvass results were only slightly better. A delivery man who left for work at 4:00 a.m. reported passing a small blue car going in the direction of the park on his way out of the neighborhood but he hadn't noticed the driver. A family living near the park might have heard a car door shut. One of Osborne's neighbors had seen a young boy come out of Osborne's house, but the description didn't fit Timmy Watts, and she couldn't be sure what day it was. A whole damned city full of people who didn't notice the world around them. Bad guys counted on that.

At 109, he found Osborne insisting on a polygraph to prove that he hadn't killed Timmy Watts. Burgess wondered if Osborne and his lawyer were unaware of the other charges, assault on a police officer and forcible rape of a minor, or whether those simply paled in the face of a murder charge. Maybe Osborne considered man-boy love part of a normal adult lifestyle, thought if you hit cops and they hit back, the hits canceled each other out.

He looked for Andrea Dwyer. Couldn't find her. Then he put the case file in order, but he was restless, so he went down to the lab. Rocky Jordan was bent over Osborne's computer, unshaven and wearing yesterday's clothes.

"Come for the picture show?" Rocky asked. "Where's the rest of your team?"

"Kyle and Perry? I'll get them."

Rocky shrugged. "Showings every hour on the hour." He fiddled with the keyboard. "This guy was a sick fuck. Knows computers, so he squirreled stuff away pretty good, but I'll find it." He nodded at a stack of photos. "You can start with those. But don't get 'em out of order or I'll kill you, Burgess. And nobody's gonna work *your* homicide. Too afraid your ghost'll show up and say they're doing it wrong."

"When's the last time you slept?" Burgess asked.

"I don't remember." Jordan rubbed his red eyes and tapped the screen. "Like I said, I don't have much yet, but it's coming. Enough to send that guy away a long time."

Burgess went to get the others. Needing to be

moving today, even if he couldn't accomplish anything. Irrationally impatient with waiting for the results of Osborne's poly, which would determine where they went next. As he passed through the lab, Devlin shoved a stack of photos into his hand. "Like I said. The Annie Leibowitz of crime scenes." He shook his head sadly. "No one ever wins prizes for pictures like these. It's a pity."

"You get anything off those clothes?"

"Purplish carpet fibers."

Maybe Jim Taylor had a purple carpet. At his desk, a small blonde woman was pawing through his papers. Burgess dropped a heavy hand on her shoulder. "May I help you?"

She jumped away with a squawk, flushing to the roots of her hair. "Detective Burgess, I had some questions for you."

"I'm busy, Ms. Farrell."

"I can wait." She edged toward the chair.

"Not around here you can't."

She gave him the smile of a woman used to getting what she wanted. "I promise not to touch anything."

"You already have." He gestured toward the door. "Now, if you wouldn't mind..." He walked her to the elevator, impressed with the way she managed a full body sulk, and waited until she got on. Then he returned to his desk, threw everything in a briefcase, and went to find Kyle and Perry.

They were part of the crowd watching Osborne's polygraph on the TV monitor. He saw with satisfaction that Osborne was puffy and bruised and obviously in pain. No doubt his lawyer had had every bruise photographed and detailed and would be howling to the media about police brutality. Osborne had a good lawyer—one of the scumbags' lawyers of choice. Despite the pictures they'd taken last night,

Burgess thought it might not be a bad idea to get all his bruises and stitches photographed as well. Cops learned to live defensively.

He cut Kyle and Perry out of the crowd and herded them downstairs to the lab. "How's it look?" he asked.

"Like he didn't do it," Kyle said. "Shows deception on almost every question except his name, address, and did he kill Timmy Watts." He sounded profoundly disappointed.

Burgess was disappointed but not surprised. His gut had been telling him this all along. Osborne was dirty, a pornographer and a criminal who did sick things to children, but probably hadn't killed Timmy Watts. If the killer was Osborne, it would have made their lives easier. But as Melia was quick to point out, the world wasn't organized to make a police officer's life easier.

"I want you to take some pictures of me," he told Devlin.

"Why? You joining a lonely hearts club?"

He thought of Chris's softness, curled against him in the night. Her generosity and startling honesty. Shook his head. "Wanted to catch these bruises while they're fresh like the other side's doing."

"Sounds like a plan. Take off your shirt."

Dani came in while Wink was taking the pictures and patted Burgess's undamaged shoulder. She looked tired and depressed. Her navy Portland PD jumpsuit was too big and reminded him of his sisters in their snowsuits. He wished he had some news to cheer her up.

When Wink finished, he went on to Rocky, revulsion churning his stomach as the pictures Rocky had pried loose from Osborne's encryption appeared on the screen. Naked male children in sexually provocative poses, often with naked male adults. None of the adult faces were shown. "Just the tip of the iceberg, Joe," Rocky said. "I'm gonna find real bad stuff in here."

It was hard enough dealing with the awful things adult did to each other. But children were so helpless. It made him want to do extremely bad things to the people who collected this trash, traded it, got off on it. He wasn't alone. That was why child molesters had such a hard time in prison. Even the most vicious killers found their crimes revolting.

"Dwyer seen these?" he asked.

"Said she wanted to shoot his fucking dick off. She was looking for you earlier. Something about one of these kids. She recognized a few of the photographs, too. Took a couple, following a hunch."

Burgess, thumbing through the ones Rocky had printed, found several of Timmy Watts sitting naked on the floor, playing with a Power Ranger. Had Osborne thought they wouldn't find these?

"It gives me the creeps thinking about guys like that, going around to parks and playgrounds, snapping pictures of people's kids," Perry said. "Kids getting their diapers changed, kids romping naked on the beach. Little boys peeing in the bushes. Pervert going around taking those pictures and the parents don't notice a thing, while he's probably bringing 'em home and jacking off."

"More like bringing the kids home and doing more than jacking off." Kyle said.

The atmosphere in the room was bleak, the mood ugly. Perry fiddled with the dirty bandage on his head. Kyle drooped on his chair, staring blankly into space. All waiting for Melia to see if he wanted them to stick with the Timmy Watts case or put more time in on Osborne and Taylor.

When Melia came in, his shirt was fresh, his suit was clean, but he looked like he hadn't slept. He dropped into a chair and closed his eyes. "Get this. Osborne and his lawyer actually thought if he passed the poly we'd cut him loose. We need to do Taylor's place. Can one of you..."

Stan hit his buzzer and won that round. The kid. He and Kyle could barely find their hands.

"Where do you want to go with this, Joe?"

"Lotta places," Burgess said. "Talk to Dawn Watts's brother, the guy who threatened Dwayne. See if anyone in that neighborhood knows who The Witch is. Reinterview that kid, McBride, and have a talk with his mother. Talk to the other kids Timmy played with, see if anyone knows who might have given him that ride to see Iris. Keep working on that damned blue car. Find the missing meth. Find the missing Martin brothers."

"Several people in the neighborhood saw Ricky Martin around on Friday. No one knows where he's staying," Perry said. "He and Jason are supposedly living in a trailer somewhere, only no one in the Watts household can recall the address or the phone number." He picked at his bandage. Caught Burgess's eye. "Effin' itch is driving me crazy." He returned to Martin. "You guys read his file? He's one sick puppy. Sounds like he's been trying to screw anything that moves since he was 13. It sucks, you know? Rape a woman, plead it down, you're out on the street before the paperwork's done."

"Think he'd kill his own brother?"

"Half-brother," Kyle said.

Perry shook his head. "His PO said nothing Ricky Martin did would surprise him. Only things that surprised him were letting Martin out for fu—" A quick glance at Melia. "For good behavior, if you can believe it—and that he hasn't been rearrested. And no, his PO has no idea where he is."

"So we see if we can find Martin. Interview Henry Devereau, Dawn Watts's brother, the one who was fighting with Dwayne. Talk to the people who made complaints to social services. Find the woman who was driving the blue car. And pray for a break."

"Sounds about right," Melia said. "Split it up anyway you want. And Joe, can you get together with Dwyer about putting Osborne in a line-up for her kid?" His eyes stayed closed, his voice distant. Another minute and he'd be asleep.

"Will do," Burgess said softly. They waited. Melia's breathing got slower. Slower. He was gone. Quietly, they left the room.

They grabbed an empty interview room and divvied up the work. "We got a bunch of people who contacted social services about Timmy. Most of the neighbors we've talked to, except this Regina McBride. His teacher. Plus a doctor who treated him, thought he was being abused. And his former social worker. And there's Mother Watts's brother."

Kyle took the social worker, the doctor, and the family near the park whose kids had played with Timmy. When he finished Taylor's apartment, Perry would try the teacher and keep looking for the Martin brothers. See the good folks at K-mart. Burgess got Henry Devereau and Regina McBride. When he finished, he'd swing by and visit Julie Gordon.

"You ever connect with Lloyd Watts?" Burgess asked.

Perry nodded. "Total blank. The Martins are slimy but smart. Watts are just slimy."

There was a knock on the door. The team heading out to Taylor's place, looking for Perry. He kicked back his chair and headed for the door.

"Hold on. When shall we three meet again?" Kyle asked.

"When the hurly-burly's done, when the battle's lost and won." Burgess said.

"What the fuck?" Perry said.

Kyle, sprawled in his chair like a long-limbed scarecrow, grinned. "Fair is foul, and foul is fair. Hover through the fog and filthy air."

"It fits, doesn't it?" Burgess agreed.

"You guys are crazy," Perry said.

"You'd remember Shakespeare, too, if the nuns had beaten it into you with a ruler," Kyle said.

"Crazy," Perry repeated.

Burgess pushed back, too, and hauled himself to his feet. He felt crazy. Crazy with impatience and irritation. Crazy to go make something happen. Crazy to find one witch, if not three. And one crime scene. "Stay in touch, okay. Either of you get something, anything, call me."

CHAPTER 26

Charlene Farrell waited outside the door, her blonde cheerleader cuteness wilted by the heat. She followed him to his car, her heels clicking loudly across the brick court and the cement of the parking garage. "Detective Burgess," she said. Rushing had left her breathless and her voice was small and squeaky. "I understand that Jeffrey Osborne's attorney is filing a police brutality complaint against you, stating that you continued to beat his client after the man was handcuffed. Is it true?"

He turned so suddenly she nearly ran right into him. "Is what true?"

"That you hit Osborne after he was in custody and handcuffed?"

"After he was handcuffed, Osborne continued to be violent. He bit and kicked the arresting officers, rammed them with his head, and attempted to escape. What do you think we should have done?"

"But did you hit him?" she repeated, ignoring his question. He reached the car and opened the door. "You really should talk to me," she said. "Tell your side of the story."

"My side of the story is well documented in my reports," he said. "There were several officers involved in the arrest. Now, if you'll excuse me, I have a job to do."

"So do I," she said, refusing to move. "And you're making it very difficult."

Burgess couldn't help smiling. She looked so hot and small and angry, standing there with her pink polished fingernails digging into the silk of her sky blue suit. He didn't envy her cleaning bills. It was bad weather for silk. "Just trying to do my job, Ms. Farrell," he said. "If that means you can't do yours, I'm sorry. Now, if you wouldn't mind, I'd love to close this door. Get the air-conditioning on." He considered himself hard-faced and ugly, but his mother had claimed that he had a disarming smile. Maybe she'd been right. Charlene Farrell stepped back and let him get away. It might have been his smile or that she wanted to try her luck with Terry Kyle, see if Kyle was a softer touch. Kyle brushed her aside like an annoying gnat and didn't even bother to smile.

He decided to take the long ride first, give himself some thinking time, so he headed west to Raymond. The part of 302 he was going to be on was ugly, clotted with motels and strip malls and places catering to the tourists who flocked to the lakes region, but just beyond it, in Naples and Bridgton, was one of the most gorgeous parts of the state. Ranks of soft gray-green hills surrounded sparkling lakes. Today he was so saturated with nastiness and irritation he was tempted to keep driving and lose himself there. He'd done it once. After he'd gone over the desk after Cote and his own department had beaten him senseless, he'd gone directly from the hospital to a camp on one of the lakes.

That time—the Kristin Marks case—he'd given it

his all and had felt righteous about blaming others when the case fell apart. This time, no one was slacking off. They were doing the job; they just couldn't seem to get past an epidemic of know-nothings and a lot of bad luck. Cases went like this sometimes. Or was he fooling himself? Had he let his ego, his certainty he was the right man for the job, get in the way? If Kyle were handling it, or another detective, might things be going differently? Would they have found witnesses, turned up better leads?

It was so damned easy to second guess yourself.

Before he got out of range, he tried to reach Dwyer again. She'd left him a voice mail that she needed to talk about the pictures. He left her a message about the line-up. He wondered what she had? Whether it would be the thing that mattered.

He'd called ahead to the Raymond police. It was courtesy, protocol, and common sense. It would be dumb to miss a chance to learn what a local department might know about a subject. Even dumber to go into a dangerous situation without backup, without someone knowing where he was. They'd said someone would meet him.

The ride wasn't soothing. Too many out-of-state drivers doing their usual dumb things—turning without signaling, jamming themselves into traffic when there were no spaces, riding each other's rear ends like life was a game of bumper cars. Despite the stifling heat, there were joggers along the roadside. He didn't get it. Why drive hours to vacation in a beautiful place, and then go jogging along an ugly road next to bumper-to-bumper traffic? There were plenty of nice side roads, less traveled and more scenic. But then, who was he to understand human behavior? He'd only been dealing with its perversities all his life.

Following his directions, he turned onto a side road and spotted a Blazer with a light bar idled along the verge. He pulled in beside it and rolled down his window. The Raymond officer was middle-aged and one size larger than his uniform. He had a bland, easy-going face. Even in Maine there were differences between the small town cop and the city cop. This guy didn't deal with Asian, Somali, and Sudanese gangs, homeless shelters and SROs full of alcoholics, addicts, the marginally socialized and deinstitutionalized, and motorcycle gangs stabbing each other. Didn't have the burden of it etched into the lines of his face.

"Burgess?" he said. "Chip Lavoie. Chief says I better come along with you. This guy you're going to see's got him some temper and he doesn't have much use for law enforcement." His voice was easy, sarcastic, a man who saw life's irony.

"Sounds like the rest of the family."

"We've met most of them, too," Lavoie said. "Guess they don't get on." He eyed Burgess's Explorer with approval, then pointed up the road. "We go up here, coupla miles, hang a left, then a right, and onto a fire road. Just a track, really. He's down the end of that. Got some pretty mean dogs." He pushed his glasses up his nose. "I gotta warn you, Sergeant. He's as likely to shoot you as ask you in." He paused. "Moody, ya know. Don't know if I'm coming along to give him a second target or to drag your ass back after you're shot."

"Thanks a lot." Lavoie's couple miles were more like five, on a road so humped by frost heaves it felt like five miles on a rumble strip. He was grateful when they finally turned off onto dirt. After that, it was a couple more miles before they finally emerged into a clearing at the edge of a small pond and into a typical Maine dooryard. Car parts, tractor parts, miscellaneous chunks of metal, and a partially cannibalized bus rested among rotting stumps in the uncut grass. Someone had made planters out of hubcaps and hung dispirited geraniums along the sagging porch rail.

The back of his neck prickled as he walked up a dirt path toward the house. The steps were punky, and he picked his way up carefully, trying to step where the supporting boards were. He crossed the porch to the door. There was only a screen. The inside door stood open. He peered into the dark interior as he knocked.

"Whatever you're selling, we don't want it."

"I'm not selling anything," he said.

"Don't need to be saved, neither. And don't leave none of your damned litachur on my porch."

"Detective Burgess. Portland Police. I'm looking for Henry Devereau."

"He ain't here."

"Mr. Devereau, I need to ask some questions about your nephew, Timmy Watts."

"I got nothing to say to no cop." Even here by the lake it was hot and the mildew and garbage stink of the place suggested that Dawn Watts's housekeeping skills were hereditary. Chains rattled, toenails scratched, and two Dobermans appeared, drooling with anticipation as they peered at him through the screen.

Burgess wasn't about to sacrifice any more of his bodily integrity to the extended Watts family. "Listen, Devereau," he called. "We can do this the easy way. You call off your dogs, let me in, we talk. Or we can do this with the SWAT team, smoke grenades, and pepper spray. I've got enough to bring you in. I just wanted to hear your side first."

"You ain't got jackshit."

"Got a bunch of witnesses who heard you threaten Dwayne Martin that if he didn't deliver on his promise by Friday something really bad was going to happen. And something real bad happened."

"I got an alibi."

"For what?"

"For that night."

"What night?"

"Saddaday. The night he was killed."

"I think we better talk," Burgess said. "Timmy wasn't killed on Saturday."

"Fuck off. I got an alibi for whenever it was."

"You'd rather have a bunch of cops busting in and tearing up your place than talking to me for a few minutes?"

"I'd rather you all sucked my dick and choked."

This was going a hell of a lot of nowhere. He was frustrated enough to call in a SWAT team, but this wasn't Portland. It would take interdepartmental cooperation and time he didn't have. Timmy Watts was lying cold and dead in a cooler up in Augusta because nobody in his slug-assed family could be bothered to plan a funeral, and his killer was laughing up his sleeve because the cops couldn't catch him. Burgess jerked the screen door open, stepped aside as the dogs rushed out, then stepped in, shutting the door behind him.

He skirted discarded clothes and junk, reached the end of the hall, where the voice had been, and stepped into a sparsely furnished, yet cluttered living room. A mountainous man in dirty overalls held up by one strap sat on a sofa facing the door, his back to the view of the lake. The rifle in the man's hands was pointed at Burgess's chest.

His heart skipped as it shifted into a different gear, the accelerated beats surging in his brain like an insistent backdrop of drums, his gut suffused with the hot acid rush of adrenaline. "Henry Devereau?"

"Who the fuck else? My house, ain't it?" The weapon didn't move.

"Mind if I sit down?"

Devereau gave a derisive snort. "Ain't no chair that I can see."

He looked around, saw that Devereau was right. "Mind if I stand?"

"Suit yourself."

"What was it that your nephew, Dwayne Martin, was supposed to deliver that he wasn't delivering?"

Devereau's grin revealed a host of missing teeth. "Five cords of wood."

"I don't think so. I think it was methamphetamine that you'd paid for."

Devereau shrugged his massive shoulders, sending his whole torso jiggling. Not a typical meth users body, but not everyone who dealt also used. "Think what you want." The gun dipped slightly but stayed pointed at Burgess.

"You have any kind of a relationship with Timmy Watts?"

"He's my nephew."

"Did you know the boy?"

"I seen him a few times. Once, when Iris come out, she brought him with her. He was a cute kid. Didn't deserve what happened." Devereau had a high, reedy voice, incongruous in his massive body, and wheezed the way morbidly fat people often did.

"You have a relationship with Iris?"

"Is that a crime? Iris is a good kid. She's not like them other thieves and whores."

Devereau had that right. A belligerent, bullying nutcase who used or sold amphetamine and was a doting uncle. It was a strange damned world they lived in. Burgess played a long shot. "I'm worried about Iris," he said. "About how she's handling this. You know she was close to Timmy." He watched Devereau's face, saw the nod, even, despite the man's monstrosity, a kind of shared concern. "When I went to talk with her, there was something she didn't want to tell me. Something she knew that maybe mattered to the case but for some reason, she wouldn't share."

He tried not to look at the gun. Tried to act like he carried on conversations all the time while staring down a rifle barrel. Tried not to let on how much it pissed him off. "I'm afraid that if that secret involves the killer, it could get her killed, too."

Devereau didn't respond, so he continued. "It looks like whoever killed Timmy might have been someone he knew. The night he was killed, Timmy was running away."

"Not as dumb as I thought," Devereau said.

"Somebody killed him, Mr. Devereau. Somebody stabbed him repeatedly with a knife..." Burgess searched for something that would move Devereau away from stubborn and uncooperative. "Timmy might have been going to see Iris. According to her, he'd run away once before and actually reached her. That's a long way for a little boy. He got a ride with someone. She says she doesn't know who. But she knows. Even if that person isn't the killer, he's likely someone Timmy saw that night. One of the last people to see the boy alive. We need to find him. Talk with him."

"You sound like a friggin' TV program. Sheesh, you got everything but the friggin' violins. You know what?" Devereau gestured with the rifle. "Why doncha take a commercial break. Come back later."

Looking back toward the door, Burgess saw that the

floor there was a different color. Darker. As though the center of the room, until recently, had been covered by a carpet and protected from some of the dirt. "What if that person is the killer? What if Iris is protecting a killer for some reason and doesn't even know it? The killer does. You want the same thing to happen to Iris?"

There was no response. Burgess didn't know whether the man was mulling it over in a slow, ponderous mind, or indifferent, or simply couldn't conceive of someone killing Iris. He hadn't seen what the killer had done to Timmy. Maybe Devereau knew the killer wouldn't hurt Iris because he *was* the killer? Timmy would have taken a ride with him. He was family, after all. It wasn't inconceivable that Devereau could have been in the neighborhood or that this man might have done something monstrous.

"Maybe *you* killed him," Burgess suggested. "Killed him to get back at Dwayne Martin. At your sister."

"Wouldn't mind killing my sister. Might, one of these days. She'd be no loss, nor any of those sons of hers. But a kid? Pathetic little kid like that? Why would I?"

"Why would anyone?"

"Preverts," Devereau said. "They're the ones that kill kids." The gun never wavered. There was something Zen in the man's ability to keep his hands calm and still while his voice and mood wandered all over the place.

"And people who lose their tempers. You've got a temper."

"You come all the way from Portland to tell me that?"

"No. I came all the way from Portland to see what you were like. See if you might have done it. Lotta people heard you threaten Dwayne."

"Ain't nobody seen me do nothing to the kid, though. Right?"

It was stifling and the place smelled bad. His knee hurt, and a fly buzzing around his head reminded him of the flies on Timmy's face. He watched the steady hands, the gun, the small eyes sunk in the fat of Devereau's face. "Timmy was a pathetic, abused little eight-year-old who tried to live a normal life and died a horrible death. He was a sweet little boy. The only light in his life was his sister, Iris. Iris is a good kid, too. And maybe, since no one in her family gives a damn, Iris might go the way her brother went. Raped and butchered."

He let it go a beat. "Iris plant those geraniums out there?"

"How'd you know?"

"Looks like a woman's touch."

Devereau nodded. "Yeah. Okay. Look. Maybe I'll talk to Iris. See what's up. I ain't promising. I'm pretty busy these days. But maybe I'll see her."

"Maybe it won't even be too late. But if it is, you can always come to the funeral. Buy her some nice flowers or something. Put one of those hubcaps on her grave."

"Screw you," Devereau said. "You can't mess with my mind. I've spent too much time around cops."

What mind? "Five cords of wood, huh. Doesn't seem worth a screaming match."

"Unless otherwise you gotta cut it yourself," Devereau said.

"I wonder what his story will be?"

"If you ain't heard it yet, you prolly ain't gonna. Dwayne don't love cops no more than I do."

"He's facing an assault with intent to murder a police officer," Burgess said. "He'd rat out anybody. Loves himself best, Dwayne does. So you've got no idea who might have wanted to hurt Timmy? No idea what Iris might be hiding?"

"Not unless it has something to do with her boyfriend. Iris prolly wouldn't want her folks to know about that."

"Boyfriend? You know his name?"

"Nah. She never said."

"Think she'd tell you?"

Devereau's shrug threw off a wave of rancid body odor. "Iris ain't much for confidences. I could ask."

"You do that. Iris tell you anything about this boyfriend?"

"Not really. Sounded like maybe he was older. She mentioned he was a teacher. Least I think that's what she said. He brought her out here once. That time she come with Timmy. When she planted them geraniums."

Burgess felt every pore go on alert. "But you didn't meet him?"

"Nope. He just dropped 'em off over to the edge of the yard there and hightailed it outta here." Devereau shook his head. "Dunno whether he was scart a me, or of them dogs. I never even seen him. Course I wouldn't, bein' in here, would I?" The tiny eyes looked puzzled. "Can't have been much of a boyfriend, though, could he," Devereau said, "leavin' her way the hell over there with all them plants and bags a soil and all."

Obviously, despite Devereau's claim that he'd seen nothing, he'd watched Iris being dropped off. "What was he driving?"

"Small car. Blue. Dark blue," Devereau said.

"You see the driver? You're sure it was a man?"

"No. I ain't sure. Only that Iris said...nope...hold on. It worn't Iris that said. It were Timmy. He said Iris had got a boyfriend, and he'd given them the ride."

"Timmy didn't say his name?"

"Nope. I think he woulda done, only Iris tole him to shuddup." Devereau shrugged. "Timmy always done what Iris said."

"Anything else?" Devereau shook his head. Burgess reached in his pocket for a card, and the gun suddenly became all business. "Just getting you a card with my phone number. So you can call if you learn anything."

"Slow and easy," Devereau said. "Take it out slow and easy and leave it on the kitchen table. And don't come back here. Next time, this gun's liable to go off in your face."

He backed through the door like a commoner leaving the presence of the Queen, and left the card on the table. On a window ledge over the sink, a pair of caged birds were making a racket. Maybe they were another one of Iris's innovations. Devereau seemed like the type to have one use for birds—shoot 'em and eat 'em. When he left, the dogs rushed eagerly past him. Not so much fierce as dumb and dangerous, like their owner. Back at the main road, he got out, leaning against the car, shaking, smelling like the inside of Devereau's house.

Lavoie pulled in behind him and came over, grinning. "You have fun in there?"

He sucked in air, purging his lungs of the stench and quelling the adrenaline surge. It hadn't gone as he'd expected, but it hadn't gone so badly, either, aside from the years it had probably taken off his life. At least he'd learned something.

Lavoie studied him. "You gonna stand there all day? It's effin' hot out here."

"Thanks for the back-up," Burgess said. "Devereau always conduct his interviews with a rifle in his hands?"

"Nah. Sometimes it's a shotgun. Unnerving, ain't

it?"

"You might say that." As he drove back down the corrugated road, an old tourist industry motto came into his head. "Make Vacationland your vocationland." Great idea. Look where it had gotten him.

CHAPTER 27

Next on his list was Regina McBride. He hadn't called ahead. The tone of her letter told him that she was reluctant to get involved. She'd emphasized that everything she knew was in the letter, that the Watts shouldn't know the complaint had come from her, and had requested Human Services not contact her. Despite what she'd said, she probably knew much more. She was observant, lived in the neighborhood, and had cared about the child. He thought the conscience that prompted the letter would keep her from closing the door in his face once he appeared on the step.

By this time, he'd realized that this was the mother of Matty McBride, sometime friend of Ricky Watts, occasional companion of Timmy, the nervous teenager who'd first told them about the confrontation between Dwayne Watts and Henry Devereau. Maybe he'd get lucky and the son would be home, too. Then he could make it a twofer. He'd been meaning to see the boy again. Matty, he recalled, hadn't wanted them talking to his mother.

The McBrides lived on the nice side of the hill,

where the streets slanted toward the Eastern Promenade. Not at the end, where grand old houses faced out to the water, but close enough to have a toe-hold on gentility. He thought about Alan Gordon's comment—that Matty and his mother were snobs with nothing to be snobbish about. Class was a funny thing. Some people didn't give a damn; some gave too many damns.

He knew she was home because he'd used the old phone trick. Called from a pay phone, then hung up when she answered. The way pay phones were disappearing, it was a strategy on its way out. He parked in front, went up the short walk, and rang the bell. No flowers here, but things were very neat. A small mud scraper brush shaped like a hedgehog sat on the bottom step. He rang the bell and waited. Nothing happened, so he rang again. A stolid, patient flatfoot, trying to do his duty.

Finally, he heard the rush of footsteps, the door flew open, and the voice from the phone demanded, "What?"

"Detective Sergeant Burgess, ma'am, Portland Police. I'd like to ask you a few questions about Timmy Watts."

She stood without response, her hand on the doorknob, a colorless, shapeless woman with unhealthy sallow skin, graying hair half-covered by a brown bandana, wearing a carefully ironed tan blouse and a pleated beige and white plaid skirt. He'd never met anyone flattered by beige, and she was no exception. She held a paintbrush in the hand she hadn't used to open the door, the bristles glistening with gray paint. She blinked like a startled rabbit. "What could you possibly want with me?"

He read from her darting eyes and clenched hand on the doorframe how much she wanted to close the door and shut him out. He had one foot inside, now he moved the other in, pressing her back a little. "May I come in?"

"Oh. Of course. Certainly." She closed the door, then took a few steps backward. "But I don't know anything about Timmy Watts. Nothing that might help you."

"You did know him?"

"Oh. Vaguely, I suppose. He was around the neighborhood. My son knew his brother. One of his brothers." She seemed to be trying to reach some kind of decision, maybe whether she could ask him to leave. He needed to move into the house and sit down. Make it harder for her.

"Would you mind if we sat down?" He rubbed his bad knee and gave her an apologetic smile. "It's been a hard couple of days."

"I don't know...I really don't think...things are kind of a mess right now. We're...the living room is...uh. Redecorating." She seized the word and repeated it, looking back over her shoulder into the dim interior. "Redecorating." Then she shook her head, as if that was wrong. "Painting. I've always liked the simplicity of painted floors. I suppose you could sit in the kitchen."

What he could see of the house was spotless. The floor waxed and shiny, the books in the bookcase perfectly aligned.

"I'll just put the brush down." She went to a closed door, opened it, went through, and closed it firmly behind her. A pretty elaborate way of setting down a brush. She struck him as the kind of woman who didn't do anything spontaneously, who had little tolerance for disorder. If her living room was a mess because she was painting, she wouldn't want him to see it.

Her kitchen was probably the most sterile he'd ever seen. There was no clutter, no crumbs. No signs of life. Nothing on the countertops, not even canisters. No teakettle on the stove. No dishes in the drying rack. No potholders or dishtowels or fruit in a bowl. No refrigerator magnets, photographs or notes. She thrust a hand toward an immaculate table with two chairs. Two. Not even a spare for company. "You can sit here," she said.

She pulled out a chair and sat down. There was no offer of coffee, tea, or even water. She simply sat and waited, looking neither pleased nor displeased, though her "what" at the door suggested displeasure. Her broad face was guarded. The expressive equivalent of beige. Her response intrigued him. Most people, faced with a police officer, got nervous. They chattered, fidgeted, tried to find out what was going on.

He pulled out his notebook, slowly opened it, and thumbed through the pages. Letting her cook. Finally she pulled in a deep breath. "Why me?" she said.

"You wrote a letter to Human Services."

"You're here because of that?" He nodded. "That was months ago. What does that have to do with anything now?" She touched her hand to her lips, as though her words had gotten away, defying her intent to stay silent.

"We're talking to people in the neighborhood who knew Timmy. Who took an interest in him. Trying to build a picture of his life."

"This really isn't Timmy's neighborhood. He lived on the other side of the hill."

So she was a snob. "You have a son named Matty?" he asked.

Her shoulders stiffened, and she planted both hands on the edge of the table, as though preparing to stand. A little color crept into her cheeks. Cold as ice, but protective of her son. "Matthew," she said. "What's that got to do with anything?"

Such a charming woman. So eager to help. So moved by the poor child's death. Some people spun in such narrow orbits. "I understand he used to spend time with Timmy."

"Months ago," she said, vehemently, shaking her head. "Not any more. That family was too much trouble. I told him to stay away from Timmy. Matthew is good with kids. He was trying to play big brother. But that Watts family is poison. Unimaginable filth and squalor. I didn't want him around them."

Not what her son had told him, was it? But boys Matty's age didn't tell their mothers much about what they did. Especially rigid, protective mothers like this. If Matty occasionally spent time with Timmy Watts, he probably didn't tell his mother. Burgess tried to tap into the reservoir of feeling that had led to the letter. "When you wrote to Human Services, you were concerned about a lack of supervision. What was the basis for that concern, Ms. McBride?"

"I should think it was obvious," she said. "The child was allowed to wander the neighborhood at all hours of the day and night. Occasionally he'd be over here at dinnertime, and when I'd try to send him home, he'd say there was no dinner at home and beg to stay. Often, it wasn't convenient. I'm a simple cook and I usually prepare only enough for the two of us. Matthew had homework, of course, and I had things to do. We couldn't have a small child underfoot."

She cleared her throat, a thoughtful expression on her face. Not like she was remembering a small, needy child, there was no softness there, or sorrow. She looked like she was evaluating what she'd just said. "A child without supervision grows up to be an undisciplined adult," she said. "And there are risks to children who are allowed to wander unsupervised. Bad influences, predatory adults, temptations."

"What was Timmy like?"

"He was a little boy, Detective. Unformed."

"I meant was he noisy and active? Quiet and withdrawn? Did he make conversation with adults? Could he play on his own or did he need constant attention? That sort of thing."

"Of course he could play on his own. He'd learned to rely on his own resources because his family paid him so little attention." She twisted the plain gold band she wore and then looked at the clock. "He liked those—what do you call them?—those Power Ranger toys. Matthew bought him some. He was very fond of Timmy." She seemed to choke on the words. "I think he identified with Timmy in some ways, with Timmy coming from such a violent home. His own father...Matthew's father...was violent."

"I understand there were many families in the neighborhood who used to look after Timmy. Do you know who they were?"

"I'm afraid I can't help you. As I said, we don't live in that neighborhood, and I'm not home in the daytime anyway." She must have sensed his confusion because she added, "I work at an accounting firm. I'm on vacation this week."

"But your son used to socialize with Ricky Watts, didn't he?"

She looked at Burgess like he'd tracked something nasty into her kitchen. "Matthew was younger then. He was attracted to Ricky's freedom. When he recognized the lack of discipline, and the criminal behavior accompanying it, he terminated the friendship."

"At your insistence?"

She hesitated. "Yes."

"I understand that on one occasion, you called on Mrs. Watts in an attempt to discuss her childrearing practices?"

"I've never seen anything like that place, Detective. The thought of a child growing up in that house..."

"That was when you wrote the letter?" She nodded. "Did you get a response?"

"You've seen the letter," she said primly. "I asked them not to contact me."

"Why?"

The tan shoulders rose and fell. "I didn't want to get involved. The family had a reputation. They're violent and uncivilized, as I'm sure you know. I didn't know how they'd react if they thought I'd reported them. I feared some kind of retaliation."

"Was there any?"

"They didn't seem to care."

"Getting back to Timmy. You don't know which families looked after him?"

"I'm afraid not."

"What sorts of things did he and Matty used to do together?"

"Watch TV. Play computer games. Matthew runs a computer class for elementary school students. Timmy was too young for it, but Matthew was teaching him some things. Sometimes, if I was home..." She checked the clock again. "I'm sorry I can't be more helpful." She pushed back from the table and stood. "I'm afraid you'll have to leave. I've got to start dinner soon and I need to run to the store first."

Burgess didn't budge. "How often would you say Timmy visited here?"

"I really couldn't say." She had pulled open the refrigerator and was checking her supplies. The inside was immaculately clean and nearly empty. It didn't look like the refrigerator in a house with a teenager.

"Once or twice? Four or five times? More than that?"

"More than that."

"So tell me more about him. What did he talk about? How did he act? Did he talk about his friends? Activities? Were there special places that he liked to go? Did he have a secret hide-out, a club house, a particular playground that he liked?"

"You'd have to ask Matthew. I really didn't pay attention."

As soon as the words were out, she froze. "No. No, that's not a good idea. I don't know what possessed me to say that. Matthew is so horribly upset already. I don't think talking to you would be good for him. Not so soon after what's happened. He's an unusually sensitive boy."

Burgess went to the window and looked down into the yard. A small but nice yard, big enough for catch or soccer passing. "Timmy like to play in the yard?"

"I didn't allow him out there. They went to the park." There was another hesitation. She sucked in air like someone struggling for oxygen. "You are not getting it, Detective," she said, "so I'll just have to be blunt. Timmy Watts wasn't wanted here. He was a vulgar child, a dirty little chatterbox with a rude vocabulary and no manners. My son liked the pathetic little wretch, so I tolerated the occasional visit. But I didn't try to make him feel welcome. Now, if you'll excuse me." She headed for the door.

It was so far from what he'd expected. True, her letter had been stiff and formal, but he'd attributed that to the nature of the communication—an attempt to convey the seriousness of the situation. He'd never expected this hard coldness. It hurt to think that, even if he'd been oblivious—and most children know when they're unwanted—Timmy Watts had played innocently here under her baleful gaze. Had played near, chatted at, even begged dinner from someone who thoroughly despised him.

On his way down the hall, he opened the door to the unavailable living room. Heard her gasp behind him as he stared in. It was, as she'd said, being redone. All the furniture was stacked in one end, the rest of the floor a gleaming dark gray. "Such a mess," she said. "I'm trying to get the floor done but in this heat it goes so slowly."

He understood too well about trying to work in heat like this. Wondered that anyone would bother to undertake such a project now. But she struck him as a person who did whatever was on her list, regardless of comfort or convenience. Or aesthetics. The living room had a lovely hardwood floor. It seemed a crime to paint it gray. But maybe women who chose beige also had an affinity for gray.

She stood beside the door, grim and stolid as a prison matron, waiting for him to leave. "I will need to speak with your son again," he said. "When would be a good time?"

"He's very busy this summer, working at Libby Insurance, doing data entry." There was another of her curious pauses, as if she'd once again said something she regretted. "You've already spoken with Matthew?"

"On Saturday. He described an altercation he'd witnessed outside the Watts's house."

She fingered the buttons on her blouse as she stared out toward the street. "I'm sure he's told you all he can. As I said, he's very upset by all this. Matthew is a sensitive boy who takes things very hard. He'd wanted to take Timmy to a movie that night. I was trying to discourage that association, so I wouldn't let him. I insisted that Matthew come out to dinner with me. It's my vacation, and we don't get to spend much time together. Then we came home and played Scrabble. He thinks if I'd let him take Timmy out, this never would have happened. I really wish you wouldn't remind him."

Her fingers worked the row of buttons like a rosary. "Please leave him alone. He doesn't need this right now."

"What movie?" he asked.

A button came off in her hand, leaving the blouse gaping over her breasts. She stared down at herself and gave another huffing sigh. Our lady of perpetual sighs. He imagined her son's life punctuated by those sighs. He imagined a closet somewhere in the sterile house holding a row of neatly ironed tan blouses. "I don't know. Some superheroes thing?"

"Where did you go for dinner?"

She looked at him coldly, her nose wrinkling like he was a piece of rotten meat. "Detective, we are not the suspects here. If we've done anything wrong, it was ever allowing that child in the house. Now you'll have to excuse me," she said. "I've got to go and change." She fixed him with a fierce gaze, her hands planted on her hips. Her blouse gaped, but there was nothing tantalizing about it. Even in the summer heat, she wore an undershirt.

When he didn't move, she said, "Detective, once again, I'm going to have to be blunt. It shouldn't be necessary, but I see that subtlety doesn't work with you people. I want you to stay away from my son. As I said, this has been very hard for him. I'm afraid it has brought back some terrible things from his own childhood that I hoped he had left behind."

She stepped back into the gloom of the hall and lowered her head, suddenly unwilling to look at him.

"Matthew was..." Her voice dropped. "His father..." Her thick throat worked as she forced the words out. "Matthew was sexually abused by his father when he was about Timmy's age. This awful business forces him to remember things he's been trying to forget. It would be unconscionably cruel for you to exacerbate that."

She shut the door with a click, leaving Burgess standing on a doorstep that gave off the pungent odor of pine-scented cleaner, puzzling about a woman so parsimonious with words and emotion, who'd managed to get both unconscionable and exacerbate into the same sentence. After a moment, he bent his reluctant knee and went down the steps. Like it or not, he was going to be talking with her son, even if it did exacerbate the boy's pain. Because the death of Timmy Watts was also unconscionable.

CHAPTER 28

He'd just gotten in the car when his phone rang. Stan Perry, reporting in. "We got a lot of stuff at Taylor's, Joe, but it doesn't look like our crime scene. But hey, you wanted to know about someone called "The Witch," right? Well, a woman named Julie Gordon just called and gave us a name. I got a location."

"And?"

"Her name's Valerie Lowe, sometime girlfriend of Jason Watts. And she's got a prior for cooking methamphetamine."

Time to hit the road again. The Witch was one of the last people reported to have seen Timmy Watts alive. Burgess wrote down the address. "Kyle with you?" he asked.

"I think he's 10-7. Deputy came by with some legal papers. Kyle went ballistic and stormed out. I haven't been able to raise him since."

"I'll swing by his place, see if he's there. We'll meet you."

He drove too fast through streets that were unusually quiet, his heart sinking when he saw Kyle's car. He parked and hurried up the stairs, banging on the door until he heard stumbling footsteps. "Who is it?" Kyle said.

"It's Burgess. Open the goddamned door."

Stripped to his shorts, Kyle looked like a concentration camp survivor. He held up a nearly full bottle of Jack Daniels. "Caught me before I could do much damage," he said.

"What happened?"

Kyle grabbed a paper off the counter and thrust it at him.

"Got this today." It was a petition to the court for leave to move Kyle's daughters out of state.

"You call your lawyer?"

"He's on vacation until next Monday. His associate doesn't know her ass from a hole in the ground, and the hearing's this Friday. Not to put too fine a point on it, Joe, I'm fucked."

"You can't spit in this state without hitting a lawyer," Burgess said. "We'll find somebody. Now get dressed. We've got places to go and meth chemists to see and no time for getting drunk."

Kyle hugged the bottle protectively against his chest. "You go see people," he said. "You go places. Take Stan the Man, he's dying to take names and bust heads. I'm staying here and getting pissed."

"The woman called The Witch. One with the blue car. Last person anyone saw with Timmy Watts? Her name's Valerie Lowe. And she's got a prior for cooking meth."

Kyle set his bottle on the counter, checking that the top was tight. "Sheesh," he said. "Guess I'd hate to miss this. I'll just get my gun."

"Clothes would be good," Burgess said.

The address was in Westbrook, way out near the Windham line. If he was following protocol, Stan would have notified the Westbrook police of their visit. Depending on what Stan had said, a Westbrook officer might or might not be there to meet them.

"Want me to drive?" Kyle asked, "given your shoulder and all?"

"You've been drinking."

"Not so's you'd notice."

"You can drive home, okay?"

"Why does it take three of us?"

"Probably doesn't," Burgess grunted. "But if I took you, Stan would feel left out, and if I went with Stan, you'd feel left out."

"Before I burned out my brain on alcohol, I used have this thing called instinct. What little is left says you expect to find more than a witness."

"This woman is Jason Martin's girlfriend. According to one witness, she was driving a blue car and talking to Timmy Watts the night he died. People we talk to keep coming back to a blue car. And if she and Jason are any way connected to the meth that was found in Timmy's room, by morning, they will have cleared out."

"Why?"

"Because the department has a leak. The papers know we found meth in Timmy Watts's room and that it disappeared from evidence control. It's going to be broadcast at some point. I'm betting on tomorrow's papers."

"How?" Kyle asked. "Who?"

"Charlene Farrell's the reporter. As for the leak, your guess is as good as mine."

"I need more than one guess?"

Burgess shook his head. "Plus, this is supposedly the residence of one Ricky Martin, career rapist and general bad actor. I'd say we need at least as many players on our team as they have on theirs."

Another day gone, another night coming on. The whole week one hot, humid blur. Darkness brought the fog back, giving lights, structures, and vegetation a surreal quality, as though they were driving through an alien landscape, not on roads they'd traveled hundreds of times. The occasional streetlights loomed like hazy balloons. They passed one of Burgess's favorite signs, "Vanity Pool" and he entertained himself imagining who might be hired from the Vanity Pool, and what they might be good for. Arm candy, maybe? Trophy wives? Maybe even trophy husbands. Maybe he could be a trophy husband. Kept by some woman who wanted him only for his looks and for sex. It had to be easier than this.

Squinting into the fog, he took a right, then his first left. It was supposed to be about four miles. Stan hadn't said, probably hadn't known, that the last two miles were on a pocked and pitted stretch of misery that knocked the hell out of his knee and wounded shoulder and nearly shook his teeth loose. By the time they pulled in behind Stan's car, he was thinking he should have stayed home and sent the kids. But deep down, he felt something significant was about to happen.

Kyle switched off the dome light. Then, quietly opening their doors, they stepped out into the thick, warm night. Burgess checked his gear, heard rustling as Kyle did the same. They walked to Stan's car and got into the back seat. Stan and another man were waiting.

"Officer Ted Bean," the man said, thrusting a hand back. "Westbrook PD."

"Joe Burgess," he said. "Terry Kyle. What have we got, Stan?"

"One blue Dodge Acclaim. One black Toyota pickup. It's not a house; it's a trailer. Not a double-wide. Good sized, rust-blistered piece of shit. Looks like the door opens into the living room, kitchen to the right, bedrooms to the left. I couldn't see in. Lights are on but the shades are down. Someone's been playing the same Indigo Girls song about a million times. There's a dog house but I didn't see a dog. Typical Martin setup. Yard's full of crap. Place smells like a litter box. How you wanna do this?"

"You check the registrations?"

"Yeah. Car's registered to her, Valerie Lowe. Truck belongs to Jason Martin."

"There a back door?"

"Yeah."

"You and Bean take that. Terry and I'll take the front. All I want to do is talk to her. Depending on what she says, what I see, we'll go from there."

"Let's do it," Stan said, opening his door.

"Hold on," Burgess said. "Place that smells like ammonia? Could be they dump their litter box out the door. Could be they're cooking meth. So, anything goes down, don't run in, okay? Let them run to you."

"Where's the fun in that?"

"Someone told you this job was fun?"

"It was on the recruiting poster. I get to serve and protect and have all the hot little honeys who get wet at the sight of a uniform."

"You're a pig, Stan."

"The honey in there," Bean said, "is neither hot nor wet, except maybe in what's left of her cranked up little brain. You see her, you'll understand why they call her The Witch. You go in there, Sergeant, be careful you don't turn your back on her. She's real squirrelly. One of our guys was out a couple weeks ago to serve an eviction notice on 'em...they don't own the place, just rent...and she damned near took his eye out."

"Thanks for the warning. Had any other trouble with them?"

"He shot at a couple hunters, back last fall. I had to come out and talk to him."

"How'd he react?"

"He was real apologetic. Claimed one of them shot first, too close to the house."

"You wearing a vest, Bean?"

"Yes, sir."

"You seen the younger brother, Ricky, around?"

"The rapist? He was living here. Haven't seen him lately. Heard he and Jason had a fight."

The four of them approached the trailer, Perry and Bean slipping around to the back, Burgess and Kyle going to the door. "You want me to come in?" Kyle whispered.

Burgess considered. She might talk to one police officer, if he approached her right, but not to two. "Stay outside, I think, but stay close, okay?"

"Right. I'll just stand here and feed the mosquitoes."

It wasn't a facetious observation. Since they'd left the car, mosquitoes the size of piper cubs had been circling, their whines so loud in the quiet night it surprised him someone from inside hadn't stuck a head out to see what was going on. Perhaps there had been a dog and it had been sucked dry. He pulled bug spray from his pocket and gave it to Kyle.

"Bet you used to be a Boy Scout," Kyle whispered.

Burgess walked to the door, standing to one side as he raised a fist and knocked. He could hear music inside and someone singing off-key. Loud and badly off-key. No one answered. He knocked again. Something crashed. The music was turned down and a raspy voice called, "Who is it?"

"Detective Burgess. Portland Police."

"This ain't Portland."

"Valerie Lowe?" he asked. "I wanted to ask a few questions about Timmy Watts."

"Go away," she said. "It's late. Come back tomorrow."

"I've driven all the way out here in the fog," he said. "It won't take long." She went back to singing. He knocked again. "Please, Ms. Lowe. Open the door."

"I don't have to," she said. "You can't make me."

"I'm not here to give you a hard time," he said. "Just to ask some questions about the boy. About when you last saw him? I was hoping you'd know where he was headed."

"That's all?" There was a crash as something got knocked over. "You just wanna know about Timmy?"

"That's right."

"Hold on."

He heard the snap of locks. The door opened the width of the chain and a woman peered out. "How do I know you're a cop?" she asked.

He pulled out his badge and held it where she could read it. "Joseph Burgess," she said. "Sergeant. No tricks, okay? I know my rights."

They all knew their rights. "No tricks."

"Hold on." She closed the door. He heard her fumbling with the chain, and it opened. She waved a hand toward the room behind her. "Might as well come in. And hurry it up, will ya? Those damned mosquitoes get in here, they'll be at me all night."

The light was poor, but even in a dim room, he could see where she got her nickname. She was gaunt to the point of emaciation, leaving her fleshless face nothing but nose and chin and jutting cheekbones. She wore loose cut-offs, short enough to show a flaccid slice of ass and a tube top. Instead of being sexy, it was pathetic. He could have counted every rib, and what remained of her breasts were two slack sacks under the shiny yellow fabric. Her long, black hair was matted and dull. She prowled restlessly around the room, picking things up and setting them down. Twice, before he asked his first question, she picked up a pack of Camels, shook one out, then shoved it back in the pack.

Finally, she perched opposite him on the arm of the sofa, a lighter in her hand, and focused on him. Her pupils were gigantic, her head rocking like a bobblehead doll. "So?"

"Friday night. The night he was killed. You were driving through the neighborhood and you stopped to talk to Timmy. Can you tell me about that?"

She tugged her top up and her shorts down, worked a finger into her ear and studied it carefully, and then looked back at him. "How do you know?"

"One of the neighbors saw you. Do you remember what time that was?"

She shook her head. "My watch broke. Coupla, two weeks ago."

"Do you remember seeing Timmy on Friday?"

"It was down near the park?"

"I wasn't there, Ms. Lowe," he said. "You were. You tell me."

"Down near the park. I was on my way out here. I saw Timmy, so I stopped to say hi. He was a cute little kid, wasn't he?"

"Do you remember what he was wearing?"

Her hands scrabbled across her chest like a pair of agitated spiders. "Shirt with these blue and red guys on it. Action guys. You know. Shorts. He had his backpack." She went to the cigarettes again. Shook one out. Raised the lighter. Lowered it again. Her nail polish was electric blue. "Mind if I put on some music?"

"It's your house," he said.

"Oh. Yeah. Right." She crossed to a stereo and pressed a button. The same song he'd heard from outside came on again. "I just love this song, don't you?" She began swaying.

"You remember anything about your conversation with Timmy?"

"Conversation?" She squinted up her eyes and peered at him. "Oh. You mean what did we talk about?" He nodded. "I asked where he was going, 'cuz of the backpack, you know. Like you said, making conversation. He said he was running away from home. So I asked him why, still just kidding like, because I didn't really think he was. I mean, you know. Kid that young, like where would he go, right?"

"What did he say?"

She held up a hand, signaling for him to wait. Crossed the room and pressed the button. The song began again. The room was dusty. A coffee table was littered with old pizza boxes and Oreo packets, beer bottles, soda bottles, and empty chip bags. A couple dusty terminals, monitors and printers were stacked in a corner. Instead of answering, she began to dance, swaying slowly to the music. Burgess realized that she must have been very pretty once and still thought she was. That her dance was a kind of seduction.

"What did Timmy say?" he repeated.

"Timmy?"

"When you talked with him on Friday. When he told you he was running away."

She looked toward the closed kitchen door. "Goddammit!" she said. "That bastard won't let me smoke in the house. How can I go outside when every goddamned mosquito in the state's waiting out there to suck my blood?"

Something was making his eyes sting, his throat

hurt. Starting a dull ache in his head. He tried again. "Friday. When you met him. Did Timmy say where he was going?"

"Oh, yeah. Right," she said brightly, giving him a smile showing bad teeth and receding gums. "Timmy." Burgess watched her agitated fingers turning the lighter over and over. "He said Dwayne was going to kill him. That don't surprise me. Dwayne's a bastard at the best of times." She picked up the cigarettes again.

"You want to smoke," he said, "we could go sit in my car."

"You think I'm stupid?" she said. "I ain't getting in no cop car."

He didn't think she was stupid. He knew she was. "Timmy," he repeated. "He say where he was going?"

She half turned away, looking back over her shoulder, an incongruous sultry look on her ravaged face. "What'll you give me if I tell you?"

He shrugged, playing along. She was making him work damned hard for one sentence. Kyle was probably bled out by now, Perry and Bean mere desiccated husks. "What do you want?"

The blue-tipped fingers flew to her waist, working at the button on her shorts. "I could use a good fuck."

Some piece of work, wasn't she? He was feeling sicker by the minute, wondering why it didn't affect her. Maybe if you lived in a fetid, airless place long enough, you got used to it. A man's voice called through the door, "Valerie? You talking to someone?"

"Oh, yeah, honey," she said, dropping her hands. "Portland cop's here. Came to ask about Timmy."

"Well, give him what he wants and tell him to get the fuck out."

"Who's that?" Burgess asked.

She looked surprised. "Jason, of course." It seemed

Jason Martin had inherited the family's social graces.

"Ricky's not here?"

She shook her head. "Ricky and me had sex a few times. Jason got mad about it and threw him out."

"When was that?"

She squinted in concentration. "Week ago, maybe? I forget."

"You know where he's living now?"

She giggled. "Some abandoned warehouse? Rooming house? But he's got plans. Gonna make some money and get a nice place. Maybe I'll move in with him."

"Val," the voice roared from the other room. "I told you to get rid of him."

Valerie Lowe did up the button with a sad look at Burgess's crotch. "Another time, I guess. You gotta go. What was it you wanted to know?"

"You were driving through the neighborhood," he said, forcing himself to speak slowly. "You saw Timmy coming down the street with a backpack. You stopped to talk with him and he said he was running away from home because he was afraid of Dwayne. Did he tell you where he was going?"

"Oh." Her face brightened. "Oh yeah. He told me where he was going."

"And where was that?"

She opened her mouth to answer. Got distracted by a stream of curses from the next room. "Ms. Lowe? Where was he going?"

She scratched her head and tipped it to one side, considering. "He said...he said...Jeez. I don't know what's wrong with my head today. I remembered it a minute ago." She fiddled with the lighter again. "Wait. I got it." A louder curse from the next room. "Yeah. He was going to go—"

The kitchen door burst open, a slightly smaller

version of Dwayne Martin looming there. "Get the hell out," he yelled. "Get the hell out."

Burgess grabbed the door handle and jerked it open, letting a rush of fresh air into the room.

"Stay with Iris," Valerie Lowe said, obliviously. "I asked him how he was going to get there. Did he need a ride? He said no, he'd get there the same way he did last time." She smiled at Jason Martin and flicked the lighter. Burgess threw himself through the door as the air around her erupted in a ball of flame.

CHAPTER 29

Even with his eyes shut, he could see the vivid red of the flames against the total black of the night. And no one can shut his ears. Valerie Lowe's screams would be seared in his brain forever. He'd used the last of his strength keeping Kyle from rushing in to save her. Only seconds after he'd dragged Kyle to the edge of the clearing and slammed him to the ground, the trailer exploded. Jason Martin hadn't stopped for her, either; he'd only saved himself. Maybe not even that. He was in intensive care.

A bad night all around. Everyone was scratched and bruised. Bean, the Westbrook cop, was nearly scalped by a piece of flying metal. They'd kept Burgess in the hospital overnight, giving him oxygen, because of his exposure to toxic chemicals. A typical, sleepless hospital night. Whenever he'd drifted off, they'd woken him to do something officiously medical. So he was alive, but he was beat, his head was pounding, and everything hurt. Waiting for the docs to say he could leave, impatience made him surly and explosive.

The papers had had a field day with the missing

amphetamine followed by the clandestine lab explosion. The Maine DEA agent sitting by his bed wasn't helping. "It was too fuckin' stupid for words, Detective," had been his first sentence. The ones following no more complimentary. "Going out there, risking four lives, without a shred of protective gear or clothing. Don't you know anything about meth labs?"

"Maybe you guys been doing training courses I just happened to miss?" he countered. "I do now. Know plenty." His throat had been scoured with sandpaper. "Next time I go into a house smells like cat piss, I'll back right out and call you, even if the owner's a geriatric with a dozen cats. Same goes for kerosene, gasoline, any other sene or lene. Hell, you're so smart, maybe I'll let you do all my jobs. You've got a real way with people."

"You shoulda called me this time."

"How? Using my psychic friend?" He looked for water. No pitcher. No glass. No nothing. He pushed the call button. "You're so smart, how come you didn't find it?"

"We were closing in. We woulda got 'em, if you hadn't blown things sky high."

"I didn't blow it. She did. Martin told her not to smoke, and she deliberately flicked her Bic. She knew what she was doing. She used to cook the stuff. Or she was so wired she didn't give a damn."

He wanted Chris, his own private-duty nurse. But judging from the phone call in which he'd dutifully reported his latest physical fiasco, Chris was as pissed at him as Agent Hamlin. He based this on her sigh, her silence, and the cryptic comment, "I don't know how much more of this I can take. If I wanted a nurse-patient relationship, I could date a geriatric." She wasn't likely to show up to dispense kindness and mercy.

He supposed, were their positions reversed, he'd feel the same way. No one takes well to a series of phone calls reporting physical and psychic damage to a loved one. He'd probably be worse. After a lifetime trying to serve and protect, he'd want to lock her up in Rapunzel's tower. All she wanted was for him to stay in one piece.

"Valerie Lowe was a tweaker and a moron," Hamlin said.

"You think I didn't know that?" Burgess felt so sick he could barely lift his head. He closed his eyes, wishing the asshole would leave. There was stuff to be done. He had no energy to waste on a pissing contest about something that was over and done. Even if it was hot news. Even if a woman was dead and it was Maine's first lab explosion. MDEA, in the person of one Jesse Hamlin, might be steamed and posturing, but none of that helped his case. He'd sat in Hamlin's chair, done undercover, knew what the man was about. He wasn't so sure Hamlin understood him. Burgess's business was with whoever killed Timmy Watts. "You here because you want something or just to see if you can make a bad day worse?"

Hamlin, in his miserable, pissy way, was enjoying himself. "You've got an attitude problem, you know that?"

Fuck his attitude. His throat felt like he'd swallowed a red-hot poker and it had gotten stuck. He was ready to kill for a glass of water, and his head was about to explode. He wanted to carry it to the sink and stick it under a tap with ice cold water. He rang for a third time, ready to request euthanasia. "So I've got an attitude problem. That and a couple bucks'll get you a Starbucks coffee."

"I can come back when you're feeling better."

"You come back here, you won't find me. I've got a killer to catch."

Hamlin shook his head. "That's not happening."

"You think I won't find him?" Burgess pushed himself up, glaring at the agent.

"I don't think they'll let you. If they let you work at all, you'll be counting paper clips or sharpening the Chief's pencils. Something nice and safe you can't screw up."

"What're you talking about? I'm the primary on a homicide."

"Were the primary. *Were."* Hamlin sounded as though Burgess's downfall gave him great pleasure. "By now, you'll have been taken off the case."

Hamlin must be jerking his chain. If it were true, Melia would have told him. He valued their relationship too much to let Burgess learn it from someone else. But Cote believed in power and control. Cote might use that power to decide that the potential taint of the missing drugs, plus the taint of an excessive force complaint, combined with his disabled condition, made him unfit to handle the case. A cop was never innocent until proven guilty but guilty until proven innocent. That's why they needed unions.

He needed to call Melia and find out what the story was. And couldn't—no, wouldn't—do it while this smug prick was sitting here yammering at him.

Hamlin talked on, nipping and snapping like a small mean dog. Burgess ignored him. When the nurse finally arrived, he opened his eyes and smiled. "Be an angel, would you, and get me some water and something for this headache?"

"You already have..." She looked for the pitcher and glass, found neither, and frowned as she checked his chart. "I'm sorry, Detective," she said. "I'll be right back."

She closed the door just as Hamlin was saying, "...spent six freakin' months undercover working on this, Burgess. Six months lying and cheating my way into their hearts, getting in place, getting connected and in one night you blunder into the middle of it and send the whole works sky high."

He didn't know whether to laugh or cry. "You knew about this?"

"Sure."

"You knew the cookers were the Martin brothers?" Hamlin nodded. "You read the papers, right, Hamlin, so you must have known the dead boy was Jason and Ricky Martin's brother?"

"So?"

"I thought you said you were a cop?" Why waste time on this when talking hurt so much? "It never crossed your mind that when someone gets killed, cops talk to the family? That we were bound to show up there and ask some questions?"

"Never thought you'd blow the place up."

"I didn't..." Burgess began, then changed tack. "You knew that trailer was a ticking bomb?" Hamlin was silent. "Knew or suspected. You tell the local cops what was going on, in case one of them accidentally walked in there, like one did a couple weeks ago serving an eviction notice? If he'd been blown sky high, would you have considered him stupid and interfering with your investigation? Or is that just me?"

"We don't go around warning people," Hamlin said. "That's not how it works. That's what undercover's all about. Secret."

"I know. One clandestine group going after another. You guys are playing cops and robbers while I try to protect the public from both of you."

"Oh, stuff it, Burgess. You've worked undercover.

You know how it is."

"I know," Burgess agreed. "But do you?"

The nurse came back with his water, poured him a glass, and gave him a small cup with medication. "Chris is outside," she said. "You want to see her?"

From her tone, he deduced Chris was not in a state of sweetness and light. "Sure," he said.

Chris came no closer than the foot of the bed, squaring off with her hands on her hips, ignoring Hamlin. "I don't know which of us is the bigger ass," she said.

"I've got the bigger ass," he said.

She almost smiled. "That's not what I meant."

"What did you mean?" Days when he longed for conversation, everyone was silent; days like this, when he longed for silence, everyone wanted to talk. Life was all about timing, wasn't it?

"You don't know?"

"Please," he said. "I don't know if I could feel worse, but a game of twenty questions just might do it. You want to yell at me, go ahead, but don't make me guess why you're so mad. It's not like I did this because I enjoy getting poisoned and blown ass over teakettle."

"I'm not talking about this." She waved a hand dismissively. "Seems like you get bashed all to hell just about daily."

He hadn't had so much as a scratch in months. "If you're not complaining because I make you worry, what's the problem?" His voice was a whisper dragged over gravel.

"You really don't know?"

"I'm a hell of a detective, but I don't read minds."

"Terry told Michelle you quit the case."

That brought him off the pillow with a roar they

must have heard at headquarters. "He said what?" Her hand flew to her chest in such a perfect imitation of an affronted dowager he would have laughed if her statement hadn't been so outrageous. If laughing didn't hurt so much. "Come on, Chris, you know better. I don't quit."

Her hands dropped to her sides and she stared at him, tears filling her eyes. "I didn't want to believe it, Joe, but Terry said..." Her shoulders rose and fell. "I couldn't imagine you abandoning that little boy. That's not like you. But Terry said..."

"You talk with Terry?" She shook her head. "So you don't know what Terry said, only what Michelle said. It's like some goddamned game of gossip."

What—had he thought her visit would make him feel better? Some days, he couldn't win. And he knew winning was important. Burgess was captain of the team that played for the dead. If they lost, the bad guys won. It made him a very bad loser. "I haven't heard I'm off the case." He jerked his chin toward Hamlin. "He says I am."

Chris turned her sharp eyes on Hamlin, settling her hands back on her hips. She wasn't a big woman, but she had an imposing physical presence. And she'd spent enough time with death and tragedy that she didn't mince words. "Why would you want him off the case? You know he's the best. Everyone knows he's the best."

Hamlin shrugged. "Not my call."

"Who are you, anyway?" she demanded. "What are you doing here?"

"MDEA, ma'am," he said. "Debriefing the detective about last night."

"Do you mind waiting outside? I need to do a little debriefing myself."

"Excuse me, ma'am," he said, "but I was here first."

Burgess loved the way her back stiffened and her head came up. "Suit yourself," she said. "Just don't get in my way." She went out to the hall, returning with a small suitcase and a stack of paperwork. "They're letting you go, but only because I promised you'd get skilled nursing care. If you don't mind my saying so, you do look a bit the worse for wear." She peeled down the covers, looking with dismay at his swollen knee, bandaged shoulder, the masses of bruises and abrasions. "I try to believe that love conquers all, but sometimes you challenge my beliefs."

"Never runs smooth," he agreed.

"Be quiet," she said. "I'm figuring out how to dress you without hurting you."

"You're a nurse. You're used to hurting people."

"You're so kind, Joe."

"Try to be." He shot a glance at Hamlin. "When I'm not blowing people up."

"Don't even joke about it. It must have been terrible."

"It was."

She had him up, dressed, and heading toward the door when Melia arrived, clean-shaven, shoes shined, tie knotted perfectly, looking like hell and wearing his bad news face.

Burgess let him get through the preliminaries, delivered a succinct assessment of his condition, and waited. He could have made it easier, but he didn't feel much like being a good sport if he was being booted off the team.

Finally, Melia said, "Got some bad news, Joe. Cote's taken you off the case."

They were standing about four feet apart, close enough for Burgess to see the tic in Melia's eye he got when he was exhausted. Burgess watched it twitch. "What are the terms? Am I suspended? Driving a desk? Banished to Siberia? Do I need a lawyer?" Melia didn't answer. "Is he actually accusing me of taking that meth? Does he seriously believe I used excessive force on Osborne? You know the meth thing's bullshit, and I had half-a-dozen witnesses with Osborne."

"He wants you to take a couple days of sick leave, so technically, you're not suspended. Yet. Kyle's replacing you. Paul was very clear that he doesn't want you bothering them. What he does about the meth, I can't say, but I don't think he's got any grounds to accuse you. Same with Osborne." Melia shrugged. "It wouldn't hurt to talk to a lawyer."

So he still had his badge and his gun. As for not talking with Kyle and Perry, far as he knew, Cote hadn't repealed the First Amendment.

"You going to be okay with this?"

This from the guy who'd made him cancel his vacation to take the case. "No, I'm not going to be okay with this. This isn't about deference to rank, or obedience, or protecting the integrity of the police department. This is about a pitifully neglected and vulnerable little boy who was raped and slaughtered. You saw it. Cote speaks for the department, but who speaks for Timmy Watts?"

What the hell? Why not say what he was thinking? It was no secret how he felt. "Cote's a miserable excuse for a man at the best of times, but this is truly disgraceful. I'm ashamed to be a member of a department that puts personal animosity before the interests of that child." Hubris or not, dammit, it was how he felt.

There was something else at stake here that mattered terribly. His honor. His reputation. He didn't mind having a reputation as fierce and zealous, even mean if it represented dedication to his job. He'd given his life to this department. All he asked in return was the chance to do his job with dignity and honor. Being taken off an investigation after his name was linked with missing drugs and excessive force charges tarnished him. Even if he was never formally accused, let alone charged with anything, the damage would be done.

"You know what he's doing to me, Vince. He could stop right here, never take it a step farther, and I'd still be damaged goods. I can't sit still for that."

Melia met his eyes, too honest to back away from the truth, but he didn't speak. There was nothing to say.

Burgess felt his self-control unraveling. He grabbed the bed rail, as though by squeezing tightly enough, he could force his anger back down. "Dammit, Vince. This isn't the time to take me off the case. We can break it. *Are* breaking it. We just need time. I don't need to tell you, we don't find this guy and he thinks he's gotten away with it, Timmy Watts will only be the first."

Finally saying aloud what he'd sensed from the moment they unwrapped the body—that a blood lust had been kindled which would, with time, rekindle. A child killer was loose in his city and they were telling him to stay out of it. He thought they asked too much.

"Kyle and Perry know everything you know, Joe? You're not holding back?"

Insult to fucking injury. Like he was some grandstander looking to be a media hero? He wasn't going to dignify that insult with an answer. He released the bed rail and let his anger take him.

"I'm going home, Vince. I'm sick. Sick of trying to do a job no one gives a damn about. Little piece of welfare trash like Timmy Watts doesn't really matter, does he? There's always another. You're the one who dragged me into this, remember? You can't ask me to take it on, ask me to change my plans, Chris's plans, because I'm the only guy who can do this, then tell me to take it off, like Timmy Watts's murder is no more than a tee-shirt. Like I've got nothing invested in this. Next time you get a dead kid, Vince, call somebody else."

Melia looked like he'd been struck. Burgess didn't care. Standing in a hospital in the middle of a summer Monday, going through the motions of a normal person, he was falling down into a black pit. All the rage and despair he'd been holding off since he'd gotten Melia's call about a dead child was sucking him down into the place inhabited by the spirits of the dead. Their small, keening voices rose to meet him as he fell.

Burgess nodded at Chris and they walked out the door.

CHAPTER 30

"It's a chance to get some down time," she said uncertainly, starting the car.

"Why would I want some down time?" He tried not to act as mean and vile as he felt, knowing it wasn't her he was mad at. She looked tired. Maybe she hadn't slept, worrying about him. She had wonderful balance, but she was a serious person. His immersion in this case, their canceled vacation, and his distance had to make her wonder if being involved with him made sense.

"You looked in a mirror lately?" she said.

"I rarely look in mirrors. You haven't noticed?"

"So you're going to be a rotten prick, even to me?"

He tried a couple of those BS calming breaths, but they only hurt his lungs. "Chris, I'll try. But I think…I know…the next couple days'll be bad. I'm gonna be a rotten prick even to me." Regardless of what he'd said to Melia, he was no more ready to quit this case than to tap dance naked down Cumberland Avenue. Not while the inside of his head was papered with pictures of Timmy Watts's body.

"That Cote. I'd like to stick an ice pick in that

bastard's ear," she said. "Pith him like a frog and stop his moronic meddling once and for all. I can't believe he's doing this to you."

"He's been living for this moment for years."

"Well, it would be hard for anyone to deal with what you did, especially when everyone knows he deserved it."

"I'd do it again."

"Maybe that's why he's locked you out."

"He's locked me out because he's too short-sighted and stuck on himself to recognize this is about a dead kid. It's because he's locked me out that I feel like doing it. Look, let's not talk about it, okay. The more I think about him, the madder I get."

That was putting a mild gloss on it. He could smell the brimstone stink of his anger. Probably she could, too. She was wise about people, wise about him. It was better that he was going home and not to the station. He wanted to pound someone so badly if he got close to Cote, the man would be chopped liver before he could purse his duck's ass mouth.

"It's only going to go downhill from here. I feel like I've bought a one-way ticket on a fast train to hell and the doors won't open."

"It's really going to be that bad?"

"Bad enough so you probably don't want to be around me."

She stared out over the steering wheel. "You want me to leave?"

"I don't *want* you to leave. I'm thinking maybe you should. For your sake."

"For my sake?"

"All right. For my sake. I'm not sure I want you seeing me like I'm going to be."

"Becoming your father?"

He reached out and put a hand over hers. Despite the heat, her hand was cold. "I'd never hit you. You know that. But I might..."

"Get drunk? Say bad words? Act crazy? Break things?"

"Yes." He didn't tell her how much, in the blackest times, he could come to love his gun. He didn't want to scare her. It was a cop's job to handle things.

She nodded thoughtfully as she whipped her little Subaru wagon around a corner like she was driving a BMW. "Joe," she said. Hesitant. "Can I ask you something?"

"Go ahead."

"You know that little teapot in the kitchen. The dumpy little clay one you think is so ugly? When you start breaking things, would you please leave it alone?"

With just a sentence, she'd sneaked under his armor and stabbed him in the heart. "You don't deserve this," he said.

"Neither do you." She snapped on her blinker and zipped in front of a van. The driver laid on the horn and Chris flipped him the bird. "Guess you're not the only one in a bad mood," she said. She pulled into the driveway, stopping so abruptly she made his brain slosh. As crazy behind the wheel as Stan Perry. "Honey, we're home."

He waited for the pain to subside. She came around and opened his door. "Whenever you're ready," she said. "I'll be upstairs, running you a bath."

"I don't want..."

"Do I tell you how to be a cop?"

"Not usually. But don't I recall, little while ago, someone was about to read me the riot act for quitting a case."

"Oh, that. You wouldn't like me half so much if I

weren't passionate about things. Admit it. And don't try to tell me how to be a nurse." She walked away, let herself in, closed the door behind her. He sat and stared at the closed door. God, how his mother would have loved Chris.

She got him out of his clothes and into the tub, then out of the tub, redid the bandage on his shoulder, and got him into bed. He settled back against the pillows and closed his eyes, reveling in the clean, cool sheets and the air-conditioned comfort, in the idea that he could actually lie here and rest, holding the reason he was able to do these things at arm's length like a difficult collar. Keep it away and control it. He heard her walk out of the room and then come back. She cleared her throat. "May I have your attention, please?"

He opened his eyes. She stood at the foot of the bed, an overnight bag slung over her shoulder, clutching her little teapot. "You've been a solitary creature for a long time," she said. "If you think you need to be alone, I have to respect that, so I'm going back to my place. I only ask this—that you'll call and let me know what's going on. I don't want to read important things about you, or this case, in the newspaper. Understood?" He nodded. "One more thing."

"Ma'am?"

"Don't you ma'am me, Joe Burgess. I can see right through smarmy cop bullshit. One more thing—" He waited. "If you need me, I'll come. You want to talk, I'm there. If you ignore me, you do so at your peril."

"Are you threatening a police officer?"

"You bet your ass I am."

"I never bet my ass. It's the only one I've got."

"You big jerk." She came and kissed him then, and, as usually happened when she got that close, he wanted her to stay. In the end, that was how they'd be able to tell if he was dead. It wouldn't be heartbeat or brain activity. It would be bring her close and see if he responded. If he didn't, he was dead. She paused at the door. "Leave 'em hungry for more, that's my motto. The door's unlocked, in case your buddies stop by." She left him with only the humming air conditioner for company.

He'd meant to think about the case, but his eyelids were heavy and his body, now that he wasn't sharing his room with a yippy MDEA agent, craved sleep. It was better than smashing things.

They came to him, Shakespeare's wicked dreams. Hand-in-hand, like Hansel and Gretel, two young children with expectant faces and hopeful eyes walked into his room and stood at the foot of his bed, as Chris had done. They didn't need speech.

He'd spent his life speaking for the dead, the battered, the terrified; he knew how to imagine for them what they couldn't, or wouldn't, say. How to tell their stories. Not so different from Missy Steinberg, the ASL interpreter. She spoke for Iris. He spoke for Timmy. For Kristin Marks.

The Watts family wasn't the sort to take home videos, so he'd never had the chance to see Timmy alive, but now his imagination, using all the bits and pieces people had given him, animated those stiff, skinny limbs and breathed life into that small butchered body. Timmy didn't so much walk as skip, a head-long dash through the houses and his neighborhood, blond hair flying, singing to himself. Timmy, sitting on the Gordon's steps, intently playing with Power Rangers. Timmy in Grace Johnston's living room, perched on a soft blue afghan, having tea. Curled up beside Darlene Packer listening to a story. Dancing giddily through his own house, merry as a demented pixie, until Dwayne's big fist knocked him down, showing a stubborn courage and optimism in the face of a life that had too often made him cringe.

Then the dream changed. Instead of Kristin Marks, Timmy Watts had a new companion. Timmy and Neddy Mallett were racing across the grass on the Eastern Promenade toward the playground, flying hair and churning limbs, voices raised in excited competition. They reached the playground and began swarming around on the equipment, climbing and swinging, calling to each other for admiration of each new feat, each height achieved, each structure mastered. Even deep in a dream, he felt an awful sense of foreboding. Someone else was watching the boys. A long, dark shadow ran across the sunlit grass, piercing the fenced area where the boys played.

From his strange dream vantage-point in midair, Burgess watched Timmy Watts see the shadow and began making the high, keening sound he, himself, had been hearing since he first stood in the park and looked at the body. It went on and on, rising and falling like a siren. Gradually, it permeated his stupor that it was his phone. He reached out and pulled it to his ear, grunting a faint, "Hello?" as he pawed through the sticky cobwebs of sleep.

There were a few seconds of quick breathing, a small sigh, and the line went dead. He looked at the clock, stunned to find he'd slept six hours. He was getting soft. No cop in the midst of a case like this took more than minimum time to sleep. But then, according to his bosses, he wasn't in the midst of this, was he?

He shaved and dressed, stood at the counter eating the remnants of steak cold, feeling like an ancient, wounded carnivore as he tore into it. He put the dishes in the sink and went to the window. While he was sleeping, his Explorer had come back. He limped down stairs. Someone had put his keys through the mail slot. Anything to keep him from showing up at the station, where he might also want to pick up papers, or his messages, or his mail. Where he might talk to someone about the case. The hot hall smelled of fried peppers and onions, his downstairs tenants' staple foods.

He went back upstairs, poured a glass of water, and sat at the kitchen table, feeling like Methuselah's father, trying to remember what Valerie Lowe had said just before she flicked the lighter. Something about where Timmy was going. He rubbed his head, as though he could massage the memory back into being. Chris's standard remedy, when she forgot something, was to wait a minute and it would be back. He sure hoped so.

He skipped along to the next thing on his mind. The images from his dream. Burgess didn't exactly believe in the prophetic power of dreams. He was a concrete guy. A concrete guy steeped in all the mysticism of the Catholic church. So what the hell was Neddy Mallet doing in his dream with Timmy Watts? As far as he knew, they'd never met, never played together. No one had ever linked them in anything they'd said to him. Yet he felt that Neddy was in danger. Was it simply that Neddy was another parentless boy in that part of the city?

He got out his notebook and found the number. Then remembered that he'd already put Andrea Dwyer on the case, and she'd been trying to reach him. They'd played phone tag all day before the great debacle. He started to dial her number, then reconsidered. If he called her at work, he ran the risk of being told not to talk with her. Better if he found another way. He dialed the Munjoy community center, asked if Dwyer was around.

"She was here a minute ago. I'll check. Can I tell her who's calling?"

"Tell her it's a secret admirer."

"She's got plenty of those," the woman said, sounding both jealous and approving. "Secret and not so secret. I'll check."

Eventually the phone was fumbled and a voice said, "Officer Dwyer."

"Joe Burgess," he said. "Unless you've been warned not to talk to me."

"I've been staying away from anyone who might do that," she said. "You'd think they didn't want this guy found. Unless maybe Cote did it himself?"

"Pardon the language," Burgess said, "but he hasn't got the balls."

"Breaks my heart to think the PC police have gotten to you, Joe."

"PC police, hell. My mother's responsible for how I talk around a lady."

"Really? Melinda Beck says you're blunt as a drill instructor."

He wasn't going there. "You ever catch up with Nina Mallett?"

"I did my best," she said. "She wasn't talking."

"I'm worried about the little boy. Neddy."

"You and me both," she said. "I don't see this as an isolated thing, do you?"

"No. Melia talk to you about a photo line-up of Osborne with your witness?"

"Did it this morning. Kid picked him without hesitation. Damn, that felt good."

One predator off the street? It did feel good. "Rocky said you took some of Osborne's pictures?"

"Yeah. A couple kids looked familiar. I wanted to

show them to Delinsky, get a second opinion. Then I took a few of some older kids. Pin-up photos. Playing a hunch. I was gonna show them to Nina Mallett, but she didn't let me get that far. She's one tough kid for thirteen. Shut me down and showed me the door."

The missing thought fell into place. "Iris Martin," he said.

"Iris Martin?" she echoed, puzzled.

"Just something I was trying to remember. So you struck out with Nina, huh?"

"You might give it a whirl. She thinks you're pretty cool."

"For an old guy."

"So? I think you're pretty cool for an old guy, too."

"You think Nina's mystery guy might have been in Osborne's photo collection?"

"Don't you? Like I said, it's only a hunch, but I was thinking..."

"...that the guy she was talking to was interested in Neddy, not Nina," he finished.

"Your gut says that, too?" Someone must have interrupted her, because she said, abruptly, "Look, I gotta go. I'll leave those pictures here at the desk, in case you get a chance to talk to Nina. And if I turn up anything, I'll call, okay?"

He weighed his options. Visit Iris Martin. Pick up those photos and go see Nina Mallett. Have that talk with Matty McBride. Iris topped the list. Maybe he could make her understand how important her information might be. He worked his way through a couple of vague people before finally reaching Missy Steinberg. He explained what he wanted and asked if he could arrange another meeting with Iris.

"She isn't here," Missy said.

"Has she gone home?"

The silence was so long he wondered if he'd been

cut off. Finally she said, "I don't know, Detective. When I came in this morning, her housemother told me she'd left. She left no note or information. We don't even know how she left, whether someone came to get her, or what. I'm sorry. I wish I could be more help. I guess you'll have to try her family."

He immediately thought of Henry Devereau, who occasionally picked up Iris for a visit. If Devereau was involved in this, had his interview stirred something up? Might Iris be at risk? He tried the Watts number. No one answered so he decided to go over there. Once he was out, he might as well knock off a few other interviews. He tried Libby Insurance, where the receptionist told him Matt McBride wasn't available. She was unwilling to offer any further information. Then he tried Mary Turner and got no answer. While he was asleep, a lot of people had disappeared.

Then, though he missed the other two, the one musketeer buckled on his sword and reluctantly left the comfort of the apartment. A full six hours of sleep didn't seem to have made much difference. Maybe it was projection, but just as last night when he felt hurried and solitary, the city had felt empty, today, when he felt slow and sluggish, the city moved at his pace again.

At every intersection, there were inexplicable delays, as though everyone's synapses had rusted or atrophied in the thick air. By the time he pulled up in front of the community center, his impatience was back and had him moving at a brisker pace. He asked the receptionist if Andrea Dwyer had left him something.

She eyeballed him critically. "You the secret admirer?"

"Yeah."

"She's too young for you."

"Just an admirer," he said, feeling unreasonably defensive. "She's a great cop."

"All right then." The woman searched under the counter, came up empty-handed. "She had it in her hand. I could swear she left it right here, but there's nothing. She must have taken it with her." His frustration must have shown, because she made an apologetic gesture. "Sorry. If I see Andrea, I'll tell her you were looking for it."

He got back in the car, his jittery sense that the day was going wrong ratcheted up another notch. He didn't think it was just frustration from being out of the loop. It was Iris Martin's disappearance. An itchy sense that more bad things were going to happen.

After an extensive period of banging, Pap Watts finally opened the door, stared at him blankly, uttered an indifferent "Yeah?"

"Detective Burgess. Portland Police. I was wondering if Iris was here?"

"Iris don't live here," Pap said. "She's at that special school."

"She didn't come home this morning?"

The man looked back over his shoulder as though he might have missed something. "I ain't seen her," he said finally. "And I been home all day."

Burgess tried to restrain his impatience and aim his words at the level of Pap's slow mind. "She left the school early this morning without telling anyone where she was going. You have any idea where she might be?"

Watts considered the question, a process so ponderous Burgess could almost see the gray matter working beneath the small, balding skull. After a while Watts shook his head. "Nope. She usta visit my wife's asshole brother sometimes. Dunno if she still does."

"Henry Devereau?" Watts nodded. "You got a phone number?"

"Dunno the asshole's number, if he got one. Not that Iris could use it anyways." Watts turned away, signaling the conversation was over, then turned back with an ugly smile. "Maybe she got herself a boyfriend. Went to lose her cherry. Be about time."

He started to close the door. "Wait," Burgess said. "Ricky Martin. Any idea where I might find him?"

Watts shrugged. "He don't live here. He was out staying with Jason, but they had words over that bitch girlfriend of his. Last I heard he was in one of them rooming houses."

"Does he have a car?"

"Maybe. He was driving a little piece of shit Jap car. Dunno if he still is." He grinned. "Prolly not registered or nothing."

"What color?"

"Dunno. Blue, maybe? You see Iris, tell her I hope she liked it. Time that girl got a taste for cock." He shut the door, leaving Burgess standing, sickened, on the garbage-filled porch.

CHAPTER 31

Julie Gordon waited by his car with her boys, holding a large shoebox. She looked at him shyly and lowered her eyes. "Detective, I...I thought you might want this." She offered the box.

"What is it?" he asked.

It was the bigger boy who answered. "It's Timmy's treasure box. Where my mom kept all the stuff he gave her. He was always giving her stuff."

He took the box and tucked it under his arm. "Thanks for remembering," he said.

"That's all I think about. Timmy," she said. "Come on, boys." Shooing her boys before her, she hurried away.

He was unlocking the door when a cruiser, lights flashing, came flying down the street, and rocked to a stop beside him. Delinsky leaned out. "Got a minute, Sarge?"

Burgess didn't know if he had a minute. He had places to go, people to see. He also had things he wanted to take Delinsky to task for. Some suggestions concerning sharper observational skills, like the change of social workers. The mean stuff he was famous for. But Delinsky's lights were on. This was clearly not the time.

"What's up?"

"Kids out playing found a rolled-up carpet with what looks like bloodstains on it."

"Where?"

Delinsky told him. Burgess knew the place. They'd found a body there once, years back. Guy killed his girlfriend, ran down the alley, and shot himself. He wanted to see that carpet, but it was an official police call. It was one thing to talk to people in his free time. Another to answer a call like he was actively working the case. His own distinction. Cote wouldn't see the difference. Delinsky waited impatiently, poised to go.

"I'm on sick leave today."

Delinsky's chin jutted toward the Watts house as he struggled between sympathy and kicking a guy while he was down. Resentment won out. Burgess had worked him hard, then made him feel bad about stuff he'd missed. "Well, you've found the perfect place to recuperate." He gunned the engine and was gone.

Burgess watched him skid through the corner, remembering, with a touch of regret, how much fun it had been to drive around in a cruiser with the siren going and the lights on. The rush of excitement, the Grand Prix feeling of racing through intersections. No one ever said it, but license to drive like a madman was part of the fun of being a street cop. He had no resentment toward Delinsky. It took time to make a good cop. When you were young, the older guys rode you hard for a reason—to make you a better cop. Their riding chafed and caused resentment at times, and someday you might look back and see the good it had done.

What he did resent was his exile. He wanted to see that carpet, the color, the stain pattern. To collect fibers and see if they matched up with what they already knew. He wanted to toss ideas around with Kyle and Perry. He didn't know what was happening. They could have arrested a suspect by now, gotten a confession. Cote could be talking to the press, gloating over the fact that the case got solved while Burgess was stuck out in the cold. In the heat. In the hellish summer heat and more hellish limbo of the information void.

He had a choice about where to go next. Check out Henry Devereau or pay a visit to Libby Insurance and look for Matt McBride. Devereau's place was a hike, so he let weariness decide. Then he checked his messages, disappointed but unsurprised to find there was nothing from Kyle or Perry. They were probably checking out the carpet. There *was* a message from the nurse at the hospital. If he still wanted to talk with Anna Pederson, she could have visitors. And Libby Insurance was on the way.

Libby Insurance had a second floor office in a building fronting on Congress Street. The door was old-fashioned, half-glass, with the company name in gold letters. He liked the sturdy, unchanged feeling of it, even though the hot corridor smelled of age and cigarettes. He walked into a carpeted area with a receptionist's desk surrounded by waved glass partitions. The woman at the desk had short hair an improbable shade of magenta and ears so full of piercings they looked tattered. She eyed him warily as she tapped on the glass-shielded desktop with a long black nail.

"Can I help you?" The words ran together in an almost unintelligible stream.

He showed his badge. "I'm looking for Matthew McBride?"

She shook her head, pleased to be unable to help.

"Not in today."

"He call? Say he wasn't coming in?"

She shrugged. "Not while I was here. Maybe he told someone else?"

"Can you check please? See if he did tell someone else?"

She shrugged dismissively. "I don't know who I'd..." She'd perfected the unhelpful answer that was supposed to send him away. Burgess didn't move. "Oh. All right," she sighed. "Hold on." She picked up the phone, punched in some numbers. "Yeah, Sheila. Got a cop out here looking for Matt. Did he...Matt, I mean...tell anybody he wasn't coming in today?" She listened, cradled the phone, and fiddled with papers on her desk.

Burgess waited. The girl was no Mensa candidate. Finally he said, "So?"

"So, nothing. Sheila says Matt didn't call."

"Is he normally a good employee? Usually comes to work?"

"Oh. Yeah." She rolled her eyes. "Matt loves to work. He's one of them gook types, comes in early and leaves late." The black nails danced on the desktop. "Geek, I mean." A few more taps as her eyes widened. "Jeez. He didn't, like, get killed or anything? I never knew anybody who got killed. Personally, I mean. There was this cousin of my mother's."

"You know if he has a car?" he asked.

"Sometimes has his mom's car," she said. "Not always. It's fuckin' beige. Beige and square. He offered me a ride home once, but hey...he's just a kid and who'd wanna be seen in a car like that?"

Spoiled little bitch. In his youth, any car was a treat. You had a car, you could go parking. He thanked her for her time and left. He called dispatch and asked if they could check on vehicles registered to a Regina or

Matthew McBride and gave the address. By the time he'd remembered he was on leave, it was too late. He'd already asked. Screw it. He headed toward the hospital.

He parked in his usual spot and went up to Anna Pederson's floor, sketching a wave at Charlie as he passed. The nurse behind the desk recognized him with a smile. "So you got my message. She's much better today."

Burgess followed her into a double room where a frail, white-haired woman lay surrounded by equipment. The woman looked up at him with bright blue eyes, didn't recognize him, and looked at her nurse. "Anna, this is the police officer I told you about."

"Investigating about little Timmy?" Her voice was little more than a whisper.

"Yes, ma'am," Burgess said. "Officer Delinsky, who lives in the neighborhood, says you are very observant."

"At my age there's not much to do besides sit and watch. I sit out on my porch." She paused. "Most people have been staying in, you know, because of the heat, but I enjoy it. It warms my bones." She plucked at her dry wrinkled skin. "Get more like a lizard every year."

"I'm hoping you were out there last Friday night," Burgess said.

The bright eyes shifted to the nurse. "When did they bring me here?"

"Saturday morning, Anna," the nurse said.

"So I was at home on Friday." Her thin fingers grabbed at the sheet and crumpled it between them. "I wasn't feeling very well."

"Anything you could tell us about Timmy would be helpful," he said. "Julie Gordon says he left her place around 4:00, and another neighbor saw him on Mrs. Johnston's porch around 5:30. He was wearing a backpack, and he told a woman named Valerie Lowe that he was running away from home."

"Not much of a home to run away from," Mrs. Pederson said. "This Valerie Lowe. What kind of car does she drive?"

"Small blue Dodge."

The old woman nodded, her fingers touching her forehead apologetically. "Sorry, officer. I'm afraid my mind isn't what it used to be." Her thin fingers massaged the wrinkled, papery skin as though conjuring thoughts from some deep place. "Valerie Lowe. Then that was the first blue car."

"There was a second blue car?"

"Oh, yes."

"Can you tell me anything about it? Did you know the driver? Was it a man or a woman?" He tried to hold back, but the questions came bursting out. The nurse gave him a warning look.

"It's all right," Anna Pederson said. "He wants to catch the person who did this, and so do I. It was bigger, the second blue car, a little darker and not so beaten up. And the driver was a man."

"Have you seen the car before?"

She nodded. "I believe so."

"Tell me what you saw on Friday night."

"Well, little Timmy was walking down the street—poor thing, with that great pack on he looked like he was about to fall over—and the second blue car came along. It stopped. Timmy walked over and spoke with the driver. Then he went around and got in on the passenger side and the car drove away."

"You're certain you saw him get in the car?" She nodded. "And it was a different blue car?" A nod. "Could you see whether the driver old or young?"

Anna Pederson smiled. "Officer, you look young to me."

He stifled an impulse to kiss her. "You can do better than that," he said.

"Younger than you."

"Might you recognize a picture?"

"I might. I doubt it, though."

"But you'd recognize the car?"

She nodded. "I might. Not too good with cars, mind you, but I've seen it before, parked near the Watts's house. Once, when I was riding with my daughter, I saw Iris get out, but the driver stayed in the car."

"Dark blue? Light blue?"

She considered. "I'd say medium."

"Would you recognize Ricky Martin?"

"I don't know," she said. "There's so many of those boys. Guess I'd recognize whether it was a Martin or not. Beyond that, I couldn't say."

"Did the driver look like one of the Martins?"

She considered his question. "He wasn't dark enough. All the Martin boys are dark."

"Do you know who Henry Devereau is? Big man? Mother Watts's brother?"

"I've seen him at the house."

"Could he have been the man in the car?"

She looked doubtful. "When I've seen him, he's in a truck. Often, he stands in the street yelling, but sometimes he talks to one of the boys. I always assumed he was buying drugs, but I don't know. Other people came there to buy drugs, too. I assume they came to buy drugs. The Watts weren't much for visiting." She shook her head, thin white dandelion wisps of hair against the white pillow. Her voice was faint and her eyelids drooped. "I don't think it was Devereau. He's too big. Too dark."

"Do you remember anything else about Timmy and the car?"

She opened her eyes again, squeezing her chin thoughtfully. "Timmy seemed to be expecting the car. He was looking up and down the street, then waved when he saw it."

He had to find Iris Martin. Whether she knew it or not, she possessed vital information. He smiled at Anna Pederson and touched her hand. "Thank you so much for your help."

"I hope it is help," she said. "I'd hate to have someone get away with a terrible crime like this. The rest of 'em, I wouldn't give you a nickel for the lot, but Timmy was a good little boy. He used to help me out sometimes. And he loved my cat."

He followed the nurse out, got back in the elevator, and went to his car. Terry Kyle was leaning against it, his tie undone, his shirt soaked through with sweat. He straightened when he saw Burgess coming. His thin face was so pale he no longer looked like death warmed over but death out walking. Sweat ran freely from his drenched, spiky hair. "Thought they threw you out of this place," he said. "Can't stay away?"

"Never could stay away from a good crime."

"There's such a thing as a good crime?"

"Challenging crime," he amended. "What keeps us in business."

Kyle gave up banter, falling silent so suddenly someone might have flicked a switch, and stared at him with red, exhausted eyes underscored with circles deep as bruises. "Help me, Joe. I need a lawyer. That associate couldn't get a continuance and she's hopeless. Put her up against Wanda's lawyer and it's bye-bye kids."

"What about Don Longley?"

Kyle looked like he'd bitten into something rancid.

Longley was an extremely talented defense lawyer, a thorn in all their sides. He attracted rats as readily as the Pied Piper and had a good record for putting those rats back on the street. He also regularly chewed up police officers on the stand and spat out their gnawed bones.

"He's vicious, never pulls punches, and is tenacious as a pit bull. And he does domestic relations," Burgess said. "He's more than a match for anything Wanda the PMS Queen and her viper of an attorney can throw."

"I just hate the thought of giving him even one cent of an honest police officer's wages."

"Then I'll pay him," Burgess offered. "Rumor has it I'm not an honest police officer. I'm a brutal drug thief with bad judgment. And I'm rich as Croesus."

Kyle uttered a three word sentence which, when the expletives were deleted, consisted of the word "that" and held out his hand. "Give me your phone."

Burgess gave him the phone, then fired up the engine, turning the air up high. Kyle's face was like a silent movie, the strain, the waiting, the nervous look as he explained his situation, the gradual spread of relief as the skin stretched taut over the bones relaxed into something almost peaceful. Kyle nodded a few times, disconnected, and got in the car. "He can see me now. Can you give me a ride?"

"I'll trade you."

Kyle leaned back against the upholstery and closed his eyes, sucking up the cold like a human sponge. His body took on an almost boneless look as he went limp. "What for what?"

"Transportation for information about the piece of carpet."

"I'd stake a thousand bucks it's connected, based on the blood stains and the color."

"Purplish gray?"

"You got it."

"Where's your ride? And Stan?"

"Stan's upstairs, waiting to see if Jason Martin will make some dying declaration. Martin told the nurses he had something for the cops. They called the station, but none of those fuckin' geniuses made the connection to our case. Hope it's not too late."

Burgess shrugged. "Maybe he wants to rat out one of his brothers?"

"Or sisters. Or parents. I just hope he rats out someone. We're all too damned beat to keep this up much longer." Kyle adjusted the vents so they were blowing straight at him. "Man, that's good. What about you? This don't look like home or sick."

"Oh, I'm sick," Burgess said. "And I've spent enough time here, it might as well be home. I was visiting an elderly lady named Anna Pederson, neighbor of the Watts, a lady who sits out on her porch a lot and watches what's going on. She saw Timmy Watts get into a blue car the night he died. A second blue car that came along after Valerie Lowe left. A car Timmy was expecting. Now all we have to do is find the driver."

He brought his car to a rocking halt. "Which connects to something else. Last thing Valerie Lowe said was that Timmy was on his way to see his sister Iris. I asked how he planned on getting there. She said the same way he did last time. When I interviewed her, Iris Martin said she didn't know how Timmy'd gotten there." He shrugged. "I didn't believe her. And now Iris Martin has disappeared."

He pointed to a prosperous brick building. "Here you go, son. Don Longley's office."

Kyle unfolded from the seat, as shaky on his feet as a Christian martyr going to the lions. "Pray for me," he said.

"Better I should pray for Wanda. That she gets religion before Longley tears her throat out. Or for your wallet."

"Your wallet," Kyle corrected. He slammed the door and headed into the building.

Burgess picked up the phone, thumbed through his notebook until he found the number for the Raymond police and asked for Chip Lavoie. When he got patched through, he explained what he needed. Lavoie reluctantly agreed to drive out to Devereau's place, see if Iris was there, and call him back. Then, imitating Kyle, Burgess turned all the vents so they were blowing right at him, and settled in to wait.

Waiting was what cops probably did the most. Break down a thirty-year career, the majority of the hours would have been spent waiting. Waiting or watching or both. There was all kinds of waiting. This was the hardest. Waiting when your nerves were jazzed up, when you were in a race with something you couldn't see or hear but knew was out there. Waiting for a break, for information, for insight, for the pieces to come together.

Cops didn't live in a Disney world where wishing would make it so. They lived in a brutal, scum-infested world where sometimes all the hard work and good will imaginable couldn't make the right thing happen. They lived in a world of yearning souls that were sometimes deeply scarred by the knowledge that people could, and did, get away with murder. Was it just stubborn pride to believe he wasn't letting that happen on his watch, when it had happened before? Was he doing enough? Could he try harder?

There was sharp bang against the window by his head. Instantly he was upright and alert, staring at Andrea Dwyer beside the car on her bike, grinning a Cheshire cat grin.

He rolled down the window, letting in a wave of briny heat and the minty scent of her soap. "Gotcha!" she said. "Or doesn't it count to catch you napping if you're on sick leave?"

"You were going to leave me something?"

"Yeah." She thumped a fist against her helmet. "Bad brain day, Joe. Must be the heat." She handed him a manila envelope. "Jolene says you're too old for me."

"I'm too old for me," he said. "I tried to tell her I wasn't after you."

"I know." Did he detect a touch of disappointment in her voice? "Show these pictures to Nina Mallett," she said. "I'm betting you get a bingo."

"We could use a bingo."

She raised her arms and stretched, lithe as a cat, and he thought, with more appreciation than lust, that she'd be a lovely sight naked. "You've got that right," she said. She hadn't missed his stare. Her radio spoke and she sketched a wave. "Never too hot for bad guys, huh? I wish they'd take a day off."

She rode away. He went back to waiting. Waiting for news. Waiting for Kyle. Waiting for the phone to ring.

CHAPTER 32

Finally it rang. "Devereau damned near shot my ass off. Next time, you can go yourself," Lavoie complained.

Burgess wasn't feeling awfully sympathetic, but he kept his opinion—that Lavoie's ass could use a little reduction—to himself. "And?"

"Girl's not there. At least, he says she's not there, and there was no sign of her."

"That all?"

"Not quite. He says she called him to come pick her up this morning. They went out to breakfast. He says she looked real nice. Wearing a blue dress. Asshole says blue is definitely her color. He tells me this while he's stroking his fuckin' gun stock like it's a pet or something. Says he dropped her off and that's the last he saw of her."

"Dropped her off where?"

"Knowlton Park. Wherever the hell that is."

"Where her brother's body was found. What time?"

"Around eleven. He says."

"She say why she wanted to be dropped off there?"

"If she did, Devereau didn't deign to share that."

"He tell you anything else?"

"She was going to meet her boyfriend."

"You get the boyfriend's name? Anything about him?"

"He didn't know the name. Said he'd only seen him once. You wanted to come by and show him some pictures, he'd take a stab at an ID. He seemed real taken with the idea of another visit from you. Guess you were a hit."

"You believe him that the girl wasn't there?"

"He let me look around." Burgess could almost hear the shrug in Lavoie's voice. "Not much to that house. Unless he had the girl stashed in one of those abandoned vehicles, she wasn't there. Sorry I can't be more help. I'd like the bastard who killed that boy caught as much as anyone."

"Thanks for going out there. I appreciate it."

He called dispatch. Asked for any vehicles registered to Henry Devereau. Gave the address. The dispatcher said, "I ran those McBride's for you. There's just one car registered to her. A tan Mazda."

She would have a tan car. He wondered about the car the son was driving. Asked them to run all McBrides, and then, since he was thinking of it, asked them to run Jason and Ricky Martin. "It'll be a while," he was told. "You want the printout on your desk?"

"Call when it's ready. I'll swing by and get it." He couldn't, but Kyle or Perry could.

As if he was reading Burgess's mind, Perry's voice came over the radio. "Joe? You seen Terry? I left him in the lobby and he disappeared."

"I took him," Burgess said.

"For immoral purposes?"

"They felt moral at the time. We'll see how I feel in the morning. Get anything from Jason Martin?"

"Took too goddamned long to get the message. He

was pretty incoherent. Kept raving about Iris and her petal file, like she collected bleeping dried flowers or something. And his brother Ricky."

"You're sure he mentioned Iris?"

"Pretty sure. Why?"

"She's missing." It all kept coming back to Iris.

"Fuck that. This case is crazy. Where are you?"

"Sitting outside Don Longley's office, waiting for Terry."

"Don Longley? You aren't going to feel good in the morning."

"He's a mean SOB. That's what Terry needs."

Perry sighed. "I guess. So how you doing? You okay?"

"Getting by."

"I'll bet you are. I've got to stop at 109, fill Vince in, then me and Terry thought we'd stop over with pizza. You wanna get your ass off the public streets, I'll wait for Terry. Come by your place in a few hours?"

"Fine with me, if you're allowed to associate with one as allegedly dissolute as I."

"Associating with the allegedly dissolute is my life's work."

"Can you pick something up for me?" He told Stan about the McBride printout. "And find me a picture of Ricky Martin."

"Roger that." Stan disconnected without waiting for a response.

Pizza. Not the best thing for an invalid recovering from toxic chemical poisoning. But it sounded wonderful. And he wasn't acting much like an invalid. He opened the envelope Dwyer had given him and spilled out five black and white photographs of bare-skinned young men, each cut off just at the first dense tuft of pubic hair. Pretty suggestive pictures to show to a thirteen-year-old girl, but Dwyer's gut instinct, like his, had been that the boy Nina was talking to was after Neddy, so choosing boys from Osborne's photo collection made sense. Boys who were the prey when they were prepubescent sometimes became the predators when they grew older. He stared at the pictures, willing them to tell him something. When they stayed silent, he shoved them back into the envelope and started the engine.

He parked across from Mary Turner's apartment and rang the doorbell. A voice called, "Wait a minute," then feet thumped on the stairs, and Nina opened the door. When she recognized him, she looked like a kid caught with her hand in the cookie jar, a mixture of fear, guilt, and embarrassment. She tried for cool, but her voice came out nervous and squeaky, a sound she knew betrayed her but she couldn't swallow in time.

"Detective Burgess?" Her eyes weren't on his face; they were on the envelope. "Aunt Mary isn't home. I'm not supposed to let anyone in when she's not here."

"That's a good rule, Nina," he agreed, "but you know who I am."

"It's just…"

"I'm sure your Aunt Mary wouldn't mind. Is Neddy home?"

"He's resting," she said quickly. "He didn't sleep well last night. The heat, you know."

"Brutal," he agreed. He stepped through the door, closing it behind him. "Got anything cold to drink up there?"

Her caretaking side clicked in before she could stop it. "I made some ice tea."

"That would be great." He waved toward the stairs. "Lead on." He followed her up, observing the skinny legs, the still narrow hips, the dirty soles of her bare feet, the glow of her hair. It was a lovely color, as rare and delicate as pink gold. They found Ned and a smaller boy sitting on the sofa, watching a movie. Nina looked at him guiltily and headed for the kitchen. Burgess sat down on the couch beside the boys. On the screen, Robin Hood, a suave and romantic fox, was wooing Maid Marian, a foxy lady. An excellent choice. He'd watched this with his nieces. Too many people fed their kids on a steady diet of graphic violence.

"Remember the boy that Nina was talking to, down at the promenade, when you saw someone putting that bag in the trash can?" he said. Neddy nodded without taking his eyes off the screen. "Can I show you some pictures, see if you recognize him?" Another nod.

Burgess opened the envelope and dumped the pictures onto the coffee table. This time, six fell out. He arranged them in two rows. "Okay. You can look now."

The little boy's eyes swept the pictures. A hand came up and stabbed one of the pictures. "That one," he said in a high, triumphant voice. "That's him."

There was the sharp intake of breath as Nina, coming toward them with a tall glass tinkling with ice cubes, saw her brother's hand and heard his words. "No!" she said, shaking her head vehemently. "No. He's wrong. I've never seen that boy in my life."

Burgess was sorry. He didn't mind tricking adults. They were the architects of their own lies. He didn't like tricking children. He took the glass from Nina, set it on the table, and swept the pictures into the envelope. "You said you didn't know his name?" She shook her head. "But he looked kind of like the boy Neddy picked out?"

She shrugged. The forced casualness of those bony shoulders touched him. Made him wish they all lived in a better world, where children didn't have to lie, and neither did cops. He lifted the glass and took a sip. It was good tea, strong enough to hold its own against the ice, and she hadn't added sugar. He hated sweet ice tea. He nodded approvingly. "Good tea."

She was looking down at her feet. "Thanks," she mumbled. She looked up quickly and then down again. There were two bright spots of red in her cheeks.

"Nina, I'm sorry," he said. "I know it seems like I'm invading your privacy. But after what happened to Timmy Watts, we have to be extra careful. It's possible that this boy isn't as nice as he seems. If that were the case...if I didn't pay attention and then something happened to you or your brother, I'd never forgive myself."

"He's nice." She turned away, tears in her voice. "He's nice, and he likes me. You don't want me to have any fun. Like everybody else. You just want me to be a good girl and good babysitter and a good big sister. Just always, boringly good." She ran from the room.

Neddy patted Burgess on the leg. "It's okay," he said softly. "Nina cries a lot. It's because she's learning to be a woman. That's what our mom did, too." His curls stuck up like a rooster's comb. He nodded sagely. "Don't listen to what she says. I seen that boy, too, and it's the one in your picture. I don't think he's nice like Nina does. She sneaked out to meet him yesterday, and he gave her a mark on her arm."

"Do you know where she met him?"

Neddy nodded. "Yeah. The cemetery."

"Can you remember something very important?" Burgess asked. The little boy nodded. "Can you ask your Aunt Mary to call me when she gets home?" He wrote his cell phone number on a card and put it on the coffee table.

Neddy looked at the card. "I can't read it. I'm not good at reading yet."

"That's okay. You'll learn. Just give that to Aunt Mary and tell her to call me."

"Okay. Are you leaving now? We're not going to get ice cream?"

"Not today. But soon, all right?"

"All right." Neddy wasn't too disappointed; he was caught up his video. "Drink your tea or Nina will be mad."

Too late. Nina was already mad. Burgess finished his tea and left. Back down in the street, he lingered a moment, staring up at the second story windows, wishing Mary Turner were home. He didn't like leaving without speaking to her. He was uncomfortable leaving Neddy and Nina alone in a house without adults. People liked to think crime happened only at night, under cover of darkness, and only to others. But it could happen any time. Anywhere. To anyone. He just had to count on Nina's natural caution and inclination to follow the rules.

He didn't go straight home. It would be a while before Kyle and Perry showed up and sitting around would only make him more restless. He was already so keyed up his skin didn't fit. And frustrated. He wanted to go downtown and check that printout. He wanted to fax the photo Neddy'd ID'd to the Raymond police and have them show it to Henry Devereau. Wanted every cop on patrol in the East End to be on the lookout for Iris Martin. He couldn't do any of those things without Kyle and Perry and knew this frustrating information void was what Cote wanted.

He went by Matt McBride's house. There was no tan car in sight, and no one answered the doorbell when he rang. He thumbed through his notes, found Regina

McBride's employer, got a number, and called there. She was on vacation, not expected back until Monday. He rang doorbells on either side and across the street, and got no response. It couldn't be his breath—they wouldn't know about that until they answered their doors. Maybe it was the hard, ugly set of his face.

He drove back toward downtown and took a slow turn around the cemetery, scanning it for signs of life. Saw nothing, but that didn't mean much. There were plenty of places to hide. Even covering the whole thing on foot, he could easily miss someone who didn't want to be found. Patrol officers had a rule— take a second look at anything that catches your attention. He saw nothing that made him take a second look. The cemetery and the streets around it were dead. The most animated thing he saw was a vagrant Styrofoam cup, rolling down the sidewalk, propelled by the sluggish breeze.

Mothers were keeping their children inside, off the stoops and sidewalks, out of the parks. Beneath the lead-colored sky, the normally vibrant city was holding its breath, waiting for something. It was waiting for him and Kyle and Perry to do their job. The ocean in the distance, so lively and sparkling on a good day, had a flat, dirty gray look, like water in a mop bucket. The hot air smelled like the breath of decay.

Timmy Watts, dead five days, lay unburied in the morgue in Augusta, while his killer stalked around the city, laughing up his sleeve at the incompetence of the cops, perhaps thinking about killing again.

CHAPTER 33

He checked his messages again, hoping for news. Iris Martin was somewhere in the city with a man she didn't realize was dangerous. Nina and Ned were home alone, and he hadn't heard from their Aunt Mary.

There was another hang-up call, then a message from Missy Steinberg, her anxiety exploding out of the phone. "Kelly Stanley, who is Iris Martin's best friend, just came to see me, saying she was afraid Iris was doing something stupid and might be in trouble. She wanted me to help her get in touch with you. After I offered to call you, she changed her mind and decided it wasn't such a big deal. But she's a reliable girl and she's concerned. I think if we meet with her together, she'll talk to you. I'm here until 5:30. Please call me."

She answered immediately. "Oh. Detective. Thank you for calling me back. Can you come now? Kelly's jumping out of her skin."

"I'm on my way." He took off, no longer tolerant of the sluggish traffic, his restless foot dancing between accelerator and brake as he worked his way out of the city, onto the highway, and off again. A pain in his stomach like the faint prick of a knife.

Kelly Stanley looked like a girl he'd had a crush on in junior high. The same shiny dark curls, cute nose, bright dark eyes. What wasn't the same was the fearfulness, the misery in the hunched shoulders, the anxious swiveling of the girl's head as she shifted her gaze from his face to Missy Steinberg's and then back to his, her small body taut. The girl he'd lusted after had been happy-go-lucky. Kelly made an emphatic gesture with her hands. Missy signed something back and put a hand over hers. "She's not sure she wants to do this."

Burgess looked directly at the girl. "I know you're scared. You think you may be betraying a confidence. But I'm worried about your friend, Iris, too. I think she's in trouble. Like you, I want to help her." Times like this, he wished he weren't so big, didn't have a scarred and scary face. He tried to put a reassurance into his voice that Kelly Stanley couldn't hear, hoping she could read it from his face and body, hoping Missy Steinberg would do a good job interpreting him.

He couldn't help remembering his interview with Iris Martin, older, more poised, yet infinitely more fragile than Kelly. Iris had just seen that awful picture, received a blow he'd hoped to cushion. Iris had been in terrible pain; Kelly was only suffering adolescent angst. He couldn't help seeing Timmy Watts's face, so like his sister's. Timmy's dead face. He didn't want to find Iris the same way.

The girl's hands hesitated, then signed. "Iris made me swear not to tell."

"Sometimes, when the matter is serious enough, or when a person is in trouble, we have to break promises," he said. He waited until Missy had finished. "If you didn't tell and something bad happened to your friend, you'd feel terrible, wouldn't you?"

Kelly's head bobbed, but her hands flew in a disclaimer. "But Iris will be mad at me."

He understood the process. He spoke. Missy translated. Kelly spoke. Missy translated. It was time consuming. It took patience. He was a cop, well schooled in patience, but a sense of impending danger filled his chest, crawled along his nerves like worms.

He tried to give her an easy out. "I know that Iris has a boyfriend, a boy she likes. I think she's gone to meet him. Is that right?"

He watched understanding, agreement, and caution follow one another across Kelly's face. Her hands rose, fell, then rose again. She signed briefly, and they fell back into her lap.

Missy Steinberg said, "She doesn't know what to do."

She knew what to do, that was why she'd asked Missy to call. She was just stuck in adolescent coyness, in the small teenage friendship circle of "maybe she won't like me" that kept her from seeing the larger life and death issues. He choked down impatience, trying gentleness one more time. "Did Iris go to meet her boyfriend? Do you have any idea where they went?"

Missy signed the question. The girl shrugged, lowered her eyes, then shrugged again, keeping her eyes on the floor.

He saw Iris's eyes, open and soulless like her brother's. Saw flies circle and land. Felt a clench of dread in his gut. Like sand through an hourglass, the last of his patience ran out. He didn't have time to tenderly nudge a frightened teenager toward cooperation. He stamped the floor hard with his foot.

Kelly's head came up abruptly, Missy turned, and both women stared at him reproachfully.

"We don't have time to play "should I, shouldn't I?" games," he said. "Iris Martin's gone to meet the boy she thinks is her boyfriend. He's not. He means to do her harm. There's still a chance I can prevent that if I can find her. If Kelly knows anything that could help me find Iris, I need to hear it now. Otherwise, I've got to get back out there and keep looking."

Missy Steinberg shot him a murderous look, but she was a professional. The same standards that made her translate fairly and accurately for Kelly required her to do the same for him. He watched Kelly's face as she followed the moving hands. Saw understanding followed by what looked like more stubborn reluctance. He opened the envelope he'd brought and pulled out the pictures. Without asking permission, he reached past Missy and laid them out on the desk. "Is one of these boys Iris's boyfriend?"

Missy frowned at the pictures. "Detective," she said, "I really don't think—"

"Don't think," he said. "Interpret. I know they're vulgar. They were taken by men who collect child pornography. I think Iris Martin went to meet one of these boys. Now please. Kelly's trying to tell me something," he said. "I'd like to know what it is."

Kelly, who'd been trying to get her interpreter's attention, stamped her own foot and began to sign vigorously, her gestures, which had previously been subdued, suddenly vigorous and elaborate. Missy watched attentively. "Yes. Yes. I think I recognize one of them. I only saw him once, the time he brought her little brother out to visit." She stabbed one of the pictures. The same one Neddy Mallet had picked.

"Thank you," he said. "Thank you, Kelly." He picked up the picture of Matt McBride. "Do you have any idea where he and Iris might have gone?"

For a minute, her hands hesitated, her chin set stubbornly, dark eyes resentful, but the moment passed. "Iris said her brother had a place. That they were going there."

"Any idea where the place is?" She shook her head. "Did she leave anything? An address? Phone number?"

"No," she said. "I'm sorry." Her troubled eyes searched his face, looking for something. Reassurance, maybe. "Is Iris...? Do you really think she's in danger?"

"I do."

"I could look in her room," Kelly offered. "See if she left any notes or anything."

It was exactly what he wanted her to do, but if he asked her to search, and then the search led to something, and then the something got challenged at trial? He couldn't take the chance. The memory of Kristin Marks and the chain of evidence errors still haunted him. "I can't ask you to do that."

Missy Steinberg followed him out the car, her feet clobbering the wooden floor, smashing down angrily on the gravel. "You're a real bastard, you know that?" she said.

"Because I'd rather find Iris Martin alive than dead?" He unlocked the door and jerked it open, his elbow just missing her face, she was standing so close.

Her focus had been on Kelly. Only then did it dawn on her what had just occurred. "You don't really think..."

"Of course I do. You think I was mean to that poor child because I enjoy it?"

Her eyes were wide with shock and concern. "Is there anything we can do?"

He hesitated. "I couldn't...can't ask you to search her room...but if you decided to, or Kelly took it upon herself to do it...and you found anything...I wouldn't mind hearing about it." He hoisted himself onto the seat and shut the door, taking off in a shower of gravel, leaving her staring after him. One more example of how he was a mean, selfish bastard with no social skills, unsuited to be a policeman. So dedicated to being hateful he'd rise from a sickbed just for the pleasure of sticking it to some poor deaf kid.

He drove home oppressed by the feeling that bad things were happening, things he was powerless to stop. A cop doesn't like feeling powerless. He got out of the car, fists clenched, breathing the way he would late at night, going through an open door into a dark building, not knowing what lay on the other side. That was how the whole day had felt—like going into a dark place, not knowing what was there. Except he did know what was there, didn't he? Iris Martin and Matty McBride. Ricky Martin. Perhaps others he hadn't yet identified. He just didn't know where to find them.

It was past time for Kyle and Perry. He sat and waited. Paced and waited. Stalking back and forth, tormenting his knee as he contemplated the exquisite torture Paul Cote had devised—to take his best detective, on the cusp of solving a case, and lock him out of the investigation, knowing that he wouldn't be able to leave it alone. Knowing that, at least in the privacy of his mind, Burgess would be putting the pieces together, unable to do anything with them. It was like locking a man up in solitary with half the pieces of a jigsaw puzzle. Doing something impulsive and stupid now would be to let Cote win. What he feared was that doing nothing would let the killer win.

Where the hell were they? He couldn't sit here

forever waiting, worrying about what was happening to Iris Martin. He called dispatch and asked if they knew where Kyle and Perry were. The dispatcher was a friend, otherwise he would have gotten nothing. "Call came in maybe forty minutes ago. A woman, looking for you, asking for help. Her speech wasn't very intelligible. We got a partial location. They took off."

"You get a name?"

"Rice, maybe? Rice Marn?"

Iris Martin. The knife in his stomach twisted. "Location?"

"Back Cove. She said more but we couldn't make it out."

"Hope they took an army," Burgess said. "Thanks for the information."

His pizza was indefinitely postponed. The Back Cove was a huge bay, as big as half the old city, circled by residential neighborhoods, Payson Park, Back Cove Park, a ribbon of green parkland along the water, and running paths. McBride and Iris could be anywhere. Or gone from there entirely. It could be a trick. He could have made Iris call to lure them over there while he took her somewhere else. He could have told her she was one place when she was actually someplace else. Iris probably wasn't that familiar with Portland.

"Did she sound frightened?"

"She sure did. We couldn't understand much of what she said, but "Help" came through loud and clear."

He put down the phone with a heavy heart. He could see her face too well, imagine her fear too vividly. Iris was smart and resilient, but being a deaf person in a hearing world put her at an awful disadvantage. Even if she could find someone to ask for help, she might not be understood. It would be easy for McBride to convince people to dismiss her pleas for help. People were all too ready to dismiss anyone who was difficult to understand, or who made them feel embarrassed and Iris, knowing that, would be sensitive to the rejection and the judgments. It would only increase her fear and desperation knowing that even if she did reach out for help, she might not be understood.

He still had his radio. He tried to reach Kyle, got no response, and tried Perry. Stan's voice came on, brief and breathless. "Stan. It's Joe. You find her? Did you find Iris Martin?"

"Iris Martin. Of course. I should have known. What's going on, Joe?"

"Not on the radio," he said. "Call me."

"Oh, right," Perry said. "I'll just ask one of these seagulls if they've got a phone."

He was breaking up badly. "I'm losing you," Burgess said. "And I can't go get a new battery. Where are you?"

"Payson Park. Wait," Stan said. "We're getting nowhere here. We don't know what we're doing or what we're looking for. It sounds like you do. Let me grab Terry and we'll come over. You can order the pizza."

"Only if you stop by the station and pick up the crime scene videos."

"Oh, right. Pizza and a movie. I should have thought of that."

"Large roni with green pepper and black olives?"

Through a cloud of static, Perry said, "I love it when someone remembers. And Terry wants—"

"Hamburg with mushrooms and onions. And don't forget that printout."

"Will you marry us, Joe?"

"Screw you," he said. He ordered pizza and sat down to wait. He couldn't sit still. He limped downstairs and got the briefcase of stuff from his car, the stuff he'd taken off his desk yesterday to avoid Charlene Farrell's prying eyes and never gotten back. He sat at the table like a man playing solitaire and began laying out the crime scene photographs.

The pizza man came up the stairs followed by Kyle and Perry, looking a little unnerved to find himself followed by two men with guns on their belts. Burgess paid the man and put the pictures away. He'd used a fan to suck cool air out of the bedroom and the kitchen was comfortable. Sweaty and limp from the heat, they fell on their food with silent efficiency.

Perry finished first. He pushed back his chair, walked to the sink, and shoved his bald head under the faucet. He let the cold water run over him until Kyle said, "My turn," and nudged him aside. Despite the exhausted slowness of their horseplay, the pungent scent of sweat, and their grim faces, they were like kids playing in the sprinkler. A second later, Kyle scooped a handful of water and threw it at Burgess, yelling "Gotcha" as the water hit him full in the face. He pictured Cote's prune-faced disapproval as the three of them romped around the kitchen, soaking the walls and counters and each other.

It ended as quickly as it had started. He handed out bath towels, updated them on Iris Martin, and they sat down to talk strategy.

CHAPTER 34

"I've got a K-Mart clerk, out by the highway, thinks she remembers a teenage boy buying a blue blanket and some kid's underpants last week," Perry said. "It stuck in her mind because it was odd stuff for him to be buying. And because she tried to flirt with him and he was kind of nasty. They're getting us surveillance tape. And Devlin says he's got a match between a print on the boy's body and one of the sets of prints on that K-Mart bag. Too bad they're not in the system."

"They finally got around to doing those storm drains," Kyle said. "We got the knife. T-handled thrust knife. No prints." He leaned back in his chair and closed his eyes. "What you got, Joe?"

So the system was working. Piece by painstaking piece. He told them about getting the pictures from Andrea Dwyer. About his talk with Kelly Stanley, her ID of Matt McBride's picture. About Ned Mallett also picking out the picture. He spread out the pictures.

Perry stabbed McBride. "Told you I didn't like that kid."

Kyle bent to look, pointed to another picture. "That's Ricky Martin," he said, fishing out a mug shot and laying it beside the other pictures. Ricky was clearly the beauty of the family, handsome in a deadly, sleepy-eyed way. Lots of prison muscle.

"So we've got to find them," Perry said.

"How?" Burgess asked. "You bring me those printouts? The video?"

"Yeah. But how does that help?"

Burgess's body felt like the football after the game. "I'm looking for a car. A blue car. There's nothing registered to Matt McBride. But what about his father? Or Ricky Martin? I'm looking for Martin or McBride there in the crowd. And maybe the car parked somewhere nearby? Looking for a break. Kelly Stanley said McBride was going to take Iris to Ricky's place. Since we don't know where that is, we're down to footwork. Get out there, flash pictures around, see if anyone recognizes Martin or McBride. Get cops checking all the rooming houses, shelters, and squats."

He couldn't keep discouragement out of his voice. His throat was still red-hot, and the pizza hadn't helped. "I don't like to think about what's happening to Iris. About what we may find. You guys got other ideas?"

"We could try the family again," Perry suggested, not sounding optimistic. Nothing about the Martin/Watts family encouraged optimism. "What about McBride's mother?"

"I went by there a while ago," Burgess said. "No one answered. Tried the neighbors. Called her work. Nada," Burgess said. "Work says she's on vacation." He shook his head. "Yesterday, when I interviewed her, she was painting a hardwood floor gray. I thought it was odd. Ugly. I didn't think about covering up blood. She stood there with that goddamned paintbrush in her hand telling me she was an informant, not a suspect, and I didn't make the connection even when I could see she was the queen of heartless bitches."

"We should have someone sitting on the house," Kyle said. He made the call.

They divided up the sheets and went through the printouts. Nothing registered to Ricky Martin, which wasn't a big surprise. A lot of cars in and around Portland registered to people named McBride. Ten were blue. Six were small. Six calls later, they'd come up empty.

Silently, they filed into the living room and put in the tape. Sat on the couch, shoulder to shoulder, watching the whole ugly scene unfold, lacking the will, despite their urgency, to fast forward through Timmy Watts's body. Burgess, sitting on the end, watched Kyle's face, the jaw working, the skin drawn tight. Kyle, who was seeing this for the first time, looked suitably sickened. It would get worse when the body was exposed.

Burgess shifted his eyes back to the screen as they began unwrapping the body. It hit him then with the suddenness of a head-on collision, a thought with sickening implications and the certainty of truth. It explained what had bothered him all along—the disparity between the uncontrolled sexual violence of the killing, and the careful, meticulous disposal of the body. Matty McBride had bought the underpants and the blue blanket, knowing they would be appealing inducements to Timmy Watts. McBride had committed the rape and the murder. Then his loving mother had cleaned up the body, dressed it in the clean underpants, wrapped it in the new blue blanket, and driven it to the park.

The tape rolled on, as they worked the body, as the blue blanket was finally peeled back to reveal the savagery that been inflicted. The tape had been unsparing, capturing them all at their heat-baked worst—Perry, red-faced, with sweat pouring off his shaved skull, Burgess gray and grimacing, even catching Dr. Lee with an uncharacteristically sad expression as he examined the boy's body. It had caught the dryness of the grass, the brightness of the blood, the moving black specks of flies.

Kyle made a gagging sound. "Can we fast-forward to the crowd scenes, please?"

Perry grabbed the remote, hit the pause button. "What's the matta? Too ugly for you? That's what a real murder looks like."

"Up yours," Kyle said, grabbing his head with his hands.

Burgess had the shades down. It was dim in the room. But in the semi-darkness, he could see the faint gleam of tears. Kyle was a father who'd spent part of the afternoon planning a desperate fight to hang on to his own kids. Now he was watching the graphic ugliness of a child's death. The paused image on the screen was a close up of the wounds clustered with flies. Kyle gagged again and left the room.

"What's his problem?" Perry asked.

"Guy's got kids of his own. He's running on bare rims. Cut him some slack, okay."

"If you say so, boss."

"I'm so far from being your boss I'm not even in the picture."

"That's bull. We don't stop being a team because Cote's an asshole."

"Then stop picking on your teammate. Save that for the bad guys...it's not like this doesn't make us all feel mean."

Kyle dropped back into his seat like he'd been flung by a careless hand. He tilted his head back and closed his eyes. "God, I feel like shit," he said.

"You and me both," Burgess said. "Only one still standing is young Stanley. Listen, I think I've got some of this figured out." The tape had just come to the crowd scenes. Perry hit pause while Burgess shared his speculation with the others.

"You don't suppose," Kyle said suddenly, "she has a company car to drive? What kind of work does she do?"

"She's an accountant."

"Name of the company?" Kyle had the phone poised.

"Elmer Littlewood Associates."

Kyle stabbed the phone keys as if force could make the numbers travel faster. He spat a bunch of instructions into the phone, gave the number, and punched end. "Joe, have we been stupid about this? Did we screw up somewhere?"

"This is how they go sometimes. We just go out like a bunch of retrievers, keep bringing things back 'til we get the right ones. We're getting the right ones now."

"No thanks to Cote," Perry said. "We gotta call Vince."

"You gonna tell him where you are?"

"He knows where we are," Kyle said.

"He knows?"

"You don't think he believed you'd stay out of it, do you?" Perry said. "We're the best, and we're a team. Vince doesn't care about politics. He wants the guy who did this. He wants the good citizens of Portland to be able to sleep at night and to stop calling him. He wants to go home and hug his twins without wondering if he's got to lock 'em up in a tower somewhere. We said we were coming over here, know what he said?"

"What?"

"He said don't come back 'til we could bring him something. Now we got something."

"Yeah. Maybe a hostage situation. Certainly another person in jeopardy. That ought to make his day."

"Joe," Kyle's voice was slow and soft. "Give yourself some credit. At least we've got a theory of the case. We're moving on this."

Perry hit play and they watched the crowd, unaware they were being filmed, react to the crime scene. It was revolting to watch the curiosity, eagerness, jostling. It could have been a crowd at a sporting event or a parade. "Hold it," Kyle said suddenly. "There!" He crossed to the screen and pointed to two young men in the crowd. Matty McBride and Ricky Martin. Martin's head was flung back, laughing at something. They were holding cups of 7-eleven coffee.

The phone rang. Kyle, expecting dispatch, grabbed it, listened, handed it to Burgess. "A woman," he said. "For you."

Burgess raised the phone. "Detective? It's Mary Turner. I found your card on the coffee table?"

"Neddy didn't give you my message? I came by earlier to show him some pictures, ask him and Nina some questions about the people they saw when they were out looking for bottles. When they found those clothes."

"I see. What was it you wanted to talk to me about?"

"Just following a police officer's hunch," he said. "I didn't want to alarm them, but I thought you ought to know that we believe one of the people they saw, that Nina spoke with, might have been involved in Timmy Watts's death." When she didn't respond, he added, "I wanted to suggest you keep them home, keep them in, until we can arrest this man."

Mary Turner dropped the phone. The knife in his

stomach twisted as he waited for more bad news. The damned police gut was too often right. "Sorry," she said, "Sorry. I dropped the phone. Oh, Detective, they're not here. Nina and Ned." There was anguish in her voice. "She got a babysitting job, and they let her bring Ned along."

"Someone she regularly sits for? Someone you've met?" The pain sharpened.

"No."

"But you got a phone number where she'll be?"

"Yes."

He picked up on her hesitation. "What is it?"

"I was looking for the baby's favorite toy. I couldn't find it, so I called the number. A man answered. He said it was a phone booth."

Burgess gagged. Another minute, he'd follow Kyle's lead and lose the pizza.

He opened his notebook. "Can you give me that number, please?" He wrote it down. "How long have they been gone?" An hour. "What did she tell you about this job?"

"She said they were a young couple. Friends of some people she has babysat for. She said that's how they got the number. That they had a small baby and knew Nina was good with babies. She said they wouldn't be out late."

"Did she seem nervous when she was telling you this? Either then, or looking back now, do you have the feeling she was lying?"

"Oh, God," Mary Turner said. "Oh my God! What have I done?"

"Please try to stay calm," he said. "Did she tell you anything else?"

"She said the man was picking her up. She was supposed to watch out the window for a blue car."

Pain as sharp as a knife. "Did you see the driver?"

"Not really."

"Could you pick him out from a photograph?"

"No." Her voice was shaking now. "No. I don't think so."

"Did you see the license plate?"

"Only the first three digits. It was a conservation plate."

"What were those numbers, Mrs. Turner?"

"Oh dear. I don't know. I wrote them down here somewhere." He heard her crashing around. A baby crying, another child whining. "Somewhere...I know I...Patrick, be quiet, I'm on the phone. Give the baby one of those cookies. Give it to him!" There was a crash and a wail, and then her shaken voice was back on the line. "Found it." She read the three digits. "Do you think..." She couldn't bring herself to finish.

"Can you call the couple Nina said made the referral and ask if they did give her name to someone? Can you do that now, please, and call me back?"

"Sure. Yes. I'll do it."

"One more thing. What was Nina wearing?"

"The usual. A tank top and shorts."

"Earrings? Lipstick? Like she might have dressed to impress someone?"

Mary Turner sighed again. The sigh of utter failure. She had set out to keep the kids safe, to provide a safe haven in a world that had dealt them so much danger. And let them slip back into it. "I'll make that call," she said.

Kyle and Perry were waiting. "Nina Mallet," he said. "The girl who found Timmy Watts's clothes in the trash can. That was her foster mother. She went out on a babysitting job tonight. The phone number she left was a phone booth." Perry started to speak, but Burgess held up his hand. "There's more. This afternoon her little brother Ned ID'd the photograph of

Matty McBride as the guy she was talking to while someone dumped those clothes in the trashcan. A woman, the boy says. And there's one more thing. The little brother also said that Nina sneaked out to meet McBride yesterday afternoon. Met him in the cemetery. And came back with a bruised arm. Here's the kicker. She took her brother along."

"I don't get it," Perry said. "Why sneak out on a date and take your brother along?"

"Easy," Kyle said. "The guy asked you to. And you want to please the guy."

"Fuckin' lambs to the slaughter," Perry said. A cold silence fell on the room.

CHAPTER 35

Melia had told them to come in, Burgess included. On his way out, Burgess had downed a handful of Tums. They weren't making any difference. No surprise. This pain wasn't about stomach acid. They sat around the table in the close-aired conference room, unwashed, unshaven and un-rested, laying it all out in brusque, staccato bits, interrupting each other, sifting through the stacks of papers, trying with tired minds to muscle what they had into something they could work. From their command center, like a misfiring spinal column, cops across the city spread out, trying to find the blue car or Ricky Martin.

Kyle's hunch had paid off. Regina McBride did have the occasional use of a company car. Her supervisor had confirmed it; given them a license number that matched the three digits they'd gotten from Mary Turner. Otherwise, they had nothing new. Regina McBride hadn't come home. A call to the Watts household had turned up no new information about Ricky or Iris. Kyle had gone over to the jail and tried talking with Dwayne Martin, but all he'd gotten was profanity. Jason Martin had lapsed into a coma.

Mary Turner had called back, but only to report, sobbing, that the couple she'd contacted had given Nina's name to no one.

The dirty gray dusk gave way to denser gray evening. Heat lightning crackled, like distant hope, off to the west, but the storm which might have broken the heat's grip on the city trembled like a scared virgin on the horizon. They watched it from the isolation of an air-conditioned room where anxiety and despair weighed as heavily as the outside air. Kyle, red-eyed and intense, shuffled through pictures and papers like a man who believed if he tried hard enough he could read invisible writing. Stan was stomping a wastebasket to death. Burgess put his hands over his ears and tried to screen them out, searching his brain for some connection he might have missed.

He picked up the six pictures he'd gotten from Andrea Dwyer and looked at them again. He used a magnifying glass, then passed the glass and pictures to Kyle. "These look like they were taken in Osborne's apartment?" Kyle picked up the glass and spread out the photos. Burgess turned to Stan. "What about Taylor's apartment?"

Perry stopped abusing the wastebasket, examined the pictures, and shook his head. "It's a modern condo. This looks like a cellar."

"We find out where that phone booth was?"

"Yeah."

"Show me." Perry rolled out a city map and pointed. "There's a convenience store on that corner, isn't there?"

Kyle set down the magnifying glass with a sigh. "It looks like cement or stone. And pretty beat-up."

"So they had what? Abandoned house? Warehouse? Someplace they could go and shoot their dirty pictures without someone seeing. Somewhere in that neighborhood?"

"Osborne knows," Perry said.

"If he'll talk. What about Taylor?" Kyle suggested. "I'll get Vince."

"What about Darlene Packer?" Perry said. "Maybe she knows something. Something she doesn't even know she knows, about where Ricky might be living. For that matter, what about the older sister. Shauna? She might turn out to be the hooker with the heart of gold if she knew her sister was in danger."

"Head of lead is more like it. But Packer's a possibility." Burgess had another idea. "Delinsky will know about abandoned places in that part of town. Delinsky and Aucoin."

Anxiety pulled them out of their chairs and onto their feet. Somewhere out there, two young girls and a small boy were in danger. No one fooled themselves that Ricky Martin's relationship to Iris would give her much protection. Even if they got nothing, it was better to be out there, looking. Perry went to find Shauna Martin and Darlene Packer. Kyle left to meet with Aucoin and work his half of the East End. Burgess got the other half and Delinsky. They left Vince Melia and Rocky Jordan working on getting access to Taylor or Osborne. Perry would meet up with them later.

Delinsky tapped the wheel with his big hands a few times, looking out into the night. "I'm sorry about this morning. I was being stupid."

"Don't worry about it. Everybody gets stupid sometimes. I've been where you are. Someday you'll be where I am. It's the same job, just the view is different, depending on where you sit."

Delinsky nodded. "Any idea what we're looking for?"

"As Detective Perry so eloquently put it, 'needle in a

fuckin' haystack.' We're looking for someplace Osborne might have used to take his dirty pictures. A place Ricky Martin might coop. Place McBride might take someone—empty house, building, warehouse."

"Gonna be a long night, Sarge. You want to ride with me or you want to follow?"

"I'll follow you." He hoped Delinsky wouldn't take it wrong. He just wanted to be alone with his thoughts. Two hours later, butt sore and eye sore from staring out into the darkness, his knee afire from hundreds of stairs, he wasn't so sure. Increasingly, his thoughts were stark neon messages flashing "urgent" through his brain. The knife in his gut was a steady pain now, another permanent fixture like his knee. Delinsky didn't look like he felt much better, and the radio had served up nothing that looked like news, good or bad.

They stopped at the top of the hill above the cemetery and looked back down at the city sparkling below them. Lights burned. Cars moved. Boats bobbed out on the water. Except for the incredible thickness of the air, the storm lurking on the horizon—nature mirroring his inner state—it might have been a normal night. A city crawling with police officers. Tension ratcheted up to an almost unbearable level, and yet things looked so normal. He wanted to get out and yell. Wake everyone up. Blow off some of the awful tension.

What do you do when you know something awful is happening but you can't find it or fix it, and fixing things is your job? Making the world safe. "Can you believe it?" he said. "Life's just humming along like nothing is happening." It had been so many hours. What were the chances the three of them, any of them, were still alive? Slim to none. But he had to hope.

"Most of those folks down there, they don't give a

damn," Delinsky said, his voice a deep rumble in the dark. "They're dead."

Pool cue hit the eight ball. Eight ball careened down the felt, slammed into a random thought, and drove that thought right into the pocket. He straightened up like he'd been electrified. "Cemetery. Maintenance shed," he said. "Crypt where they store bodies in the winter? Kyle said cement or stone."

"Say what?"

"The cemetery. In Timmy Watts's treasure box, he had a small American flag and a ribbon from a memorial wreath. Neddy Mallett said his sister Nina met McBride yesterday in the cemetery. Cemeteries have crypts. Vaults. Whatever they're called, right? So, where would it be?"

"This is Aucoin's turf. Let's see what he knows."

Minutes later, there were five of them standing there. Remy Aucoin was a fairly new policeman, but he came from a police family, and he'd grown up in the neighborhood. Aucoin dug through papers in a battered briefcase and pulled out an old map. "Eastern Cemetery," Aucoin said, spreading the map out on the hood of his car. "Let's take a look."

"I'll call Vince," Kyle said. "Let him know where we're at."

They identified all the places that seemed to offer possibilities and split the list, Aucoin and Perry going for the maintenance shed, Burgess and the other two heading for the crypt.

Police officers are supposed to be fearless, but only the stupid or careless truly are. Good, healthy fear is what keeps you alive. As Burgess crunched his way down the glass-strewn sidewalk in the pungent darkness, guided only by the occasional streetlight, his looming sense of dread intensified. His vest and collar felt too tight. He unsnapped his holster, checked his gun, replaced it. Didn't want a repeat of the fiasco with Osborne.

In the distance, thunder rumbled. Jagged streaks of lightning danced across the sky. Car tires hissed on the dew-damp pavement. A motorcycle revved its engine and tore off into the night like an angry bee. Sirens screamed and blue lights flashed as the oblivious city went about its business. Kyle stumbled and muttered a curse as a howling ball of fur scurried across the street. Delinsky moved silent and almost invisibly beside him.

Their destination was a black iron door leading to an underground room built directly into the hillside. In childhood, he had passed it often, wondering what mysteries lay inside. He'd felt the delicious shiver of danger at contemplating seizing the big ring that served as a handle and pulling. Once or twice he'd tried. It had always been locked, never revealing the cold, dark room that lay beyond—the room his mother had told him was for storing bodies in winter when the ground was frozen too hard for burial. On a winter night after one of his parents' more violent fights, when the smashing of dishes and the sound of blows had subsided, he'd found his mother unconscious on the kitchen floor. For a second, he'd thought she was dead, imagined them bringing her here and shutting her up behind this door. Across the years, the memory of that silent, bloody kitchen was as vivid as yesterday.

Now he studied the door. It was a bad situation. There were no windows and only one way in. No way of knowing what lay on the other side, who they might find. Whether Martin or McBride might be armed. Positioning the others to his right, he grabbed the handle, using the door as a shield. Slowly and ponderously, the heavy door began to move. He opened it a few inches and stopped, peering cautiously through the opening. It was absolutely black. He pulled harder. The door resisted. Moving quickly across the opening, he signed for Delinsky to trade places.

Delinsky seized the handle and pulled. The door gave suddenly with a sharp creak, scraping loudly over the cement sill. He held his breath, listening, detecting no sounds in the darkness. Using the doorframe as a shield, he stuck his flashlight around the edge and snapped it on. Cold, musty air streamed past as he illuminated the cavernous darkness. A high-ceilinged stone cave lined with stone racks along the walls for coffins. Some trash, stubs of burned candles, and a torn sleeping bag spoke of occasional human occupancy.

He stepped in, letting the flashlight travel around, checking tier after empty tier. Burgess doing one side, Kyle and Delinsky the other. Moving back toward the farthest corner.

Kyle's light stopped on what looked like another ragged sleeping bag. With an exclamation, Kyle rushed forward, fumbling with the zippers, pushing back the filthy, rotting cloth to reveal some curly brown hair, a bare shoulder in a blue dress. Kyle's scrambling fingers burrowed through the hair, searching for a pulse.

"Alive," he said. "Alive. Alive. Delinsky. Ambulance."

Delinsky had already stepped outside and was calling. "I'll get the car," he said, taking off at a run.

Kyle supported her while Burgess peeled the filthy bag away. Together they carried Iris Martin outside, laid her out on the blanket Delinsky had spread on the sidewalk, and began working at the bands of duct tape that wrapped her like a mummy.

It hadn't been a matter of simply confining her. The placement and amount of tape was sadistic, covering her face like a thick mask with only a minute space for breath, her arms pulled back until they were nearly dislocated and then bound there, her legs bound from thigh to ankle. She had left that morning with high hopes and a pretty blue dress to meet the man who'd done this to her.

Despite the heat of the night, her skin was cold from the chill of the crypt. Burgess wondered if McBride had planned to leave her there. Wrap her up until she was helpless, then leave her to die a slow, terrifying death.

Delinsky returned with scissors from his first aid kit and began cutting away tape, loosening her arms and legs and then going carefully to work on the tape across her face. There was no way to remove it without hurting her but he was as gentle as he could be. Burgess and Kyle worked the tape off her arms and legs, wincing as the pieces pulled free from the bruised white skin. When they could, they folded in the sides of the blanket and wrapped them around her.

Delinsky cursed and murmured as he worked, a profane running litany of what he was going to do with McBride when they caught him, mixed with gentle endearments designed to support the unconscious girl's courage. Burgess heaved himself to his feet and called Melia to report on what they'd found and request a crime scene team. Then he called Perry.

"Nothing here, Joe. We're going to check out a building at the other end."

Medcu arrived and they sent Iris off to the hospital, Burgess explaining to them about her deafness. Delinsky followed in his car, to be there to get her story if she was able to tell it, and to provide a familiar face when she woke among strangers. Burgess suggested Delinsky call the school, see if someone could find Missy Steinberg and send her to the hospital. Iris was going to need all the support she could get.

He stood a minute, regrouping, watching the ambulance pull away. Then they turned things over to Rudy Carr and his crime scene team and went to join Perry.

"I don't know whether to laugh or cry," Kyle said.

"Me neither." Any satisfaction he might have taken from finding Iris Martin was erased by the fact that they still had two more children to find, so many hours had passed, and they were running out of places to look. He was stumbling over his own feet and Kyle wasn't doing any better. Anyone watching would have taken them for a pair of drunks looking for a private corner of the cemetery to finish their bottle.

Suddenly, the quiet of the graveyard was shattered by a voice yelling, "Stop! Police!" followed by the unmistakable sound of a gun. Like Siamese twins, he and Kyle hit the ground.

"That way," Kyle said. Here, away from the streetlights, the night was black as despair. But they could both hear the thudding footsteps heading in their direction. "Now, if they don't shoot us by mistake..."

Burgess grabbed the radio. "Perry? Aucoin? What the hell's happening?" and gave, as best he could, their location.

"He's heading right toward you," Perry yelled. "And he's got something like a small cannon."

"Who? Which one?"

"Ricky fucking Martin."

The footsteps were getting closer. Burgess shut off the radio. Silently, he and Kyle moved apart, loosening their guns, watching for movement in the darkness. Then, suddenly, Martin was right in front of them. Abandoning his vow to never tackle anyone again, Burgess dove at Martin's legs, executing a neat take-down, while Kyle grabbed the body.

Martin was a wild man, gouging, thrashing, kicking, and swinging the gun like a club, inflicting damage wherever he could, all the while roaring, snarling, and spitting. His shirtless torso was so slippery it was like wrestling an octopus. It didn't stop until Kyle used his heavy flashlight on Martin's shoulder and arm, flailing until the roars subsided.

It took both of them to get his arms behind his back and get the cuffs on. Only then, shining the light on his face, did they see why he was so slippery. He was coated with blood, his eyes wild and unfocused. Burgess called for backup and a transport van. Martin went on cursing, spitting and trying to bite. Kyle grabbed him by the hair, hauled his head back and raised his flashlight. "You don't settle down, I'm going to ram your teeth down your throat. You hear?"

Martin tried to jerk his head free, spat at Kyle, aimed a foot at his crotch. Kyle sidestepped, nodding. "Okay, brother. If that's how you want it." He kicked Martin in the balls and when Martin bent over, brought his knee up into Martin's face. The man went down, scrambled up, and lurched at Kyle again. Kyle landed another kick and a few punches and this time, Martin went down and stayed down. "PCP, Joe? Angel dust?" he asked.

"Looks like it." Burgess raised the radio. "Can we get some help over here? Martin is out of his mind."

At that moment, Martin roared up, knocked Kyle onto his back, then went after him with his feet. Burgess hauled him away, pounding him until the man lay silent on the ground. There was no satisfaction in it. Martin would just keep rising up like a Zombie until they could get a sedative into him. He put a foot on the man's neck and raised the radio. "Stan? We got him."

"Dead or alive?"

"Alive."

"That's too bad."

Perry should know better. They might share the sentiment, but you kept a comment like that off the radio. "You find McBride? The kids?"

"It's bad, Joe. Worse than bad. You better get over here."

The knife in his gut went deeper. "Stan says it's bad," he told Kyle. "We'd better get over there."

Around the perimeter of the cemetery, blue lights were descending on them like mutant fireflies. He and Kyle hauled their prisoner to his feet, marched him to the street, and handed him over to the approaching officers with a string of warnings about his condition. Then they went to find Perry.

CHAPTER 36

Perry and Aucoin stood at the door of an old brick building, ringed by uniformed officers. The door was open and dim light from inside spilled out. Aucoin looked sick and green, Perry not a hell of a lot better. As they came up, he said, "Sheesh, Joe. It's a bloodbath in there."

"The Mallett kids?"

"He looks like he's gone. I can't tell. She won't let me near him. Take a look and you'll understand, but be careful. She may be only a kid but she's got the biggest fuckin' knife you ever saw."

Burgess started toward the door. "And watch your feet," Perry added. "It's slippery as hell in there."

It *was* a bloodbath. The average human body contains about twelve pints of blood and most of the contents of Matthew McBride's was pooled on the floor or ran in glistening red streaks down the walls. McBride's mutilated remains lay in the middle of the floor, the close air saturated with the mingled smells of blood and death. It didn't take a crime scene expert to see what had happened. Two men totally strung out on drugs had gotten into a disagreement they had resolved with knives. Ricky Martin, already the bigger of the two, bulked up with prison muscle and made out-of-control violent by drugs and steroids, had won the fight and not known when to stop.

Beyond the body, a naked, bloody Nina Mallett crouched like something feral against the far wall, making a low growling sound. In her hand, she held a mean-looking knife. Her naked brother lay on the floor at her feet, his face swathed with bloody silver duct tape. In the dim light, Burgess couldn't tell if the boy was breathing. Wrapped like that, it would have been difficult.

He took another step into the room. Then another. The girl's eyes fixed on him, glittering with terror. Her growling grew louder. He wondered what they'd given her, whether there was any chance of making a human connection. Keeping his voice calm and steady, he said, "You know me, Nina. Joe Burgess. We talked this afternoon, remember? Is Neddy all right?" He took another step, bringing him closer to the body on the floor, the ancient bricks around it slick with blood. He felt his feet sliding.

He stopped. He had to get close enough to Nina to get the knife while trying not to mess up the crime scene or fall on his ass.

"Neddy's dead," she said, dully. "Everybody's dead."

"I don't think he's dead, Nina. But we have to get that tape off his face so he can breathe." He studied the inert figure. Detected no movement in the chest. Neddy Mallett certainly looked dead. But he couldn't let her think that.

"No," she said. "No. He's dead. That big, dark man killed him. He killed Matt, and he killed Neddy, and he wants to kill me. But I'm not letting him." With a shaking hand, she swung the big bloody knife in a wide arc in front of her. The parts not covered with blood gleamed lethally, even in the poor light.

"That man can't hurt you," he said. "The police have him. They've taken him away. You're safe now." He watched to see if she understood. There was no comprehension on her rigid face. "Let me take you out of here, Nina, you and Neddy."

She shook her head vehemently. "You stay away from me. Stay away," she screamed. She didn't recognize him. Wasn't seeing anything but the horror.

"Nina. Your brother needs our help." He kept talking in a steady, soothing voice, trying to penetrate the fog of her terror.

"No. No. Keep away." She slid along the wall, away from him, her head bobbing in a litany of refusal. "No. No. No." She stopped suddenly as her foot came up against her brother.

She looked at Neddy, then at the knife. "This is all my fault. It's always all my fault. I'm bad. That's what my father said, too. That it was my fault. I'm hopeless. I don't listen. I don't mind. And see what happens?" She wasn't talking to him. She was talking to herself. She slid a finger along the razor sharp tip of the blade. Her skin split and blood gushed out. "I should use this. I should..."

He lifted his foot, trying not to think about the gaping, gutted thing that had been McBride, trying to get to her and get the knife away before she hurt herself further. Focusing on her, he hadn't seen the single bulb hanging from the ceiling. As he stepped carefully over the body, he hit it with his head. It swung wildly back and forth, the chain creaking, casting crazy shadows around the room. Nina screamed, an arcing, lingering sound, and curled into a deeper crouch, throwing her hands over her head. He leapt across the remaining few feet of floor, slipping on the scummy, bloody bricks, twisted the knife from her hand, and thrust it onto a high window ledge, momentum slamming him hard against the wall.

He rebounded and turned. Stan Perry, right behind him, handed him a blanket. He bent to the cowering girl, wrapped her up, and swung her into his arms, handing her back to Perry. Then he knelt and began tearing at the tape masking the small boy's face with clumsy, blood-drenched fingers, breaking nails and splitting skin as he clawed it loose. The second it was off, he scooped up the almost weightless child and rushed him out the door. Skidding on the precarious floor, jamming his bad shoulder into the doorframe, finally making it back out into the night where he handed the boy off to the nearest set of arms.

Unburdened, he stumbled around the corner of the building and tried to heave that knife up out of his gut. The smell of the place told him he wasn't the first one to have that reaction or choose that spot. Then he staggered back to the crowd that stood outside the door, centered around Lt. Melia. Behind them, working in pools of light supplied by officers with flashlights, EMTs bent over the two children. He felt lightheaded. Disembodied. Almost beyond the realm of thought or feeling. He passed the group without speaking, walking out into blackness and the silent rows of stones, feeling a million years old and thoroughly sick of the human race.

He probably hadn't been in that room more than two minutes, but they'd been a long two minutes. Whatever else this day brought, he'd acquired a hideous new image for his brain to serve up when he tried to sleep. McBride hath murdered sleep. This was what Regina McBride, in her desperate and misguided efforts to protect her son, had brought him to.

They weren't done with her. She would be charged and tried, but perhaps this was punishment enough. Although punishment enough, his sick sense of humor suggested, would be to make her reassemble her son's body and then clean the room. She liked things neat and clean.

Footsteps crunched toward him over the dry grass. A flashlight beam trained on the ground illuminated only a pair of blue legs and dark, shiny shoes. The legs came up to him and stopped. "Excuse me, Sarge. I'm sorry to bother you." The voice halted, then resumed. "I know you're...that is, I don't guess you want to talk to anyone right now, but..."

He wanted to say "spit it out, Remy," but didn't. This wasn't an easy night for any of them.

"The little girl...she was asking for you. She..."

"What about the boy?"

"EMTs think maybe a massive drug overdose?"

"Is he alive, Remy? Is he alive?" His voice, even to his own ears, gratingly harsh.

"Just barely, sir."

Probably drugged him to keep him from fighting back like Timmy Watts had done. McBride had been a quick learner, hadn't he? Quick and smart and already a monster. Assaulted by his father. Taken up by pedophiles and gently nurtured in the way he should go. Ricky Martin and Matthew McBride had been an unlikely pair of predators, but maybe it was the simple pleasure of predation that brought them together. The thrill of the hunt. The sating of lust. Young girls. Young boys. What did it matter? To be so bad so young, they hadn't had much in the way of natural inhibitions. Drugs had taken care of what was left.

He now understood what Jason Martin, seized by conscience on his deathbed, had tried to tell them. Not petal file. It wasn't some clue hidden in a book of dried flowers. He'd meant pedophile. How like the Martin family to keep it to themselves, even when one of their own was affected. But one of their own had been involved as well. And the family had perfected the art of protecting criminals.

His mind, long trained in putting together the jigsaw puzzles of crime, had automatically begun assembling the pieces. But he didn't want to think about this yet. He wanted to think about the children. Who would put their pieces back together? Iris, bound and helpless and left in a crypt to die. Nina Mallett, twice forced to witness horrible deaths and left believing she was responsible. Little Ned Mallett with his cockscomb of rusty hair, barely alive. Just barely was something. What if they'd been any later?

Could they have been earlier? This was no time for second guessing. As he could have told any raw recruit, it was important to learn from your mistakes, equally important not to beat yourself up when your best wasn't good enough. When the world proved itself imperfect. They'd done their job. Done it despite Cote's interference, Bascomb's malice, and so much public indifference. They'd pushed and probed and plodded. Found the killer and saved three victims. This time he wasn't walking away no matter how much anyone screwed up the evidence. Was he sick to take some pleasure in that?

He wanted to drag Captain Cote into that blood drenched slaughterhouse and scream in the man's face, "You see! You see! We did it despite your best efforts. If you'd had your way, Kyle and Perry would still be combing through Payson Park, I would have sat home playing solitaire, and they all might have died horrible deaths." He wanted Cote up close and personal with the stench of severed guts, his immaculate person slimed with blood.

"Sir?"

He pulled himself back. "Nina's asking for me?"

"Yes, sir."

"Then I'd better come." Aucoin offered a hand and Burgess wasn't too proud to take it. "Remy..."

"Sir?"

"This is probably the worst thing you'll ever see."

"I hope so, sir."

He followed the bobbing flashlight and slim figure back to the teeming noise and commotion. Adrenaline-deprived now, he felt dull and logy. Distant. Melia met him. Set a hand on his shoulder. Solid, steady, conveying volumes that didn't need to be spoken. "Joe." Just his name, hanging a long time in the night air, then, "You did it. Thanks."

The credit wasn't his. "It's team work, Vince. Thanks for letting me back in. But what about Cote? How'd you..."

"I didn't ask."

Burgess understood the enormous risk Melia had taken. If Melia's gamble, his faith in them, hadn't paid off, it could have been his ass as well. That was what kept them loyal. Knowing that Melia was good police. That he understood what they were all trying to do and what it took, sometimes, to get results.

"It's not neat and tidy but you did a hell of a job. No one can fault us on this."

"He'll find a way."

"Let's worry about that tomorrow. How you doin'?"

"Give me another five, I'm gonna fall on my face."

Melia laughed. "That'll be the day."

"I've gotta go see the girl."

"Go home, Joe. Get some rest." Melia patted his shoulder again and turned away. Burgess nudged his tired legs into motion again, heading for the pool of light surrounding Nina Mallett. Just one pool now. Ambo had already taken Neddy away. Behind him, Kyle and Perry were taking charge of the scene. He should have been helping. Had to admit he had nothing more to give.

She was lying on a stretcher, covered with a clean white sheet, the blood streaking her pale face and arms giving her the look of a savage painted for war. Her bright hair was vivid against the white. Her eyes were closed and she looked utterly spent, her face finally peaceful. She looked so small and fragile. The EMT, a comfortable-looking middle-aged woman, smiled up at him. "Another one of your waifs, Joe? She was asking for you."

He nodded. "I'm the only person here she knows."

The EMT nodded. "Sweet little thing." Burgess's mind flashed on Nina crouched against the wall, hissing and snarling, clutching that enormous knife. Sweet wasn't an adjective he would have chosen. "She's in remarkably good shape, considering. We're just going to take her in, check her over. They'll probably send her home."

He almost laughed aloud at the absurdity of it. Mary Turner was a nice woman who cared about Nina, probably as good as the state could do. But sending the girl back to a houseful of children and a distraught caretaker after the experience she'd just had? With her brother lying on the cusp of death? What she needed was a long, long sleep, some intensive short-term therapy and then a course of long-term therapy in a setting where she'd be carefully watched. Not a bin. Just a place where she couldn't wander at will or fall through the cracks, or be immediately subsumed back into the life of a little mother, a place where she could come to understand she wasn't to blame for the bad things grown-ups did. Nina needed to finish being a child.

"You want to ride along or meet us there?"

"I'll meet you," he said. "I'll need the car. It's looking like a long night."

"Hold on," she said, swiping at his forehead with a piece of gauze. "You've got a couple spots could use some stitching. And you might consider a shower."

"You got something against a natural man?"

"Joe..." Her voice soft with affection. Cops and EMTs worked together a lot. "You're filthy, you stink. You should find a mirror before you go anywhere like that."

He watched as they loaded the girl into the ambulance, then went back to Melia. "Thought I'd take a ride over the hospital and check on my kids," he said. "Unless you need me here."

Melia gave him a weary smile. "You weren't listening when I said go home?"

"Guess I wasn't. Guess I'm still not, huh?"

"Guess not. Let me know what's up, okay?"

"Cote know what's happening?"

"Beats me. I haven't been able to reach him. Dispatch hasn't been able to reach him. He's gonna be some pissed when he finds out what a PR op he missed."

"He's always pissed." He turned to leave. "I'll call you."

"Joe? Soap and water? Clean clothes? Please? I don't want you in the paper looking like that."

"I don't want my picture in the paper, period. And Vince? Keep an eye on Terry. He was about to drop three hours ago."

"They're my people, too, Joe."

"What about a warrant for the McBride place?"

"Rocky's working on it."

"I want to be there."

"You and everyone else." Melia cleared his throat. "Soap and water. Clean clothes. That's an order."

Burgess set off on the long uphill walk back to his car, using the heavy flashlight to light his way along the rows of ancient stones. The thunder and lightning had gotten closer and as he reached for his door handle, the first fat raindrop hit. Just as he'd predicted, the weather had refused to break until Timmy Watts's killer was found.

He switched on the interior light, looked at his clothes and hands, peered into the mirror. Melia and the EMT had been kind. He looked like something from a slasher flick. The Creature from the Blood Lagoon. He turned off the light and picked up his phone. It was time to call Chris. After that, time to keep moving. Put as many hours as he could between himself and the horror before he collapsed.

She answered on the first ring, a worried, breathless, "Joe? Are you okay?"

"Can you meet me at the hospital?"

"You're hurt again? More?" Worry shifting to panic.

"Not me. I have to check on some people. I just wanted to see you. Maybe we could sit a while. Have coffee."

"Why don't you just go home?" Irritated now because he'd scared her.

"Because I've got three hurt kids. A suspect who's out of his mind. Another body on my hands, and a search warrant to execute."

"Doesn't sound like you've got time for me."

He felt her pull away, getting ready to put down the phone. "I need you," he said. "In the midst of all this bad stuff, I need something decent and good to keep me going. Please?"

"Decent and good sounds like Wonder Bread."

"Chris, I am drenched with blood from head to toe, I've got a little six-year-old boy hanging on by his fingernails and a thirteen year old girl who thinks it's all her fault. I've been tap dancing around a man who was gutted like a deer, and I am starved for the wholesome goodness of Wonder Bread."

He heard her take a deep breath and slowly let it out. "You are the craziest man I've ever met, Joe Burgess."

"I hope so."

"You want me to bring you some clothes?"

"I want you to peel off my clothes and make my body sing, but I have to ask for a rain check."

"That's right. It is raining, isn't it? Where shall I look for you?"

"Try the ER. Don't rush. I've got to shower and change."

There was another call he had to make. He got out his notebook, found the number for Henry Devereau, and dialed. Devereau answered, predictably surly. "Who the fuck's this?"

"Burgess. Portland Police."

"Oh. That asshole. So?"

He kept it short. "You remember the other day I said your niece might be in trouble? Well, someone tried to kill her tonight. Wrapped her in duct tape, stuck her in a crypt, and left her to die. She's at the medical center. You might drop by. Let her know someone cares."

There was silence on the other end. He thought Devereau'd hung up. Was about to disconnect when the man said, "She gonna be okay?"

"Physically." He turned the phone off and the engine on, and headed across town, driving on autopilot, but that was okay. The horse knew the way.

CHAPTER 37

Crouched in a basement corner, she looked like a rat, eyes glittering, hands curled like paws, her dull brown clothes coated with gray dust and cobwebs. She blinked a few times, her head swiveling from one flashlight beam to the other, but didn't speak.

"Regina McBride?" Kyle waved the paper at her. "Detective Kyle, Portland Police. This is a warrant to search the premises."

She blinked again, still silent, then a paw uncurled and she snatched the paper. Her teeth seized her bottom lip, biting hard. Her eyes blinked again as Kyle held out a second paper. "A warrant to search your car." She grabbed it and thrust them both into her pocket.

"You need to come upstairs with us now," Burgess said. "We have to talk with you about your son."

"Where is Matthew?" she said, straightening up, hands falling to her sides. "What have you done with him?"

More like what have you done with him? And what has he done with himself? "I'm afraid we have some bad news," he said.

Her body fell back into its defensive crouch. Her hands came up and her head started swiveling again. She took a step toward Burgess, and then another. He could see both hands and both pockets. Her sleeves were short. There was no visible weapon. Yet she moved with a definite sense of menace and he knew what she was capable of.

He shifted his flashlight to his left hand, leaving his right hand free and took another step back toward the stairs. Kyle, feeling it, too, moved closer.

"Mrs. McBride? If you could step upstairs."

"Don't you dare!" she exploded. "Don't you dare tell me what to do in my own house. You can step upstairs if you want. You've already invaded my home and my privacy. I will come up if and when I please. For now, I prefer to remain down here."

"Suit yourself," he said. "I'll send an officer down to stay with you."

"That's not necessary."

"Routine procedure, ma'am." No way was he leaving her alone. She might try to flee. Destroy things. Set the house on fire. Ruthless women were rarer than ruthless men, but they existed, particularly where their children were involved. He took a step backward. "Detective Kyle, could you send an officer down." He shifted his attention back to her. "Is there a light down here?"

"What have you done with Matthew?"

"When you're ready to come upstairs, we can discuss your son."

"We can discuss my son right here, Detective. Matthew is innocent. Whatever you may think, he isn't involved in what happened to that little boy. I told you. I was with him that night. Except when we went out to dinner, he never left the house."

She should have saved her breath. Despite her

meticulous housekeeping, the forensic team, on a preliminary walk-through, had noted fibers to match the bloody carpet and traces of blood. Matt's room, a typical teenager's hole, hadn't been cleaned at all. There, in addition to a blood stain under the carpet suggesting the stabbing had begun there, they'd found a 6-pack of empty Coke bottles, one with blood and traces of hair. They'd find much more.

Burgess was always grateful for stupid criminals, but this one surprised him. Why get rid of one carpet and repaint one room, and neglect to do the same with another? Had she thought the attack was confined to the living room? Where had she been while it was taking place? He doubted he'd hear the answer from her.

The thud of feet on the stairs announced Delinsky's arrival, Kyle behind him, carrying a light bulb he screwed into the empty fixture. When bright light flooded the room, Burgess felt a sense of relief. It had made his skin crawl being in the dark with her.

She stared at Delinsky, then back at Burgess. He didn't know where she'd been hiding, but her head was covered with cobwebs. "You can't leave me down here with him."

"Your choice. Stay here with Officer Delinsky or come upstairs."

"You can't leave me alone with a black man."

"Your choice," he repeated, starting up the stairs. Some ingrained instinct kept him from turning his back on her. Kyle was at the top of the stairs, and Burgess two steps up, when she suddenly started yelling at Delinsky.

"It's all your fault," she screamed. "Your fault. If you hadn't always been going around sticking your nose into people's business, no one would have thought about Matthew."

Her hand plunged into her pocket, rustling the papers, and came out with a knife. She lunged at Delinsky. The blade, powered by rage and insanity, slashed right through his shirt. As she pulled back, preparing to strike again, Burgess launched himself off his step, carrying her to the floor. He twisted her arm, trying to force the knife out of her hand. Before Kyle could even get down the stairs, Perry had pushed past, flown off the stairs, and twisted her arm behind her back.

"It's okay, Joe. I got her. I got her," he said. Burgess let Perry handle it. Happy to defer to that youthful energy. He'd had enough crazy people today. Deftly, Perry flipped her onto her face, grabbed her other arm, and looked at Delinsky. "Your cuffs?"

Dazed, Delinsky got them off his belt and handed them over. Then he sat down on the steps, hunched defensively, his arms wrapped tightly around his middle. When Regina McBride was secured, Kyle knelt beside him, pulled Delinsky's hands away, and untucked his shirt. He loosened the vest, checked underneath, and straightened with a grin. "Score one for the good guys," he said. "Nothing a Band-Aid can't fix."

Delinsky was still in shock. "You mean I'm not dead?"

"You feel dead?" Kyle asked.

With the trepidation of a man expecting to find a gaping hole in himself, Delinsky slipped a hand under his vest. His fingers scrabbled around, around again, and came out, two fingertips streaked with blood. "Hot damn!" he said. "Hot damn!" He thumped his vest with a fist, his voice low and full of wonder. "It was so hot, I wasn't going to wear it. My wife made me."

On the floor at their feet, Regina McBride squawked

and thrashed. Perry put an admonitory foot on her back. "Lie still," he said. He shot a wicked grin at Kyle and Burgess. "Remember when this was a peaceful little city? Now even the accountants carry knives. Selling real estate is looking better all the time."

"You'd hate it, Stan," Burgess said.

"Yeah," Kyle agreed. "There aren't half as many chances to get laid. Women don't get all hot and bothered over a real estate broker, but tell 'em you're a cop..."

"That's another thing. It's been a pretty dry summer. It's not so bad for you guys. You've got girlfriends. But night after lonely night..."

"You're breaking my heart," Burgess said. "If you didn't love 'em and leave 'em like some Downeast Don Juan, you'd have a girlfriend. Been too hot for sex anyway."

"No fuckin' way!" Perry hooked his thumbs into his belt, thrust his pelvis out and swayed his hips, grinding his foot back and forth on Regina McBride's arching back. "It's never too hot for sex."

"Let me up!" their prisoner squawked. "I will not listen to this filthy talk."

"Shut the fuck up, lady," Perry said mildly. "Talking about filthy. You just stabbed a police officer."

Someone's head appeared at the top of the stairs. A woman's voice said, "What's going on down there? You guys doin' a circle jerk or what?" Andrea Dwyer's shift had ended hours ago, but the case involved kids and she'd wanted in.

"Oh, hi, Dwyer," Perry said. "Lady down here just stabbed a police officer. You want to take charge of the prisoner and search her, you being a female officer and all? And ask someone to bring Delinsky a Band-Aid?"

"A Band-Aid? You've got her face-down on the floor in handcuffs when all he needs is a Band-Aid?"

"Honeybun," Kyle said, and Burgess knew the endearment was carefully chosen, for Kyle didn't have the ingrained sexism many cops did, "clever Officer Delinsky was wearing a vest. Otherwise he'd either be on his way to the ER or heaven. I hope you're wearing your vest because we're about to hand you the accountant from hell, and she's probably got more knives hidden in her panties."

"Honeybun and panties? You're some kind of anachronism, you know that, Kyle?"

Kyle swept her a graceful bow. "I've never been called an anachronism by a more beautiful colleague," he said.

"Thin ice," she said, "and sinking fast."

They grabbed her elbows and hauled Regina McBride to her feet. Delinsky, still holding himself together as though he didn't quite believe he wasn't hurt, stepped down to let them pass, then followed them up the stairs. They stood by while Dwyer searched Regina McBride, then put her in the living room and left her with Dwyer and another officer to wait for the transport van.

Melia was in the front hall, directing the search. Burgess called him into the kitchen. "Vince? We need you."

He steered Delinsky to a chair. "Despite our foolishness down there and our jokes about the Band-Aid, this is very serious," he said. "You're right to be shaken by it."

They got Devlin in to photograph the slashed shirt, then had Delinsky take off the shirt and got pictures of the vest and the wound. Plodding through the careful collection of evidence—this time, of the attempted murder of a police officer—they were all so punchy they could barely function. Burgess ached for a cup of coffee.

Dwyer stuck her head around the door. "She says she needs to go to the bathroom."

Burgess shook his head. "Let them deal with it down at the jail."

"That seems a bit harsh."

"Dwyer, I don't care if she wets her pants, okay. This woman, after her son raped and murdered a small boy, cleaned the body, dressed it, and drove it to the park. She got rid of the clothes and the carpet, and painted over the bloodstains. Then she had the nerve to tell me that she'd never liked Timmy Watts because he was dirty and had a poor vocabulary. This is not June Cleaver. This is a mother so protective she carries knives in her pocket in case she needs to kill a few police officers. Her comfort is not one of my priorities."

"As you wish," she said. "I thought *we* were still supposed to be civil."

"Don't give me that look, Dwyer. You want to take her to the bathroom, go ahead. Just be prepared to shoot her if necessary."

Perry looked at Kyle and shrugged. "Did you know Burgess has a reputation as a hard-nosed cop? I wonder where he gets it?"

"Beats me," Kyle said. "He's always been very nice to me."

"Me, too." Perry nodded solemnly. "I've got an idea. Let's do something nice for him." Melia smiled faintly, an indulgent father watching his children play.

Like a bad actor simulating thought, Kyle tapped a finger against his forehead, then rubbed his chin with his hand. "I've got it!" he said. "Let's give him a present."

"Nice idea," Perry said. "Can you think of anything

Burgess really wants?"

Kyle turned to Melia. "Lieutenant, we want to give our friend Joe a present. You got any ideas?"

"Got one," Melia was working on bland, but the lines around his mouth betrayed him. He patted his pockets, searching for something, finally reaching inside his sport coat and pulling out a small paper bag. He held it up triumphantly. "This."

"No way, Lou." Perry gave a vehement shake of his head. "Not nearly grand enough. Joe Burgess is our special friend. He needs a special present."

With a flourish, Melia handed him the bag. Burgess pulled out a pair of fluffy pink handcuffs. "They're beautiful," he said. "Thank you. I know Chris will appreciate them just as much as I do." Delinsky looked like he thought they were crazy.

"Wait. Wait!" Melia held up his hand, shaking his head in disgust. "That's not what I was looking for." He patted his pockets again. Found another one that rustled. Pulled out a second small paper bag. "Sorry, Joe. This is what I was looking for."

Carefully, because the faces around him had now grown serious, Burgess opened the second bag. Inside was a plastic, Zip-loc bag full of what looked like dirty rock candy.

Perry looked at Delinsky. "Cover your ears, son," he said. "I'm about to confess to conduct unbecoming." Delinsky put his hands over his ears. "A few of us paid a visit to fat Wayne Bascomb recently, bit of routine follow-up. We were concerned about some missing evidence. Things like that make all of us nervous, street police and detectives. Next thing you know, cases start going down the drain, it gets even less worthwhile to spend our waking hours chasing down bad guys. We wanted to be sure Wayne understood how concerned we all were." His twinkling eyes went around, soliciting agreement. They all nodded.

Burgess felt dangerously close to tears. The effect of too many hours out, too intense an evening. He turned toward the window, looking to reassert control. Saw his face reflected back at him, stitched and battered, eyes shining, grinning like a madman.

Perry leaned back nonchalantly against the doorframe. "Fat Wayne, he says he doesn't know what I'm talking about. He doesn't see the problem. It's just the one thing that's gone missing, what's the big deal?"

"Gee, Stan, that makes sense to me," Kyle said, "What *was* the big deal?"

"Well, I saw then that Fat Wayne just didn't get it. If one of our most meticulous officers brings in a crucial piece of evidence in a high profile case, and that goes missing, what faith do we have that the everyday stuff won't start disappearing? So I say maybe he hasn't looked hard enough. That he should check again, see if that stuff is in the back of a locker or something." Perry passed a big, bruised hand over his bald head. "Fat Wayne just shakes his head and says it isn't there. So I ask him how he knows?"

"Because he's already looked very carefully?" Kyle asked.

"That's what I asked," Perry said, "but he says he just knows. So then I ask, and you know I'm a detective, so I'm pretty good at asking questions—"

"Hey," Kyle interrupted, "when do we get to the good part?"

"The good part?"

"The part about the conduct unbecoming?"

Delinsky looked like he thought they were all crazy. They were, of course. Crazy from exhaustion. Crazy from exposure to violent, crazy people. Crazy from knowing that no matter how bad you imagine things can get, in the cop business there's always someone who takes it one step farther. Punch-drunk crazy and taking refuge in the company of their brothers.

"I had brought my nightstick." Perry's voice got low and soft. "Moving it from my locker to the car, so I happened to have it in my hand. Actually, a number of us did. Why, you even had yours, Kyle, as I recall."

"I've been out of the room for the past five minutes," Melia said.

"Right, Lou. You and Delinsky are doing something upstairs. We're just here in the kitchen, talking to Joe."

Perry's grin was manic. "I'm tryin' to give Fat Wayne a little advice. Fat Wayne, you know, hasn't got many friends. So I'm saying how bad life can get when people lose confidence in you. How your car can break down, stranding you places, maybe go off the road into the water. How a guy's gun can jam when he's at the range, blow his hand off. Just, you know, talking to him about the risks. He says well that won't happen to him. I ask does he have some guardian angel or what? He says he's got friends where he needs 'em. I woulda thought there in that room was where he needed friends, wouldn't you, Kyle?"

"I would," Kyle agreed. "I did. But Fat Wayne gets this stupid expression on his face and says, are we threatening him?"

"Who's telling this story?"

"Sorry, Stan. Pray continue."

Burgess's eyelids were dropping. He pulled out a chair and sat down. "Tired, Sarge?" Perry said. "I'll make it quick. Then we can all go home and go sleepy-bye. The Lieutenant won't mind if we don't write our reports until morning. I told Fat Wayne a threat implied something that might happen in the future if the desired something didn't happen first. That there was nothing implied or future about this. This was a promise. He handed over the missing meth or I promised a boatload of bad shit would be coming down."

"I thought Bascomb would wet his pants," Kyle said happily. "He looks around and says, you guys all heard that, right? And everybody says no. That was when—"

"Yeah," Perry interrupted, "Fat Wayne pulled the stuff out of his desk drawer, rolled up inside a fuckin' Playboy magazine."

"We never," Kyle began.

"Laid a hand on him."

Burgess stood and bowed solemnly to his colleagues. "Words fail me," he said. "I think you know how much I appreciate this." He handed the bag back to Melia. "Maybe you'd better keep it. I might lose it again."

A commotion in the next room turned their heads toward the kitchen wall. A gun went off and a bullet exploded through the plaster, bounced off the cupboards, and landed with a metallic clang in the spotless aluminum sink. Burgess considered the miracle that none of them had been hit. "I told her to shoot McBride, not us. Sometimes they just won't listen."

CHAPTER 38

Hospitals in the dead of night are spooky places. In the dimmed down rooms, machinery hisses and pulses, monitors flash, IVs drip, patients moan and stir. The corridors have a bright, echoing emptiness that seems both harsh and desolate. Burgess hated the smells, the sounds and lights, the way it could trap him in a net of memory. No one had made him come, but he was here, walking the corridors with the painful stiffness of a very old man, the burden of exhaustion weighting every step.

Portland's meanest cop could have gone home to bed. He longed for rest, soft sheets, for the sheer delicious act of getting horizontal with every acid-filled muscle fiber and every swollen, bruised piece of his body. But he couldn't rest until he'd checked on his children.

He disliked the expression "every cloud has a silver lining." His take on it was the opposite—that every silver lining was surrounded by a big dark cloud. Yet life still possessed the capacity to surprise him, and occasionally, even in his line of work, the surprises were pleasing. The room he'd just left contained such a surprise. There Iris Martin lay deeply asleep, her small hand clasped tightly in the huge, grubby fist of her slumbering uncle. Devereau might dwarf the chair, snore like a chainsaw, and stink up the room, but he had come because Iris needed him, and he had stayed to reassure her.

In the face of the mass of abominable violence the degraded citizens of Portland had visited on each other during the past week, it was a small thing. But hope is made of small things. In a life filled with so much inhumanity, it was the small acts of love and grace that kept Burgess connected to his humanity. His humanity and the humanity of those around him. Like Stan and Terry and Vince in the kitchen. The hot pink handcuffs and the small bag that helped restore his honor. Melia's courage in letting him back into the investigation.

The only sound in the corridor was the shuffling of his feet. It carried him back to a shabby rooming house and one of his rare visits to his father. He'd knocked on the door. Heard shuffling steps and the door had opened to an older, ravaged version of his own face, the reek of booze, the charming Irish joviality. A ratty bathrobe and mottled feet in ragged slippers, a swollen purple hand reaching out to pull him in. His father had been the age then that he was now. Looked decades older. The sound of slippered feet ever after that made him cringe.

He heard footsteps behind him. A soft voice called, "Detective?" He turned to find Charlene Farrell standing there. "I heard about what happened tonight."

"I don't want to talk about it," he said.

"I wasn't going to ask you to." She looked young and tired, and something, maybe weariness, had taken the brittle edge off. "I knew you'd come back to check on the victims." He started walking. "Look. Detective.

I'm not here to bother you. Honestly. I just wanted to apologize."

"For what?"

"Misjudging you?"

He turned on her suddenly. "I thought that was your job."

"Excuse me?"

"It's what you do. What your paper loves to do. Ignore the thousands of good things police officers do every day. The lives we lead. The risks we face. Only waiting for a mistake, or something you can call a mistake, to rub our faces in it. What about you? About what you do? About that picture? You're young, at the beginning your career, and you've already done something more unthinkable than anything I've done in thirty years. And there's no one out there to call you on that."

"My editor approved that picture."

"As if two wrongs make a right," he said. "Now, if you'll excuse me—"

"Dammit," she said. "I'm trying to apologize and you won't give me a chance."

"Write me a letter," he said. "Write my boss a letter."

"I don't want to write *to* you," she said. "I want to write *about* you. The people you've helped. The difference you've made. Like today. Tonight. Captain Cote tries to shut you out of the investigation. Without you, your insight, experience, persistence, who knows what might have happened."

"Who have you been talking to?"

She smiled. "I have my sources."

Then surely they'd also told her about his reputation with the press. "Please don't write it, Ms. Farrell. It can only make things worse. For me. For a lot of other good people." She started to speak. He held up his hand. "One other thing. It's never just one of us. It's a team thing. I didn't catch a killer and I didn't save those kids. The Portland Police did."

"You really believe that?" she said.

He walked away from her then. Walked until he came to Neddy Mallett's room. The boy looked so small and so sick. Smaller because of the enormous stuffed moose that lay beside him.

Chris was sitting in a chair beside the bed, reading. She set down the book, came over, and put her arms around him. "Hi, honey," she said. "How was your day?"

"I wouldn't want a rerun. How about you?"

"If this is going to be a long-term relationship, I may have to take up knitting. I need something mindless to do when my head is all full of worry about you." She pulled his face down to hers and kissed him.

Burgess had never had sex in a hospital room but he was willing to consider it. "Why would you worry about me? I was with Stan and Terry. They look after me."

"The Three Stooges," she said.

"You have no idea," he said.

"Yeah. Maybe you can help me with that." She tightened her grasp. "It is over?"

"Except the paper work. You wanna go away somewhere this weekend?"

"Like where?"

"I know where there's a nice cottage on a lake. We could borrow a canoe."

"It sounds heavenly," she said. "But I'll believe it when I see."

"You check on Nina?"

"An hour ago. They're going to keep her down for a

while."

"Was she..." He was supposed to be able to deal with ugliness. Couldn't bring himself to ask.

But she knew. "No, Joe. Neither of them were. None of them. You guys got there in time."

"The Three Stooges."

"Oh. All right. I know you're not Stooges. I just wish..."

"I know you do. You always will. But consider this. If you were Iris Martin, or Nina Mallett..." He touched the wild red curls. "Or Ned...who would you rather have on your side, The Three Stooges or Paul Cote?"

She stepped up beside him, pressing her hip into his. "Oh, Joe," her voice dropped into that lower register. He reached down and took her hand. "That's not fair."

"And life is?"

Reluctantly, he stepped away. "I'm going to look in on Nina."

"You coming back?"

"To you? Always."

"Idiot."

"Only an idiot would come back to you?" She picked up the moose and threw it at him. "Portland officer assaulted by moose," he said. "Yes. I'll be back."

He sat in the chair beside Nina Mallett's bed, holding her limp hand in his. He uncurled the fingers with their chipped pink polish, one of them bandaged where she'd cut herself, and heard her voice, back there in that horrific room. "It's all my fault. It's always my fault. I'm bad. I'm bad. I'm bad."

It was a terrible time to be a child. He and Terry and Stan, and even the righteous Vince Melia, were such imperfect guardians of the small souls entrusted to their care. Even sworn to serve and protect, they could only do it one incident, or one bad guy, or one street corner at a time.

Just for tonight, he ought to have been able to enjoy some satisfaction that things had come to a good end. He'd done his job. Timmy Watts's killer had been identified. Matt McBride's killer had been caught. Regina McBride, monster and maker of monsters, was behind bars. So were the vicious predators Osborne and Taylor. And the three children were alive. The runaway train of predation and abuse had been stopped. Now it was time to tend to the injured. Sooner or later they would wake up and begin to feel their pain. He had little confidence that someone would be there to help them deal with it.

He knew Melia had stopped at church on his way home. For Vince, the certainty of the Baltimore catechism was still there. It was wired in Burgess, too. There was a deep place where the certainty and the possibility of redemption dwelled and could be comforting. But there was a parallel place that was dark with doubt and cynicism, a pool that got stirred up when children and other innocents were the victims.

Police officers don't cry. They're supposed to be the ones who are there when ordinary citizens need comfort and security. Sitting in the dimly lit room, listening to the quiet rhythm of Nina Mallett's breathing, Burgess became, for a private moment, an ordinary citizen. Then he wiped his eyes and heaved himself back up out of the chair. It had been a long day, a long week, a long year, a long life. And tomorrow he would get up and do it again.

THE
JOE BURGESS MYSTERIES

Playing God
The Angel of Knowlton Park
Redemption

Turn the page for an

excerpt from

REDEMPTION

A Joe Burgess Mystery
Book Three

Kate Flora

The two boys on the curb shot out into the street so abruptly Burgess had to stand on the brakes to avoid hitting them. It was seven a.m. Saturday. Columbus Day weekend. The weather was perfect. The city was quiet. And even as he rocked to a stop, shoved the truck into park, and rolled down the window, he knew from the wild look on the taller boy's face and the single gasped word, "body," that his day, and probably his weekend, was lost.

In the rearview, he watched Nina and Neddy cease their happy chatter about school and the upcoming picnic and go quiet, their bright heads still, their faces wary. Body was a word they knew too well.

It was no prank. The taller of the two, a gangly kid with a lamb's pelt of curly dark hair, freckles standing out against his pale, drained skin, was wide-eyed with alarm. "Excuse me, sir," he gasped, his fingers tightening around the window frame to steady himself, "There's a...Do you have a cell phone? We need to call the police. There's a body in the water."

"I am the police," Burgess said. "I'll park and you can show me."

He pulled to the curb and turned to the kids in the back seat. "Stay in the car. I'll just be a minute." He'd hoped they hadn't heard, but Neddy's coxcomb of red hair was pressed up tight against his sister, his eyes squeezed shut, and Nina wore the stricken look he kept hoping time would erase.

Cursing quietly, he followed the boys out onto the wharf, wishing he could have just made a phone call passing this to someone else. But he was a cop, a homicide detective here in Portland, Maine, and the boy had said body. A few minutes earlier or later, the boys would have stopped another car and he could have gone on with his day. He might have made it out of cell phone range before word went up the food chain and came back down to him, making it someone else's problem.

Neddy and Nina didn't need this. They'd already been through more trauma than a combat vet. This was what they got, Burgess feared, for hanging around with him. He tried to keep his personal and professional lives separate, but trouble had a way of rising up and smacking him in the face. This was a perfect example.

His girlfriend, Chris, wanted to adopt these two foster kids, rescue them from the crap that life that thrown at them. After what they'd seen and had done to them, it was no simple task. Endearing as they were, Nina and Neddy were damaged. First, from having witnessed their father killing their mother. Later by being the targets of a disturbed and violent pedophile. He wasn't sure he was on board for another thing in his life that was this demanding. His day job—hell, his day, night, weekend, whole life job— was demanding enough.

The boys, moving with herky-jerky eagerness, led him out the wharf to a spot where two fish poles and some gear were propped against a railing, and pointed down into the water. "Down there," the tall boy said. "Do you see? Floating on bottom, there in the seaweed?"

"Is it really a body?" the smaller boy asked. He was blond, pink-cheeked and blocky, and tended to stay behind the other boy.

Burgess followed the boy's pointing finger, peering down through foam and flotsam into the choppy green water. Lot of times, you looked into the water, you couldn't be sure what you saw, but this one was pretty clear. A man's body—at least, it looked like a man—face-down, fully dressed, and shifting with the currents down there on the murky bottom.

REDEMPTION

**available in
print and ebook**

Kate Flora first developed her fascination with people's criminal tendencies as a lawyer in the Maine attorney general's office. Deadbeat dads, people who beat and neglected their kids, and employers hateful acts of discrimination led to a deep curiosity about human psychology that's led to twelve books including seven "strong woman" Thea Kozak mysteries and three gritty police procedurals in her star-reviewed Joe Burgess series. Her first true crime, Finding Amy, has been optioned for a movie. Her second, Death Dealer, will be published in September 2014.

When she's not writing, or teaching writing at Grub Street in Boston, she's usually found in her garden, where she wages a constant battle against critters, pests, and her husband's lawnmower. She's been married for 35 years to a man who can still make her laugh. She has two wonderful sons, a movie editor and a scientist, two lovely daughters-in-law, and four rescue "granddogs," Frances, Otis, Harvey, and Daisy.

CPSIA information can be obtained
at www.ICGtesting.com
Printed in the USA
FSHW011953141020
74857FS